# THE LONG PATROL

### A WWII NOVEL

## CHRIS GLATTE

# PROLOGUE

July 1942, Solomon Island chain, Guadalcanal

COLONEL ARAKI SQUATTED beside Captain Toryu with his pistol drawn. He looked into the dark jungle, but couldn't see more than a few feet. The night's torrential rain had stopped. The rising mist gave the jungle an eerie feel. The foreigner, the gaijin told him the village was there only yards away, but to him it looked like any other miserable part of this miserable jungle.

Silent as a snake, the gaijin was beside him, his whisper in his ear startling him. *The man moves like an apparition.* In the mist, the image made him shiver. He suppressed the feeling. "We have the village surrounded, Goro. We are ready for your order to assault."

The scowl from Colonel Araki went unnoticed in the darkness, but the tone of his voice gave little doubt to his displeasure. "Do not presume to use the familiar with me, Mr. Welch." He said the name as if he'd stepped in dog shit.

He heard the foreigner swallow and caught the slight movement of his head nod. He looked at his watch, straining to see the translucent dials. The watch was a gift from his father upon his commission into the Army. He remembered Thomas Welch being nearby when his father presented the watch to him. Many hundreds of miles and countless hours of hard victorious battles had passed since that summer day in Tokyo. Now he was reunited with this gaijin, whose entire race he'd come to despise. "Tell the men we attack in five minutes."

Captain Toryu nodded and passed the word to a waiting Sergeant, who scuttled away in silence.

The time passed slowly. At the stroke of five minutes the jungle erupted in noise as six Nambu machine guns opened fire. The guns were joined by the sharp cracks of rifles. All along the line Colonel Araki could see the winking of muzzle flashes through the gloom. The tracer rounds had been removed to keep the machine guns' locations hidden. The flat firing Nambus were stable platforms. The veteran gunners swept their sectors back and forth. The villagers had little chance of survival.

The thumping of knee mortar rounds arcing through the air and landing in the village accompanied the guns. Colonel Araki wanted to bring the heavier 81mm mortars, but the two-day walk through the thick jungle would slow them down too much. The heavy mortars were left behind and the light 50mm knee mortars brought instead. He could tell they were more than sufficient.

The attack was over in minutes. The mortars and machine guns stopped as abruptly as they started and his men rose from the jungle like wraiths. Keeping low they advanced into the village, firing at any movement. In minutes, they'd gone through each hut completing their grisly work.

Colonel Araki stood in the center of the village his pistol ready. He had yet to fire the weapon and was itching for a target. The huts were smoking, some destroyed and on fire. The flames lit up natives sprawled in various death poses. Their flowing blood looked like black tar against their dark skin.

Welch trotted up to him with a worried look on his face. "Report," Colonel Araki barked.

"The attack's a complete success, Colonel."

"Then why do you look troubled?"

Welch broke eye contact. He had streaks of blood across his face, not his own. "The Captain isn't among the dead."

Colonel Araki gritted his teeth. "You said he would be here, you assured me he would be here."

In desperation Welch said, "He must be close, perhaps he slipped out only minutes ago." He pointed to the dark jungle, "Perhaps a patrol could…"

Colonel Araki cut him off, "He's gone, he moves even better than you through this jungle. Finding him will be impossible." Welch stammered and started to speak. Araki's hand moved in a blur cuffing his face with a loud smack. Welch yelled out in surprise. "You've failed me gaijin." Welch dropped his eyes to the ground. To continue speaking would bring more pain. Once the man's mind was made up there was no changing it.

Colonel Araki raised his pistol. For a moment Welch thought he'd shoot him and he felt his bowels loosen, but instead Colonel Araki found another target for his rage. He strode to the edge of a burning hut. His men surrounded a native woman and her squalling infant. As he approached, the men sprang to attention.

Colonel Araki addressed a sergeant, "what do we have here, sergeant?"

The sergeant, a stocky man with bowed legs and hard eyes gave a quick bow. "A survivor, sir. A captive."

The woman clutched her crying baby to her bare chest. He noticed the child had much lighter skin than his presumed mother. Colonel Araki scowled, "These heathens are disgusting. This child's wail is grating on my nerves, sergeant." The sergeant nodded waiting for an order. "Take the baby from her breast."

The sergeant didn't hesitate as he slung his rifle and ripped the baby from the woman's arms. She screamed, tears streaming down her bloodied face, pleading. The sergeant held the baby away from his body like holding something foul. Colonel Araki put the barrel of the pistol against the infant's screaming face. The woman leaped at him, but the soldiers were ready and grabbed her. He pulled the trigger spraying blood and gore onto the sergeant who dropped the lifeless body to the jungle floor.

The woman dropped to her knees clutching for her baby. Colonel Araki safed his weapon, pulled out a white cloth and wiped blood from his hand and the gun barrel. He holstered the weapon and started to walk away. The sergeant spoke up, "What should we do with her?" he leered.

The colonel turned, "That's the men's reward for a well-coordinated attack, sergeant. Have your fun then dispose of her. Be quick about it."

The sergeant smiled showing mangled teeth in the firelight. He gave a quick bow and said, "Hai."

The woman looked up from her lifeless son as the soldiers pulled her towards a partially destroyed hut. She saw Thomas Welch approaching the officer who'd just killed her baby boy. She pointed and screamed his name. Welch froze, the color drained from his face as he met the eyes of his accuser. Her hatred was palpable. He strode to the knot of men and in Japanese addressed the sergeant dragging her, "Sergeant." The soldier scowled at Welch. "Be sure she doesn't survive." She struggled to break away, to get at him, scratch out his eyes, but the men pulled her into the dark hut. It was the last time he saw Captain Morrisey's wife.

# 1

T hree months later, October 1942 off the coast of Guadalcanal

ELEMENTS of the 164th Regiment of the American Division worked their way down the cargo net ladders to the undulating landing craft. The air was muggy and Private O'Connor thought his Irish ass would melt.

He wondered how a boy born and raised in the woods of Oregon ended up in this hot corner of the world. The men around him were from the mid-western part of the country, North Dakota mostly. He had no idea how he'd ended up with these cornhuskers, but here he was.

He looked down at his next step waiting for the man beneath him, Private Dunphy to move his hand. "Come on Dunphy, hurry your ass up."

Dunphy scowled at him and kept his methodical pace, not daring to release his hand to give him the finger. One false move and you'd either fall twenty feet to the bottom of the landing craft assuring broken bones or you'd miss and sink to the bottom of the blue Pacific, pulled down by the sixty pounds of gear on your back.

O'Connor had seen it happen, the young kid from South Dakota's capital. He couldn't remember his name. He'd sunk like a rock, struggling to release his pack as he shot to the bottom. Even if he'd managed, he went down so fast the pressure probably killed him before he drowned. The vision was still firmly imprinted in his mind. The look in the young man's eyes as he disappeared into the blue abyss was haunting. He glanced at the green island a mile off and wondered what other experiences he'd soon be unable to forget.

The official name was Guadalcanal, but everyone called it 'the Canal.' The fighting had been going on since early August. The 1st Marine Division had landed unopposed and pushed inland to seize the newly constructed Henderson airfield. Of course, the Japanese had their own name for it, but to the Marines, it was Henderson.

Henderson was the key to the whole operation. If the Japanese owned the island they'd use the airfield to launch attacks directly against the shipping lanes around Australia and use the island as a rally point for a full-on invasion. The allies were determined to stem the steady advance of the Imperial Japanese Army and Navy. They sent nineteen thousand Marines to secure the airfield and the island.

The Marines held off relentless Japanese attacks over the next few months and inflicted heavy casualties, but they took casualties of their own. The jungle was as dangerous as the enemy soldiers, causing mounting casualties from malaria and dengue fever, foot-rot and some diseases the Navy docs had yet to name.

The entire world had heard of the Marines holding off three times their numbers on the miserable little island. Guadalcanal, a name ninety-nine percent of Americans had never heard before the summer of '42, was now a household name.

The men of the 164th Regiment were no exception. They'd heard all about the hell they were being sent to. They'd been acclimated to the stifling tropical environment on the island of New Caledonia. They'd spent months training in the jungles, learning the sights, smells and sounds of the harsh environment where they'd meet the enemy.

Now it was October 13th, 1942 and the 164th was offloading troop ships and heading to the beaches at Lunga Point, the same place the Marines had landed three months earlier. No opposition was expected, the Marines had secured the area, but there was the ever-present danger of artillery and marauding Japanese aircraft.

As O'Connor finally jumped from the ladder to the boat he hoped they'd get a move on. Sitting in these damned boats made him feel like a sitting duck. One well-placed artillery shell and they'd all die instantly, shredded shark meat.

He lined up behind Dunphy and watched the last man from the rope ladder enter the boat, Sergeant Carver. Carver was his platoon Sergeant. He was a big man, everything about him was big, his hands, his eyes, his jutting jaw. Even his eyebrows were big and bushy.

Sergeant Carver noticed O'Connor eyeballing him and in his flat Midwestern accent said, "Whaddya lookin' at Private? Eyes front, pay attention."

O'Connor looked away staring at the back of Dunphy's helmeted head. He clutched his rifle checking the plastic cover. His M1 was his most prized possession. Of course, it wasn't his, he was only borrowing it from the Army, but he thought it was the finest weapon he'd ever held, even more than his trusted Winchester he shot deer with back home.

Carver pushed him in the back knocking him into Dunphy who scowled. Carver yelled to the squad, "Keep your fucking heads down, when the gate comes down haul ass and get to cover. I know the Marines have made things all safe and sound for us, but they're Marines so who knows."

O'Connor grinned. Carver's disdain for his Marine brethren was well known. He detested the way they strutted around like they were something special. He'd been in the Army since his 18th birthday. To him it was the only military branch that made any sense. He did what was asked of him, never complained, always delivered and never asked for special treatment. The Marines were always striving for the limelight, trying to be the golden boys of the armed forces. When there was real work to be done they called in the Army. And now, here it was again, the Army coming to the rescue to finish kicking Tojo off this shithole island.

The boats' throaty motor went from idle to full throttle and the brick shaped boat plowed forward. The sea was calm this early in the morning, barely any chop. It was a smooth ride all the way to shore. O'Connor waited for the thumping of artillery, but it never came. When the boat ran up on the beach, he lurched into Dunphy. "Get off me, hick."

The front gate slammed open and thumped onto the beach. Sergeant Carver was yelling, "Go, go, go."

O'Connor was glad to be moving. He jumped off the gate and felt his feet sink into the sand of the canal. There was no opposition, but they still sprinted to the tree line and took cover. O'Connor laid against the roots of a huge palm tree. He unwrapped his rifle and checked the breech. He looked around at the others doing the same.

Dunphy was beside him, he stood up and held his rifle against his hip, the barrel pointed to the sky, like he was posing for a Remington commercial. He looked around, "Shit, what are we hiding from? there's nothing but palm trees and beach."

The landing craft backed away and headed back to the transports to bring more of the 164th. O'Connor heard clapping and laughing. He peeked around the palm tree into the shadowed jungle. There were soldiers in raggedy uniforms, no, not soldiers, Marines. They were laughing, clapping and pointing. O'Connor felt his face redden wondering what the hell was so funny.

"Nice job Army. You saved us all from the big bad Japs." There were one hundred Marines milling around tents. O'Connor felt like an idiot, he stood and studied the Marines. They didn't look like the proud men he'd seen a couple of months ago. Most of their uniforms were ragged and torn. Their boots were worn, some with gaping holes. They were thin, like wraiths from a Halloween nightmare. Most were unshaven, some with full beards, the less developed only sporting wisps of uneven growth. They were all dirty, the kind of dirty that would never completely disappear. O'Connor wondered if he'd look like that in a couple of months. He shivered despite the oppressive heat.

Sergeant Carver stood up, "All right, let's get to our rally point." O'Connor trotted with his squad. "Set up over there," he pointed to a thinned out area one hundred yards west of the Marine camp. He yelled, "Clear out a spot for our gear, it's coming with the next wave."

O'Connor got to work pulling undergrowth from the area. The dirt smelled rotten, like dead decaying animals. He wondered what could possibly make such a foul smell. Dirt was supposed to smell like dirt. He heard Private Crandall yell, "Goddamn, this is shit!"

O'Connor looked over his shoulder at the Marines who were laughing and pointing and falling over themselves. "Goddammit, were grousing in the Marine's shit trench."

O'Connor and the rest hurried to the waters' edge, stripped off their soiled tops and tried to wash. Sergeant Carver saw his platoon in the ocean, "What in sam hell you doing? I told you to clear an area for our supplies." He pointed to where they'd been.

Dunphy spoke up, not wanting to miss a chance to mess with Sgt. Carver. "You sent us to a shithole...literally. That's the Marines' latrine we were digging in, genius."

Carver took the ten steps to Dunphy in five strides and pulled up close. They were nose to nose. Dunphy didn't back down even though Sgt. Carver outweighed him by thirty pounds of muscle. Instead he sneered at him. Carver growled, "You got something else smart to say?"

Dunphy didn't, just stared back, not intimidated. Sergeant Carver growled, "Your attitude's gonna get you hurt, slick." He looked around to the other men who were watching the confrontation with interest.

Dunphy came from a rich family, joined to piss off his parents, but never thought he'd actually be put into a normal unit. He didn't think his parents would allow that to happen, but it did. His parents made sure he went into a regular unit to teach their spoiled son a lesson.

He may have been a private, but he thought of himself as a general and let everyone know his disdain for their lower class. He also let it be known that he was a champion boxer and could best any man that cared to try. A few had and he'd been true to his boast. He was light on his feet and his jabs were lightning fast and powerful.

The platoon knew that eventually Carver and Dunphy would come to blows. They were split 50/50 in the betting pool. Carver had the brawn and the street fighting experience, Dunphy had the benefit of professional training.

Sergeant Carver wanted to take Private Dunphy down a notch, but now wasn't the time. Now was the time to get squared away. He pointed, "Move further west until you find a less shitty spot and clear it out." He turned back to Dunphy and yelled, "Now!" Dunphy leaned back, the force of Carver's voice startling him. He turned and with the others put his wet top on and moved away from the latrine area.

Sergeant Carver looked to the Marines who were still laughing. He walked to them and was confronted by another Sergeant, his counterpart. Sergeant Carver pointed, "Why're you shitting in the boonies, why don't you have proper latrines?"

The Marine gunnery sergeant smiled showing brown, tobacco stained teeth, "The Japs blew 'em up couple nights ago. They come by almost every night, drop their bombs and skedaddle."

Carver put his hands on his waist, "Well shit." The gunny nodded, agreeing with his sentiment.

There was yelling from the beach, "Sergeant Carver." He turned and saw his commanding officer tromping up the beach from a just beached landing craft. Carver looked at the Marine, "Don't ask me why he wasn't in the first wave with his troopers." The gunny spit out a long stream of black tobacco juice and made himself scarce.

As Lieutenant Caprielli trudged towards him, Sgt. Carver stiffened, but didn't salute. Caprielli looked him up and down, "It's protocol to salute your commanding officer, Sergeant."

Carver snapped off a crisp salute, "Sorry, Sir. It's common for Jap snipers to shoot officers. They figure out who's who by seeing who gets saluted."

Caprielli cringed and pulled Carver's hand down. He looked around wondering where the shot would come from. He pulled Carver behind an idling jeep and crouched pulling Carver with him. He pointed to the landing crafts beaching and dropping their front gates. "Our supplies are on those boats. Have the men start offloading them to that spot there." He pointed to the same spot the Marines were using as a latrine.

Carver said, "I've got the men clearing an area out over there," he pointed, "the spot you're looking at is a latrine."

Caprielli nodded, "Well, okay. the other spot looks fine, but get the men moving, we're sitting ducks on this beach."

Carver stood up, "Yes Sir. Don't we have tractors or something to help with the offload?"

Caprielli shook his head, "No, there's only a couple of jeeps. This beach isn't big enough to build harbor facilities. The men will just have to grunt it out."

"Yessir." Carver went to tell the men the good news and Lieutenant Caprielli got in his jeep and trundled away along the beach. Carver had no idea where he was going.

HOURS later the equipment and supplies were moved to the relative safety of the sparse jungle. O'Connor sat on a box of rations and pulled heavily on a cigarette. He had his shirt off, as did the entire company. He was dripping with sweat. The heavy labor had taken its toll. He felt like his limbs were made of concrete and the heavy air made his lungs feel like they were pulling oxygen through taffy.

He looked around at the others, they looked as haggard as he felt. His red hair was darkened with sweat. Suddenly he heard a loud Siren. The Marines, who were three hundred yards up the beach scrambled and jumped into foxholes disappearing like mice when a hawk's shadow passes over. O'Connor looked around, knowing the Siren meant air raid, but he had no idea where to go. They'd been so busy offloading supplies they hadn't had time to dig their own holes.

He grabbed his rifle, put his helmet on and dove to the only cover he could, the boxes they'd just off-loaded. A minute later the throaty sound of airplane engines starting up added to the Siren. He looked towards the sound and figured it must be Marine fighters from Henderson field scrambling to meet the threat. He hoped they'd get up in time and kick the crap out of whatever was coming.

As he laid there he noticed the box he was lying next to was labeled '20mm ammunition'. He wondered what would happen if a bomb landed nearby. Would it explode the ammo and tear him to shreds? He didn't want to find out. He grabbed his M1 and took off towards a thick grove of palms. He heard someone yelling for him to take cover. He thought, *no shit*. He was halfway to the palms when he heard the distinctive sound of incoming. He hadn't heard the enemy bombers, but he sure heard their whistling ordnance.

He wasn't going to make it to the trees, he threw himself to the ground and quick crawled to a small depression. He felt, rather than heard the first bomb impact. His body quivered as the shock wave pulsed through him. It was followed by more bone jarring explosions. He dropped his rifle and pulled the edge of his helmet down tight around his ears. Time seemed to stand still as the bombs thumped and thundered. It was less than a minute, but it felt like an eternity.

He heard the distant sound of airplane engines leaving the area. He looked in the direction he thought the bombs had hit. He was surprised to see smoke rising far from his position. He'd thought they were right on top of him, but they were three hundred yards away. He'd never been in any real danger. He went up on his elbows and wondered what it would be like when they were landing within yards, or feet, or inches.

He started to get up, but Sgt. Carver yelled to stay down. The Siren was still wailing. He looked up at the sky, but couldn't see anything through the palms. Soon the same whistling sound of impending doom. He went flat pulling his helmet down. This time the impacts were closer. His body shimmered and bounced on the fetid ground. He wondered if the dancing dirt beneath him would be the last thing he saw.

This wave of bombs didn't last as long, but they'd been close enough to knock palm fronds onto his bare back. He cringed every time thinking a tree would crush him if a bomb didn't kill him first.

This time when the bombs stopped the Siren's wail also stopped. *Is it hit or is the raid over*? O'Connor decided he'd stay down until given the all clear.

He heard feet beside him, he turned his head and saw Carver's size elevens. "It's over, get your ass off the ground."

O'Connor sprang up with his rifle at the ready. He looked at Carver and nodded, "I'm okay." He said it as if confirming it to himself.

Sergeant Carver shouldered his rifle and slapped his back hard.

"Course you're okay, they weren't aiming at you, they're aiming at Henderson, dumb-ass."

Oconnor nodded still shaken up. "We gonna dig in now, Sarge? Feel like my ass is hanging in the wind."

"Yeah, it's time to move up to our positions south of the field." He pointed with his thumb where the smoke was rising.

"We're going closer to the field?" O'Connor looked like he'd eaten something rotten. Sergeant Carver scowled and walked away yelling for his soldiers to gather their shit and form up. O'Connor found his shirt covered with a fine layer of dirt and various unidentifiable bugs. He shook it out and put it on. It felt gritty and hard against his sweaty body. He found his rucksack and swung it onto his shoulders. He formed up with the others in a ragged combat formation and tromped through the shredded forest toward Henderson field.

The closer they got the more bomb craters they encountered. Some were still smoldering. They came to the edge of the jungle and looked out over the expanse of Henderson. The Japs and then the Marines had done a good job of fleecing the jungle. The field was flat with not a single living plant growing within its borders. It looked like a moonscape, it even had the craters.

As they skirted around to the south they watched the fighters that had gone off to intercept the bombers coming in to land. They landed two at a time, the powerful F4 Wildcats looked like dangerous predators. They sent up plumes of choking dust and taxied to parking. They stayed spread out, not making themselves easy targets for any uninvited guests.

O'Connor nudged Dunphy who marched beside him, "Love to get my hands on one of those."

Dunphy guffawed, "You wouldn't get off the ground, you'd kill yourself and anyone nearby. Besides, you have to be an officer to be a pilot."

O'Connor shrugged, "Doesn't look that hard."

"You have no idea, there's more to it than you think."

O'Connor looked at him sideways, "You've flown before? You're shitting me. If you were a pilot you'd be in one of those."

Dunphy kept his eyes forward. "Forget about it, Red."

Dunphy always called him Red, unoriginal, but probably inevitable. O'Connor watched the graceful planes landing and parking. He wasn't going to let Dunphy ruin his fantasy. He'd only seen a handful of airplanes in his life and none as sexy as the Wildcats.

They finally got to the southern edge of the airfield. The company was ordered to dig in. They didn't have to be told twice. The recent bombing and their move closer to its target was incentive enough to get busy. Soon every soldier had dug a deep hole. Some of the men had cut down large palm trees and were using the thick trunks to cover the tops.

O'Connor was pleased with his hole, but not to be sharing it with Private Dunphy. He looked up at the sturdy cover and wondered if it would be strong enough to withstand a direct hit. After seeing the size of the bomb craters, he had no illusions. He only hoped for relative safety. He'd soon find out if his efforts were enough.

## 2

Once their positions were consolidated on the southern end of Henderson field with clear fields of fire and zeroed mortar crews there wasn't much to do. O'Connor was exhausted. He slumped to the bottom of the hole. Beside him Private Dunphy napped fitfully, unable to get comfortable. "This fucking hole's disgusting. How am I supposed to sleep in here?"

O'Connor closed his eyes and leaned back. "You can't complain; you didn't do shit. If you wanted it comfy you should've helped."

"Fuck you Red, I helped plenty." He held up his palms, "Look at my hand, those are blisters."

O'Connor laughed, "First time?" Dunphy picked at his hands. "Look I don't like it any more than you. Were in a hole." He pointed to the overhead palm logs, "You think those'll sustain a near miss?"

"How should I know?" he reached up and pulled on one, it was solid. "Pretty sturdy, doubt it'll take a direct hit."

"I'm gonna try to get some sleep, when're we up for outpost duty?" When there was no answer, he looked over at Dunphy who shrugged. "You're worthless, you know that?"

O'Connor sighed and stood up poking his head through the slot between the palm logs. He looked around and spotted Sgt. Carver talking with Lt. Caprielle. "I'm gonna go find out."

Dunphy punched him in the leg, "Don't make work for us, asshole, they'll tell us when it's time. Why you so damned jumpy?"

O'Connor ignored him and hopped out of the hole. It was evening, the day was winding down, but still hot and humid. It felt better out of the hole, there was a slight breeze. He stopped to relish it. The entire company was gone, hidden in their holes waiting for the next bombardment. O'Connor stretched his back and trotted over to Carver who was walking away from Lieutenant Caprielli. When he saw O'Connor he said, "What you doing out of your hole?"

"Sorry Sarge, have to take a leak real bad. Can't hold it."

"Well hurry up and get back in your hole."

He nodded. As he veered towards a nearby bush he asked, "What's the guard duty schedule tonight? Am I on?"

"Nope, the observation post's already out there...don't worry you'll get your turn."

"Yes, Sarge." He took his leak and slithered back into his hole. It was getting dark quick. He was amazed how fast night came in the jungle. He looked towards the jungle. The thick green was now deep black. It looked nothing like his forests back in Oregon. The jungle was thick and daunting, he couldn't see a path through. He figured there was though, there always was, animal trails probably snaked through everywhere.

He loved traveling through forests, loved finding their secrets. Every forest was different. He supposed even though this was jungle it was still a forest, still wild country. He stared into it, wishing he knew its secrets. He wished the enemy wasn't lurking out there hunting him, he'd like to explore this place properly.

He watched the edge of the jungle not ready for the utter darkness of the foxhole. He could hear Dunphy's soft breathing. The jungle's blackness seemed impenetrable, but the longer he focused on it the more features he could pick out. His hole was twenty yards from the edge, he knew the OP was just inside the jungle. He thought how terrifying it must be for that pair. *Wonder who drew the short straw?*

The sounds alone were terrifying. They'd been on New Caledonia for a couple of months so they were used to the exotic locale, but this jungle was different, more alive and more deadly. Every sound was an animal, some new secret waiting to be discovered. He knew from the forests back home that animal sounds were a good thing. If the animals were going about their normal routine it meant there was nothing unnatural out there disturbing them, like Japs. Most of his hunting success was because he could move through the forest without disturbing the wildlife. He could sneak up on his unsuspecting prey and the first they knew about it was when the bullet or arrow sliced into them. *Wonder if Japs hunt?*

He kicked where he knew Dunphy was sleeping, "Dunphy, wake up, hey Dunphy." He kicked him again harder.

He felt him stiffen coming awake, "What is it? Japs?"

"Nah, just a question, you think the Japs have any hunters? I mean you think they have any stealthy hunter types that could be sneaking up on us right now?"

"What the fuck you talking about? You didn't wake me to ask me that did you? Did you? I finally get to sleep and you wake me with that?"

O'Connor continued, "I don't think they do, they live in cities. All they are is a bunch of city slickers…like you." He grinned, "Bet they're clumsy as hell, could hear 'em coming a mile away."

Dunphy started to respond, but was cut off by the wailing of the air raid Siren. "Shit, not again." O'Connor looked towards the airfield, all the lights were out, he pictured the pilots running out to man their fighting machines. He listened for the tell-tale engine noises of the Wildcats or the bombers. *Would the fighters launch at night? They wouldn't take off without lights, would they? Wouldn't the lights be perfect aiming points for the Japs?*

Five minutes passed, he heard nothing from the airfield, but he did hear the dull, distant rumble of approaching aircraft. Then he saw spotlights erupt from the jungle and slice into the night sky searching for the bombers. The anti-air started flashing from various points around the airfield. The light was chaotic, he could see tiny explosions in the dark night sky. He hoped they'd find their mark so he wouldn't have to test his hole. He longed to see the flames of a dying Japanese bomber, but nothing. Then he heard the distinct whistle of approaching bombs. He hunkered back into the hole and held his M1 tight to his chest. He adjusted the chin strap of his helmet. *Looks like the Japs are throwing us a welcoming party.*

This time the bombs were much closer. The sides of the foxhole flexed and caved in with each terrifying impact. He thought he'd be buried. A flash of panic coursed through his body, *Should I get out? Save myself from suffocation?* He didn't bolt, he knew it would be suicide. The ground above him was being shredded. He understood why there weren't any plants alive around Henderson, the bombs were more effective than a scythe.

He tried to count the impacts, but lost count after twenty. The bombs seemed to be falling closer and closer together making it impossible to distinguish one from another.

As suddenly as it started, it stopped. The only sound that of diminishing engine noise. O'Connor wondered if anyone was hit. He got his answer soon enough when he heard screaming coming from his right towards the airfield. The screaming sounded far away, but he realized his ears were ringing and he couldn't judge distance. The wounded man or his nearby buddies were calling for a medic. He wondered if he knew the man. *Was he in his platoon, his company? Would he die? Lose a limb? Be paralyzed?* A minute passed and finally the screaming faded to a whimper.

O'Connor put his head above the foxhole and was amazed to see his world was still intact. How could anything survive after such a thrashing? He could see the silhouettes of the Marine F4 Wildcats in the distance, pushed up against the jungle for protection. The one building in the entire area was still standing. The hut, or 'the pagoda' as it came to be called was standing defiant and untouched by the bombing. The airfield had taken a number of direct hits. The Marines were already firing up tractors and men with shovels were dashing around filling the holes with surplus piles of dirt made for the occasion. He had no doubt the airfield would be ready to launch fighters in the morning.

A soldier was running past. Dunphy, who was up watching too, reached out for him, "Hey, what's going on? Who got hit?" the soldier kicked off his hand and kept running without answering. "I need to figure out what the hell's happening?" said Dunphy.

O'Connor felt a deep fatigue rush over his body. He slumped into the hole and pulled his rifle close. He'd never felt anything like it, he had to sleep *now*. He shut his eyes, but the flashes of exploding bombs wouldn't leave his vision. Finally sleep overtook him, but it was fitful, filled with starts and stops.

## 3

————

O'Connor woke when he felt Dunphy's boot in his ribs. He nearly jumped out of his skin; whatever dream he was having playing out in terrifying form. "Get up. Something's happening."

O'Connor sat up and peeked over the edge. Men were shuffling about stretching. He hopped out of the hole and felt his back spasm. He was nineteen, but felt like eighty. He wondered how the older Dunphy felt. Dunphy sprang from the hole without so much as a grunt. He looked around taking in the scene. Men were gathering around a tattered tent. A Sergeant was trotting from hole to hole giving instructions. When he got to them he said, "Eat K-rats and form up at the tent in fifteen minutes for a patrol."

O'Connor looked to the jungle. It looked green and almost inviting, completely opposite from the night before. They were finally going out on a combat patrol. He felt his bowels loosen at the thought. He remembered the latrine area from the day before. He trotted toward it, loosening his belt on the way.

By the time he got back Dunphy had eaten a K-rat and was gearing up. "Hurry up chump, you're gonna miss the show."

"Had to take a shit."

Dunphy nodded, grabbed his M1 and watched his foxhole mate open a K-ration. "Enjoy your breakfast, mine was spaghetti, or something resembling it."

O'Connor ignored him and slurped a can of peaches. They were a delicacy in the jungle, he hadn't planned on opening them, but the upcoming patrol was occupying his mind and he hadn't realized what he was doing until it was done. He couldn't very well reseal them, once opened they had to be eaten. They tasted amazing. Maybe it would be his last meal; not a bad one.

They joined the gathering group of soldiers and waited for the briefing. Lieutenant Caprielli was standing at a table and yelled "Tenhut." The room snapped to attention as Captain Simmons walked in. He was a short balding man. He looked to be in his early thirties. "At ease, men." He stood beside the lieutenant and gathered some papers. He looked over the men, "Last night was a typical night on Guadalcanal. The Japs bomb us every day without exception." He looked around, "That was actually a light night, usually they do it more than once. Sometimes their ships will run by the coast and hit us with naval guns…not ideal."

A sergeant raised his hand when he sensed a pause. The Captain pointed at him, "Sir, I thought our navy was handling the Jap navy."

The Captain looked at the floor and shook his head, "Not true Sergeant. The situation's confused. Sometimes the ships we see are ours, sometimes theirs. From what I hear it's an even fight. The Japs are spread thin though, they'll run out of ships before we do, but don't count on support from our squids. In fact, the Japs continue to land more troops on the other side of the island almost nightly. We're trying to interdict, but it's a big ocean and we haven't had much luck so far." He took a sip of warm water. "We're not facing worn out troops, we're facing fresh, seasoned soldiers. We can expect to be hit any day. They know we're here, they know we're untested. There's little doubt they'll hit the 164th. They think we're green and weak. We're gonna prove 'em wrong."

He paced up and down the table. Lieutenant Caprielli had to back out of the way. The Captain pointed to the jungle, "We're gonna make our presence felt today. The NCOs will brief individual squads, but were sending out patrols. We need to find the enemy line. It's essential for us to know how close these troops are to mounting an attack."

Another sergeant spoke up, "Are we attacking, Sir?"

"We're waiting to assess the situation. We just landed yesterday, we need time to figure out how things work here. Get our bearings. We'll stick it to 'em soon enough."

He grabbed the edge of the table and looked out over the sea of young faces. "The Marines have been fighting on this island since August. It's our turn. I know you'll do me, the Army and your families proud. Make no mistake, the enemy is relentless and brutal. Kill them when you find them, have no mercy, give no lenience. They won't give you any. Good luck and good hunting."

With that he left and was replaced by Lieutenant Carprielli. "Break up into your platoons. You'll be briefed by your sergeants."

O'Connor saw Sgt. Carver and went to him. His platoon was milling about making small talk. Carver yelled to get their attention. "I want 1st and 2nd squads, the rest of you back to your holes."

O'Connor looked at the men around him. The other members of 2nd squad looked like deer in headlights. *Are they ready for battle?* He knew they were, they'd been training endlessly for months, now it was the real deal. He was ready, he hoped the others were, his life depended on it.

SERGEANT CARVER GATHERED BOTH SQUADS. Lieutenant Caprielli spoke, "Men, our first patrol. Our first time being tested." He looked from man to man, "I'm sure you're all wondering how you'll perform out there. You're well trained. When in doubt fall back on your training. If everyone does their job it'll go off without a hitch." He gestured to Sgt. Carver who listened with his burly arms across his chest. "Sergeant, make sure the men are loaded out correctly. We kick off at 1000 hours sharp." He looked at his watch and walked back towards his tent.

Carver watched him go. "Okay, just like we practiced back on New Caledonia, this is a light patrol, meaning, don't bring a lot of shit. One canteen, no food, full complement of ammo, your K-bar, a basic load-out. I want each man carrying at least two grenades. Morgan bring the BAR, the rest of you your rifles. Clear?" There was a smattering of nods and 'Yes Sarge'. "Clear?" he yelled it this time.

"Yes, Sergeant," came the chorus.

"Meet back here at 0945 looking sharp."

The squads broke up heading to the makeshift armory to fill ammo pouches with clips and grenades. As O'Connor filled his bag he thought he'd throw up. He wondered if anyone else was nervous. He looked around at the young faces, none of them seemed scared. Some were even joking around. An M1 clip fell from his hand and landed in the dirt. He bent to pick it up, but Private First-Class Morgan said in his deep voice, "Don't pack that one unless you plan to unload it and clean each bullet. You don't want your M1 jamming when you need it most."

O'Connor nodded and placed it away from the pile. He didn't tell him he'd undoubtedly shot more than Morgan. Morgan watched him fumble another one. He put his hand on his shoulder. "Relax Red. Believe me the jitters will go away as soon as we step off into the jungle."

O'Connor nodded, "You've been in combat?"

"Nothing like the Marines here, but I was a cop before. Doubt it's much different." He smiled, "At least out here you know who the enemy is." He paused and stopped pulling ammo. "When the shit hits the fan your training takes over. Kinda go into auto-pilot."

O'Connor nodded. That's what everyone always said 'Remember your training,' but he didn't feel his training was all that good. He'd spent his life living in the woods living off the land. His parents never had real jobs, they lived meal to meal, tending gardens and shooting game. His little sister knew more about stealth and staying alive in the wilds than any of these yahoos and she was ten years old. All they showed him in boot camp and subsequent training was how to use different weapons and how to follow orders from someone who'd likely get him killed.

For the first time he realized he wasn't nervous about facing the Japs, he was nervous about facing the Japs with a bunch of city slickers. He looked around the group, the only man he thought he could rely on was Sgt. Carver and maybe Pvt. Crandall. Crandall had been a trapeze artist or some such thing and seemed like all the traveling around from town to town had hardened him more than the others. Dunphy was probably a good boxer but he was sure he'd become totally useless when the bullets started flying. He'd never worked a day in his life.

He finished gathering his kit, looked at his watch and went to the rally point waiting for 0945 to come. The day was sweltering, he'd already soaked through both his undershirt and his blouse top. He had a couple minutes so he laid out his tarp and stripped his M1 Garand. His M1 was the one thing he loved about the Army. He'd shot a lot of rifles, but nothing felt as smooth and comfortable as the M1. He'd qualified expert without even having to try. He caressed each piece inspecting it for any dirt then put it back together marveling at how perfectly everything fit into place.

At 0945 everyone was standing with their weapons slung. Sergeant Carver stood next to Lt. Caprielli. "The sergeant will put you in battle order. Our orders are to probe and find the enemy line. Once we do, we break contact and get back here. Clear?"

"Yes, Sir."

Carver boomed, "I want 2nd squad up front with Crandall on point." O'Connor saw the color drain from Crandall's face. O'Connor had told Carver back on New Caledonia of his hunting experience, but for some reason he never let him take point. He wasn't sure he wanted to, but he thought he'd be good at it. Crandall wasn't bad, but he'd gotten them lost a few times in the thicker jungle.

O'Connor was placed in the middle of the squad behind Dunphy. He couldn't seem to get away from him. 1st squad would hang back and cover any hasty retreat. They formed their line and Carver said, "Keep your interval, no bunching up. Keep the man in front of you in sight. If he stops, you stop, speeds up, you speed up. No talking and be sure nothing's making noise on your uniform. Hopefully, the Japs won't even know we've been there." O'Connor almost laughed out loud. From his experience these guys were anything but quiet.

They walked past their foxholes, the barbed wire was pulled back and then they were in the jungle. It was like turning off a light. One moment they were in a bright sunny morning the next they were in a greenish black jungle. The smell changed from dried out dirt to wet loamy decay. The smell permeated O'Connor's senses.

The trail they walked was narrow. He wondered if it was a human trail or a game trail, probably both. He watched Dunphy's back. He was walking upright his gun slung like he was on a Sunday stroll. O'Connor glanced back and could just make out Morgan with the big Browning Automatic Rifle. He saw his teeth flash as he smiled. He turned back around and listened for anything out of the ordinary. The squad consisted of twelve men. They weren't hunters, they were loud. He couldn't hear anything but them.

Suddenly Dunphy crouched down holding up his fist. O'Connor immediately did the same. He looked to either side of the trail. The jungle was so dense there could have been an enemy soldier within spitting distance and he wouldn't have known it. Following the trail was stupid. It was obvious, the Japs would ambush them any second. Dunphy signaled to get off the trail. He did the same for Morgan and went to his left as Dunphy went right. He pushed into the jungle parting foliage until he'd made himself a small pocket. He was off the trail, but only just. He tried to keep Dunphy in sight, but his green uniform was hard to pick out. He found his silhouette though and listened and watched.

Two minutes passed before he saw Dunphy come back on the trail. O'Connor noticed he'd brought his rifle off his shoulder, it was a start. They advanced another fifty yards. The trail started to peter out and the jungle opened up a little. Dunphy, who was paying more attention now went left and he directed O'Connor to the right. He, in turn pointed left to Morgan. He felt much better getting off the trail and into a combat spread. The underbrush was thick, but manageable. The jungle was buzzing with clouds of mosquitos. He looked at his hands, he counted 6 of the little blood suckers doing their thing. He ignored them and kept listening and watching. Dunphy off to his left was making a racket swatting them off his exposed skin. O'Connor gritted his teeth, that kind of thing would get him killed. He wondered if he should try to get his attention when he noticed the man in front of Dunphy was crouched with his fist up.

He immediately stopped and sent the signal back, but Dunphy was oblivious and kept walking until he was next to the soldier. O'Connor thought it was Corporal Hooper. He watched Hooper jump in surprise. Hooper reached out and grabbed Dunphy's sleeve pulling him down. Dunphy tried to back up to where he should be, but Hooper held him and pointed. O'Connor tried to see what he was pointing at, but the light was too dim, it looked like more green jungle. He readied his rifle wondering if it was the enemy they'd spotted.

Dunphy looked back looking for O'Connor. O'Connor was crouched behind a tuft of thick grass not moving a muscle. He watched Dunphy trying to find him, getting some satisfaction from his obvious distress. He leaned forward pushing his face through the grass. Dunphy saw him and signaled to take cover. He passed it along and dropped to his stomach, his rifle pressed against his shoulder pointing right.

Then there was a pop, the sudden sound made him jump. It was difficult to figure what direction it had come from, the jungle seemed to swallow sound. Then another and another. It was coming from the front and it was gunfire. He rolled out from behind the tuft and searched for targets. He could see Dunphy lying flat, crawling to his left away from Hooper.

He heard Sgt. Carver yell from the front, "Morgan we're peeling back to you, be ready with the BAR."

Morgan yelled one word, "Yes." He pulled the bipod down and adjusted himself behind the big Browning. O'Connor watched Dunphy try to rise and take off, but Corporal Hooper yelled at him to stay put until the others to his front were by him. They'd practiced this peel, but it was dangerous to run through your comrades when they may be firing at pursuing enemy. There was a good chance for friendly fire casualties. They'd trained not to fire until all friendlies were behind, but if the Japs were hot on their heels they'd have to shoot.

The firing became more intense. He heard the distinctive blast of the M1 then the ping as the clip emptied. Someone had just fired all 8 rounds in a few seconds. It was answered by a machine gun. Tracers came out of the jungle like angry bees. O'Connor looked for a muzzle flash, but the machine gun must have been firing from cover, probably a bunker. Then he saw Carver, Crandall and McDougal running like Olympic sprinters. Carver dropped into a crouch and emptied another clip the way he'd come.

He slapped another clip in as he sprinted past Corporal Hooper and Dunphy. "They're right on our ass, give 'em grenades." Hooper unclipped a grenade from his harness, pulled the pin and chucked it as the men sprinted by him, then he was back on his rifle. He was halfway through his clip when the grenade went off. He used the distraction to jump to his feet and start running. He saw Dunphy still on the ground, he ran to him and yelled for him to get up. Dunphy was fumbling with something at his belt. He stood up and O'Connor saw something drop to the ground. Dunphy took off pushing Hooper in front of him, "Grenade" he yelled.

They got ten feet away when the grenade went off. Hooper yelled and fell, his rifle spinning away. O'Connor was the next in line and he sighted down his rifle waiting for a target. Dunphy was trying to get Corporal Hooper onto his feet. Hooper was clutching his ass, screaming. He put an arm around Dunphy's shoulder and hobbled back.

Out of the dark jungle O'Connor saw what he was waiting for. Two men burst out of the bush and were charging with their impossibly long Arisaka rifles with bayonets attached. They were charging, trying to skewer Dunphy and Hooper. They'd catch up to them in seconds, stab them with the long blades, then they'd come for him. He sighted on the nearest man's chest. He put pressure on the trigger and it bucked in his hand. The thirty-caliber bullet went supersonic and entered the Japanese soldiers' chest and exited pulling blood and gore with it. The man dropped and didn't move. The next man didn't miss a beat, he was almost upon the two men. O'Connor adjusted and shot twice. Both bullets hit within centimeters exploding the man's chest. He went from full sprint to hitting an invisible wall and flying backwards. He landed on his comrade.

O'Connor pulled both his grenades, pulled the pins and hurled them one after another. There was movement in the dimness where the Japanese had come from, but he didn't wait. He got on the other side of Hooper and now they could run.

O'Connor waited for the bullet that would end his life, but instead he heard his grenades explode then the powerful thumping of Morgan's BAR. He got beyond Morgan and saw Carver directing them to the rear. "Get him out of here."

When they got back to the end of their squad, Lt. Caprielli was moving forward. He saw the wounded man and called up men from 1st squad to take over. O'Connor was glad to be away from him; three men together was too easy a target. He ran back to the line. Morgan's BAR was still thumping.

He ran in a crouch until he was behind Morgan. He threw himself to the ground and crawled forward until he had a clear view of the jungle. He saw the crumpled forms of the two men he'd killed. They were a greenish blotch on the jungle floor. He searched for targets, but didn't see any. Morgan was still hammering away. Sergeant Carver yelled from O'Connor's right, "Covering fire, Morgan, fall back to the trail."

Morgan sprang to his knees and collapsed the attached bipod. He lifted the heavy gun and started running to the rear. O'Connor sighted down his M1 and fired into the darkness until he heard the clip ping. Carver yelled, "Fall back!" O'Connor smoothly loaded a new clip. He stuffed the empty clip into his pocket and took off for the trail. He ran hunched over waiting to get shot. He decided he didn't like running away. The thought of getting shot in the back terrified him.

When he got to the narrowing jungle he saw the rest of his squad crouched, guns pointing back the way he'd come. No more shots came from the jungle. Sergeant Carver got them up, "All right let's get back down the trail." He looked around, "Where's first squad?"

Private Troutman said, "The L-T took 'em back down the trail couple minutes ago."

Carver shook his head, "Okay, looks like were tail end Charlie." He pointed at O'Connor, "you cover our tail. Keep up."

O'Connor nodded and watched the squad filter past him towards the jungle path. They were trotting and soon disappeared onto the narrow trail. O'Connor backed away looking for any enemy. Nothing. He turned and found the trail. He trotted a couple feet then turned and listened and watched. Nothing. He couldn't hear the squad; they weren't wasting any time running home. He turned and ran to catch up. The thought of being alone in the jungle scared him.

After fifty yards he caught sight of the back of a soldier, he couldn't tell who it was. He stopped and crouched watching the back trail. He felt sure no one was following.

Minutes later he caught up to both squads. They were crouched waiting for him. Carver saw him and raised his eyebrows. O'Connor shook his head, there was nothing following. Sergeant Carver looked to Lieutenant Caprielli, who nodded. Sergeant Carver called to the line, "1st and 2nd squads coming in with wounded."

"We heard you coming a mile away, come on in." They stepped out of the dark jungle into the bright midday sun. They covered their eyes and squinted. The sun was brilliant after the darkness of the jungle. The rolled barbed wire was put back into place once they were inside.

Lieutenant Caprielli and Sergeant Carver double timed to the head-quarters tent. Corporal Hooper was helped to a jeep, thrown onto the hood and carted back to the medical tent near the beach.

O'Connor went to his hole and sat on the edge. He took off his helmet and took a long pull from his canteen. He drained it and started on another. It was warm and had a chemical taste, but it was the best water he'd ever tasted.

Dunphy sat beside him and put his head into his hands. He rubbed his short dark hair. O'Connor put his hand on his shoulder. "Don't sweat it, could've happened to anyone."

Dunphy looked at him sideways, "What the hell you talking about?"

O'Connor stared, "Thought you were feeling bad about wounding Hooper. I was saying it could've happened to anyone."

"Wounding Hooper? He made me fumble that grenade. The stupid spic could've killed us both. Getting his ass blown off was what he deserved."

O'Connor played it over in his head. He didn't remember it that way. "You're something else, Dunphy." O'Connor ejected the bullet in his chamber and started stripping his M1.

Dunphy pointed, "You're a pretty good shot with that thing. Saw you bag those two nips back there." He kept stripping and cleaning the rifle. "You learn how to shoot like that in the Army?"

O'Connor wasn't interested in talking with Dunphy. The stupid son of a bitch couldn't even admit when he'd almost gotten someone killed. O'Connor was sure he'd say something he'd regret.

"Stern silent type now? Shit, last night I couldn't get you to shut up, now you're tight lipped."

O'Connor stopped cleaning and looked at him, "Why you call Hooper a spic? He's as white as you or I."

Dunphy only smiled and shrugged. "He's a loser, got hit, he's a spic."

"He got hit because you dropped your own grenade. You wounded him, it was your fault, I saw the whole thing."

"Really? You sure about that? Sure about what you saw? Cause that's not what happened. He hit my arm and I dropped the grenade. I'm surprised I didn't get hit." He paused and picked up a colorful furry caterpillar. "I pushed him away, probably saved his life."

O'Connor couldn't argue with him there. He pointed at the critter crawling from one hand to the other. "You know this island has a thousand different poisonous creatures that can kill you?"

Dunphy kept playing with the caterpillar. "This thing's not dangerous. Look how pretty it is. It's harmless."

"A lot of times the colorful ones are the most poisonous. Their colors draw their prey in, they want to be found so they can attack." Dunphy flicked it off his hand. "Mother Nature's a bitch."

Sergeant Carver was making his rounds from hole to hole. When he got to theirs he pointed at Dunphy, "You almost got Hooper killed today."

Dunphy started to protest, but Carver grabbed a fistful of shirt and pulled him close, nose to nose, "He told me you dropped your grenade. It's your shrapnel in his ass." His voice went an octave lower, "You better watch your shit soldier or someone may drop one near you." He pushed him away ignoring his reddening face. He looked at O'Connor. "Good shooting today. You did good." O'Connor couldn't help beaming, feeling like a school boy getting kudos from the teacher.

Dunphy stood up and walked away shaking his head. O'Connor thought he heard him mumble, "Spic."

Carver watched him go, "Sorry to put you with that prima-dona prick. If he gives you any trouble you've got my permission to beat the hell out of him." O'Connor grinned and Carver continued, "I'm not kidding, whip his ass." Carver stood up and went to the next hole. He turned back, "Keep your helmet close, this place gets shelled regularly." O'Connor nodded.

# 4

The rest of the day was spent fortifying their position. The holes were reinforced with more palms. Soon O'Connor's hole resembled a bunker, something he hoped would withstand the bombing he knew would be coming. They were dug in on the eastern side of the airstrip and depending on the wind the Marine fighters were either landing or taking off right over them.

He couldn't help stopping his work and watching the graceful killing machines coming and going. They called themselves the Cactus Airforce but to O'Connor they were the most beautiful machines he'd ever seen. He didn't know what their missions were, he assumed fending off Japanese bombers and that was a beautiful thing. He wasn't looking forward to being on the receiving end of another bombing run.

Their positions were strengthened with the addition of more thirty caliber water-cooled machine guns. They'd already proved highly effective against Japanese attacks by the Marines and O'Connor felt better about their position with their presence.

As evening came the company stopped filling sandbags and settled down for chow. They were hot, sweaty and black with dirt and dust. O'Connor lost count how many times he'd drained and filled his canteen. The water was from a nearby spur of the Tenaru river. It was silty and tasted terrible especially with halazone purification pills added, but it was wet and cooler than the thick muggy air. Surviving on this island without fresh water would be a difficult task. Fighting without it, impossible.

As they were eating their K-rations, swatting flies and smashing mosquitos, the quiet was shattered with the sound of a freight train passing overhead. "Incoming! Take cover, take cover!"

O'Connor looked around for his helmet, it was lying ten yards away, he lunged for it. He slapped it on and leaped for the foxhole. Dunphy was already inside peeking through the slit at him. In another second he'd be safe inside but before he got there a huge blast hit him from behind and he was lifted and tossed like a rag doll over the bunker. He flailed his arms and landed hard, knocking the wind out of him. He lay on his back stunned, trying to get his breath back. As he stared, the dust cleared momentarily and he saw the blue sky dotted with puffy clouds. He was dying and the world didn't care.

Across the sky something streaked, seemingly on fire. He marveled at the speed. He watched it arc then land near an F4 Wildcat, which immediately burst into flames. He shook his head, coming back to the world. He remembered seeing his hole fly by beneath him. He turned onto his stomach and started crawling the way he'd come. He could see the outline of the bunker. It was dim through the dust and smoke. It seemed like a million miles away; he'd never make it.

He kept crawling. It was worth a try. Another nearby explosion lifted him off the ground then slammed him back down. He felt like a toy being played with by an unruly child. He felt something hot on his leg. He kept crawling, ignoring the burning pain. After an eternity which was actually seconds he found himself at the lip of his bunker. He poked his head through, then his shoulders then he fell to the bottom like a slug.

"Jesus Christ, you're on fire." O'Connor didn't move. He wondered what the man in the hole with him was saying. The ground shook with another close hit. The man pulled his tunic off and jumped onto O'Connor and started slapping and pounding on him. The man had clearly lost his mind. O'Connor tried to push him off but he was too weak, he felt tired and just wanted to sleep. He wanted this maniac to leave him alone. Blackness finally took over and he dropped into a dark place.

WHEN HE WOKE he thought he must be dead. He tried to move. The pain lanced through every fiber of his being. He was definitely not dead. "Welcome back, asshole."

He turned his head and saw Dunphy sitting beside him. He was shirtless and so dirty he looked like one of the dark-skinned natives. "Wh-what happened?"

"Jap Navy paid us a visit. They cruised by the beach and shot their big fucking naval guns at us." He looked around. "You were on fire, your pants mostly. I got most of it out before it got to your skin, but doc says you may have some second-degree burns. He rubbed some kind of salve on it." He bowed his head. "Some of the others weren't so lucky. We lost Wright, Victorino and Spalding. They're dead." He paused and stared as if picturing it, "Along with you, eleven other guys were wounded. You're wounded the least." He slapped his arm and O'Connor gritted his teeth, "So consider yourself lucky."

O'Connor mumbled, "If this is lucky, fuck luck."

"If you'd seen what was left of the others you'd understand. Their parts...they, well you couldn't tell where one person ended and the other started. Mashed up like stew or something." He pulled his K-bar out and jammed it into the ground, "Fucking Japs."

Another soldier slid in next to O'Connor. He had a red cross on his arm. He dropped his rifle and looked at his wounds. "How you doing, Pal? Glad you're awake; that's a good sign." He poked and prodded, "Think you had a concussion too, along with your burns. Both will heal with time. We're not able to get you to a hospital ship. Not sure you'd be safe anyway; the Jap navy seems to have taken up residence. You just need a day or two, then you'll be ready for duty. We'll get you to the rear for a couple days, just waiting for a jeep...okay?" He didn't wait for an answer, but sprinted off to check on more men.

O'Connor nodded, "Doc sure has a lot to say."

It wasn't long before a jeep pulled up and Dunphy and the driver were lifting him onto the hood.

The ride to the rear was short and painful. The driver and a medic lifted him off the hood and helped him to a cot. The other wounded men were far worse off than he was; he felt he didn't belong there. Men were covered with seeping bandages, most unconscious. His wounds paled in comparison. He was embarrassed. He decided he'd take the first opportunity to rejoin his unit. He was taking the medic's time away from these men who needed the care more than he did. He decided he'd just take a nap then slip back to his unit.

DUNPHY WAS BACK in his hole. Their patrol had run into the Japanese line far closer than they'd expected; only a couple hundred yards. The thick jungle made the distance seem farther. The Japanese would have as much trouble traveling through as the soldiers, but they'd gotten far closer than expected. Command thought they'd be hit any time. They'd put outposts to the edge of the jungle as an early warning system. Everyone was on edge. With O'Connor at the aid station, Dunphy was alone and as much as he loathed the hayseed, he'd rather have him beside him. The kid could shoot. *He dropped those two Japs with three shots.*

He was thinking about his predicament when the first mortars started raining down. At first, he thought it was another artillery strike, but someone yelled "Mortars, take cover." He hunkered down as the line of explosions worked their way toward his position. It was like an advancing hail storm, coming at him with purpose. He cringed with every impact. He looked up at the logs over his head. *Would they stop a direct hit? Would he survive such a thing?* He doubted it would end well.

There were some close impacts, but soon the mortars passed his hole. He heard desperate calls for medics. At least one soldier had been hit. He wondered who. He heard the L-T call to Sgt. Carver to get the OPs in. Dunphy knew what that meant; a Jap attack. He gripped his rifle and took deep breaths. He closed his eyes and tried to control his breathing. He thought about how his boxing coach prepared him for matches. Control the breathing, picture the fight, picture winning the fight, beating the opponent to hamburger. He pictured the soldiers O'Connor had shot, then pictured himself pulling the trigger.

There was an eerie silence when the mortars stopped dropping. *Maybe that was it, maybe it was just more harassment and they wouldn't attack.* The silence was broken as the engines of multiple fighters from the airfield were cranked. They were getting airborne, never a good sign.

Dunphy peeked over the hole towards the jungle. He saw the last of the OP sprinting back to their original holes. He poked his head higher and called to one, he thought it was Crandall, "Hey, hey Crandall. What'd you see out there?"

Crandall didn't look at him but slid into his hole fifteen yards to his right. He popped up, "They're coming, right on our ass. The whole Jap army."

Now their own mortars were firing. The outgoing sounded good. The explosions lit up the jungle. The mortar crews were walking their shots back, giving the Japs their own medicine. Dunphy had his rifle out and scanning. He pulled four grenades off his battle harness and placed them within easy reach. He looked to his right and saw Crandall and Troutman sighting down their M1's sights.

The Japs would have to cross fifty yards of open ground before getting to their holes. He hoped it would be enough. The thought of hand to hand combat terrified him. As if on cue he heard Sergeant Carver yell, "Fix bayonets. Hold fire until you hear the machine guns."

Dunphy tried to remember where the machine guns were. There were two to his right and three to his left. He was in the middle of the company. He took a deep breath. The mortars were still working the tree line and he thought he could hear screaming. Then there was a whistle and the jungle seemed to come alive. Where there had been nothing now there were green clad soldiers. The shrill whistle kept blowing, carrying on the humid air over the sound of falling mortars.

Dunphy sighted on a Jap's chest and was about to squeeze the trigger when he remembered his orders; wait for the machine guns to open up.

He didn't have long to wait. Up and down the line the thirty calibers opened up, their distinctive staccato cadence a welcome sound. He watched Japanese falling all along the line, but for every man down there seemed to be three more. He fired at his man, but the shot went high. The Jap hunkered and kept coming. Dunphy adjusted and fired three more shots; the man went down. He found another target right behind the first and dropped him, a spray of red mist from his chest. Another target, he shot and spun the man around, his shoulder shredded. He found another, but this one went down before he could shoot. The Japs were being decimated by their withering fire, but they were getting closer. He heard pings as men around him burned through their clips. He wondered how many more shots he had and cursed himself for not knowing.

He fired and missed and his clip pinged. He ejected the clip, grabbed another and slapped it home, just like training. There were targets everywhere. He burned through another clip. He stopped seeing the men he was shooting. He was shooting at uniforms and colors instead. They'd halved the distance. Mortars were still falling amongst them, tearing limbs from bodies, but another couple yards and the mortars would have to stop for fear of hitting their own men. Dunphy went through another clip and slid another home, but before firing again he grabbed a grenade, pulled the pin and hurled it. Before it exploded he had another in hand and threw it. He had his rifle sighted on another soldier when his grenades went off in the middle of a pack of soldiers. They were cut down with hot shrapnel. He could see their red insides exposed as they fell.

He was in a rhythm. All fear had left him and he was on automatic pilot. Find a target, fire, move to the next. He was in the zone, the place he lived when he boxed, the place where he won.

All his efforts though were only delaying the inevitable. The Japanese were going to be on top of them. They would get to their holes and it would be hand to hand. He threw his last two grenades and slammed his second to last clip into the M1. The explosions ripped a hole in the advancing line. He noticed Crandall and Troutman scrambling out of their holes to meet the screaming soldiers. Dunphy thought that was a good idea; he'd rather fight them hand to hand in the open. The hole was too constricting, one grenade and he'd be shredded.

He was about to hop out, but there was a looming soldier only feet away. He was leveling his long Arisaka rifle. Dunphy didn't aim, but shot from the hip until his clip emptied. He sprang out thinking he'd be shot by the big man, but when he got out he saw him grimacing and shuffling backwards, trying to keep his intestines from spilling onto the ground.

Another soldier filled his vision; this soldier bent low running at him full speed, his rifle and gleaming bayonet aimed at his guts. He only had time to jump out of the way. The man flashed by him and Dunphy hit him with the butt of his rifle, sending him to the ground. The soldier tried to roll to defend himself, but he was too slow and Dunphy sank his bayonet into his spine. The soldier tensed like a spring. Dunphy pulled back trying to dislodge it, but the bayonet was stuck in the tensed soldier's bones. He tugged and yanked, but it wouldn't come loose.

He saw another Japanese soldier coming for him, an officer. He held a sword over his head with both hands. It shimmered in the late evening sun, dulled by dripping blood. He gave one last pull then released the M1 and confronted the charging officer. His boxing instincts kicked in. He had to get in close on this guy to keep him from using his sword.

Instead of backing away from the threat, he charged. The Japanese officer brought the sword down hard, but Dunphy was too quick. He got inside the sword's arc and the officer's arms came down on his shoulders. The enemy was overextended, off balance. Dunphy was crouched and once the man was exposed he sprang up hard. His steel helmet shot into the officer's chin and he reeled backwards. He still held the sword so Dunphy pulled his helmet off and charged him. The officer's eyes went wide; he was reeling and wouldn't get the sword up in time. Dunphy swung the steel pot, aiming for the side of his head, but instead it slammed into his neck. There was a sickening crunch and the Japanese officer went down. Dunphy pulled his K-bar, the only weapon available and jumped onto him. He led with the knife and he felt it enter his guts. The sensation of sticky warm blood turned his stomach.

He rolled off the officer and looked around. All along the line there was fighting, mostly hand to hand. He looked for a weapon. He saw a Japanese rifle and picked it up. It felt odd and foreign, but good. To his right Crandall was in the fight of his life. He had two Japanese thrusting and jabbing. He was parrying and dodging, but those weren't good odds. Dunphy aimed at the nearest man and pulled the trigger, but nothing happened. "Dammit," he looked at the rifle and saw the bolt action. He pulled it back and felt the satisfying sound of a round being chambered. He aimed again as the soldier was thrusting. He fired and he was surprised at the kick. The bullet destroyed the soldier's head, blowing it apart. He'd been aiming at his chest.

He chambered another round and was aiming at the next enemy when he sensed movement to the side. He spun the rifle around and fired, hitting the charging soldier in the leg. The impact sent him spinning backwards. He screamed like a wounded animal. There was another right behind him and Dunphy knew he didn't have enough time to chamber another round. As the soldier thrust, he parried, slapping the enemy's gun away, but he recovered. This one was light on his feet and well balanced. They circled, the soldier thrust and Dunphy parried, testing each other. Dunphy was used to sparring, used to finding his opponent's weak points and using them to his advantage.

He went on the attack. He feinted high and when the soldier went to parry he stepped under and slammed the butt of his rifle into the man's balls. He felt them crush under the assault. The soldier was stunned, but held onto his weapon and tried to bring it down on Dunphy's head. He moved to the side reaching for his K-bar. He cursed, realizing he'd left it in the officer's gut. He spun away and came up on the balls of his feet. The Japanese soldier was slow, his crushed balls slowing him down. Dunphy was about to finish him, but he bumped into the back of another enemy fighting an American. They both jumped in surprise. The distraction was enough to allow the first soldier time to spin around. Now Dunphy was caught between two enemies.

The second soldier thrust his bayonet into the chest of the G.I. and screamed as he looked into the dying soldier's eyes. Dunphy had his hands full. He had to kill the first man quick or face two of them. He went to thrust, but his foot slipped on something slick and he fell onto his back. The first soldier loomed over him, his eyes crazy with kill lust and revenge. Dunphy couldn't move. He tried to roll, but whatever had made him fall wasn't allowing him to move well. He saw the point of the bayonet coming down fast. He waited for the pain of the impact and the cutting of his vital organs. This was it.

He shut his eyes, but the pain never happened. He opened his eyes and the crazed soldier was replaced by blue sky. He scrambled off the gore he'd slipped on and stood up looking for the soldier. There was a smoking hulk off to the side. He guessed that was the Jap. He saw Troutman working the bolt of a captured Arisaka, smoke wafting from the barrel.

He didn't have time to thank him as the second soldier was on him. He'd dropped his weapon and reached for the first thing he saw, the dropped Samurai sword. It was heavier than it looked, but perfectly balanced. The handle was soaked in blood making the leather slippery. He was no swordsman, but it couldn't be that much different than boxing. He'd tried fencing as a child, but didn't like all the formality. He much preferred the raw power of the well-placed punch.

He held the sword with two hands. The soldier was bigger than most, burly and menacing. His bloodied bayonet was coming straight for him. When the Japanese saw the sword, his eyes turned hard. He recognized his officers' weapon.

He took a balanced lunge and Dunphy stepped to the side. He took a short thrust trying for the big man's shoulder, but missed. The soldier feinted right then went low, Dunphy barely evaded the slice. He took a step back then attacked. He swung in a low arc, the sword clanged against the rifle. Dunphy was sure the sword would break, but its tempered steel took the shot without so much as a scratch. The soldier followed the attack with one of his own, thrusting then slicing upwards to catch his arm. Again Dunphy sprang away on light feet. As he did so he jabbed at the Jap's hands and cut him. The soldier grit his teeth and used the pain to fuel his attack.

It came like lightning, but Dunphy expected it. He feinted left, the soldier following then went right and brought the sword down hard. The blade went through the man's arm like it was cutting through warm butter. The soldier screamed, but held onto the rifle with his other hand. The detached arm and hand still clutching the rifle.

The wounded soldier kept coming, but the fight was over. He made a clumsy attack that Dunphy easily avoided and brought the samurai sword down on his head. It traveled down his body cleaving it in half to his sternum. He pulled the sword and watched the halves of the man fall to either side.

He looked up for the next fight, but there were no more. Soldiers littered the ground all around him. He held the sword at the ready, breathing hard, ready to take on whatever they could throw at him, but there was no one left. To his right Troutman still had the Arisaka rifle. He was down in a crouch sighting down the barrel, swinging back and forth searching for targets. The chatter of the machine guns was absent, Dunphy wondered how long they'd been silent, *had they been overrun?*

The sounds of wounded men assaulted his senses. He heard desperate pleas for medics and the gurgling sounds of men's final breaths. He stayed tensed and ready until Crandall walked up to him and put his hand on his shoulder. Dunphy swung around with the sword and almost lopped his head off. He stopped in the nick of time when recognition came to his heightened senses.

Crandall said, "Christ, it's over, it's over. They're all dead or retreated. Put that damned thing away." Dunphy stared and realized how close he'd come to killing the man he'd saved only minutes ago. He dropped the sword in the mud and blood and sank to his knees beside it.

He looked out over the masses of dead. He felt as tired as he'd ever felt. If the Japanese decided to come again at that moment, he was sure he wouldn't be able to lift a finger to stop them. They'd been on Guadalcanal for less than a week, but it felt like an eternity.

## 5

O'Connor woke from his black sleep to the sound of thumping mortar rounds exploding. He thought for a moment he was dreaming until he felt the ground shudder slightly beneath his cot.

His surroundings flooded back to his consciousness and he sat upright forgetting his injuries. He winced and yelled out when he felt the bandages on his legs stretch and pull against his singed skin. He was forced to lie back down.

He closed his eyes and tried to catch his breath. The mortars were getting louder and soon they were falling so close together there was no distinguishing one explosion from another. He took a deep breath, he had to get up, get back in the fight. His unit was in the shit and he was laid up, useless in this damned infirmary.

The men around him were also awake listening to the barrage. They looked at one another trying to find solace from their fear. If the Japanese attacked and broke through they'd be just as dead as the men on the line. The Japanese weren't known for showing mercy even to the wounded.

O'Connor saw the man to his right trying to sit up. He'd been gut shot. He could tell by the way the medics treated him he wasn't expected to make it. It wasn't stopping him from trying to join the fight though. O'Connor was much better off than him, only slightly wounded. He grit his teeth and came to a full sitting position. The move made him cry out involuntarily and he cursed himself for his weakness.

He sat on the side of the cot and felt dizzy. He held his head and rubbed his temples until the world stopped spinning. When it did the nausea came and he threw up whatever food, mostly bile, that was left in his stomach. He ignored the others and stood up. He swayed and had to sit down to keep from falling over. The jarring caused more pain, but the pain focused his resolve. He used it to stand again and walk. Each step brought more pain and with it more focus. The nausea was gone, replaced by sheer purpose. He went through the medical tent flap and was immediately greeted by a medic. "Whoa, soldier where you think you're going?"

O'Connor looked at him with daggers, "Where's my weapon?" The medic backed up a step, seeing his dark glare. He glanced behind him at a stack of rifles against a fallen palm tree. O'Connor pushed his way by him and grabbed the first rifle. He pulled back the breech; it was loaded with a full eight round clip. He slammed the breech forward with a satisfying click. Beyond the weapons he saw ammo satchels. He slung the first one over his shoulder and started walking towards the sound of falling mortars.

He took it slow since running was out of the question. He was barely able to walk a straight line, but the louder the explosions got the more sure-footed he became. He'd walked one hundred yards when he tripped on a root and sprawled. He hit hard, knocking the breath out of him. The pain was more than anything he'd ever felt and he thought he might pass out. If the Japanese came they'd bayonet him where he lay, but at least he'd have his rifle. If he was going to die he'd like to have a gun in his hand, not a wad of bandages.

He felt hands under his arms pulling him up. He came back to reality and got to his feet. He looked at the man who'd helped him; it was Corporal Hooper. He smiled at him, "Hooper. Where'd you come from?"

He motioned behind them, "I was back at the damned infirmary too. When I saw you limp by I figured you could use some backup. That medic gave me some trouble, but I finally convinced him." He rubbed his knuckles, they were scratched.

From the front they heard their own mortars countering the Japanese then the chatter of thirty caliber machine gun fire. They looked at one another, "Sounds like an attack," said Hooper. They held onto each other as they limped towards the fighting. They couldn't see the front line yet, but they could see the entire Marine air squadron launching from Henderson field. O'Connor wondered if there were bombers coming or they were simply getting out of harm's way.

The gunfire from the front was one solid sound. There was no pause, no single shots, just the constant sound of concentrated fire coming in and going out.

They were halfway to the front line when stray bullets started smacking trees and whizzing by like angry bees. They started using the downed trees and bomb craters for cover as they went forward. No use getting hit way back here without getting into the fight.

They got to a large bomb crater at the eastern edge of the runways and poked their heads up. O'Connor was still a bit fuzzy from the pain, but he could see the Japanese were in amongst the company's slit trenches and foxholes. As he watched soldiers started coming out of their holes and engaging hand to hand. He could see the gleaming steel of bayonets from here. His gut turned, thinking what his comrades were facing. Hand to hand combat was the most terrifying thing he could think of on the battlefield. The thought of having to do it in his condition almost made him sick again.

A bullet snapped, O'Connor hunkered down, but Hooper thumped him on the shoulder, "See that hole? The one straight in front of us?" O'Connor lifted his head and nodded, "If we can get to that I think we'll have a good line of sight on these suckers, be able to lend some firepower."

O'Connor nodded and launched himself out of the hole. Crouching was too painful so he stayed upright and shuffled as fast as he could to the hole, Hooper right on his tail. They threw themselves into cover. They doubted any Japs would be paying attention to two injured soldiers behind the line, but there were so many stray bullets around they could easily be hit.

The exertion and their wounds took their breath away. When they were ready they crawled to the top of the crater and peered over the lip. They brought their rifles up. It was a good firing platform. The hole wasn't deep. It provided cover, but didn't force them to fight to keep from falling to the bottom. They searched for targets, but found the scene too confused. It was difficult to discern the enemy from friend-lies. They couldn't shoot without possibly hitting one of their own guys.

Hooper nudged him, "If any bust through, we'll pop 'em." O'Connor nodded and watched the scene over the sights of his M1. Every fiber of his being wanted to jump up and join the fight, but he knew he'd be a liability in his wounded state. He wouldn't last ten seconds against an uninjured enemy.

They watched the gruesome battle in frustration without firing a shot. O'Connor watched men die, Americans and Japanese alike. He felt guilty, but deep down he was also relieved not be involved in that hell. Hooper said, "To the right, see those guys, they've busted through." O'Connor swung his rifle and found the targets. Five or six Japanese were past the line of foxholes and slit trenches and were running towards the rear. "Bastards are heading for the hospital, they'll butcher those guys."

O'Connor found his target and tracked him as he ran. They were sixty yards away and running from left to right. He'd have to lead them like a sprinting deer. He pulled the trigger, but his man kept on running, albeit a bit faster. O'Connor adjusted and fired again. This time the man went down. He fired at the next man and brought him down with three shots. Hooper got to the end of his clip, the "ping" seeming to echo. He'd dropped a man too.

There were three more, but they dropped and found cover searching for the unknown shooters. O'Connor saw a pith helmet pop out of a depression in the ground, probably another bomb crater. He shot but missed, sending the helmet back out of sight. He opened the breech and saw he only had one more shot. He popped out the remaining bullet and loaded another eight-round clip being careful not to catch his thumb in the breech.

He brought the M1 to his shoulder again and searched where he'd seen the man. "Where are they?" asked Hooper.

"About seventy yards out." He pointed, "They're in some kind of depression, I saw his helmet but missed."

Hooper went up on a knee to get a better look. The air beside his ear ripped with a near miss. He dropped down, "Shit, that was close." He lay on his back and took a deep breath, "They're maneuvering on us, trying to flank us." He rolled onto his stomach, "You stay here, I'll go to the other side of the hole in case they come up that side. If you see something, sing out."

O'Connor didn't like the fact they were being hunted like the wounded animals they were. He thought he saw movement where the helmet had been. He gripped his rifle and waited. Suddenly a Japanese soldier was up and running off to his right. He swung on the man, but by the time he was pulling the trigger he was already in another closer hole. The original spot he'd been looking at was now empty. He'd fallen for the bait and now he had no idea where the other soldiers were.

"You saw that guy, right?" he asked Hooper.

"Yeah, but he got cover before I could shoot. You get him?"

"Nah, too quick, I think he was bait for the other guys to move. I don't know where they are."

"You got any grenades?"

"Nope, wish I did, but I left the hospital in a hurry."

"If those nips get much closer they'll be able to lob grenades at us. We gotta get the upper hand."

O'Connor looked around the hole there wasn't much to it, but off to his left the ground rose up slightly. He wondered if he'd have a better view from there. "I'm moving over to that mound, see what I can see." Hooper didn't answer. O'Connor slipped backwards ignoring the pain of his burnt legs scraping over the dirt. He rolled to his left until he was abreast of the high ground then crawled up until his head was just beneath the horizon. He reached up and pulled a dirt clod down, then another until he'd created a V shaped slot to look through. He slid his rifle through the slot, moving it almost imperceptibly forward.

When he was in position he pulled himself up to the rifle and looked down the sights. He almost cried out. Two hulking Japanese soldiers were twenty yards away hunched over making their way down a slight depression caused by monsoon rains. They were almost upon them. O'Connor had a perfect shot. He pulled the stock into his shoulder and shot through his eight rounds in seconds. The Japanese didn't have a chance and never knew what hit them. The thirty caliber bullets tore into the front man and continued through the second man finally stopping in the stinking mud of Guadalcanal.

O'Connor didn't have time to celebrate. He felt the thunk of a bullet beside his head. He was sprayed with dirt and rocks. He knew the next shot would kill him, but he couldn't make himself move. The welcome sound of Hoopers' rifle sang out. Then Hooper yelled, "I got him, I got that Jap son-of-a-bitch."

O'Connor rolled to the bottom of the hole and tried to control his breathing. It was coming in short spurts, he was hyperventilating. The near miss had shaken him. If he hadn't changed positions they would've killed them with grenades or just come over the top and riddled them with bullets. He closed his eyes and got control of himself.

Hooper hobbled over and went up to the lip O'Connor had just abandoned. "Holy shit, you laid those suckers out." He got onto his knees, "Looks like the battle's over." He gave a low whistle while shaking his head. "Looks like a scene out of Dante or something." He dropped his rifle to the ground, "Bodies everywhere. We better go help."

O'Connor didn't hear his last words as he'd passed out. His body and mind had done what were asked, but now the stress and his injuries took control and he slipped into a black dreamless sleep.

## 6
------------

O'Connor regained consciousness back at the aid station. His head felt like it was being crushed between two vises. He stared at the green tent ceiling illuminated by low light. It was dark out. He heard movement beside him, someone was sitting next to him. He tried to look, but even the slight movement made him cringe. "Who's there?"

A face came into view, looming over him. "Hey, it's me, your foxhole mate."

O'Connor was surprised. He wouldn't have believed Dunphy could survive the attack. "What are you doing here? Where am I? What's happening?"

"You've been out for a couple hours I guess. Hooper brought you back here then found the platoon. That's how I knew where you were. You're back at the aid station."

O'Connor closed his eyes. "Are you wounded?"

"Nah, not really, couple scratches. After the attack they pulled our platoon off the line. Guess they thought we needed some rest." He gestured behind him, but in the low light it was lost on O'Connor, "We're camped over there, near where we landed."

"What you doing here?"

"Like I said, I was in the area. Thought I'd check on you. Something wrong with a guy checking on his squad-mate?"

O'Connor forced his head to look over, "No, guess not. Just didn't figure you'd be the one to do it."

Dunphy stood up and slung his rifle. He picked up his helmet and put it on. "Yeah well, I wasn't doing anything else."

As he walked out O'Connor said, "Hey, Dunphy." He stopped and looked back, "Thanks for stopping by." Dunphy nodded and walked back to his bivouac area.

THE JAPANESE AIR FORCE bombed the airfield again that night, but the sound and rumble seemed distant and far away, almost harmless. O'Connor opened his eyes at first light, feeling like he'd slept for days. He felt good for the first time in a long while. He figured he got eight or nine hours of sleep, which didn't seem like nearly enough, but his body felt good.

A medic was working on the man beside him. He got his attention. "Hey, when am I getting out of here?"

The medic startled and looked at him, "Damn, you're finally awake. Never seen anyone able to sleep through so much noise. Thought something was wrong with you. Thought maybe you'd gone into a coma or something."

O'Connor sat up on his elbows, "What're you talking about? I just fell asleep a couple hours ago."

The medic grinned and shook his head. He came over and lifted the blanket to look at his burns. "You've been asleep for two days. The battle was three days ago. You've slept through four air raids and one naval bombardment. Pretty damned impressive."

O'Connor shook his head, "What? I've gotta get outta here. Where's my unit? I've gotta rejoin my unit."

"Well your wounds aren't healed, but between you sleeping and the burn salve, it's looking pretty good. You can stay another couple days, but if you wanted to go now I'll bet the doc will approve."

O'Connor whipped the sheets off and swung to a sitting position.

When his feet hit the floor, he felt dizzy. He put his head in his hands and waited for the world to stop spinning. "Take it easy. Your body took a hit, so take it slow or you'll end up back here in a hurry." He went to the foot of the cot and handed him his pants. "That stunt you pulled, you know during the attack? Pretty stupid." He pointed to another medic making rounds down the other aisle, "Gerry said you and that corporal, the one gave me this," he pointed to the remnants of a black eye, "Killed some nips coming straight for the aid station. Said you two probably saved our bacon."

O'Connor remembered the skirmish. It seemed like a long time ago. He pictured the two charging Japs lined up in his sights, the way they looked when his bullets tore into them. They'd been flung back like rag dolls.

When he felt better he pulled his pants on, careful not to scrape along the bandages. The medic said, "Doc hasn't given you the okay to leave. You may be jumping the gun."

O'Connor continued to dress, pulling on his dirty t-shirt. "Not waiting for the okay, just gonna walk out of here. I'm fine."

"You can't go against a direct order; you'll spend the war in Leavenworth."

"Then you better get the doc in here to release me before I up and leave."

The tent flap opened and a man dressed in a filthy white apron walked in. He was drying his hand on a towel. He was tall and wore Captain's bars on his shoulders. He stopped at the entrance letting his eyes adjust to the dimness. The medic looked up, "You're in luck, that's him. That's Captain Wolski, he's a surgeon. He can release you."

O'Connor got to his feet. He felt unsteady, but he willed himself to attention, determined to show the captain he was good to go. The medic raised a hand and got his attention. He waved him over. As he approached O'Connor snapped to attention and gave him a crisp salute.

Captain Wolski gave him a lazy salute back, "At ease soldier." He looked him up and down, "Going somewhere?"

"Yes Sir, back to my unit, Sir."

Wolski nodded and looked at the medic who shrugged. "Have a seat soldier." O'Connor sat, wincing as the skin around his burns tightened. "You can stand a few more days here, Son. Your body's still healing. Another day or two would do wonders for you."

O'Connor replied, "With all due respect Sir, I'd like to get back to my unit. I feel fine, I'm ready for duty."

Wolski put up his hands in surrender, "Alright, alright, it's against my better judgment, but I'll allow it only because you probably saved our asses the other day."

O'Connor went to stand, but the Captain pushed him back down. "Now listen, that wound could get infected in this jungle environment. You need to keep it clean and change the bandage at least once a day. This is important. I don't want to see you back here in a week with a septic leg I need to amputate. Fact is, I was going to release you today anyway. the Division's short men and the outcome of this misadventure's still uncertain."

O'Connor stood up and this time Captain Wolski let him. O'Connor saluted and Wolski gave him a crisp salute back. "Good luck, son and good hunting."

O'CONNOR WALKED WITH A SLIGHT LIMP, but with each step he felt better. He guessed it was loosening up. The day was bright and sweltering hot. Sweat was pouring off him. The aid station had been hot, but the direct sun pounding on his green uniform made him feel like an ant under his ten-year-old sister's magnifying glass.

He flagged a passing jeep and asked where Baker Company was bivouacked. The driver told him to hop in; he was going there now. He threw his pack in the back and took the empty front seat, his rifle propped between his knees.

The jeep driver looked him over, "You been at the aid station?"

"How'd you know?"

He shrugged, "I don't know you've got that antiseptic smell I guess."

"Sorry 'bout that. I've been out of it a few days. What's the situation?"

He steered around a large mud hole, the Willie's jeep bounced over ruts sending shots of pain throughout O'Connors' body. The driver said, "Shitty. We stopped the Japs from overrunning Henderson, but now they're giving the 1st Marines hell again. They've been probing the last day or two. The brass thinks they're trying to run their tanks up the coast road straight to the airfield. We're planning something, maybe our own assault."

"With the Marines?"

He shook his head, "Scuttlebutt says they're too tired for an assault. It'll probably be us, the 164th."

O'Connor pondered that. Would his injury make it hard for him to move through the jungle? He thought he'd be fine sitting in a foxhole, but how would his wound feel if he was forced to walk and run on it? He guessed he'd find out soon enough.

The jeep braked to a halt and the driver pointed, "There's the CP, they'll know where you belong."

O'Connor waved and approached the tent. He stuck his head in and a sergeant sitting behind a card table looked up at him, "What can I do for you?"

O'Connor thought he recognized him, but couldn't place his name. "Private O'Connor, reporting for duty. I'm in 2nd squad, Baker Company."

The sergeant looked at him closer, "You the guy who took out those Japs heading for the aid station?"

O'Connor looked down, "I wasn't alone and why does everybody keep bringing it up?"

"Yeah, Corporal Hooper was with you." He looked sideways at him, "You mean you don't know?" O'Connor only stared. "Those Japs were carrying satchel charges. The big sergeant had a diagram of the entire area and a big red X marked over the aid station. Those savages were gonna blow it up sure as shit, but you and Hooper stopped 'em."

O'Connor felt embarrassed with the praise. The sergeant continued, "The LT's not here, but I'm sure he'll want you back with your squad." He pointed, "2nds over there somewhere, maybe two hundred yards."

He grinned, "Just listen for Sergeant Carver's voice, he's always chewing someone out."

"Thanks, Sarge." O'Connor walked down the line of tents searching for his squad-mates. He recognized Private Troutman sitting outside drying his socks over a pathetic fire. "Hey, there you guys are."

Troutman looked up from his chore, "Well shit. Look who it is." He leaned into the tent, "Red's returned from the dead."

O'Connor punched Troutman's arm as he entered the tent. The smell of rotting feet and sour bodies struck him. He'd only been gone a couple days, but they looked like different men. Someone grabbed him around the neck as he entered and gave him a noogie. "Welcome back, asshole." It was Private Crandall, but he had a set of stripes on his arm, Corporal Crandall.

O'Connor shucked him off, "Whoa, corporal huh? You must've blown the right guy." Crandall punched him in the arm. "You guys miss me?"

He went over and slung his gear onto an empty cot. "You guys are living in high style. Cots?"

The man in the cot next to him pulled the sheet from his face, "They figured we needed a break after the other day."

The mood sobered as each man remembered the Japanese attack. O'Connor sat down and looked at the man. It was Dunphy. He looked like he'd lost weight and his skin was pale. He lit a cigarette and took a long pull. He blew smoke towards O'Connor. O'Connor nodded through the blue haze, "Yeah, I heard."

As dusk was descending there was another air raid siren. They rolled off their cots, grabbed their rifles and trotted to the slit trenches behind the tent line. The Japanese bombers normally attacked the airfield, but you never knew if they'd switch things up and go after the beach.

O'Connor was next to Dunphy as the bombs dropped around Henderson. Dunphy lit a cigarette and offered O'Connor a puff. He took a long drag and blew it out. O'Connor stood up and put his head on the side of the hole. "The attack the other day…heard it was bad."

Dunphy didn't respond at first. O'Connor let the time pass, he'd talk if he wanted to. O'Connor sat next to him. Dunphy blew smoke out his nose and nodded. "Yeah, bad as it gets I guess." He kept smoking. It was all he was going to get out of him.

THEIR SLEEP WAS INTERRUPTED one more time during the night by an artillery barrage, but it wasn't meant for them. At first light Sgt. Carver stormed into the tent and in his booming voice yelled for them to form up in ten minutes.

They stood at parade rest with the rest of the company as Captain Blade addressed them. "Men, the 164th is moving up the line to support the 1st Marines. We're expecting the Japs to try another thrust from the east. We're expecting them to run infantry supported by tanks up the coast road. That's good tank country and we're sure they still have em. The 1st Marines need assistance on their right flank and were going to provide it." He let that sink in. "The rest of the day will be spent moving and digging in. Your sergeants will fill you in on the specifics." He paced, "The Japs tested us and we rose and beat them back decisively, but they've still got a lot of fight left in 'em. Have no doubt we'll be in for more of the same. You men performed marvelously and I'll expect the same in the coming weeks and months." He put his hands on his hips and squared up, "That is all."

O'Connor leaned towards Dunphy and whispered, "What happened to the other Captain?"

Out of the side of his mouth Dunphy said, "Japs skewered him in his foxhole."

The sergeants dismissed them and they melted back to their tents to collect their gear. As they were packing, Private First-Class Morgan said, "What's with that guy? Is that really his name? I mean *Captain Blade* sounds like some comic book hero or something."

Corporal Hooper spoke up, "I don't care if his name's Captain Marvelous. He's a good officer, cares about us. Can't say the same about the LT."

Dunphy laughed, "Don't get me started on that guy. Heard he never ventured from his hole during the attack, just cowered."

They collected their gear and went back to the main supply area to meet up with their transports. As they were standing beside the truck waiting to load, a man in white knee-high socks, clean khaki shorts and shirt and a floppy jungle hat walked past holding his head high. The men watched him, staring like he was something from another planet. Private Mcdougal in his flat Midwestern tone said, "Who in the hell is that?"

## 7

Thomas Welch walked past the green clad soldiers with his chin held high. He'd show them how a proper Englishman carried himself even out here. He'd kept a clean set of clothes buried deep in his pack just for this day; the day he came out of the bush and presented himself to the Americans.

He sauntered up to a man with sergeant stripes and asked him in his heavily accented British, "Hallo, could you direct me to your commanding officer?"

The sergeant unslung his Thompson submachine gun and squinted at him. He looked him up and down twice, "Who the hell are you?"

Keeping his arms close to his sides he gritted his teeth, "That's none of your business. I'd like to speak with your commanding officer. I have information he'll want to discuss."

Not to be intimidated, Sgt. Carver growled, "If I'm taking you to the brass it sure as hell is my business." He took a wide stance blocking his way.

He harrumphed, "Very well, my name is Thomas Endicott Welch the Third. I'm a member of the British government, who happen to be your allies and I've urgent news for your commanding officers."

"Wait here. You guys keep your eyes on him, don't let him leave and don't hurt him." He spun and walked off towards the end of the truck line.

As the minutes passed the men of the 2nd squad surrounded Thomas Welch and grinned. They stared at him like he was a prize cow at auction. The sight of someone not covered in grime was awe inspiring. O'Connor was the first to speak, "How could you come out of the jungle looking so clean?"

Before he could reply, Sgt. Carver came trotting back and put his grimy hand on his clean shirt. "Come with me. Captain Blade and Lieutenant Caprielli will see you now."

Thomas took a look around at the men and gave a curt nod, "Very good. Lead on Sergeant."

Captain Blade and Lieutenant Caprielli were seated behind a makeshift desk made from oil barrels and a large plank of splintered wood.

When Thomas Welch entered he gave a smart British style salute, palm facing them. The two officers looked at one another then returned his salute. "Are you military or are you saluting out of courtesy," he hesitated, "Mr. Welch is it?"

He dropped his salute, "Ah well, let me explain. When all this nastiness started," he gestured at the jungle, "my higher-ups decided it would be a good idea to give us military rank in case the Japanese captured us. Guadalcanal is a British territory and as such has British rules. I am a part of the provincial governing body that oversees this territory."

Captain Blade nodded, "I thought all the civilians left, thought only natives were still here."

Thomas Welch nodded, "Yes, most did. The plantation owners left months before hostilities started, leaving many locals out of work in the process. Made for difficult governing, but back to the point. We were instructed to stay on the island and do whatever we could to foil the Jap's efforts."

"You mean you're partisans? You've been fighting the Japs?"

He shook his head, "Not the way you imagine. They're much too well equipped; they'd annihilate us in a matter of days. Our armaments are few and our ammunition scarce. That's not to say we're not armed, we are, but we don't have enough men or guns to take on the Japanese army in a head on fight." He smiled, "We'll leave that to you blokes. We've been fighting them by reporting their whereabouts and movements. We have radios we use to communicate with Australian forces. Much of the information you have about Guadalcanal no doubt was derived from our reports." He looked at them hopefully.

Captain Blade nodded, "Yes, we were briefed about you guys before the invasion, told to keep an eye out for you. I'd forgotten all about it. The Marines have been here since August. Why didn't you come forward earlier?"

"This is the first time we felt we could make it through the lines undetected. Besides, being behind the enemy gives us some advantages as far as watching the Japs."

Blade nodded and looked at the ground trying to remember something, "What do they call you? Watchers?"

"Coast-Watchers, yes. We're referred to as Coast-Watchers." He smiled, "Seems a silly name, like we're bird watching or something. Fact is, we're in danger nearly every second of the day. We're either dodging Japs or your incoming artillery and aircraft."

Captain Blade nodded, "Well, yes, sorry 'bout that, but there's a war going on. The sergeant said you had some important information for us?"

"Yes, quite. Can we confer with your commanding generals so I don't have to repeat myself?"

Blade smiled, "We're kind of in the middle of a major move, not sure now's a good time."

Welch grit his teeth, "I can assure you your generals will want to hear what I have to say before you make your move. It can shorten the battle by months."

Blade looked at Caprielli then back at the smiling Englishman. "Okay, I'll see what I can do for you, but if you're jerking me around there'll be hell to pay."

"I'm sure they'll find it worth their time."

～

AN HOUR later Thomas Welch sat on a fallen palm log and faced General Thornton and Colonel Sinclair. Because of the urgency and the short notice, they too sat on fallen logs and stumps like a Boy Scout troop around a campfire. General Thornton spoke first, his rough, low voice the reason for his nickname, 'Thorny.' "We hear you have some vital information for us?"

Welch expected some polite chitchat, but these impetuous American's liked to get straight to the point. "Yes, well as you know, I'm a part of the coast-watchers here on Guadalcanal. Until recently we've been feeding reports to Australia who I hope has been relaying them to you." He paused hoping for some confirmation. When no one spoke, he continued. "Our radios are old and the wet jungle climate wreaks havoc on them. My own stopped working two weeks ago, the last working unit stopped working only two days ago. As luck would have it, the timing couldn't have been worse. My area of responsibility was the southern region of the island. I had to retreat far into the bush, as we all have, to avoid capture. We were effectively corralled to the center of the island. With you Americans here, they stopped actively looking for us and we ended up within a square mile area. Since we were so close we decided to team up. We've been essentially one unit since mid-September."

Colonel Sinclair smiled and interrupted. "Get to the point, son. We've got an attack to lead."

Welch reddened, but continued, "Yes, quite. Well, we noticed something about the way the main Japanese force has set themselves up and we think they've put themselves in a pickle without knowing it." He picked up a stick and started drawing in the sand.

Colonel Sinclair looked at the general who nodded. Welch continued, "We're sitting here," he poked the stick and made a hole in the sand, "my blokes are here," another hole with a perimeter around it, "And your forces are here, generally." He looked up to see if they were following. "The Japs used to be here to the west, but now they've shifted a large part of their force here. Basically, they've leapfrogged their lines further southwest." The American officers were looking with interest now. "So, as you can see they've placed themselves right in front of our band of guerrillas."

Thorny leaned in, "Are you suggesting you have a force that can attack them from the rear?"

He shook his head, "we're not strong enough to cause them much damage, they'd sweep us aside in a jiffy. But right here," he plunged his stick into the sand in front of the hole representing his men and drew a long line behind the Japanese force, "Is a peculiar land structure. It looks like normal jungle from the air and you wouldn't know anything was peculiar about it until you tried to pass through. It looks a bit thicker than the jungle around it, but that's because it's hiding a deep canyon. The vines and grasses have grown together and connected the steep canyon walls. It looks like you're walking on normal ground until you find yourself sinking through the vines. It's impassable, the natives use ladders they've hacked from the jungle to cross it, but without them it's impossible, particularly if being pursued by a strong enemy force." He grinned, "We can sit on the other side and snipe them as they get stuck. They'll be ducks on a pond."

Colonel Sinclair looked up from the sand drawing, "What kind of weapons do your men have and how many are you?"

"We've got our rifles from before, Enfields, one Lewis machine gun left over from the first war and we've managed to sneak a few rifles and ammo from the Japs. Our boys love getting the best of the Japs. As far as numbers, we're relatively small, one hundred fifty trained men."

"Natives?"

He nodded, "Yes, but many were local police before the Japs arrived and have weapons training. The others are eager and quick to learn and are excellent in the jungle. Not up to your Marine standards, but stout fighters when the chips are down."

Thorny looked at Sinclair then back to Welch, "We're Army. The Marines are up that way a bit."

"Ah, yes. Beg your pardon." He spun his hat in his hands. "So, what do you think? Will you consider my plan?"

Thorny cleared his throat, "Sounds interesting, but I can't base an entire attack on some crazy land feature that may or may not be there."

Welch spluttered, "I can assure you on my honor it is there. I've seen it with my own eyes, tried to walk across it even. Before the war. It's a perfect trap and the best part is they don't know it's there."

"Yeah, well neither do we. With all due respect, I don't know you. I've got a call into my intelligence people and they're checking on your story." He held up his hands when Welch started to protest, "Now hold it, it's standard procedure. It won't take long, but until I get confirmation on you, I can't let you wander around my lines."

"You actually believe I'm working for the Japs? Have you lost your mind? I'm British, obviously. I'm an ally."

"That'll be all, Mr. Welch." They stood up and Thorny gestured behind him to a waiting soldier. "Sergeant Frank will escort you to your temporary accommodations."

Welch looked behind at the smiling soldier. He looked like he'd been cut from granite, "Right this way, Sir."

Welch looked back to the officers, "This is daft. We're wasting time. If you attacked you could cut the Jap force in half. You'd have them on the run."

Thorny nodded, "Oh we're attacking, but we're attacking our way based on solid intelligence."

Welch raised his voice, "Intelligence you got from your higher-ups who no doubt got it from our radio reports." The General raised his eyes to Sergeant Frank, who nodded and put a large hand on Welch's shoulder. He guided him from the area and directed him to a nearby tent. Sergeant Frank nudged him in and stood guard outside, his weapon slung over his shoulder.

Colonel Sinclair stood next to Thorny, only coming to his shoulder, "Interesting fellow. What do you think of his plan?"

"Probably has some merit, but it's thin. Have some of our intelligence guys talk with him. I want to know more about his men. Might be nice to have some local talent guiding us through this god-awful place. Thinking it may be a good idea to send a small squad out to make contact. Organize them into a fighting force we could use."

Sinclair nodded, "I'll get on it, take them some weapons and ammo. Keep the Japs on their toes."

Thorny nodded, "Yes, having an active guerrilla squad behind them would definitely keep 'em on their toes. We'd need a unit that could be on their own for a while. Good jungle fighters. Any come to mind?"

He thought about it a moment then nodded, "Yes, Sir. A platoon in Baker Company, Captain Blade's company. They were hit the hardest during the Henderson attack the other night, yet they had the fewest casualties. Real hard fighters I was told. They'd be up to the task."

"Good, but you can't send a whole platoon, needs to be smaller to slip through the Jap lines. Send a squad."

## 8

Thomas Welch sat on the bunk and watched the sweat dripping from his nose pool onto the dirt floor. It was a balmy day and with the tent flaps closed there was no airflow. Hours passed and he could hear the constant din of an army in motion. There were countless trucks hauling equipment and men. He even heard a few Stuart tanks clanking by. The officers weren't pulling his leg, there was a big operation in process. He told himself that was why his plan had been snubbed. Once something's set in motion it's almost impossible to stop. He should have come a day or two earlier.

He heard talking from outside the flap and then it was flung aside allowing the bright afternoon sun to stream through. Two men came in and the second one rolled up the flap and tied it in the open position. "Hot as hell in here. Mind if I keep this open?"

Welch didn't respond only stared, then said. "You here to interrogate me?"

The first man spoke, "I'm Lieutenant Smote and this is 1st Lieutenant Tormac. We're with intelligence G2, but we're not here to interrogate you. That sounds bad. We're here to ask you questions about you and your men. That alright with you?"

Welch smiled not seeing the distinction, "Whatever you Yanks call it. Get on with it."

Smote sat on the bunk across from him and looked at a clipboard he held on his lap. "We confirmed your identity. Thomas Welch the third. Born in London on August 10th, 1917 to Madelaine and Geoffery Welch. Joined the foreign service after attending college. You were originally sent to Tulagi, but just before the Japs started this, you were sent here to be an assistant to a Captain Morrisey. You were here two years before the Japs invaded. You report to Captain Morrisey." He looked at Welch with stony blue eyes, "That sound right to you?" He nodded. Smote continued. "Now that we know who we're dealing with…welcome to the 164th."

Welch took a long pull from his canteen. He'd been conserving the luke warm water wondering if he was a prisoner or not. Now that he knew he wasn't he quenched his thirst. "Can't say I feel welcome, Lieutenant."

Smote handed the clipboard to Tormac who held his pencil poised, ready to take notes. "Did Captain Morrisey send you to us? Was the attack plan his idea?"

Welch smiled, how to play this? "Morrisey knew I was coming here, but he didn't think you Yanks would go for the plan…guess he was right."

"Do you think Morrisey would welcome our help in the form of guns, ammunition and men?"

Welch flared, "I know we would. Look, I'm the man standing before you, I'm the man that risked his life coming through the Jap lines."

"Okay," Smote paced, "Would you be willing to risk your life again and take a squad of our men through to your camp?"

Welch brightened, "Yes, yes of course." He looked Smote in the eye, "For what purpose?"

Tormac's hand was writing in a blur, but stopped with the question. Smote answered, "To link our men to yours. To help you out, to re-supply and set you up to become an effective fighting force. We'd also want some of your natives to join our main lines, they'd be invaluable guides. Could save countless lives with their knowledge of the island."

Welch smiled, "When do we leave?"

THERE WAS two hours of daylight left when Lieutenant Caprielli gave Sgt. Carver the news. Carver stared as he listened to the details. When he told him everything he knew, Carver nodded, *what kind of cluster-fuck is this?* "Okay. We better get our shit together if we're leaving at dark. I'll have Corporal Hooper get the men packed, they'll bitch about the extra weight, but sounds like we'll be gone for a while. You'll be down a squad, they gonna reinforce you?"

"They're rolling 1st squad and the rest of 2nd squad into 2nd platoon. I'll be leading this expedition." Sergeant Carver looked at the Lieutenant with a flash of anger before he gained control. "They're taking your platoon?"

Caprielli shrugged, "I'll get it back when we return." Carver nodded, but in his head, he groaned. Going into the jungle with only twelve men was bad enough, but being led by the Lieutenant made the situation ten times worse. How would he keep the men alive if he had to watch every move Caprielli made? He hid his feelings. "I'll get started on the packing."

The Lieutenant said, "Make sure the men have the carbines for this one. I don't want anyone weighted down with a rifle." Carver looked at his Thompson sub-machine gun. "I don't care what you bring Sergeant, but bring plenty of ammo. You'll be the only one carrying the forty-five caliber."

Sergeant Carver nodded. At least that made sense, maybe he was coming around. "Yes, Sir."

Two hours later they were watching the sun set. They sat beside their stuffed packs. O'Connor wondered how he'd be able to move through the jungle with such a heavy pack. It was going to be slow going and murder on his sore legs. He'd taken the bandages off. He wouldn't be able to tend to them in the bush and besides, he was mostly healed.

The Lieutenant brought the Brit around to meet them. He seemed like an okay guy, if not a bit too chipper. He'd exchanged his tropical whites for olive drab army pants and top. He kept his floppy jungle hat, though. Instead of his captured Japanese Arisaka rifle he carried one of the new M1-Carbines. They packed a smaller punch, only thirty caliber, but they held more rounds in the magazine and were feather light compared with the 30.06 M1 Garand. He'd been given a crash course shooting at floating coconuts as they bobbed in the ocean waves. He thought the weapon a marvel of ingenuity and fell in love with it.

O'Connor liked the carbine too, but he missed the power of his Garand. To compensate he'd brought along his sidearm .45. He'd won it in a poker game on the ship ride over from New Caledonia. The heavy caliber round would put an enemy down even if he hit him in the arm.

He looked the squad over. They'd only been on the island a little more than a week, but each man looked like a combat veteran of many years. They'd been bombed, strafed, shot at and they'd killed men with bayonets and knives. Despite this, O'Connor was worried, these men weren't jungle fighters. His years of hunting had taught him to move like a ghost through the woods, but these men were mostly from the farms and cities of South Dakota. If the Japs heard them tonight they wouldn't have enough firepower to fend them off.

O'Connor convinced Sgt. Carver to let him be point man. Carver had wanted Hooper, but he'd convinced him that his injury would make it hard for him. Carver agreed and gave the job to O'Connor. Now as he sat at the edge of the darkening jungle he wished he'd kept his big mouth shut. *I could get these guys killed.*

Sergeant Carver put the men in the order he wanted for the patrol. He wanted them to stick close together. The dark jungle would be even darker at night and he didn't want anyone getting lost. Welch had tried to get them to go during the daylight. He was convinced he could get them to the village without being spotted, but the higher-ups wanted them traveling at night so that's what they'd do.

O'Connor hefted his pack and kneeled beneath its weight. He watched Sgt. Carver in the dying light. Carver nodded at him and he took his first step into the jungle. Dunphy followed staying close and so it went until the squad disappeared into the darkness.

O'Connor's senses were on full alert. He concentrated on every step being as silent as he could. He'd schooled Dunphy on walking silently and he was happy to see that the lesson had some effect. He could hear him, but he didn't sound like an elephant, more like a clumsy dog.

The first couple hundred yards were the toughest. The jungle was thick, but it soon opened up into more open palms. O'Connor thought it was probably part of a deserted plantation. Dunphy touched his arm and he crouched, waiting. He scanned his front. The palms swayed in a warm, light breeze. It would be beautiful if it wasn't so deadly. Soon he heard footsteps coming from behind. He kept scanning forward until someone came up beside him. It was the Brit and Sgt. Carver.

Welch whispered into his ear, "This is the Witherspoon place. Looted long before the Japs got here. There weren't any Japs here when I passed through the other day."

O'Connor nodded, thinking, *today ain't yesterday, asshole.* Carver slapped his arm and motioned him forward. O'Connor nodded and moved like a cat on a prowl. The entire column was up and moving again. O'Connor could see a building looming out of the murky darkness. The Witherspoon place looked like it must have been quite the spread in its day. Now it looked dark and foreboding. He led the squad around the back. When he was beyond it, the wide open plantation terrain gave way to more jungle. It wasn't thick, in fact it reminded him of what he'd see in Oregon; tall trees with thin underbrush. Perfect spot to find a deer. He hoped Japs didn't think like deer.

To his front he heard something that didn't sound right. He crouched and each man in line did the same. He pictured Dunphy crouching and trying to figure out why he stopped. O'Connor could hear the men as they bumped into each other, stopped and crouched, too loud. He strained his ears searching for what had spooked him. Had he imagined it? He'd heard something, but didn't know what, something out of place. His hunting senses were buzzing, but there was nothing.

He was about to move when he heard it again, the low murmur of someone whispering. He couldn't be sure how far away, but there was someone ahead and there were only Japs out there.

As he strained, Sgt. Carver appeared beside him. O'Connor was impressed he hadn't heard him coming. *Is Sarge a hunter? A Jap hunter, no doubt.* Carver touched his shoulder and O'Connor pointed forward and signaled he'd heard talking. Carver was still beside him, straining to hear. There it was again. Carver squeezed his shoulder and signaled for him to fall back. O'Connor nodded and started backing up. He almost yelled when the world lit up with the light from a flare, but he bit his tongue and froze. *The Japs must've heard us; they're searching for us. I knew these sons-of-bitches would get me killed.*

He moved his eyes and saw Carver lying on the ground motionless. Having the big man near him was calming, kind of like his father's presence on a hunt.

The flare sputtered and sizzled as it descended, making the jungle dance with crazy shadows. When it extinguished and darkness and silence returned, Carver and O'Connor crept back down the line until they were gathered around the Lieutenant and Welch.

Carver whispered, "We found their line, not where they're supposed to be." You couldn't see his eyes in the darkness, but everyone knew he was glaring at Welch.

Lieutenant Caprielli mulled things over, he needed to decide. "Let's keep moving. We'll head ninety degrees from our current direction and get around the edge of them."

Carver shook his head, "Sir, it's too risky. Why don't we fade back to the plantation and see things in the light of day? We're liable to run into them out here in the dark and we've got no support, totally on our own."

Lieutenant Caprielli scooched closer and whispered in Carver's ear, "I'm in charge, sergeant. Don't question my orders, follow them." It was whispered, but everyone caught the gist.

Sergeant Carver's face turned red, but no one could see it in the darkness. Without responding he grabbed O'Connor's shoulder and said, "Take us due east for a quarter mile. We'll reassess our position."

O'Connor nodded and was about to head out when he heard the Brit, "Going east isn't a good idea. We'll hit the river soon enough. With the recent rains it's high and impassable."

Carver leaned in, "Tell it to the LT. I'm only following orders." He signaled for O'Connor to move out.

O'Connor moved to his left sensing Dunphy following him. So far no one had gotten themselves lost, a minor miracle. They stayed in the same single file formation as before, but now O'Connor could tell they were making more of an effort to be quiet. The Japs were close and everybody knew it. Their stealth gave O'Connor hope that they might live to see the dawn.

The jungle was spread out and easy to maneuver through. He took one careful step after another. After an hour he came to the bank of a meandering river and halted. Carver was beside him again. He'd have to compare notes, no way Carver learned to be so quiet in the big city.

As O'Connor searched for any unwanted guests, they were joined by Lieutenant Caprielli and Welch. The others faced away from each other and watched the dark jungle to either side. Caprielli pulled out his map and under a red light and poncho searched for their position. "This river shouldn't be here," he whispered to himself.

Carver couldn't help himself, "Yet here it is."

Caprielli brought the map to Welch and pulled his poncho over both their heads. He pointed to where he thought they were. Welch took a long look at the map and chuckled. "This map is wrong, they've put the river in the wrong place and misnamed it. This is Alligator Creek. Of course, there aren't any alligators in the area, it was named by someone who didn't know the difference between an alligator and a crocodile." He slid his finger over, "The map says it's the Tenaru, it should be here." He put his finger where Caprielli thought they were. "Could be an old map and the river's meandered, but more likely it's just wrong. I'd put the map away. I know this island; I can get us there without all this nonsense."

Caprielli folded it up and stuffed it in his front shirt pocket. "I'll keep it. Can you get us there tonight?" Welch looked him in the eye, under the red glow they both looked like devils from a Halloween horror, he nodded.

When they came out from under the poncho Sgt. Carver stared at Caprielli. There was little doubt how he felt about him bypassing his opinion. He didn't say a word, only stared. Caprielli tried to meet his gaze, but turned away. In the darkness he was able to keep his dignity. "Welch is going to lead us from here," he whispered.

Sergeant Carver almost spoke, but decided to hold his tongue. Trusting this unknown Brit was folly as far as he was concerned. He didn't think he would knowingly give them away, he'd be just as dead if he did, but he didn't trust him to lead the patrol through the jungle without bumbling into Japs. He'd much prefer the stealth and obvious skill of his new point man, O'Connor. He moved close to O'Connor and spoke in his ear, "Stay right next to him. I don't want him stumbling into the Japs."

O'Connor nodded and waited for Welch to move out. When he did he was right beside him. Welch moved well, it was obvious he was comfortable in the jungle. O'Connor reminded himself that he'd been evading Jap patrols for months now.

They followed the river south, upstream. Where he was from in Oregon most rivers flowed west, but this one flowed due north, something he'd never seen. He shook his head. *I'm not in Oregon anymore.*

They were moving along a well-worn path beside the slow river. He was by no means a veteran of these parts, but when he hunted these were the trails he'd set up on, well used game trails. He didn't like the feeling. He tapped Welch who stopped and listened. "Think we should get off this trail." It was a statement not a question.

Welch shook his head, "This is a native trail, Japs don't use it." He followed along, but his sixth sense was buzzing and he'd learned a long time ago to listen. He was about to stop Welch again when the world behind him erupted in gunfire and bright flashes.

He dropped to his belly, pulling Welch down with him. He spun to the flashes, only yards away put his carbine to his shoulder and fired in quick succession. The noise was deafening as more shots rang out deeper in the jungle. His squad was getting hit hard. He fired at the new muzzle flashes. The air above his head came alive with buzzing bullets. He rolled to his left back towards his squad. He pulled Welch along, but he was dead weight, he wondered if he'd been hit. As the fire continued he yelled, "Welch, you hit? You hit? Move your ass." He got no response.

He pulled his gun up and fired at the flashes. On the third shot his carbines' firing pin slammed onto an empty chamber. He cussed, shucked off his pack and dug into his belt for another magazine. He pulled out the old and slammed another in, priming the weapon. He aimed more carefully, trying to judge where the enemy's body would be in relation to the flash. Answering fire from his squad petered out as they retreated. He realized he was cut off, alone with Japs all around him, his only ally a dead or wounded Brit. A feeling of panic started to rise in his gut, but he suppressed it and fired again.

He was about to pull the trigger again, but thought better of it. He had to get away from the area quick. No shooting had come from the river behind him. It was his only chance. The Japapanese continued firing. He wanted to kill them, pour fire into them, give his buddies a chance, but it would be the last thing he did. Instead he reached out and pulled his pack along the ground towards the river. He wasn't trying to be quiet anymore. Once the Japanese stopped firing he'd give his position away, but as long as they kept firing he could make all the noise he wanted.

He grunted and pulled the unwieldy pack along. With each step he got further away from the ambush. He wondered if any of his buddies had survived. He'd heard screaming, but not anymore. They'd been hit hard. It had been a perfectly orchestrated ambush. The thought made him feel uncomfortable, *were they waiting for us?*

The firing was slowing down. There was no return fire. He hoped that meant the squad had successfully disengaged themselves from the fight. He imagined them running like hell back to the deserted plantation, the enemy hot on their heels. It wouldn't be a bad place to make a last stand.

The quiet descended like a shroud over a death's head. The firing had ceased, the jungle sounds ceased, so he stopped moving and strained to hear anything over the ringing in his ears. It was unnaturally quiet. Finally, like a far-away train approaching, the jungle started waking again. First the chirps and snaps of insects then the unknown night bird calls, he thought he even heard the call of a monkey. *Does this place have monkeys?* Soon it was as if the firefight hadn't happened, the jungle returned to normal.

O'Connor didn't move. His pack was in front of him. He could sense he was close to the river, but he couldn't be sure how close. It may as well be a mile since the noise of dragging the pack even a foot would bring the Japs onto his position.

He rested his carbine on the pack and waited for a target. He had no doubt they'd pursue him. He'd walked right past the ambush without ever seeing them. They'd let he and Welch pass first to let the main force walk into the kill zone. How had he been so clueless? Why hadn't he sensed the Jap ambush? Then he remembered he had, but Welch wouldn't get off the trail. O'Connor gritted his teeth. The poor son-of-a-bitch was laying out there dead or dying; he'd paid the price for his mistake.

It wouldn't take long for the Japs to come for him. They'd probably already found Welch and were searching for him. He wondered how many there were. The main force must have pursued what was left of the squad, but how many stayed back to finish off the point man? He felt his bowels loosen as he remembered the stories he'd heard of how Japs treated prisoners. Long torture and slow agony as you prayed for death. He decided they wouldn't take him alive. He felt along his belt until he found a grenade. He pulled it and laid it next to the pack. If he was wounded in the next couple minutes, he'd end it with the grenade. Use the Jap playbook against them and take a few with him. He felt better with the grenade; it eased his mind to know he wouldn't suffer at the hands of these savages.

Minutes passed with no sound to his front. He wondered if they'd all joined the chase. The night calm was shattered again with gunshots from down the trail. The heavy sound of rifle fire then the tinny sound of return carbine fire, then the heavy thumping of a Thompson sub-machine gun. He grinned, at least Sarge was still in the fight.

He used the firefight to make more ground towards the river. He pushed backwards until he was at arms-length from his pack then pulled it towards him, moving slow. He repeated the process three more times until the jungle to his front changed. He focused and read-justed his firing position. Someone was coming towards him. He felt sweat sting his eyes as it dripped down his furrowed brow. If he opened up, it would be minutes before the whole Jap army descended on him and he died.

He reached for the grenade, maybe he should throw it as a distraction, pull the Japs away from him. He dispelled the thought since he wouldn't be able to throw it far enough. In the close jungle, it would be a clear signal of his whereabouts. He felt along his belt and put his hand on the cool handle of his K-bar knife. If it was one man and he got close enough, the knife would be just the thing. His mouth went dry as he pictured himself driving the knife into a man's belly.

He carefully pulled it from its sheath and gripped the handle. It felt cold and deadly. *Can I kill a man with a knife?* He'd soon find out. He made a plan; if it was more than one man, he'd open up with his M1 and sprint for the relative safety of the river. If it was one man he'd kill him with the knife. He took a deep breath hoping it was more than one man.

The darkness to his front took on a shape, dim at first then becoming more distinct. It was the unmistakable silhouette of a man, one man. He released his grip on the carbine and licked his lips, it would be the knife. He tried to control his breathing as the soldier advanced ever closer. The Jap was being cautious, each step silent, his eyes scanning for him like an owl searching for mice.

When he was only feet from him he stopped and turned back the way he'd come. It was perfect. He had his back to him, it was now or never, there wouldn't be a better chance.

His muscles coiled. He launched himself at the man's back. He drove his knee into the soldier's back and with his left hand grabbed his head and pulled back, stifling a yell. His right hand held the blade and he drove it down toward the man's chest, but something slowed his hand, something wasn't right. Something about the way the soldier carried himself, the way he moved, the way he smelled. Something was wrong.

He pulled the man to the ground and put the knife to his neck. Better to kill him on the ground, less sound of falling. The man was gagging, trying to talk. Then he recognized English words, the reality of the situation now clear. He put his face close to his and whispered, "You stupid Brit, I almost killed you."

Welch was breathing hard, his second shave with death even closer than the first. His eyes were wide, "Right, it's me so get off and let's get out of here?"

O'Connor kept the knife at his neck. He looked the way he'd come, straining to see lurking Japs. "Thought you were hit."

Welch pushed his hand from his jugular and sat up, "Grazed my forehead, must've knocked me out, probably our own chaps returning fire." He reached up and felt his forehead showing off the gash.

Even in the low light, O'Connor could see it had bled a lot. "You've lost a lot of blood. You okay to move?"

"Head wounds always bleed a lot, I was moving until you knocked me over."

O'Connor grinned and nodded, "Come on. Let's get to the river. We can stay near the bank and float along, use the bank for cover if they get too close. We can float all the way to the ocean, our guys are set up on the west side."

"That's where I was headed when you jumped me."

## 9

They crouched along the river bank, guns pointed back the way they'd come. O'Connor still had his pack, but Welch had lost his in the fighting. O'Connor leaned in close and whispered, "Watch the jungle." Welch nodded. O'Connor dug into his pack and pulled out his heavy rain poncho. He folded it then tied the ends closed with cord from his pack. He laced the remaining cord through the grommets spaced at ten-inch intervals along the side and cinched it off as tight as he could. Welch looked over his shoulder wondering what this crazy hillbilly was doing besides making a lot of unwanted noise.

O'Connor placed his pack next to the river's edge and slid into the water. The bank was steep, but the water only three feet deep. He pulled both ends of the poncho under water and stepped on them. The belly of the poncho floated to the surface with trapped air. Then to Welch's horror O'Connor started splashing furiously beside the poncho pulling air into the makeshift float. He was making a hell of a racket, but after a few seconds the poncho was floating high.

O'Connor pulled his pack over and keeping the edge of the poncho under water wrapped it around and through the shoulder straps of the pack. He slowly released the pack testing its stability. The buoyancy floated the pack halfway out of the water. Satisfied, O'Connor whispered, "Let's go, we'll put the carbines on the pack, keep 'em out of the water."

Welch backed towards him, "I'm not getting into the river." O'Connor stared, it was their only chance. "It's called Alligator Creek for a reason. It's infested with crocodiles." O'Connor looked at him funny. Exasperated, Welch explained, "Whoever named it didn't know the difference between a crocodile and an alligator."

O'Connor looked around, were they coming at him now? He didn't see anything except black water flowing to safety. "We'll have to take our chances. I haven't seen any crocs though. If we stay here the Japs'll get us for sure. I'd rather take my chances with the crocs"

Welch had seen crocodiles attack and kill on land and in the river, they were terrifying predators. The thought of being slammed then rolled and stuffed under a river ledge until tender, terrified him. He sat on the edge weighing his options. O'Connor had his hand out wanting the carbine. Welch's mind was made up when a flare popped overhead and he heard Japanese voices. They were close. He ducked down and slid into the cool water. He kept his carbine pointed back to the lit-up jungle. The flare seemed to hang forever. When it was almost out he saw a shape emerge only yards from him. There was no doubt it was a well-armed Japanese soldier searching for them.

The light extinguished at the perfect time. The Jap kept coming, but he stumbled and fell, blinded by the sudden darkness. Like a viper striking, O'Connor lunged out of the water and drove his razor sharp K-bar into the neck of the soldier. He cut his spinal cord and without a sound the soldier died.

O'Connor pulled the dead soldier into the water, pushed him under and sent him downstream. Welch shook his head, "The blood will bring the crocs."

"Well now they'll have something to eat besides us."

Welch shook his head, "You don't understand. They go into frenzies, like sharks."

O'Connor slipped deeper into the water and started floating downstream. Welch made his decision, he handed his weapon over and slid in behind him. He fingered the knife he had at his side, it would be a small defense against a croc, but it would have to do.

The pack was floating well on the poncho and Welch and O'Connor gripped the edges like a raft. They could float like this for a long time, all night if need be. With every passing foot they drifted further away from the ambush site. Another flare popped back where they'd been and tracer fire arced into the night slashing across the river well upstream. Either the Japs were jumpy or they'd found some stragglers.

O'Connor stroked closer to the bank and Welch followed. They heard Japanese voices yelling from upstream. "Let's keep close to the bank in case we have to get out in a hurry." Welch nodded. The bank was steep and the jungle leaned over it dipping vines and branches into the water like fingers feeling the passing coolness.

O'Connor figured the Japs had found their entry point. There'd been a lot of blood and trampled jungle. They could hardly miss it even in the darkness. O'Connor wondered how close the river trail was. He remembered it being close most of the way. If the Japanese suspected they were in the river, they may be moving down the trail to get in front of them. "We have to move faster, Japs'll be coming down the trail fast, can't let 'em get in front of us."

They pushed the pack in front and started kicking underwater to propel themselves. They had to move away from the bank to avoid the overhanging jungle. They were more exposed, but they were moving much faster now. The darkness was their only cover. The effort had them breathing hard. They dipped their heads to keep the sweat from dripping into their eyes.

They were making good time, but after thirty minutes they needed rest. The poncho was losing its buoyancy, despite forcing more air into it. O'Connor suspected the para-cord was loosening in the water. Their carbines were dangerously close to being submerged. He pointed to the near bank, "Gotta retie the poncho. Let's get to shore." Welch nodded.

They pushed into the bank and worked their way downstream until they found a relatively flat spot where the bank sloped into the river. They pushed the pack onto the muddy bank and lay still, listening. After two full minutes O'Connor said, "Keep watch upstream while I retie this." Welch nodded and pulled himself out of the water. The water dripping from him made the bank muddy and as he tried to crawl up he felt himself slipping back into the river. He dug in with his finger tips and pulled himself until he could see upstream. He realized he was lying beside the trail they'd walked up earlier; the trail he'd deemed safe.

He wondered what time it was. He looked at his watch, but even in the dim light he could tell it was beyond repair. Another victim of Alligator Creek. He thought the sun must be coming up soon, they'd been at it a long time. He watched the trail and listened to the young O'Connor working on the poncho. He wondered where he'd learned that trick, was it something they taught in the Army?

Minutes passed. It felt good to be out of the water. He felt his eyes growing heavy as a thick wave of exhaustion swept over his body, threatening to send him to blissful oblivion. He shook his head trying to shake the fatigue. Here he was in a desperate situation and he was having trouble staying awake? Bugger that. He bit his lip, the pain keeping him in the here and now. He heard something coming. Boots pounding on the muddy path, the Japanese were double timing down the trail. O'Connor was right, they were trying to cut them off.

He looked back to O'Connor who heard it too and laid still beside the pack, his body half in the water. Welch realized he'd left his carbine on the pack. Their only chance was to lay low and hope the Japanese passed without seeing them. From the sounds it was a sizable force. Welch scooted himself deeper into cover. He hoped it would be enough, the trail was only feet from his prone body.

He kept his head down, but kept one eye open. He watched as the Japs' cleft toe boots landed only feet from his head. He tried to keep count, but lost it after forty. The pounding boots sounded like thunder, but he was sure they'd hear his own beating heart. He tried to control his breathing. It took all his concentration to keep from hyperventilating. His mantra; breath in, breath out, slow it down. After an eternity the troops stopped coming. He laid there until he couldn't hear the boots at all. He lurched when O'Connor touched his boot and pulled him towards him. It was time to get on with it.

He pushed his way back and when he hit the mud he slid into

O'Connor who stopped him from splashing into the river. He put his mouth next to Welch's ear, "Let's stay here till daylight, sun should be coming up in an hour." Welch didn't like it. He wanted to get as far away from the spot as possible. He shook his head, but O'Connor persisted. "Too many Japs looking for us downstream. We'll lay up in cover and wait. We need to rest."

They slid into deeper cover along the bank and pulled branches and vines around them until they looked like part of the jungle. O'Connor whispered, "Try to get some sleep, I'll keep watch." Welch closed his eyes thinking it would be impossible to sleep.

He woke with a start when O'Connor poked him hard with a stick. The darkness was gone, replaced with early morning light. He thought it a lovely morning until he remembered his situation. A feeling of dread overtook him. He itched all over, the drying mud and the crawling bugs taking their toll. Instead of itching he moved his head and met O'Connor's eyes which were gleaming from behind a thick layer of vines and mud. Something had him spooked. He followed O'Connor's eyes as they scanned towards the river. His blood froze. The dead Jap soldier O'Connor had killed and pushed into the river the night before was hung up in the branches swaying back and forth in the current only yards away. From the river came the lazy form of a large crocodile. His snout and yellow eyes gleamed in the morning light, his eyes focused on the easy meal caught in the branches.

Welch started to move, but a high-pitched Japanese voice coming from the trail stopped him. He didn't move a muscle. The soldier's voice brought others until there were many. They were getting closer; they'd seen their comrade. Any second they'd be down by the river beside their hiding place.

Another voice, this one in charge. It was easy to discern an order even in a foreign language. O'Connor was on his stomach and could see two soldiers coming down the slick embankment. He hoped they would be too preoccupied with their dead buddy to notice the scuff marks on the bank pointing to their positions.

The soldiers came down the bank between Welch and O'Connor. They were pointing at the body and yelling. They didn't notice the dark form in the water sink out of sight. One soldier took off his small pack and handed his rifle to the other man and waded in. O'Connor lost sight of them as they walked past him, but he heard one enter the water. He saw four more soldiers on the trail, their weapons at their waist watching the scene.

The first soldier got to the body and tried to pull it loose, but the branches held him tight. He pulled out his knife and started cutting and slashing at the vines, but the current, the depth and the awkward dead weight were too much. He called for his comrade to help. The second soldier put down his pack and his buddies' and laid the rifles on top. He waded out to help.

They almost had the body free when the first soldier yelled and there was a great splash and a massive dark shape. He had time to look at the second soldier, terror and confusion on his face before he was pulled beneath the dark water. The second soldier screamed and half swam half ran for the shore. His eyes were wide, yelling at the top of his lungs. He was three feet from the bank when something big came from behind him and landed on his legs and back. The soldier reached out and his hand was the last thing anyone saw of him.

The yelling from the soldiers on the bank intensified and they started shooting into the water at unseen targets. Maybe they'd get lucky and hit the crocs. Even if they accidentally hit their own men, it would be a mercy. The man in charge yelled an order and two grenades were thrown. The water geysered when they exploded, but only bubbles and dead fish surfaced. A few more shots, then another order.

Two more soldiers came to the shore looking at the deadly water, their guts roiling. The dead soldier in the branches had been shredded by the grenades and was nearly free. One soldier stood at the ready, his rifle pointing into the river covering the other man who went in fast. He yanked on the body and it came loose. He pulled him onto the bank. The other man grabbed him under the arm and they hauled him up to the trail dropping him at their sergeant's feet.

They inspected the body. O'Connor wondered if the grenades had shredded him enough to hide the mortal knife wound in his back.

The sergeant stood and looked out over the water searching for his lost men. He yelled an order and the remaining troops started to form up along the path. A sudden burst of gunfire erupted in the distance. The soldiers tensed and dropped to their knees pointing their weapons toward the sound.

O'Connor knew the sound of carbines meant his squad was engaged with the Japs again. The sergeant gave another order and the soldiers double timed it towards the sound of battle, dragging their dead comrade with them.

## 10

O'Connor waited a full ten minutes before he moved a muscle. The Japs had been close enough to touch, but they hadn't seen them. It was a minor miracle. He moved his eyeballs first, then slowly turned his head. He couldn't see anyone, but if they were on the trail he wouldn't know until he was fully exposed. He looked to where Welch was hiding, but couldn't see him. He was completely covered, just a mound.

He moved onto his stomach so he could see the trail. It was abandoned; the Japs were gone. He crawled higher up the bank until he was on the trail. He looked both ways, they were alone. He turned back to the water, remembering the beasts that had taken the Japanese to their watery grave. He saw movement; the mound was coming alive. He could see Welch's head taking shape as the leaves, vines and dirt slid off. He made eye contact with O'Connor who gave him a thumbs up.

He returned the signal, but didn't smile. He crawled up next to O'Connor and whispered in his ear. "Let's get outta here." O'Connor nodded and pointed into the jungle. Welch shook his head and pointed down the trail towards their lines.

Gunshots from the plantation continued. They were still in the fight. O'Connor pointed, "We're going to help out the squad. They need us, we can come up behind the Japs and surprise 'em."

He started to crawl away, but Welch grabbed his belt. "That's suicide. They can take care of themselves."

O'Connor pushed his hand away and came up onto his knees. He inspected his rifle being sure to check the barrel for mud. He wiped it with his shirt, getting the mud off the moving parts as best he could. "We'll take 'em by surprise. Put down a steady field of fire and move around a lot; we'll confuse 'em, give our guys a chance." Welch started to protest, but O'Connor's eyes took on a red intensity, "I'm going to help my unit. You come with me or go it alone." He didn't wait for a reply, but moved across the trail into the jungle. The sounds of gunfire were sporadic, but he could still discern the pop of the carbines and the occasional burst from a Thompson. Ammo wasn't a problem as long as they hadn't lost their packs. He could hear the Brit behind him. He didn't need him, but was glad he decided to come along.

With each step the sounds of fighting grew louder. A new sound, a machine gun started hammering away. The Japs had upped the ante; the squad wouldn't last long with that pinning them down. O'Connor hunched lower, but increased his speed. Even though he was almost running he was still quiet. Welch, who'd been walking jungle trails for years was keeping up, but making more noise. With all the gunfire O'Connor didn't think it would matter.

The machine gun stopped, probably reloading, but O'Connor steered them towards the area. He was about to pass around a jeep-sized rock when the machine gun opened up again. He dropped to the ground, it was directly in front of the rock. He'd almost blundered into the crew. He looked behind him at Welch and signaled that he was going to toss a grenade over the rock and he should too.

Welch nodded and pried a grenade from his belt. It was mud covered, he hoped it worked. They got to their knees and faced each other. O'Connor looked into Welch's eyes and bobbed his head as if in cadence. He mouthed, 'One, two, three,' then pulled the pin, released the lever and tossed it over the boulder.

Welch's was right behind, but wasn't thrown as hard. It bounced precariously on the top then toppled down the other side. There were two closely spaced explosions. The machine gun stopped and there was screaming. O'Connor sprang around the rock and emptied his carbine into the three men sprawled in a low depression. The grenades had done their work, the men had smoking holes in their bodies.

O'Connor kicked over the machine gun, the barrel was bent and smoking. He came back around the rock and crouched looking at Welch, "We've gotta keep moving." He heard more firing and saw the muzzle flashes and smoke from the main Japanese position. In the commotion of the fire fight the Japanese hadn't noticed their machine gun's silence, but that wouldn't last and someone would investigate. A bullet whizzed off the rock next to his head and he pulled back squinting from the rock dust. He'd almost been killed by his own men.

He signaled Welch to follow him and he went back the way they'd come, then moved laterally to get behind the enemy line. He found a thick patch of bush and went to his knee. He pulled two more grenades and placed them within easy reach. "How many you got?" he asked Welch. Welch reached down and pulled his last grenade and held it out for inspection. O'Connor nodded, "Throw yours to the right, I'll put one in the center and left. When they go off we'll unload with our M1s and skedaddle over there." He pointed back to the dead machine gunners' rock. "That's where we'll meet. Got it?" Welch's eyes were wide, but he nodded.

O'Connor put his carbine down and hefted the first grenade. He pulled the pin, then carefully put it back on the ground careful to secure the lever. He picked up the second grenade and pulled the pin. He looked back at Welch who was looking at him funny. He hadn't armed his grenade and O'Connor looked at him wondering. Finally, Welch shook his head and nodded. He pulled the pin.

O'Connor threw his grenade, then reached for the second before the first landed. Welch thought how easy it would be to drop his grenade at this cowboys' feet and surrender to the Japs. This soldier was going to get him killed, but instead he hurled his grenade towards the firing right flank of the Japanese line intentionally short and picked up his carbine.

The grenades went off seconds apart and the shooting stopped. Two Japs were hit and screaming and the others looked around in panic wondering what happened. O'Connor picked up his carbine and shot into the Japanese lines, sweeping his weapon back and forth where he thought they'd be.

Welch took off towards the rock without firing. He slid in beside the boulder and panted. O'Connor had expended his magazine and was running back to the rock. Welch watched him bob and weave in a crouching run. It would be so easy to lift his carbine and end this right here, but now he was committed. The Japs would never take his surrender, they'd string him up and fillet him for days. Instead, Welch raised his M1 and fired a few shots back toward the Japanese line.

O'Connor slid in beside him and pulled another magazine from his pocket and pushed it into place. It made a satisfying 'click.' He looked back the way they'd come, there was firing coming their way, but nothing concentrated. *They're worried about hitting their own men.*

The fire coming from the plantation intensified. Bullets cracked and whizzed through the branches, but not directed their way. A Japanese soldier rose from the ground fifteen yards away and saw them crouched there. He rose up and charged. His gun with the glinting bayonet was leveled at them. The soldier yelled and pulled the trigger, but he shot from the hip on the run and the single shot went between them. Welch instinctively pulled his carbine to his shoulder and quickly shot four rounds into the advancing man, but he kept coming. The tiny holes in his tunic shone bright red in the morning sun. He re-aimed and pulled the trigger again, this time the man's head snapped back and he fell to the side only feet away, his eyes staring.

Welch looked at the gun then at O'Connor, who said, "That's why I prefer my Garand." Welch nodded and reloaded. "We gotta move. Let's make a run for the plantation." The rock behind them started taking hits and the ricochets were coming dangerously close. "Let's get away from this death trap." He pulled on Welch's sleeve and ran to the other side of the boulder. "When I say go, I want you to take off to that cover," he pointed at a stack of downed palm trees at the edge of the plantation. "I'll cover you, then you do the same for me. I'll be coming as soon as you find cover so make it quick."

The bullets were much more concentrated now. The rock was chipping and soon a dust cloud of rock surrounded them. "Now!"

O'Connor yelled and leaned out and fired towards the Japanese line. He walked his fire from right to left until his magazine was empty. He turned just in time to see Welch dive behind the pile of wood with bullets sending dirt geysers on his heels.

He swapped magazines and saw Welch pop up and start laying down fire. O'Connor took off in a low crouch. Bullets were buzzing by him like angry bees. He gritted his teeth and kept running, concentrating on the wood pile. Welch was sending a steady stream of fire downrange, but the Jap fire was intensifying. He made the log pile and laid on his back as rounds flew over and into the pile. He felt like he was on the inside of a drum head.

Welch came down and lay beside him. "Getting kinda hot. Anymore bright ideas, Private?"

O'Connor shook his head, "Don't think we'll find better cover than what we've got right here. We can hold them off if they don't bring anything heavier." As if in answer they heard the distinctive sound of a mortar shell arcing their way. "Shit, mortars. We gotta leave." O'Connor went to run directly away keeping the wood pile between himself and the Japs, but the ground in front of him erupted with the impact of a 50mm mortar shell and he was thrown back into the pile. He slammed hard and lost his breath. He lay there gasping.

Welch leaned over to shield him, "Are you hit?" he yelled. O'Connor was only able to gasp and grunt for air. Welch assumed the worst and came off him to look for wounds, but another shell landed and sent dirt and jungle onto them. He leaned over the struggling Private. He lay on O'Connor, his ears ringing knowing the next shell would be right on top of them. Any second now his world would end. It made him angry to think how ridiculous it had become.

But the next shell never landed. Instead the shooting seemed to slacken from the Japanese lines and intensify from the plantation. Welch heard the Japanese yelling. He risked raising his head and saw the back of a Japanese soldier running the way they'd come. Another soldier entered his vision, this one much closer. He went to raise his rifle, but the uniform was different. This was an American soldier.

The soldier went to one knee and aimed at the fleeing soldier's back. He shot three times and as Welch watched, the man's back erupted in two new holes and he pitched forward his rifle flying through the air. The American stood and turned to the wood pile. Welch recognized him from the squad. He thought his name was Crandall.

Welch stood up holding his carbine over his head, "Hey, it's us. Welch and Private O'Connor. He's hit, needs help, mortars."

Crandall's smile at seeing them alive faded when he heard his friend was hit. He ran and leaped over the wood pile with ease. He landed next to O'Connor and gave him a once over. O'Connor got his breath back, "Get off me Crandall, I'm fine, just had the wind knocked out of me." He pushed him away.

Crandall grinned, "You're a sight for sore eyes and make no mistake. We got the Japs on the run, but when they regroup they'll come at us like a freight train. Your attack from the rear got 'em flustered, allowed us to advance without being noticed. Got close enough to nail their mortar crew. Thank Christ they didn't have that thing up and running earlier." He looked over the wood pile and waved at someone. "You able to run? We gotta go. Sarge's signaling us, we gotta go now."

O'Connor hopped to his feet and nodded, "Lead on." As they cleared the wood pile they saw more guys crouched next to trees and rocks covering their withdrawal. They ran past them and they followed in turn. When they got close to the plantation it was pockmarked with bullet holes, it looked like a deranged flock of woodpeckers had been unleashed.

Sergeant Carver was standing in the doorway his Thompson smoking. He tilted his helmet back, "Well, I'll be, thought you fuckers were long dead."

Lieutenant Caprielli was aiming his carbine out a window, his eyes like saucers. He gave a curt nod to them.

O'Connor only smiled, but Welch reached out and shook the sergeant's hand. "Jolly good to see you, thought our goose was cooked back at the wood pile."

Sergeant Carver looked him up and down. He was covered with mud and dirt, his white teeth shining like beacons. Carver dropped his hand, "Let's get our shit and find someplace to hole up. When the Japs realize how thin we are they'll come back pissed. We don't wanna be here." He glanced at Lieutenant Caprielli who nodded. He grabbed Welch by the shoulders, "You know this island, any place you know we can safely powwow?" Welch looked at him sideways not understanding the word. Carver rolled his eyes, "Someplace we can make a plan without getting our balls shot off."

Welch's eyes lit up and he raised a hand in recognition, "Ah," then he put his hand to his chin and thought about it. After a few seconds he looked around at the plantation and nodded. "Yes, follow me. It's close, we should be safe there." He pointed behind him, "There's an old mine on the edge of this property. The mine shaft's old and out of use, but it's safe. In fact, old Smiley used to give tours."

"Smiley?" Caprielli asked.

"Yes, the chap who owns this plantation, Smiley Witherspoon. He's a good chap, but he was one of the first to flee." He looked around at the shot-up building, "Break his heart to see it this way."

Sergeant Carver gathered the men for a quick head count. They'd lost two men in the ambush, Private Skinner and Private Markos, whittling their twelve man squad to ten. They'd had no choice but to leave them to rot in the stinking jungle. He nodded realizing it could have been a whole lot worse. "They're all here, Sir."

Caprielli nodded and they moved out.

## 11

The bedraggled squad shouldered their packs. They were much lighter now; they'd used a lot of ammunition. They filed out the back door and trotted after Welch who kept waving them onward. The fast pace felt wrong, there were Japanese soldiers throughout the jungle, but they kept up and kept their eyes on the jungle.

They were following an overgrown trail. It was probably well used when Smiley was running this place, but the jungle was reclaiming it. If Welch hadn't known about it the trail would be impossible to find.

They traveled at a trotting speed for a quarter mile before the trail opened up onto an open patch of land. Welch stopped at the edge and crouched. Lieutenant Caprielli ran forward and Welch pointed at the edge of the jungle. Lieutenant Caprielli strained and finally saw the dark hole in the side of a small hillock. The entrance was half covered with old wood that had once been on hinges, but they'd rusted and the door had leaned over. Caprielli nodded and motioned O'Connor and Crandall forward. They stayed low and crossed the low grassy field. When they got to the mine entrance Crandall moved the wood and stepped inside. O'Connor kept his carbine ready. Crandall disappeared into the blackness, but came out in seconds and waved the others forward. Lieutenant Caprielli nodded at Sergeant Carver and they went across, leaving plenty of space between each man.

At the entrance they crouched and Crandall said, "It's clear, far as I can tell. Pitch black in there."

Welch pushed his way past and went inside like he owned the place. Caprielli tried to grab his sleeve, but he slipped by. The Lieutenant was about to send someone in after him when he saw a soft glow coming from inside. Sergeant Carver entered and waved them inside, "He's found some light."

Entering the mine was like entering the inside of a musty old closet. The smell of wet earth tinged with some kind of metallic tang was oppressive. The mine shaft went straight for ten feet then turned a corner to the left. The soft glow was coming from around the corner. Welch poked his head back around and held up an old-fashioned kerosene lantern. It threw crazy shadows behind him. "Old Smiley always keeps a tin of matches and plenty of kerosene in his lamps."

The others gathered around the light, it was downright cozy and since the Japanese would have a hard time finding the place they felt relatively safe. Sergeant Carver wasn't taking any chances though, "Crandall, go to the front and make the entrance disappear. Wipe any sign of us and keep watch." Crandall trotted around the corner. Carver took Lieutenant Caprielli's shoulder and pulled him aside. "Think it would be a good idea to lay low here awhile. The men are beat and could use some chow and some shuteye. It's nice and cool in here, be a good place to rack out for a few hours."

Caprielli nodded. He looked at his watch which was still ticking despite the jungle's best efforts to corrode anything with moving parts. He returned to the men, "Alright we're gonna stay here and get some food and rest. Break out what you got, lay out your ponchos and get some sleep. We'll rotate the guard on the hour."

The men didn't need coaxing; they tore into their packs and pulled out their K-rats. They hadn't eaten since embarking on the doomed mission. The sound of tin cans being opened was quickly followed by slurping and burping, then light snoring.

Sergeant Carver, Lieutenant Caprielli and Welch sat around the lantern and talked quietly. Caprielli said, "We'll roust the men at 1400 and try to get around these Japs again. Any ideas on how we can do that?"

Welch's face went white in the yellow glow, "Surely you're not thinking of continuing the mission after what's happened?"

Carver glared, "Of course we're continuing the mission. We haven't accomplished it yet."

"But things have changed, you've lost men, you're understrength." He looked down realizing how weak the argument was.

The Lieutenant continued, "You're not obligated to stay with us, but your knowledge of the land could be the difference between success and failure."

Carver grumbled, "Didn't help us much last night."

Welch's face went from white to red as quick as a light switch turns dark to light. "You can't blame me for that, that trail's normally clear. It's the same one I took to get to your lines the other day."

Caprielli put a hand on his shoulder, "Easy does it." He waited for Welch's color to come back, "Is there another way through?"

Welch thought about it, then hesitantly said, "We could cross the river. I know of a decent fording spot, but there are crocodiles."

Carver grinned, "Crocodiles? Why they call it Alligator Creek?" Welch glared and Sergeant Carver continued, "I haven't seen any crocs, or gators, for that matter." Welch told them about their early morning experience with the Japanese. Carver shook his head, "Shitty way to go, even for a Jap." He looked at the Lieutenant, "Sounds better than risking the trail again."

Caprielli nodded, "Yeah, we'll watch for crocs. I'd rather fight them than Japs." Welch played the scene of the two Japanese soldiers being taken by the crocs and wasn't sure he agreed.

At 1400, Sergeant Carver rousted the men and they grumbled and stretched, farted and belched. They shuffled gear, getting ready for the coming move. They were glad not to be moving back up the trail.

They crouched at the entrance to the mine. Each man wanted to stay in the shaft; it was quiet, safe and the perfect temperature for sleeping. Carver touched O'Connor's shoulder. He nodded and pushed the cover aside and reentered the hostile world of Guadalcanal. Welch told him what bearing to follow to get to the ford spot and he moved from cover to cover. He saw no sign of enemy soldiers. The going was easy, the jungle was thick overhead, but the ground cover sparse. They could move quickly and quietly. It wasn't long until O'Connor came up against a well-used path. He kneeled and waited for counsel.

Sergeant Carver conferred with Welch who said the crossing was only a couple hundred yards down the trail. Carver directed O'Connor to stay to the side of the trail and take it slow avoiding any more ambushes. O'Connor gritted his teeth, blaming himself for leading them into the ambush the night before.

His pace was slow, every step thought out and calculated for noise control. He stopped several times when he thought he heard something, but it was always nothing. He was regaining his trust in his stalking abilities.

He'd gone a quarter mile when he heard the distinct sound of water babbling over shallow rocks. The river flowed deep. He hadn't known it to have any shallow rapids, but the sound was clear. He crouched and waved Sgt. Carver up. Welch came too and nodded, "That's it, that's the crossing. It's shallow and easily crossed here, but it's usually croc infested because other animals cross here too."

O'Connor smiled, predators in the Oregon woods hung out at spots like this too and for the same reasons. It was nice to know no matter where you were in the world, animal behavior was generally the same.

Sergeant Carver said, "I'm more concerned about the predators on two legs." He waved for Lieutenant Caprielli and pointed out the fording spot.

He nodded and pointed at Crandall, "You and O'Connor move across. The rest of us will cover you. Signal when it's safe to cross."

Crandall and O'Connor nodded and moved to the edge of the river. It was muddy limiting their view of the bottom. O'Connor was the first to enter. The water went up to his knees. He got his balance and took a tentative step. The bottom was mud covered rocks. He moved carefully not wanting to fall in and make a lot of noise.

With each step the water got deeper until it was over his belt. It wasn't cold, but cooler than the air. It felt good. With each step he felt more exposed. When he was halfway across he felt like he had Japanese crosshairs on his back. Any passing patrol would see him instantly; he wouldn't have a chance. He quickened his pace. Corporal Crandall entered the river and followed.

They rendezvoused near the bank on the far side. Crandall was jumpy looking over his shoulders in jerky movements. O'Connor said, "What's the matter with you? Calm down."

Crandall took a deep breath, "Sorry, that story about the crocs has got me spooked."

O'Connor nodded, "Yeah, but I don't think they like all the shelling. I heard someone saying they've pretty much disappeared with all the bombing."

"What about the ones that ate the Japs?" O'Connor shrugged. He went up onto the bank to investigate. He didn't want the rest of the squad to come over without clearing this side. The Japanese might be waiting for the main force just like last night.

He went twenty yards each way and came back to Crandall who was crouched on the bank. "It's clear. Signal the others."

Crandall waved them over and they entered the river at fifteen-yard intervals. They sloshed across quickly, nervous about crocs and Japanese. Welch was almost running and kept looking over his shoulder for the coming river monster.

Safely across, Sgt. Carver put O'Connor on point and they moved out. There was no trail on this side and the jungle was thicker. O'Connor felt better about this side. He moved with more confidence. With every passing step he felt more in control. He was sure he'd sense any Japs in the area long before they saw him.

He slipped into an efficient routine. Take stock of the world, take five quiet steps, take stock, five more. He had to remind himself to stay vigilant.

Two hours passed, this was the time when point men got sloppy. Sergeant Carver had already asked if he needed a break, but he'd shaken his head. He was in his element, wanting to keep the men safe, making up for getting Markos and Skinner killed.

He sensed something in the jungle ahead. He crouched and searched from left to right. Everything looked okay, but he couldn't shake the feeling; something wasn't right. He sniffed the air and listened for anything different. He was sure something was out there despite the lack of evidence. He'd learned to trust his instincts and they were buzzing now. He felt something big crawling up his pant leg, but ignored the tickling sensation.

He motioned for the others to get down and he sensed more than heard them going to their bellies. He brought his arms out of the backpack's shoulder straps and laid it beside him. He didn't want the squad to advance until he figured out what was bothering him. He looked back at Sergeant Carver and signaled that he was moving forward to take a look. Carver nodded and passed it along to the Lieutenant. The men were poised, their weapons trained on the surrounding jungle.

O'Connor crept forward. His steps careful and quiet, his carbine at the ready. There was a thicker portion of jungle to his front. When he got to it he went to his knees then his belly and slithered underneath the low vines and branches. It got darker and he heard something off to his left, someone was there. He brought his rifle up and aimed into the bush, but he couldn't see the source. Then he did. Bloodshot eyes set deep into the blackest skin he'd ever seen were staring at him. His eyes adjusted and the form took shape. A man crouched, an old bolt action rifle aimed at him. His reaction was to shoot, but this wasn't a Japanese soldier. A crucial second passed when both men could have killed the other, but instead, they only stared.

O'Connor didn't move, his aim never wavered. The man spoke. It was English, at least the words were, but he couldn't understand what he was saying. The words were all jumbled up and crazy. O'Connor went up to his knees, still aiming. The man moved his rifle harmlessly away and took a step towards him. He broke into a broad smile, the yellowed teeth looking bright against his black skin. Another man came out of the jungle appearing out of nowhere. He was younger and didn't have a smile on his face. He looked more menacing and kept his ancient rifle pointed at O'Connor's gut.

O'Connor put out his hand in greeting, then called to the others behind him. "Got some natives up here, Sarge."

Welch came sprinting forward and burst onto the scene. The smiling man smiled broader and the younger man pointed his gun to a harmless angle. Welch was bursting, "Eloni and Fau, I was wondering if we might run into you blokes." They hugged and slapped each other on the back.

Lieutenant Caprielli said, "What the hell's going on here? Who are these men?" Upon seeing the officer both natives sprang to attention and gave him smart salutes, palm out. Lieutenant Caprielli didn't know what to do. He saluted them back. They both smiled and said something Caprielli couldn't understand. Welch said, "These are some of my men." He pointed to the older, "This is Eloni Finau and this young chap is Fau." He pulled them into hugs, "They're some of the chaps we're trying to find. We're in good hands. They can take us directly to their village."

Lieutenant Caprielli asked, "What's that they're speaking? Sounds like English, but it's not."

"Ah, yes it's Pidgin. I've lived here for years. I'm fluent. It's quite easy to learn being English speakers already. It's basically a mix of their language and ours, weighted towards ours." Caprielli looked uncertain, "Don't worry, I'll translate." As if to prove it, "He just said, welcome to his island."

Sergeant Carver butted in, "Ask him how far to his camp."

Welch said, "I know how far it is." Carver glared at him and Welch asked. "He says about two kilometers that way," He pointed.

Lieutenant Caprielli shouldered his carbine, "Tell him to lead on."

# 12

The squad moved much faster with the native guides. They led them to a trail that would be invisible unless you knew it was there. They moved along it at a trot for almost a kilometer, then the trail went up for another half kilometer ending on top of a hill. One moment they were moving along a jungle trail and the next they were in a small meadow surrounded by thatched huts and dark people wearing very little clothing.

The villagers gazed their way, but mostly went about their business. To be in amongst friendlies was a good feeling. The men relaxed and slung their rifles, feeling safe. A group of three topless women walked past them and giggled as they looked them up and down. Private Dunphy took off his helmet and bowed, "Ladies," he said.

They tittered and bounced away. The one on the end looked back at him. Dunphy put his helmet back on and whistled. Corporal Hooper punched his arm, "What you whistling at? Those are the homeliest women I've ever seen."

Dunphy pushed him away, "How long we been on this shithole island Hoop?" Hooper shrugged. Dunphy continued, "Couple weeks. Before that, New Caledonia and before that a stinking troop ship. I haven't seen a woman in months and certainly not a topless one."

Corporal Hooper shook his head, "They're still ugly. They'd have to be the last women on earth. Even then I'd have to close my eyes."

"Ha, that's why you never get any. Too picky. The ugly ones are the most appreciative." He mimicked slapping an ass as he gyrated.

Sergeant Carver put an end to it, "Can it Dunphy. Hands off the merchandise." He pointed around the squad, "Understand?" They all nodded. "Go have a seat over there while we figure out what's happening."

The squad, sans Sergeant Carver, Lieutenant Caprielli and Welch, went to a tree in the center of the village and took their packs off. They sat down relishing the rest. O'Connor put his head on his pack and watched the puffy clouds drift by. The evening brought a breeze and its caress felt good against his sweat encrusted skin. The stress of leading the squad through the jungle left him with each slow breath he took. A line of half clothed women came to them holding flasks made from animal hides and the men drank the cool water. O'Connor thought he'd died and gone to heaven.

SERGEANT CARVER, Lieutenant Caprielli and Welch were escorted into the largest hut. Upon entering they were inundated with a thick pall of foul smelling smoke. A man sat in a makeshift chair a long pipe in his hand spewing thick tendrils of smoke. He was as black as Eloni, but his skin was wrinkled deeply giving him a look of old leather. He was powerfully built. Even sitting he had a presence that couldn't be ignored. His dark eyes looked them over through the smoke. He directed them to sit. They looked around for chairs, but settled for the hard pack dirt floor. He spoke to Welch calling him by name, "Mr. Welch, you leave alone and you return with Marines."

Welch smiled, "Chief Ahio I bring you soldiers, not Marines. These men are very good soldiers, like the Marines."

Ahio spoke, "Soldiers, Marines, is all the same, Americans."

"Yes, Americans. They've come to help us kill the Japanese."

He smiled, showing off only a black hole, no teeth were visible. "That's good. There are plenty to kill, more arrive all the time."

Welch translated for the others. Caprielli said, "Ask him how many and where."

He asked and Ahio answered, "Japanese have landed three thousand soldiers off Cape Esperance. They moved their forces to the edge of the Matanikau. Some are still close to us, but the larger force has moved east to the river. Big loud tanks too."

Caprielli was beaming. Getting this kind of intelligence would not only help his men, but his career as well. "Is he sure about this? Can we trust him?"

Welch scowled, "Of course we can trust him, these people are loyal to us; they've no love for the Japanese, believe me."

Caprielli addressed Carver, "Sergeant we've got some elevation here, see if we can relay this information to Division from here."

Carver got to his feet and slung his Thompson, "Yes, Sir. He left, leaving Welch. Welch continued to speak in Pidgin and they laughed and back slapped. Lieutenant Caprielli looked around the hut. There was something on the far wall hanging from strings attached to a pole. He squinted trying to see what it was in the dim light.

Ahio saw him looking and broke into a wide smile. He reached back and grabbed the pole. The objects swung wildly, appearing to be medium sized balls. Caprielli reached his hand out to stop them from spinning. He pulled his hand back fast when he realized they were shrunken human heads. Disgusted he said, "What the hell are those?"

Welch said something to Ahio and they both laughed. He slapped the Lieutenant on the back, "Those are what you think they are... shrunken human heads. Don't forget these islands have only been occupied by the commonwealth for the past one hundred years. Head-hunting and cannibalism were rampant for many thousands of generations." He smiled at the heads, "These were passed down from Chief Ahio's grandfather, possibly the last relics from those days. They're a national treasure."

Caprielli scowled, "Not for those poor souls."

Welch shrugged, "Our influence turned them away from such atrocities. Before the Japs arrived, these islands were well managed and behaved societies. Honestly, if they thought the Japs would win they'd turn us in to save their own skins. They're loyal as long as we're supplying them with goods and showing progress."

"That sounds pretty flimsy."

Ahio put the shrunken heads back against the wall and spoke to Welch who translated. "He's asking when you plan on visiting the next village…where Captain Morrisey is."

"We'll sleep here tonight and go in the morning. The sooner we meet up with him the sooner we can plan some guerrilla attacks."

After Ahio heard the translation he clapped his hands and spoke excitedly. "Ahio says his hunters killed a wild boar today, they will feast and celebrate your arrival."

Carver reentered the hut, "Sir, Crandall went up a tree and was able to relay the message you wanted sent out. He talked with Lieutenant Smote. He wants you to check back in when you find Captain Morrisey. He also sent his thanks for the info." Lieutenant Caprielli nodded, *this mission might turn out alright after all.*

THE SMELL of cooking boar meat permeated the village making the hungry soldiers salivate. They hadn't had a hot meal since arriving on Guadalcanal. Villagers hustled about preparing for the big night. They wanted to build a big bonfire, but Welch reminded them of the danger of air attacks and they settled for a small fire under cover of a thatch roof with no walls.

The soldiers sat around the fire. Chief Ahio assured them the perimeter was well guarded by his best men. The soldiers took it with a grain of salt and held onto their carbines anyway. Women were entering the circle of men to refill gourds with water. Dunphy stared at the women, smiling and waving. One in particular caught his fancy. She was homely by western standards, but younger than the others and shyer.

When she entered the circle, he held up his empty gourd for a refill. She walked over and kneeled beside him, holding her animal skin flask out. He handed her his cup, but when she reached for it he pulled it back, teasing her. She looked at him and he smiled. She gave him a small smile back then looked down in embarrassment. He reached out and lifted her chin. He looked her in the eye then held out his cup and she poured. "Thank you," he said.

She nodded and left the circle. He watched her all the way and was happy to see her look back at him just before disappearing in the darkness. He took a drink of water and Private O'Connor leaned close, "I'd be careful if I was you. She looks like jailbait to me."

"Out here? There's no such thing. Besides she looks old enough to me."

"I wasn't referring to her age, but her being Chief Ahio's daughter. Doubt he wants your grubby hands on her."

"My hands are clean," he spit, "mind your own business, Red."

The night went on and soon they were feasting on wild boar. Parts of the animal were passed around and the men would tear off a chunk and pass it along. Dunphy stood up and mumbled he was going to take a piss. He wiped his greasy hands on his pants and left the circle of light. The darkness was complete. He stopped and stretched his back waiting for his eyes to adjust. He went to the edge of the village and took a piss. He stared up at the stars which were darting in and out of cloud cover. The jungle noises were almost deafening. With a full belly and relatively safe position he pondered the island. He wondered if people vacationed here before the war. He doubted it.

He finished and turned back towards the village. His eyes were adjusted and he could see the women and children huddled in a group waiting for the men to finish eating. He realized they were waiting to eat whatever was leftover. He spotted the girl he'd teased and watched her. Back home he wouldn't have given her the time of day, but he hadn't been with a woman in a long time and he was used to being with women. His family money, his position in society and his handsome features were magnets for shallow treasure-seeking young ladies. He'd never sought them out, but they'd always found him and he'd grown accustomed to the touch of a woman. He craved that touch now.

As he watched, she stood and took her flask to get a refill. Now was his chance. He watched her and followed. She stopped at a barrel that looked like it once held wine. She twisted a knob and refilled her skin.

He came up behind her and when she turned she let out a yelp. He put his hand over her mouth and his finger to his. "Hey, it's me, don't be startled."

When she recognized him, he took his hand from her mouth. Her dark eyes shone in the night. He couldn't decide if it was fear or excitement. He smiled and took a step back. She relaxed, "You're pretty," he said, thinking the direct approach would be best.

She said something he couldn't understand. He smiled, "I think you're beautiful." She smiled and he reached out to touch her cheek. She pulled back slightly. He took that as a good sign and he kept his hand there. She looked into his eyes and he gave his best bedroom eyes back. He caressed her cheek and stepped closer. She said something and he put his finger on her lips. "It's okay. We can have some fun."

She didn't understand his language and he didn't understand hers, but there was no doubt of his intentions. He leaned down and kissed her tenderly on the forehead. She looked surprised and tried to turn away, but he held her cheek and lifted her face. He kissed her lips, but she didn't kiss him back. He kissed her again and this time she responded and kissed him back. He smiled inwardly, *now we're getting somewhere.*

They kissed in the darkness, then she broke away, smiled and led him by his hand around the outside of the village. He looked behind him at his squad still scarfing down wild boar around the fire. They wouldn't miss him for a while. He followed this island girl and she led him to a hut. The inside was as bare as the other huts, but it had a pile of military style blankets mounded on a makeshift thatch bed.

She pulled him towards it and she sat down in front of him. She looked into his eyes and started unbuttoning his pants. This girl wasn't as innocent and shy as she pretended. His eyes rolled to the back of his head as she worked her magic. Soon he was lying beside her under the itchy wool blankets. It was hot, but the sweat that dripped from both their bodies mingled and made their lovemaking even more powerful.

## 13

Sergeant Carver woke before light to the sound of yelling. He gripped his Thompson and aimed towards the commotion, but he didn't see any flashes or signs of combat. The yelling was in Pidgin and it sounded like the head honcho, Ahio. He ignored his stiff muscles and joints and trotted to the yelling coming from a hut. He kept his weapon ready, but didn't enter. More yelling and someone came running out the door pulling on their shirt while their carbine dangled from their shoulder. Sergeant Carver gritted his teeth and put his shoulder down knocking the running man off his feet with a perfect open field tackle.

He stepped over the figure and leaned down to see who he'd leveled. He recognized Private Dunphy gasping as he struggled to catch his breath. He put his boot on Dunphy's chest and held him there. Chief Ahio came storming out, pulling behind him his naked daughter. He saw Sgt. Carver holding down his daughter's lover and started yelling in Pidgin. Carver put his hand up for silence, but the tirade continued. Carver yelled, "Welch, get your ass over here!"

A bleary-eyed Thomas Welch stumbled over, pulling on his shirt. He'd been getting the best sleep he'd had in days and was none too happy about the interruption. He saw the situation and spoke in rapid-fire Pidgin to Ahio, who fired it right back. "Your bloke there," he squinted in the pre-dawn darkness, "Dunphy, was caught in bed with Ahio's daughter, Lela. It seems the chief's upset."

Carver guffawed, "Yeah, I figured out the upset part on my own." Dunphy started to struggle against Carver's boot, but he pushed harder pinning him there. "Stay down there, lover boy. You're in deep shit and I'm not in the mood."

"Let me up goddammit, Sarge." Carver let his Thompson move forward, the barrel swinging back and forth across Dunphy's chest. He stopped struggling.

Lieutenant Caprielli arrived and Carver filled him in. Dawn was quickly approaching, the sounds changing from night animals and insects to awakening day animals and insects. He looked at the half disrobed Dunphy, the woman standing in the doorway with an Army blanket wrapped around her and the scowling Chief Ahio. He put two and two together. "Let him up, Sergeant."

Dunphy shot to his feet and stood beside Carver with gritted teeth. Carver looked him in the eye wanting him to strike him, willing it with all his might. He yearned to have an excuse to pummel the cocky rich boy and there was no better reason than self-defense.

Caprielli pushed Dunphy away, "At ease soldier, you're already in trouble." He pointed to a stump twenty feet away, "Sit over there while I figure this shit out, Private." When he didn't move, he yelled, "Now!"

Dunphy snapped out of it and went to the stump. He put his shirt the rest of the way on and slung his rifle. He sat down heavy and ran his fingers through his hair.

Lieutenant Caprielli told Welch, "Tell the chief we're sorry for any indiscretion and we'll punish Dunphy for his actions."

Welch translated and listened to Ahio's heated response. "Chief says Dunphy's going to have to make it right by marrying his daughter."

Dunphy heard and sprang to his feet, "Marry her? That's ridiculous…"

Carver strode across the space and pushed him back onto the stump, he hit hard. "Shut the hell up or I'll shut it for you."

For once Dunphy listened and didn't speak. Lieutenant Caprielli said, "Tell the chief there can't be a wedding. He's a soldier. He can't stay here and he can't take her back to our country. It's impossible."

Welch raised his eyebrows, but relayed the argument. The chief eyeballed Dunphy, pointed at him and spoke. Welch translated. "He says Dunphy disgraces his village, his daughter and himself by his actions. He demands marriage or punishment by his means."

Caprielli squinted, "What kind of punishment we talking? Not burning or head shrinking or anything like that I hope."

Welch asked and responded, "He says he needs to stay in the village and work as a... well I think he means, slave. He says he must do this or his men will join the Japanese and kill all of us."

Carver looked around looking for any aggressive moves by the natives. Most were listening to the exchange and their postures changed from peaceful to alert. Carver held his Thompson in both hands, ready.

Caprielli put both hands up, "Whoa there, take it easy. We can figure this out." The other members of the squad gripped their rifles and looked around at the men they'd feasted with only hours before. Even being outnumbered three to one their carbines would make short work of the lightly armed natives. "Let the chief know I'll have to think about it. Just give me a minute."

When that was done he waved Carver and Welch over. He asked Welch, "Is this guy for real?"

Welch nodded, "Undoubtedly, I've never known him to bluff. He's quite a serious fellow, good fighter too. We can't afford to upset him or we risk losing the natives across the whole island."

Lieutenant Caprielli shook his head, "I can't just leave Dunphy here as a slave. He's a United States soldier. It's disgraceful and probably illegal."

Sergeant Carver spoke, "Why not? The shitbird deserves it; probably do him some good. We'll give him a week. Our mission with Morrisey will take at least that long to accomplish. We'll pick him up after that. It's for the good of the mission."

Caprielli pinched his lower lip and kicked dust with his foot. "There's no chance we come back next week and find Dunphy's shrunken head is there?"

Welch smiled, "Unless the young private does something horrific, there's little chance of that. White men are held in high regard by these people; they consider us their betters. To have one as a slave is a huge coup and will completely compensate them for their bruised pride."

Caprielli looked over at the sulking Dunphy. After a minute he nodded, "What about the Japs? Will he be safe here?" he realized the stupidity of the question before he finished the sentence. They were all in danger, they were on Guadalcanal surrounded by hostile Japanese soldiers. "Alright, tell Ahio he's got himself a new slave."

They shook hands on the deal. Sergeant Carver kneeled down in front of Dunphy and told him the good news. Dunphy turned pale. "What do you mean a slave? You can't do this; you can't make me stay." He looked into Carver's steaming eyes, "What if I just marry her? I mean it's not like there's a preacher here, it won't be a legal marriage. I'll just fake it and tell her I'll be back to get her after the war."

"Bullshit! She doesn't deserve that. It's an order. You've jeopardized this entire mission and unless you want to marry the girl for real, you're gonna do it." He put his finger to his chest, "If you fuck this up you won't make it back to Division for the LT to court-martial you. I'll be sure you don't make it back, understand?"

Dunphy stared into Carver's hateful eyes. He meant every word and he had no doubt he'd carry out the threat. He pondered his plight. If he refused, the best-case scenario was getting court-martialed back at Division and spending years in prison. Worst case, Sgt. Carver would drop a grenade beside him while he slept. A week of slavery? Well that was a total unknown, but he'd be done in a week, he'd have a bed every night, probably food too. *What's the worst that can happen?*

# 14

The squad left the village an hour later without Private Dunphy. O'Connor turned before entering the jungle and saw Dunphy surrounded by villagers. He was an asshole, but he hoped he'd be okay. He shook his head, the smart S.O.B. was actually getting a week's vacation away from combat patrolling. His smile disappeared when he thought how much could happen in a week's time.

They walked in single file following three native men with old bolt action Lee Enfield rifles. Despite the corrosive effects of the jungle environment, the rifles were in surprisingly good condition. The natives thought of them as prized possessions and took care of them accordingly. O'Connor looked at his own weapon, *taking some abuse out here, but basically brand new.* The Marines landed on the canal using similar weapons as the Lee Enfields, bolt action Springfields. *How'd those guys stay alive with those relics?* He silently thanked the Army for sending him into battle with the M1.

They followed a trail that was well used. The guides kept a fast pace supremely confident in their abilities to avoid any Japanese patrols. The way they moved soundlessly grew O'Connor's respect.

These guys had been hunting their entire lives, moving silently was bred into them, they didn't know any other way.

At one point they slowed and stopped, waving the rest of them down. O'Connor passed the signal and waited. He had no doubt if they stopped there was a real threat out there somewhere. He strained to see and hear anything, but there was nothing, only jungle. After five minutes the guides signaled them up and they continued. O'Connor wondered what they'd seen. *Maybe they're acting on instinct and sensed something.*

They marched unimpeded for three miles. The trail led down to a valley with a raucous creek bouncing through. The guides bent down and drank handfuls of water. The rest of the men filled canteens, dropped Halazone tablets in, waited the ten minutes it took to kill any diarrhea causing bugs and drank their fill. The water tasted cold and sweet, even with the Halazone. O'Connor dipped his hat and poured it over his head. He closed his eyes relishing the coolness as it flowed down his body. He wanted to sit down and soak his aching feet, but the guides waved them forward and they started climbing the other side of the valley.

The trail steepened and soon they were slowing down. Their packs weren't as heavy as before, but they were still more than they were used to carrying. After a mile the guides stopped and gave whistles that sounded like jungle birds. There was an answering whistle and they stood up and advanced into a clearing. Ancient trees hung over the clearing. The trees' upper branches formed an almost solid roof above. The village would be invisible from the air.

In comparison to Ahio's village this village was immense. The same thatch huts were everywhere. They were bigger and looked more maintained. The village seemed rich and thriving, or at least it had been before the Japanese invaded and cut off supplies from the coast.

Chief Ahio's guides greeted the other villagers in excited Pidgin, no doubt telling the tale of the white slave. It would boost their prestige in the area and they held it over the others in obvious pride. These villagers were similarly armed with old rifles and pistols. The men without guns had long knives with wood handles. There were at least three times more villagers than Ahio's and they all gathered around the newcomers with interest.

From a central hut, a tall white man wearing wrinkled and torn beige pants and a short sleeve button down shirt emerged. He put his hands on his hips and took the scene in. He strode up to Lieutenant Caprielli, his long legs covering the ground quickly. He stopped in front of him and smiled through a thick dark beard. The man was immediately likable. He extended his hand, but the lieutenant saluted him instead. Morrisey grinned and gave him one back then extended his hand, "Courtney Morrisey at your service. You can call me Court or if you prefer, Captain."

Caprielli took his hand and smiled, "It's an honor to meet you, Captain. I'm Lieutenant Caprielli and this is Sergeant Carver. I think you know this man." He gestured to Welch who was keeping himself well back.

Morrisey locked eyes with him and nodded, "Thomas Welch, I was wondering where you got off to." He gestured to a group of native men standing behind the group and they stepped forward and took Welch by the arms.

Welch lifted his chin in defiance, "It had to be done. We have to join the war."

Morrisey said something in quick Pidgin and three natives took Welch into a hut. One man stayed inside with him and the other two stationed themselves on either side of the door as guards. Caprielli watched, wondering what was happening. Welch was under his command; he couldn't let this man, Captain or not, simply arrest him for no reason he could see. "Excuse me, Captain, but Welch is under my command and he's been most helpful in guiding us to you. Please explain yourself."

Morrisey nodded, "I suppose I owe you an explanation," he gestured back to the hut he'd come from. "Come inside."

Caprielli nodded to Carver, "Get the men situated and fed, have the gear separated and ready for dispersal." Carver nodded and Caprielli ducked into the hut. He poked his head back outside, "Have Crandall climb a tree and transmit that we've found Captain Morrisey and his village."

The inside of the hut was filled with furniture that had seen better days. On a table in the corner a huge radio was partially covered by a tattered canvas poncho. Morrisey sat on a padded rocking chair and tilted it back and forth. It creaked and groaned with each slow pass. He picked up a glass from a side table and held it out to him, "Something to drink?"

"Is it alcohol?" he asked hoping.

He shook his head, "Afraid not, we ran out of that some months ago, even before your Marines landed. It's water." Caprielli shook his head no. He took off his jungle hat and wiped his brow. "You chaps find it hot here, no doubt?" Caprielli looked at him like he was crazy. "I've been here so long it seems normal to me. I can't remember what a cool breeze off the channel feels like. I suppose I've gone native by now."

Caprielli couldn't tell if he was remorseful or simply stating a fact. He said, "I suppose you can get used to anything."

Morrisey stared at him and took a sip of water. "Yes, quite right." He stared at the Lieutenant until he fidgeted under the gaze. "Mr. Welch left this village without my consent." He placed the water on the side table. "In fact, I expressly forbid him to leave."

Lieutenant Caprielli said, "He came to us asking for help, said your radio was dead and needed our assistance. Is that not the case?"

"Our radio gave up the ghost a week ago, that's true, however I never asked for assistance from the Americans, or anyone else. He went AWOL essentially, so he's under arrest. I'll figure out how to deal with him later."

Caprielli wasn't sure how to take that, "Why wouldn't you want our help? I mean we're all in this together, we're allies with a common enemy. We've come to supply you with weapons and ammo and to link up with you to harass the enemy from the rear."

Morrisey kept rocking, "Your small group brought us weapons and ammo? Have you stowed it somewhere?"

The lieutenant shook his head, "We only brought what we could carry and we used some of the ammo getting here. Each man brought two extra M1 Carbines. They're broken down in their packs. It's not a lot, but it's better than what you've got." He pointed at an old Lee

Enfield propped in the corner. We could teach your men how to be guerrillas, how to strike the Japs and live to fight another day."

The Captain laughed, "I doubt you could teach us much about that. These men have grown up here, they're better guerrilla fighters than you and your men could ever be."

"I'm sure we could teach them something about tactics; they've never been through formal training, have they?"

"Their training has been hands on I should think." He clapped his hands, "Tell you what. We've got a patrol going out this evening to hit a group of Japanese that are getting too close. My amateur natives found them yesterday while blundering around the jungle. Would you like to tag along and take any notes on what you think needs improvement?"

Caprielli could hear the sarcasm in his voice. He looked him in the eye, "I meant no disrespect. I'm only relaying what we were told of your capabilities." He smiled, "I'd love to tag along, would you like to take your new carbines?"

He considered it, but shook his head, "Probably not this time. The men should have weapons they know." He stood up, "We shove off at 1500." He looked at his watch, "Three hours from now."

Lieutenant Caprielli stood and nodded. Before he left he said, "I meant what I said about Welch. He's been helpful to us. He seems a good sort."

"You don't know the man like I do, Lieutenant. He's been a thorn in my side for some time now. He's gone too far this time."

"You mind me asking why you don't want our help? If I'm getting kicked out of here without completing my mission, my superiors are going to want an explanation." He squared up his shoulders to Morrisey, "I suspect your superiors will too."

"Until I get a direct order from Australia telling me to follow American orders I'll continue with the mission given to me, 'report enemy activity, engage when victory is assured.' Surely you can understand that?"

"What if you heard it from a higher ranking American ally? That countermands your last order. You'd have to follow orders."

"Lieutenant, I never said you couldn't join our guerrilla force. I'm simply not able to give you command over it. You're welcome to stay, but seeing as I outrank you, I'm in command here, as I've always been. Have your men outside this hut, combat ready at 1445." With that he drank the last of his water and said, "Dismissed."

Out of habit, he snapped to attention and saluted. He cursed himself for falling into the trap. How did he come under his command? He'd pushed the man too hard and it backfired. He'd have to get on the radio and tell his superiors the situation. He wasn't relishing the conversation.

THE SQUAD FORMED up outside Captain Morrisey's hut at precisely 1445. His men had gotten fed and even bathed in the nearby creek. They felt refreshed and after last night's feast and long sleep, rested.

A ragtag group of twenty natives formed up too. They wore loin-cloth shorts, some in bare feet, others in thin treaded sandals and nothing else. Their dark bodies were lithe and strong without an ounce of fat. They'd been forced to eat less with the Japanese invasion, their normal food supply routes cut off, but they'd managed to stockpile canned meats and vegetables from Australia and they'd raided some of the abandoned plantation stores. Morrisey made sure to document everything they'd taken in order to compensate the owners upon their return. They were acting out of necessity; they weren't looters.

As they waited for Captain Morrisey, Lieutenant Caprielli thought about the conversation he'd had with Colonel Sinclair over the radio. He'd told him to stay with Morrisey and his merry band of cutthroats until ordered otherwise. He was to offer the squad's services in what-ever manner he saw fit and the extra radio was to be given to him with all the batteries he thought he could spare. Caprielli wasn't sure what to make of it, but his command authority was cut out from beneath him just like that.

The Captain emerged with his rifle slung over his shoulder. He was dressed in the same dirty top and pants as before, but had on a different hat. He looked through the thick tree canopy, "It'll rain tonight, which will make the going harder." He said it in English for his American friends' benefit. The squad looked to the sky, but couldn't see what he was seeing.

At exactly 1500 he nodded to the native who seemed to be the acting sergeant. He nodded back and loped off into the jungle. The others followed in a loose line. The squad unslung their carbines exchanged glances and followed.

Morrisey hung back with Lieutenant Caprielli, "Your men move well for inexperienced jungle fighters, but keep to the rear. Let my men lead; they know this jungle better than their own mothers.

The Lieutenant nodded and waved his men forward. "Follow their lead." He let O'Connor and Carver pass then fell into the line. Morrisey trotted forward.

After twenty minutes of fast patrolling the natives stopped and crouched. The squad did too and watched as silent commands were issued. The guerrillas spread out, their rifles unslung. Morrisey waved the squad forward putting his finger to his lips. They crept forward and crouched in a line to either side of the Captain. He lifted his hand and pointed. The squad followed his gaze and they saw a small group of Japanese soldiers sitting around a tiny fire about twenty yards away. It was obvious they were going to spend the night.

O'Connor strained to see any guards, but couldn't find any. *They must have men watching for intruders.* His question was answered when he saw a native dart out of the jungle like an arrow from a bow. He had his long knife out and he grabbed his target, a snoozing soldier O'Connor hadn't noticed. He put his hand over his mouth and expertly buried his blade into the back of the man's neck, angling up into his brain. He lowered the twitching man to the jungle floor and crouched beside him. He pulled his dripping blade out and wiped it on the enemy's green uniform. He looked to where O'Connor was watching and gave him a toothless grin. A shiver went up O'Connor's spine despite the heat.

At that second the sky opened up and the rain came down in sheets. Everyone and everything were instantly soaking wet. The ground went from solid to soup in seconds. O'Connor couldn't see anything further than a couple of feet. He felt someone pulling him back. It was Morrisey whispering, "Let's get you blokes a better view."

He gathered the squad up and had them follow him to the left, angling closer to the group of Japanese. Morrisey's men had disappeared like ghosts. Morrisey pointed and crouched, the others followed suit. The Japanese were only fifteen yards away, scrambling to get ponchos over themselves. The presence of enemy soldiers so close made the Americans nervous. The Japanese soldiers were oblivious to their impending doom. Each squad member had his weapon trained on them. Morrisey pushed O'Connor's barrel down and shook his head. He pointed to the Japanese, then his eyes, "Watch."

The hapless soldiers were wet and bedraggled, miserable lumps under their green ponchos. They were desperately trying to keep their fire going. One soldier held a large jungle leaf over the flame, but the fire looked to be doomed to a wet death. There were eight of them, each man looked thin and pathetic.

Out of the jungle there was sudden movement. The guerrillas attacked with raised knives and short sword-like weapons. They didn't make a sound as they converged on the Jap soldiers and drove their knives and swords into spines and skulls. A soldier yelled out and reached for his rifle, but was stopped when his head was cut from his shoulders with a vicious cut. It was over in seconds. The soldiers were alive, then dead, like someone had flipped a switch.

The guerrillas cleaned their weapons and put them back in their belts. They quickly went through the dead soldiers' belongings keeping things of interest and tossing the rest. Three men collected weapons and ammo and any food they found. The Japanese soldiers were well stocked with rice and dried fish.

The squad watched the butchery in silent fascination. The operation had gone off without a single injury. Indeed, it didn't appear anyone had even broken a sweat. twenty minutes later the bodies were dragged and piled into a shallow rain filled pit. They were covered with jungle leaves and vines until they were invisible. Captain Morrisey explained, "We don't want them to be found or they'll start looking for us. We want the patrol to simply disappear and never be heard from again. A bit of psychological warfare."

Carver spoke up, "What do you suppose they were doing out here? They're a long way from the coast."

Morrisey nodded, "Probably looking for the other two patrols we dispatched." He watched his men working, "They're getting closer. We think they may have used triangulation on our radio transmitter before the batteries went dead so they have some idea where we are. I'm surprised they still care about us; we haven't sent out a signal in over a week. I'd think you Americans would be their priority."

The clean up was done and the guerrillas started patrolling back towards home. They used a different route, avoiding any chance of being ambushed. The going was harder, the ground was soft and muddy. Each step sank deep and had to be pulled free with a sickening sucking sound. Their footprints immediately filled with seeping water. If anyone was following them they'd be easy to track.

Sergeant Carver brought it up to Morrisey. "Don't worry, I've got two men behind us covering our passage. We haven't found the Japs to be especially good trackers, but just in case, we always make it hard for them."

With the extra precautions it took longer to get back. It was full dark when the lead guerrillas whistled to the perimeter guards and they entered the village. The rain hadn't abated, but the center of the village wasn't muddy.

It was a relief to be on relatively solid ground. O'Connor knelt down and picked up a swath of dirt. It was muddy, but not bad. Morrisey came over, "The Melanese have lived here for thousands of generations they know a thing or two about drainage." He kneeled down and pointed, "Notice how the center is slightly higher? That little bit of relief is all it takes to keep the area from getting too sticky. There's also an assortment of bamboo pipes three feet down that act as drainage, like gutters on your American houses. They need to be tended every ten years or so, I hear it's quite a difficult job." He smiled at Caprielli who was listening in, "Not bad for a bunch of heathens, aye Lieutenant?"

Caprielli only nodded. Morrisey continued. "Your men can take those two huts over there, they'll be protected from this squall. There's a fire built, they can dry off inside. Why don't you and Sergeant Carver come into my hut for a debrief? It's warm and dry inside."

## 15

The squad felt like they were on vacation. The village was patrolled night and day by Morrisey's men. He assured them they needn't worry about being surprised by Japanese soldiers. If there was a threat his men would warn them with ample time. Lieutenant Caprielli offered his men up to rotate through the guard duties, but he declined. His men would do it anyway, not trusting the safety of their families to strangers.

They ate their own K-rations, they'd brought enough for a few weeks, but the natives insisted on them sharing their food as well. It was mostly rice and dried meat they'd stockpiled before hostilities, but the added calories were welcome.

It had been a day since the deadly patrol that had killed the eight enemy soldiers. The men had cleaned weapons, dried out clothing and generally sat around relaxing. The sounds of distant combat were constant, but they didn't feel guilty knowing their brothers in arms were being barraged and bombed almost daily. The drone of aircraft was a common sound and they spotted the planes high overhead, mostly bombers delivering deadly eggs to Henderson field.

The squad was told to be ready for another patrol scheduled to leave at noon. They showed up at 1145 ready to go. Sergeant Carver was chewing on a piece of grass, his dark eyes shrouded by heavy brows. O'Connor spoke, "Hey Sarge, what's the scoop?"

He spit out the grass, "Shaddup, you'll know soon enough."

Lieutenant Caprielli and Captain Morrisey came out of the hut. Morrisey was sporting his new M1 Carbine. He'd shot it the day before and was pleased to have a weapon that could fire at such a rapid rate. The other carbines were put together and passed around, but most of the natives stuck with their trusty Lee Enfields. O'Connor noticed a few of them were using captured Japanese Arisaka rifles. He supposed shooting their own ammo back at them was sweet justice.

Captain Morrisey addressed the gathered men. "We're going out for an extended patrol. If everything goes well, we'll be back here this time tomorrow. If there are no questions, we'll start..."

Sergeant Carver interrupted, "What's the target?"

Morrisey smiled, "Ah yes, not used to working with outsiders. Sorry. We'll be patrolling along the ridgeline to our west." He pointed. "There's a long ridge that's very good for observing the enemy, particularly the enemy navy. Some of my messengers have reported increased naval activity and were going to find out whether or not the Japs are trying to bring in more troops and if they are where and how many. Your radios should be able to talk with your blokes and give a running account. Should be most helpful to your troops, I should think."

Sergeant Carver nodded, "Grab more ammo for the extended operation and be back here in two minutes." The men dashed off to their huts and filled their belts with more bullets and grenades.

Morrisey spoke, "I'm not expecting any serious run-ins, Sergeant."

Carver shrugged, "Better safe than sorry, Sir."

Three minutes later they were entering the jungle. Once again, the guerrillas set a fast pace, using trails only they could find. The men weren't used to the quick pace, it made them nervous to be moving so fast behind enemy lines, but they kept their mouths shut and relied on their native guides. They'd done pretty well for themselves up to now.

The rain had stopped, but the ground was still saturated. The trails became muddy with the added foot traffic. The men in the back, suffered the most, having to slog their way through the churned up ground. Sergeant Carver had them rotate positions to keep from exhausting half the squad.

After an hour they stopped as the guerrillas talked in low murmurs. The squad used the stop as a water break. They were angling towards the high country, away from the water rich valleys. Their blistering pace sapped their physical reserves which in turn sapped their water. Each man carried two canteens, but at this rate they'd be drained before sunset.

They were at the base of the ridge they would be patrolling. It looked like a spine poking up from the islands' middle and spanning almost to the western tip. It wasn't the highest point of the island, but it was higher than anything surrounding it by five hundred feet. The jungle thinned out as the ridge rose. At the top of the spine the foliage was almost nonexistent. They'd have to be careful of enemy aircraft, or any aircraft for that matter. Their own forces would assume them to be Japanese, they were on the wrong side of the line.

The patrol went up the ridge much slower. Not only was it steeper, but it was more exposed. This was the type of patrolling the American's were accustomed to.

With the loss of the shady jungle canopy the sun beat down on the men like an incessant furnace. The natives didn't seem to notice, but the squad was quickly dripping sweat and breathing hard. When they were halfway to the top, Sgt. Carver pulled on Lt. Caprielli's sleeve and pointed at the men. They were falling behind and clearly struggling. Caprielli trotted to Captain Morrisey's side and spoke and pointed. Morrisey nodded and called for a short break. The natives looked at him in confusion. Morrisey spoke some Pidgin and the natives grinned and nodded, making their hair flop. Caprielli grit his teeth, the pompous ass was making fun of them.

After their ten-minute break they continued towards the ridge. Once on top they patrolled to the westernmost edge. The occasional views to the sea were breathtaking. The sea was calm with varying shades of blues and greens. They could see the scarred beach where troops and supplies were still being ferried and thrown into the grinder. To the east, the edge of Henderson field was just visible. As they watched, two Marine Corsairs lifted off and banked towards the sea gaining altitude. Even from this distance they could make out the heavily laden undercarriages, bombs and rockets.

The ridge was easy walking and the natives increased their pace to a steady trot. The squad tried to keep up, but were soon left behind. Carver grumbled to Caprielli, "What's Morrisey trying to prove?"

Caprielli shook his head, "Don't know Sarge, but if we keep to the ridge we can't miss it." Carver nodded and rolled his eyes, *no shit, Sir.*

He was about to speak it out loud, but stopped himself. Lieutenant Caprielli wasn't his favorite officer. He thought some of his decisions were downright dangerous, but he seemed to be coming around the longer they had their asses hung out here in the bush. He thought a couple more weeks with the natives and he might shape up to be a decent officer.

They made the far point of the ridge an hour later. Morrisey and his men were crouched around a tiny thatch hut built into the hillside facing the invasion beaches. They were watching the uninhibited view of American naval vessels slowly cruising along the coast. It was the afternoon; the sun was beating down and the squad was haggard.

Caprielli said, "Sarge, get the men off the ridge into cover and set up a perimeter."

Carver glared at him, "Already on it, sir." He paused, *can't he see that?* "The men are short of water, sir. Most are down to half a canteen."

Morrisey took a break from scanning the sea with his binoculars and turned to the sergeant "Your men can top off over there." He pointed to a large barrel half dug into the ground beside the hut. The barrel had a lid, but the natives had placed huge jungle leaves around it, their points aiming towards the top of the barrel. The evening rainwater would be funneled into the barrel assuring constant fresh water.

Carver smiled, "All right, looks like you can drink down your canteens and refill over there." The sound of lids being unscrewed and loud gulps ensued.

Caprielli went to Morrisey's side, "Quite a view."

Morrisey took the binoculars from his eyes and handed them to the Lieutenant. He put the strap over his head and pulled them to his eyes. He scanned the sea, watching the ships unloading their cargos of men and war material onto barges which ferried back and forth. Morrisey touched his arm and pointed, "Look over there, Jap zeros."

Caprielli swung the glasses and found the silver Zeros slashing through the air heading towards the offloading ships. "They're making a run on the transports; our guys must see them."

As if in answer, tracer rounds and anti-aircraft guns opened up on the streaking planes. From this distance they couldn't hear the distinct firing, only the dull throbbing of far-away gunfire. The two Zeros dove toward the sea. It looked like they'd continue straight into a watery grave, but at the last second the nimble fighters pulled up only feet above the waves. The sea around them erupted with geysers from the cruisers and battleships trying to protect their defenseless transports.

The zero to the right slowed and fell behind his leader, they were in echelon attack. Caprielli couldn't tell if they were carrying bombs or only on a strafing run. With all the fire erupting around them he couldn't believe they were still flying. It looked like suicide. Even if they were successful, there was little chance of escape.

As he watched, tiny flashes from the lead Zero's wingtips winked, "They're strafing the transport." He watched in morbid fascination as the Zeros' deadly 20mm cannon ripped into the side of the transport. He could see chunks of the ship falling into the sea. The pilot only got a three second burst off before the plane suddenly and violently shifted and dipped to the left. Guns from the transport itself ripped into the left wing and sheared it in half. In an instant the Zero was lost in a great geyser of sea water.

Caprielli lifted his right hand in a fist and cheered like he was watching his West Point Army football team scoring a touchdown against Navy, "Yeah, got him."

The second Zero opened up. He was higher than his dead comrade, his cannon fire sliced into the bridge of the ship which erupted in glass, metal, fire and smoke. It was a devastating attack lasting only seconds. The Zero flashed over the crippled bridge then went even lower and flashed away across the sea followed by tracers. "Shit, the second one's getting away," Caprielli lamented.

Carver shook his head, "Don't think so, look to the zero's two o'clock." Caprielli pulled the binoculars from his eyes and found what

Carver was pointing at. "Those two Corsairs we saw earlier will make quick work of him if they have any more ammo."

Caprielli put the binoculars to his eyes and found the two Corsairs angling down towards the fleeing enemy fighter. They were in a perfect position behind and higher than the Jap and they'd be coming directly out of the sun. The Japanese would never see what hit him. The lead Corsair was gaining fast. When he was close enough he opened up with his six, fifty caliber machine guns. It took less than a second, the Zero exploded in mid-air, the wings folded backwards, the engine and propeller skipped along the sea like a child's skipping stone. The Zero's fuselage came to rest on the beach. Caprielli whooped, "Hot damn, got him. Those Marines sure can shoot." The Corsair pulled up and made a lazy victory roll over the beach before turning towards the ridge they were standing on.

Lieutenant Caprielli dropped the binoculars and ran to the top of the ridge and started jumping up and down, waving to the Corsair pilot as he came closer and closer. Carver couldn't believe what he was seeing. The Lieutenant was acting like an ass. He yelled, "Get down, get down, he'll think you're a Jap." But it was too late, the pilot had seen him and instead of continuing his turn towards Henderson, he lined up on the ridge.

Marine Lieutenant Griff McPhearson was piloting the Corsair. He'd just had the easiest kill of his career and that, following the successful bombing of the Jap stronghold off Cape Esperance, was making his day bright. Now another opportunity to kill the enemy was presenting itself. As he was leading his wingman, 2nd Lieutenant Terrance back to Henderson he caught a flash of something out of the corner of his eye. A Jap was on the ridge jumping around like a lunatic. He called Terrance, "Got a target on the ridge at my two o'clock. You got any more ammo?"

The response was quick, "Roger. Got a half load of fifty, I'll follow you in."

The Corsairs lined up on the ridge. Caprielli saw the gull shaped wings in silhouette as they streaked straight at him. He heard Carver yelling, but he was frozen in place, transfixed by the approaching fighters. The last thing he saw was the winking on the leading edge of the wings. The fifty caliber bullets walked up the ridgeline tearing rock, plants and flesh. The blue Corsair flashed over the cowering squad then rode the ridgeline until disappearing over the edge and out of sight.

The second Corsair unleashed his six fifty caliber machine guns into the dust cloud of the shredded ridge, but 2nd Lieutenant Terrance had more ammo to expend. Using his rudder pedals, he yawed the aircraft side to side spreading his deadly ordnance across a wide swath.

He put the plane into a shallow climb and looked over his shoulder. The ridge was covered in a thick layer of dust and debris, he wondered if he'd hit anything.

The roar of the strafing run and the heavy throb of the passing Corsairs was gone in an instant, replaced by the sound of falling rock and moans of pain. Sergeant Carver lifted his head from behind the boulder he'd dove under, but he couldn't see more than two feet. The dust was as thick as smoke. He could hear moans coming from the hut area, but when he tried to move, the choking dust sent him into a coughing fit. He lay back down and pulled his bandanna from around his neck and pulled it over his face. He took a deep breath, testing. He could hear the departing Corsairs, they'd had their fun and were returning home. He got onto shaky legs and went to the ridge to search for the Lieutenant.

With each passing second the dust became less as it settled back to earth. The white powder settled on him making him look like an ashen ghost. He went to where he thought Lieutenant Caprielli would be, but there was nothing there. He backtracked searching the torn up ground for any clue. The dust had settled thick, erasing any signs of blood. He took a step and his boot sank into what felt like soft sand. He looked down and lifted his boot, it came up sticky and wet with blood. Entrails caught on his boot tread lifted from the ground as if he'd stepped on chewed gum.

He backed away a step and leaned down. He'd found what was left of Lieutenant Caprielli. He shook his head looking further down the slope for the rest of his body, but the dust was still too thick. He looked to where the hut and the rest of his men should be. There was no doubt the Lieutenant was dead. He needed to focus on the living.

He stumbled his way to the hut. The dust wasn't as thick here. He heard the soft gurgle of water as the shredded barrel drained its last drops of lifesaving water. He'd have to deal with that later, his priority was finding and treating survivors.

The first man he came to was a native, the hole in his chest looked like he'd been hit point blank with an exploding grenade. His lifeless eyes were covered in white dust, giving him the look of a crazed zombie. He went to the next man who was face down. He wore a uniform; one of his men. He touched his shoulder and shook him gently, hoping he was only stunned. When he got no response, he turned the man over. His face was gone, replaced with seeping gray matter and white bone. He was unrecognizable. He reached for the man's neck and found the chain with the dog tags. He pulled them over the soldier's head and wiped the congealed blood, trying to read the red outlined letters. It was Crandall. He gripped the dog tags and shook his head. He went to the next inert form, another native whose head was gone, only the jagged spine sticking out of the neck. Besides that, the body was perfectly intact. *Jesus, am I the only survivor?*

A moan off to his left was coming from the hut. The dust was almost settled now and with it came the heat of the day. He poked his head into the surprisingly intact hut. The western wall was gone, but other than that it was undamaged. Inside, however looked like a butchers' shop. The grass walls ran thick with blood and the ceiling dripped. A native stared up at the ceiling one leg was gone and he had a deep gash in his neck which exposed the round pipes of his arteries and esophagus. Carver thought that must be where the majority of the blood came from. The dead native's normally black skin was dull and gray; devoid of blood.

Another moan from underneath the dead man had Carver pulling the body over and to the side. The skin was dry and cold. Underneath he found the source of the moaning. Captain Morrisey's eyes were closed; he looked as though he were having an afternoon nap. There wasn't a drop of blood on him. Carver felt his pulse and checked for chest rise. "Morrisey, wake up, wake up. Are you hit?" When he got no response, he slapped him across the face, "Wake up!"

He moaned in protest then shot up like he'd been electrified. His eyes were wide as he took in his surroundings. "Wh-what happened?"

He tried to stand, but Carver pushed him back, "Whoa there, take it easy. You were knocked out, give yourself a minute." He held him in place until he could focus. "You're okay, we were attacked by those Corsairs."

Morrisey shook his head looking around the hut. His eyes rested on the native's lifeless body. "Makala," he said. His mouth downturned and a tear formed in the corner of his eye. "Makala, my friend."

Carver didn't recognize the name or the man. He surmised it must have been the native who'd reported the naval movements. He'd been stationed here to observe and report. "I'm sorry about your man. You're the only survivor I've found so far." He squeezed Morrisey's shoulder and exited the hut. With his voice cracking he called out, "Anyone alive?"

When he got no response, he sat down and put his hands over his eyes rubbing them. *What the fuck am I supposed to do now?*

He heard a voice, "Sarge? Is that you?"

He stood up, "Yeah it's me, where are you?" He saw a hand waving from down the slope. He took three steps and peered over the side of a short eight foot cliff. Private O'Connor and Corporal Hooper were huddled against the wall covered in a fine mist of white dust. Carver's relief at finding some of his squad alive made his voice crack. He wiped dust out of his eye, "You, you guys okay?"

They nodded. Corporal Hooper said, "We were told this was the latrine. We were taking shits. What the fuck happened?"

"Never mind that, let's get you up here." He reached down to give them a hand. The rock cliff was an easy climb and soon they were standing beside Sgt. Carver, surveying the scene. O'Connor said, "Oh my God."

## 16

---

The rest of the day was spent sorting out the dead and assessing what supplies remained. The water barrel had been drained except for a half a gallon at the bottom. The barrel wasn't repairable; they'd have to fill up their canteens as best they could with whatever rain fell.

Of the eight natives, five were killed. They were laid next to one another awaiting their final journey back to the village. One of the unharmed natives had already left to get help. The American's had been hit the hardest. Most didn't have time to take cover. The heavy caliber bullets simply ripped them apart. The original patrol of twelve was cut down to four, not including Welch. Carver, O'Connor, Hooper and the absent Dunphy were all that remained. They buried Crandall, Doc, Troutman, and what they could find of Lt. Caprielli, on the coast side of the ridge and marked the location on the map. They'd pass along the coordinates to graves registration when they were in contact with Division again.

The somber day was made a little better by the clear view they had of both the American and the Japanese positions. They were specks from this distance, but with Captain Morrisey's powerful binoculars they were able to see enemy fortifications despite the thick jungle and heavy camouflage. It took careful scanning, but Carver identified three low slung bunkers. He marked them on the map.

In a stroke of luck Crandall hadn't been carrying the radio when he was riddled with fifty caliber fire. It had survived the onslaught. O'Connor cleaned the dust from its delicate parts, turned it on and was greeted with the happy sound of static. The frequency hadn't been moved so when O'Connor spoke into it he got an immediate response from Lieutenant Smote back at Division.

He handed the piece to Sgt. Carver. "Mother, this is Falcon 6. Over."

The response was clear, they were within the radio's six-mile range and had a clear line of sight to the beach. "Falcon 6 this is mother. That you Lieutenant Caprielli? Over."

"Mother, Falcon 6. Negative. Lieutenant Caprielli is KIA. This is Sergeant Carver, I'm in command. Over."

"Falcon 6, Mother. Understand Lieutenant Caprielli is KIA. What is your position and situation? Over."

Sergeant Carver told him about the past thirty-six hours. When he got him up to speed Lieutenant Smote asked, "Falcon 6, Mother. Your coordinates put you on the ridge overlooking our area of operations, yes? Over."

"Affirmative, Mother. I can see everything from up here. Over."

"Outstanding. Can you see enemy installations, bunkers, artillery, that sort of thing? Over."

"Affirmative. I have visual on three probable bunkers and can direct artillery fire. Over."

"Shoot an azimuth on all and we'll relay the coordinates to the Navy. Over."

"Roger. On it. Over" Carver yelled for Hooper to take himself east along the ridge. Once there he shot an azimuth to the targets and brought the numbers back to Carver who shot his own azimuths. With the two separate points the rest was simple geometry. The targets would be at the points where the azimuths met. He called in those coordinates.

Smote relayed the first set of coordinates to the waiting big guns of the Navy. Carver used Captain Morrisey's binoculars to look for the billowing smoke of the guns. The distance was far, but he could see the plume of smoke, "Shot out," he called. He found the first bunker nestled against a hillside in the jungle. He'd almost missed it when he'd first scanned the area, it was well camouflaged, but he'd caught the movement of a soldier relieving himself and marked it as a target. He watched now, waiting to correct the naval fire. There was a black plume of an exploding 203mm shell in the jungle a hundred feet to the west of the target. He looked at his map and was in the process of a correction when Morrisey was next to him. Carver said, "Add fifty and right one hundred." He waited for the read-back. When he got it he continued, "Fire for effect." Carver kept his eyes on the bunker this time as Morrisey called it out, "Shot out."

Carver watched the explosion hit beside the bunker, "That's it, fire for effect." The rolling thunder of big guns finally reached them. The white plumes of smoke belching from the cruiser obscured its sleek hull, barely discernible on the horizon. Carver handed the binoculars to Morrisey who put them to his eyes and watched their handy work. The explosions hit in quick succession sending large plumes of black dirt and green jungle skyward. In amongst the dirt and debris there was a bright flash followed by a larger explosion.

Morrisey said, "That's it, targets done. Secondary explosions; I'd say they found some ammo."

Sergeant Carver relayed the battle damage assessment. The bunker was reduced to a pile of smoking rubble; no signs of the Japanese soldiers were visible.

The next target was another bunker, but this one was closer to the allied front line. Carver called in the coordinates, but the Navy was done for the day, they'd be taking up defensive positions away from the shallow strait in case the Japanese decided to show up during the night. Ever since the costly naval battles of late Summer, the US Navy held a healthy respect for the Japanese Navy's ability to maneuver and shoot at night.

This target would be handled by the artillery section assigned to Sgt. Carver's own regiment. He watched the bunker and Morrisey watched for the tell-tale smoke indicating a shot out. He didn't see it, but Carver saw the impact. It was followed by the dull thump of the shot then the explosion. The shot was close and the correction was minimal. Carver beamed with pride, his boys were shooting well. The lighter guns scored direct hits on the bunker, but the thick Japanese concrete withstood the impacts. Carver wondered what it must be like inside that tomb with 105mm shells slamming into it.

He called in another round and the bunker disappeared in a flourish of exploding ordnance. When the dust cleared the bunker was still there, but the front had a gaping hole with smoke billowing out of it. It looked to be on fire. He could see the ant-like forms of Japanese soldiers disgorging from the dark hole like cockroaches from light. He spoke into the radio with urgency. "Give 'em another volley, troops in the open."

He handed the binoculars to Morrisey who'd given up on seeing the artillery position. He watched as the rounds fell amongst the Japanese troops, tearing them limb from limb and in some cases, vaporizing them. "My God," he whispered.

Carver said into the radio, "Nice shooting; spot on. That ruined their day." He signed off in the fading light.

The sun was setting on the horizon and Morrisey and Carver watched it sizzle into the sea. Captain Morrisey rubbed his face and scratched his beard. Sergeant Carver knew he was thinking about the men he'd lost. "Real sorry about your men, Captain."

Morrisey watched the sun, "Yours too." He ground his teeth, "What a fool of a man, your Lieutenant Caprielli."

Sergeant Carver didn't want to kick the man while he was down. He'd already paid the ultimate price. "Damndest things happen in war." He shook his head. "What're you planning on doing?"

He sighed, "When my men return for the bodies, I'll return with them to the village. There'll be a lot of sadness. The men were well-loved and will be sent off in high fashion. Feasting and dancing will help them along their way. Your men should come too; we'll honor your fallen, along with your Lieutenant, who is blameless in death."

"My orders are to stay here and keep calling in these strikes as our guys slug it out down there. I can't leave this post." A cool breeze came up from below, carrying with it the smell of the sea. "The higher-ups didn't mention it, but I'm sure they will. Are you still planning on waging your own private war up here, or will you join us?"

Morrisey stood up and crossed his arms. The sun's final sliver slipped beneath the sea. "You can see what joining up with you has done. I've lost more men in the last two days than the previous six months. I'll harass the enemy as I see fit. I won't become a pawn for your generals down there." He motioned towards the beach with his head. The word 'generals' came out like a curse word.

Carver stood beside him and extended his hand, "I don't blame you, Sir, not one bit. I'd like to ask you one more favor though." Morrisey cocked his head waiting. "When you take your dead out tomorrow will you take Corporal Hooper back with you? I need him to fetch my soldier, Private Dunphy. It hasn't been a week, but with my KIA I'll need every man I can get up here."

Morrisey nodded, "I'd forgotten about that bloke. He can come along and we'll escort him to Chief Ahio's village, but I can't guarantee your Dunphy will be released."

"There's nothing you can say? Don't you hold sway over his village? I can't just abandon him. He's an asshole, but he's my soldier. I'm responsible for him."

Morrisey nodded, "I quite understand. I do have some influence and I'll see what I can do, but once a decree has been laid down it's not easily overturned, even by myself."

Carver nodded. "By the time Hooper gets there, Dunphy will have served five days. That's a working week back in the U.S."

Morrisey smiled, "I doubt Chief Ahio will see the distinction, but like I said, I'll see what I can do."

# 17

Private Dunphy watched his squad leave the village without him. He couldn't believe this was happening, *they're really abandoning me to these people?* Not a single man gave him a parting glance. Not even O'Connor, with whom he thought he'd formed a bond. They'd been through a lot of shit together yet he didn't so much as flinch when his sentence of slavery was passed down. *This is total horseshit. I'm a member of the U.S. Army for God's sake, and a Dunphy.*

The thought of his parents flashed through his mind. They'd never believe the predicament they'd put him into. *Why'd they let me join? Why hadn't they apologized and pulled him out of that recruiting line?* He tried to remember what caused the rift, but couldn't. He shook his head, *all this and I can't even remember what I was mad about.* If he had the chance he'd undo whatever he'd done to get himself here.

With his squad gone he looked at the villagers. They were milling around giving him quick glances. When he tried to make eye contact they'd look away like scared children. *Maybe this won't be so bad. I'll use my Dunphy confidence and make them work for me for the next week.*

He lifted his chin and pointed at the Chief who was standing outside his hut chewing on a shoot of grass. He walked up to him and said, "Now see here, I'm no one's slave. The way I see it this will be a week's vacation away from the Army." The chief stared at him only catching a few words. Dunphy pointed to an unused hut, "I'll stay over there out of your way. You won't even know I'm here."

The Chief yelled, "Nogat spik."

The harsh voice stopped Dunphy. He raised his hands, "I don't know what you're saying, darkie, I..."

"Nogat tok." And the Chief slapped Dunphy across the face with his big hand.

Even though Dunphy was a trained boxer, he never saw it coming. He whirled around and fell to his knees. He put his hand to his mouth and pulled back blood. His blood boiled and he came up swinging. He gave the Chief a quick right jab to the chin then a shot to the belly. The Chief's eyes went wide and he reeled backwards. Dunphy went to press his advantage, but four men grabbed him and wrestled him to the ground. More natives gathered around and started clubbing him with thick lengths of wood. He tried to cover himself, but the blows were coming from every direction. He screamed and took the beating. It was over in less than a minute, but seemed an eternity.

The Chief stopped the men with a quick word. He kneeled and lifted him by the hair. He looked into his bloody face and shook his head, "Nogat," then he pinched his lips together, "tok." He tilted his head as if asking, "Understand?"

Dunphy nodded, *guess I'm not allowed to talk*. He picked himself up off the dirt. He felt like he'd been in the worst boxing match of his life. He didn't think anything was broken, but he knew he'd be sore as hell in the morning. He looked at Chief Ahio, who nodded and said, "Em tasol. Tekewe."

The native men grabbed him under the arm and took him to the hut he'd pointed out. Once inside the men stripped him down to his underwear. They laughed and pointed at his shaking white legs. He clenched his jaw, but didn't let his anger get the best of him. He doubted he could take another beating.

They folded and stacked his clothes and left him alone. He looked around the empty hut. He wondered if they'd bring him something to sleep on; maybe some of those furs he'd seen in Ahio's hut. He looked at the ceiling and could see two large holes that would do nothing to stop the torrential rains that were sure to come during his stay. *I wonder where my rifle is?*

He peered out his rickety door and saw the men trotting back across the compound towards him. He backed away and looked for some kind of weapon. He shook his head; it would be useless to fight them. There was no escape; he wouldn't last an hour without shoes, clothes, or a weapon. Even if he got away they'd easily track him then he'd get another beating. If by some miracle he found his squad they'd only turn him around and send him back. He took a deep breath and closed his eyes. He was just going to have to accept his sentence and live out the week with these heathens. *At least I'm not fighting the Japs,* he thought.

The men burst through the door, smiled and threw a garment onto the ground in front of him. He picked it up. It was the same loincloth they wore. They mimicked him putting it on and he nodded. He took off his underwear and slipped it on. He tied the cord and looked down at himself; he'd gone native. The others smiled and nodded their approval.

AFTER TWO DAYS living with the natives, Dunphy started to get the feel for their language. It wasn't as difficult and foreign as he first thought. A lot of words were English and the rest were combinations of sounds that made sense. For instance, 'Thank you' was 'tenkyu.' Dunphy found if he closed his eyes and listened to the flow of the language he could pick up the gist of most conversations. He was able to avoid more beatings with his newfound language skills. After the first day he was beaten two more times for not doing something when asked. *Perhaps the key to learning languages quickly is simply a matter of having it beat into you,* he mused.

His days were spent doing menial tasks for his captors. He'd be awakened early, before light with a jab to the ribs. He'd pull firewood from the great stacks behind the village and bring it to the cooking stations. He'd help serve breakfast, which usually consisted of boiled roots and some unknown dried meat. Once the men were served, the women ate. Then it was his turn. The portions were small, leaving him hungry. When he was done, he'd police up dishes and clean them. Then the men would drag him along for the daily hunt. He wasn't allowed a weapon and still didn't know where his M1 was. He would follow behind trying to stay as quiet as possible. It didn't seem to matter how careful he was, he always got withering looks as he made his way through the narrow jungle paths.

When the men found their prey, whether a snake, a lizard or a pig, he would be the one to carry the bulk of it back to camp. He cringed when the natives draped a huge snake as big around as his leg and so long they had to wrap it around his neck three times. The weight was too much for one man so the tail was strung out to two more men behind him. He carried the bulk of the ghastly thing around his neck. The awful feel of its skin was soon forgotten as he struggled to walk under the burden. By the time he got back to the village his legs were shaking and felt like noodles. There was no rest for the weary, though. With close supervision and the occasional smack to the back of the head, he learned how to skin and prepare a snake for eating.

After the hunt, he was put to work patching and repairing huts. Since he had no idea how to even start such a project, he would end up standing by and holding tools or handing them things they needed. He spent a lot of time moving back and forth between the creek filling flasks for the working men. The natives yelled at him whenever he wasn't moving fast enough. They were worse than his drill instructors back in basic. They took great pleasure in ordering a white man around, something none of them had ever done and would probably never do again.

At midday the men would lay down for an afternoon nap. The days were hottest during this time and an hour of rest out of the direct sunlight was a relief. He was never allowed the nap though. He would be put to work doing menial tasks like stacking fire wood, or rewashing already clean dishes.

In the evening he was put to work preparing the evening meal. He was constantly scolded by the women who tittered and laughed at his clumsy hands and terrible culinary skills. The women were harsher than the men with their cutting remarks and hateful eyes. They never struck him though; he was still a man.

On the second night he laid down on the palm fronds he'd collected and closed his eyes. His body was exhausted and sore from his beatings and the hard work. Any thought of escape was gone. He was too sore to even contemplate running and he had no place to go. He'd wait for his squad to return.

He was almost asleep when he sat bolt upright with a terrifying thought, *what if the squad gets ambushed and killed? What if they never return? Will I ever leave this place?*

He decided that would be a fate worse than death. He groaned and lay onto his aching back, but before he could close his eyes there was someone coming through the door. He pretended he was asleep; they couldn't make him do more work at this late hour could they? *They have to let me sleep, don't they?*

The intruder took two quiet steps towards him. He opened his right eye. This was unlike them; usually they'd burst in and kick him, not sneak. *What's this all about?* He almost jumped when he felt small hands touch his chest. He knew immediately it was a woman. He sat up quickly trying to see in the pitch blackness. The hands caressed his chest and then pushed him to his back. The soft voice said, "Sikrapim bel bilong."

He shook his head; this was how he got into the predicament in the first place. He tried to push her away, but she was persistent. She had his loin cloth off in an instant and massaged his manhood until there was no going back. He shut his eyes and stopped resisting. She straddled him. It only took a couple of minutes before the lovemaking was done. He was breathing hard, sweat coming off him in tiny rivers. He couldn't believe he'd gone so fast in his battered state. During the lovemaking his aches and pains had disappeared, but when she laid beside him they came flooding back and he moaned. She took it as pleasure and she nuzzled into his neck and they were both asleep in minutes.

WHEN ONE OF the natives burst through his door before light, he sat up in a panic. He looked around the dim room, but the woman was gone. She must have left during the night. *Or had it been a dream?* He sighed in relief. He had no idea what Chief Ahio would say if he knew he'd been with his daughter again. Probably cut his balls off and hang them next to his shrunken heads.

He stood, every muscle in his body protesting. He felt around for his loin cloth and wrapped it around his waist and tied it. He was getting used to the comfort of these simple garments. The native said something in Pidgin which he took to mean, 'go get firewood'. When he went in that direction and there was no yelling, he'd guessed right.

It was just getting light; the air was the coolest it would be which wasn't saying much. He pulled the loin cloth to the side and pissed into the jungle. His spray went in all directions until it settled down. He shook his head thinking about the woman who'd visited him. He was convinced it was Lela, Chief Ahio's daughter, but in the darkness, he couldn't be one hundred percent sure. He shuddered as his stream came to a halt. He was about to continue to the wood pile when he heard talking coming from his right. He hesitated trying to listen. He thought he recognized Chief Ahio's voice and another familiar voice he hadn't heard in a while.

His curiosity peaked; he took a few steps towards the conversation. The voices were easier to hear now, speaking in Pidgin, he couldn't decipher every word, but he definitely recognized the second voice. He carefully peered around the corner and confirmed his suspicions. Thomas Welch was across from Ahio talking quickly. They were twenty feet away, he couldn't make out anything they were saying in their rapid fire Pidgin. He wondered if the squad had come back early for him. His hopes rose and he was about to approach and ask that very question, but his instincts told him not to disturb them. Welch wasn't here for him. There was something else going on and he had the distinct feeling it was meant to stay between Welch and Chief Ahio. As Dunphy watched, Welch pulled the the M1 carbine he had slung over his shoulder and with two hands held it out to Chief Ahio. He smiled and took the weapon, holding it up and feeling the weight.

Dunphy felt better. He'd witnessed one of the reasons they were out here in the first place; to arm the natives with better weapons. Welch was helping his squad complete the mission.

He watched for another ten seconds as Welch took the Chief through the ins and outs of the carbine. Dunphy put the incident out of his mind and went back to what promised to be another long day of back breaking work.

## 18

The men spent the night on the ridge. As darkness enveloped them, Carver thought about the men he'd lost. Out of the twelve that started he only had four left. This mission was fucked up the moment they stepped out of the Division's shadow.

The original mission to bring the natives together as an effective guerrilla force wasn't happening. He picked mud out from under his fingernails, *hell, Morrisey's got 'em better off than we ever could. They'd probably win the war by themselves if they were left to it.*

He remembered hearing Welch's crazy idea to launch an attack toward the mountains where he said a large number of Japs were. He'd been ignored and as far as he could tell there was no such Japanese force. If there was they'd be in amongst them on this ridge. He wondered about that. He'd have to bring it up to Welch when he saw him again. *If I see him again.* Morrisey didn't seem too pleased with him. He wondered if he'd suddenly disappear. He didn't think Morrisey operated that way. He was usually a pretty good judge of character, but he'd been wrong before.

He lay down and tried to get some sleep, but the vision of Lieutenant Caprielli's body in pieces, scattered across the ridge kept popping into his head. He'd never had nightmares or been affected by death, but there was something about the Lieutenant's torn up body that was keeping him awake. Maybe it was the stupid way he died, jumping around like some high school cheerleader. *What the fuck was he thinking?*

He sat up grabbed his carbine and crawled to the nearest hole. O'Connor whispered, "Who goes there? Identify."

"It's me, numbnuts."

"Sorry Sarge. What are you doing here? It's not time to switch."

He crawled into the hole with him and looked out over the valley below. The occasional flash from a distant gun in the jungle made the battleground almost beautiful. There was a sliver of a moon and its glow made the distant ocean glimmer. Carver thought he could see the shape of a navy ship's silhouette, but he was probably imagining things. "I can't sleep. I'll take your watch. I was going to be your relief so I'll take two shifts." He put his big hand on O'Connor's shoulder, "Go get some sleep, son."

O'Connor nodded and crawled back the way Carver had come. He was glad for the early call; he was barely able to keep his eyes open.

WHEN MORNING CAME the men tore into C-rations and had breakfast. They were stiff and groggy. Sergeant Carver wasn't the only one having trouble sleeping. Hooper tore open a hard D-bar and tried to tear off a chunk. The thing looked like a hard hunk of shit. It was supposed to be chocolate, but tasted like bitter cocoa. Its one attribute was its high calorie count. The villagers had been supplementing their rations with rice and dried meats, but now they were back to their C-rats and D-bars. "Never thought I'd miss that smoked iguana or whatever the hell that stuff was."

O'Connor nodded as he spooned something resembling food into his mouth. "We've got enough food to last us a long time now..." He trailed off remembering the reason for the extra food.

Carver sat down beside them in the growing light. "Morrisey's men should be back any second to take their dead. Hooper, I want you to go with him. He's gonna take you to the other village to get that dumb ass Dunphy."

Hooper nodded, "I'm ready when they are, Sarge."

As the sun came up the shadows across the lowlands lit up the smoking battlefield. Carver put the binoculars to his eyes and scanned. He could barely make out parked vehicles of the 164th Regiment. He glassed forward until he spotted holes he knew to be foxholes on the front line. He continued glassing towards the Japanese lines. There was no movement, which wasn't a good thing. The Japanese were happy to sit back in their fortified positions and kill the exposed G.I.s and Marines as they tried to advance.

He put the radio to his ear and tried checking in, but nothing happened. There wasn't any static. "We got anymore batteries, Corporal?"

Hooper shook his head, "We have three more back in the village."

Carver cussed, *should've thought about that yesterday*. He hoped the natives would be bringing them this morning, otherwise their mission was over. He thought maybe that wouldn't be such a bad thing. Getting off the mountain and into his old unit would be a relief. With only the four of them he felt like his ass was hanging in the wind. What could four men do?

He heard the sound of aircraft and looked up to see a flight of fighters circling above the sea. He put his glass to them, carrier based F4 Wildcats. He hadn't seen any carrier based aircraft for days. With them back in the fight maybe they could punch through the Jap lines and kick them all the way to Cape Esperance.

The din of the distant airplane engines increased and he looked towards Henderson field. He could see B-17s lifting off and scratching for altitude out over the sea. Seven of them circled and formed up under the watchful eye of the Wildcats. He wondered if Division was trying to call him for bombing targets. He clenched his fist. He could see a plume of dust in the Japanese rear area. It was probably a large contingent of vehicles, but he was powerless to tell the bombers about them. He wondered if they would see it on their own.

Ten minutes later his question was answered; the bombers veered towards land lining up on the Japanese front line. They were almost flying directly at the ridge. When they were nearing the line, he could see their bomb-bay doors open and tiny black shapes tumbled towards earth. The five hundred-pound bombs plowed into the jungle sending great geysers of dirt and trees high into the air. If they were on target the Japs were catching hell. He'd endured the same thing the first weeks stationed around Henderson. There was no feeling more terrifying or helpless than waiting for a string of bombs to hit. Under his breath he said, "Fuck you Tojo."

He heard Hooper say, "looks like Morrisey's guys are back."

He let the binoculars dangle from his neck and turned. There were ten men with somber faces, some carrying handmade stretchers. The others had their hands full of the rest of their gear. He grunted, "O'Connor, see if you can find the radio batteries."

O'Connor threw the C-rat box into the bottom of his hole and went to the men. He started rifling through bags. He found the batteries and brought a fresh one to Carver. He tried to contact the regiment again and this time he got a weak response. The bombers were circling back to the airfield lining up for landing and rearming.

Lieutenant Smote's voice crackled over the radio, "Where you been, Falcon 6? Over."

"We're running out of batteries up here. Over."

"Good to have you back, we're making a push soon, you have any targets for us? Over."

He put the glasses to his eyes again and scanned. "I can't see anything except dust from the bombers. I can't see the line. Over."

"Understand, target obscured. How about movement behind the line? Over."

He glassed that way and shook his head, "Nothing moving. Saw a dust cloud a half hour ago, probably vehicles moving, but it's gone now. No targets to report. Over."

"How far behind the line can you see? Over."

"About a mile behind their front line. The land makes a southerly turn, can't see anything after that. Over."

"Wait one. Over."

He waited, continuing to glass the area for targets. He was limited, the battle lines had slowly moved west. If this push was successful he'd be unable to call out more targets.

The radio came to life in his hands. "Falcon 6, are you able to move? Over."

He looked at his two men, they were tired, but physically fine. "Affirmative. We're able to move. Where do you want us to go? Over."

The radio crackled out coordinates. "It's the next hill to the west. It's not far as the crow flies, about four miles, but it looks like you'll have to traverse a valley between the ridge you're on and the hill. Do you see it? Over."

There was a copse of tall trees blocking his view of the hill, but he knew which one he was talking about. He confirmed it with a quick look at his topographical map. It was an ancient map, the year on the bottom, 1921, but big land masses were easily identified and the ridge and the hill were there. "I know the hill. Over."

"We think you'll have a good view of the Jap's rear from there. Over."

Carver traced the distance from the hill to the Japanese held area to the west. He gave a low whistle. "That hill's damned close to the Jap lines. Do we know if it's occupied? Over."

"There's been nothing suggesting it's being used by the Japs. Can you get there? Over."

He nodded, "Can do, Sir. We'll leave at the earliest and report in when we get there. Over."

"Roger," was the only response.

He handed the radio to O'Connor and walked to Captain Morrisey who was supervising the loading of his fallen men. The corpses had lost their lustrous black skin, replaced with graying bloated and cracked skin.

Sergeant Carver told him of his new orders. Morrisey held his hand to his forehead, shielding the sun and looked towards the distant hill. He scowled, "That hill's cursed, Sergeant."

Carver squinted, "Cursed, sir? How do you mean?"

"My men won't go near it. I went up there a couple years ago to see what all the fuss was about. Couldn't get anyone to come with me. It's superstition, but I must say the place did have an eerie feel to it. Probably influenced by all the dire warnings I got."

"So your men won't know if the Japs are sitting up there?"

He shook his head, "Fraid not, but I'd be surprised if they aren't. It's high ground and close to their troop concentrations I should think. Why wouldn't they be there?"

Sergeant Carver sighed. "Well that's where we're going."

He pulled the binoculars from around his neck and held them out to Morrisey who shook his head. "Keep them, Sergeant. I'll get them back when you're off that hill."

"Thanks." He put them back around his neck. "I'm not leaving until Hooper gets back with Dunphy. I'll need all the men I can get for this one."

The dead were loaded, a native at each end of a stretcher staring straight ahead. "If your chap's ready to go, we'll be heading back," said Morrisey.

Hooper spoke up, "Ready when you are, Sir." He had his carbine in his hand. "Lead on, Macduff."

Morrisey laughed, "Didn't peg you as a Shakespeare fan, son."

Corporal Hooper looked at him, "Shakespeare? Nah that's from a comic book. Think it was Batman."

Morrisey shook his head, "Of course." He took a long stride and the whole procession moved down the ridge towards the village.

Carver called to Hooper, "Don't dilly dally, we need to move off this position ASAP." Hooper waved his acknowledgment.

The distant sound of another artillery strike filled the morning. Carver put the binoculars to his eyes and watched the 105mm rounds walking back and forth along the Japanese line. He thought the Japs must be dug in deep, he couldn't see any movement at all, only the great dirt and fire geysers tearing up the earth. When the artillery stopped, he watched in morbid fascination as the American line moved cautiously forward. He passed the glasses to O'Connor who was watching for any unwanted guests coming up the ridge behind them. "The big push is starting."

O'Connor took the glasses and lay down to better support his arms. He scanned back and forth then whistled. "Looks like an army of ants from up here." He continued watching for five minutes. "Looks like a cakewalk. Far as I can tell they're not meeting any resistance."

He handed them back to Carver. He held them for another five minutes. "I think you're right. Maybe they bugged out?"

ON THE GROUND Captain Blade was leading his Baker Company against the Japanese front line. His company was wedged against the sea on his right and Able Company on his left. He was dreading this morning, he knew he'd lose men today, but he'd be damned if he'd sit in the rear like some traffic cop. He took the term "combat leader" literally. He was in the mix, leading them to battle.

They'd advanced twenty yards over the chewed up jungle and hadn't taken any fire. He expected the chatter of the deadly Nambu machines guns, but they were silent. He kept moving forward; maybe they'd caught them sleeping. He increased his pace, the men followed. Thirty yards and still nothing; no resistance. He held his Thompson sub machine gun at the ready as he started passing foxholes he assumed were Japanese forward observation posts, they were empty. *My God, the Japs have bugged out.*

His heart raced and he waved his men forward. They were gaining more ground than they'd gained in three days of hard fighting. He could see the looming shapes of bunkers still in the distance. He expected the dark gun ports to start winking deadly fire at him any second. His radio man tapped him on the shoulder, "Sir, the colonel wants an update."

He kneeled down letting his men continue forward around him. "Keep advancing, Lieutenant," he said to one of his platoon leaders. "Don't out-pace Able Company, no gaps."

He was almost giddy when he spoke with Colonel Sinclair. "Sir, we're not finding any resistance. It looks like they pulled back last night. Over." He listened to the Colonel, Yes sir, I can see the bunker line ahead, but we're taking no, repeat, no fire from them." He listened, "Yes, Sir, we'll take the bunkers and report. Over."

He handed the radio back to his radioman. He stood up and yelled to his slowing men. "Move forward, move to the bunkers!" He took a step then heard the unmistakable sound of incoming artillery. *Shit.* His men were in the open running towards the bunkers still three hundred yards away. He screamed, "Take cover! Incoming! Take cover!"

He pushed his radioman into the crook of a fallen palm tree and tucked in behind. All around him men were scrambling for cover. This section of the advance was on the edge of a pre-war coconut plantation. The ground was churned up by multiple artillery and bomb strikes. Coconut trees lay everywhere uprooted and torn apart by direct hits.

Captain Blade held his helmet tight over his head as the first 105mm shell landed amongst his men. The ground shook and he felt himself lifted off the ground then slammed back down. The first was followed immediately by another and another. He couldn't hear himself, but he screamed. They'd been lured into the open to be cut apart like rag-dolls by pre-plotted artillery fire.

The artillery kept falling all along the line. He lifted his head to try to assess what was happening. He saw one of his men, *was it Reynolds?* He was thrown into the air, his torso a mass of blood. He grit his teeth and saw another man staring at him with wide eyes fifteen feet away. He looked like a scared child. He thought the man's name was Travis, but he couldn't be sure. There were so many young men out here. He tried to give him a reassuring look. He tried to smile, but it came off like a grimace. Suddenly the boy disappeared in a red hot flash. Blade was covered with dirt, debris and human parts. He yelled a long desperate, "Nooo!"

When the dirt cleared he looked to the spot; there was nothing, only a smoking hole. He felt tears fill the corners of his eyes. He was helpless, the dirt piled on him, trying to suffocate him. He put his head down and screamed into the rotting jungle floor.

The barrage lasted 7 minutes. It was the heaviest artillery barrage any of the men had seen. When it ended it seemed the entire world took a deep breath. Captain Blade lifted his head, dirt cascaded off his helmet. He looked forward trying to shake the cobwebs out of his head. His ears were screaming, like a tidal wave siren was going off inside his skull. He couldn't catch his breath. He was hyperventilating, the weight on his back making it hard to breathe. He put his arms beneath himself in push-up position and pushed his torso up. Dirt, leaves and jungle slid off him. He extracted himself, found his Thompson which was still clean beneath his body. He tried to yell an order, give a command, but it only came out as a moan.

Something snapped past his head, *was that a bee?* Another went by. He saw the downed tree in front of him erupt like some invisible hammer was smashing it. He was confused, then his head cleared and he realized what he was seeing. On his knees he looked through the settling dust and saw the darkened gun ports of the bunkers winking with light. All along his shredded line men were dazedly standing, getting their bearings, then being cut down by ruthless machine gun fire.

Pouring through the gaps in the bunkers were Japanese soldiers with fixed bayonets on their rifles. Captain Blade shook his head and finally found his voice, "Fall back, fall back!" He reached for his radioman who'd been lying beside him. He found him under the dirt and gave his arm a pull. It came out of the dirt easily, too easily. He held his severed arm. He needed that radio, had to get more men up here to stop the attacking Japanese. He dug out the rest of his radioman and using his K-bar knife cut the straps of the backpack. He pulled the radio, it was slick with blood. He put the headpiece to his ear, but he couldn't hear anything except the ringing in his ears. He lifted the radio and turned it towards him. He dropped it and cursed, there were three large smoking holes in it. "Fall back, fall back!" he screamed again.

Men started hearing him and started reacting. At first, they wobbled and trotted, but as their heads cleared and the adrenalin kicked in they started running. "Back to your holes, back to your holes!"

The eyes of the men running past him weren't human; they were scared animals. If he didn't reign them in they'd run all the way back to Australia. He grabbed a man running past and threw him to the ground, yelling in his face. "Covering fire!" Blade popped up and laid a long burst towards the charging Japanese. He didn't know if he hit anything, but he slowed them down.

The man he'd pulled down was still wide-eyed, but the crazy was being replaced by the eyes of a soldier. He put his M1 to his shoulder and emptied his clip into the Japs. Soon other men were joining in, dropping behind cover to shoot the screaming Japanese, then falling back to another position. Most of the men were still panicked, but the Japs weren't advancing as fast now that they were taking casualties.

Blade stayed with the soldier covering each other and moving back, shooting, moving. The line of enemy soldiers was close. Blade aimed from behind a big palm and was surprised to see a Japanese soldier only yards away coming straight for him, bayonet leading. He pulled the trigger and five forty-five caliber bullets slammed the soldier backwards into another charging soldier. This one scrambled over his fallen comrade and lunged. Blade leaned back behind the tree and watched the bayonet and rifle glance off it harmlessly. As the soldiers' momentum moved him past the tree, Blade backstroked him with the butt of his Thompson. The soldier's head crumpled like an overripe melon, sending his eyes squirting from his skull.

Another screaming Japanese soldier was on him. Blade only had time to turn his head enough to see that he'd take the bayonet in his gut. He braced for the impact, but it never came. The soldier covering him was standing in front of him pumping rounds into the Japanese soldier's body. Blade slammed another magazine in and primed his weapon. There were targets everywhere. He knew he would die soon, like so many of his men had today, but he was done running. He'd die in place beside this soldier.

He chose his targets, firing in short bursts to preserve ammo. He'd take as many of the bastards with him as he could. The M1 of the soldier beside him pinged and he yelled, "Last clip, Sir."

Blade shot at a running man who disappeared behind a downed log. He sighted on another soldier to his left who was ramming his bloody bayonet repeatedly into one of his men. He pulled the trigger sending him to hell. Another Jap in the open, running hard, he led him slightly and pulled the trigger. Only one shot and the pin slammed against an empty chamber. He reached to his ammo belt, but he knew he was out of ammo. He pulled his K-bar and put his hand on the soldier's arm, who was busy burning through his last clip. "It's been an honor serving beside you, soldier."

The Japanese went over them like an ocean wave around a delicate sand castle, leaving only death and destruction.

SERGEANT CARVER WATCHED the advance from his vantage point on the ridge. From this distance the men were mere dots, but those dots were advancing unopposed. He felt a knot form in his stomach, something didn't feel right. It was too easy. He fanned the binoculars to the bunker line. He could barely see two of the low-slung concrete structures. They looked like children's toys. He'd directed artillery onto them earlier, but they proved to be too thick and well-built. Even with 105mm shells raining down on them, they were still operational.

He scanned further west searching for the Japanese forces, but his view ended with the curving point of land. He couldn't see anything beyond the bunkers. *Why would the Japs give up the bunkers?*

He pondered calling Division to tell them his fears, but thought better of it. He was a lowly sergeant; they wouldn't be interested in his gut feeling. Besides, the advance was in full swing and it would be a mistake to stall it.

His fears were realized when he saw the first shells falling amongst the troops. They were out in the open getting shredded by zeroed in artillery. He didn't want to watch, but he couldn't pull the binoculars away. His knuckles turned white as his grip tightened.

Behind him O'Connor turned to the dull thump of artillery. "Holy shit, are those our guys under that?"

Carver dropped the binoculars and they swayed beneath the neck strap. He rubbed his forehead, "They're getting torn to shit. It's a trap." He quickly brought the glasses back to his eyes. "When the arty stops they'll probably send a counter-attack. Get over here and get ready on the radio. We'll call it in when we see those yellow bastards."

The barrage seemed to last forever, neither of them had seen such a devastating display of Japanese firepower.

Finally, the barrage stopped. Carver watched the bunkers knowing what was coming. "Get ready on the radio."

"I'm ready, Sarge."

Carver pointed, "There they are. Get them on the horn and give them fire-mission Alpha; they're at the bunker complex. It's close to our guys, but it's the only chance they've got." O'Connor called it in and waited for confirmation. It was taking too long; the troops would be mixed soon. "What the fuck's taking so long?"

"They're checking, I don't know." Carver's grip on the binoculars threatened to crush them. O'Connor listened intently to the radio; they'd finally come back with a reply. He gave Carver a wide-eyed look, "Say again." He listened, his own hand squeezing the headset, "We've got Japs in the open streaming past the bunkers, our guys need the fire support or they'll be overrun." He listened and threw the headset down. Carver looked at him with narrowed eyes shooting daggers. "The fucking pricks won't fire, think they'll hit our troops."

Carver's face turned red, "Why the hell we up here if they're not gonna listen to us, goddamnit?" He pressed the glasses to his eyes. "Our guys are retreating, they're in full retreat. The Japs are right on their tails…oh my God." He handed the glasses to O'Connor and took the radio handset. "Mother, this is falcon 6. Fire mission Alpha minus one hundred."

The response came back, "Negative Falcon 6. That's on our troops. Fire mission denied."

"I can see the battle. We're in full retreat. You rear echelon types better fix bayonets 'cause they'll be at your doorstep in minutes."

There was a twenty second pause, then the response, "Roger. Fire mission approved. Standby for shot out." fifteen seconds passed. "Shot out."

Carver watched as the 105mm howitzer shell exploded amongst the tiny dots below. "That's it. You're right on 'em. Pour it on."

The barrage lasted 6 minutes, he spotted the shells along the Jap advance which finally broke and ground to a halt. The counter attack ended in the same spot they'd occupied the day before. On paper the lines hadn't moved, but it was clearly a Japanese victory.

The two companies of the 164th were cut to half strength. Able and

Baker companies were melded into one company. The attack had left the Division weakened by a full company and they hadn't gained a yard.

Sergeant Carver felt drained by the whole experience. "We've gotta get to that hill before we make another push. We've gotta find that Jap artillery or we'll never take this shitty island."

"Why aren't our guys shooting counter-battery?"

Sergeant Carver gruffly replied, "Must be out of range, that's the only explanation. They don't feel obligated to keep me up to date, private." He pulled a C-ration from his pack and walked off a couple yards, "Keep watch, I'm eating lunch."

## 19

Corporal Hooper and Captain Morrisey's men were back to the village by midday. As they entered they were met by the entire village. They formed a solemn line and watched as the procession walked by. There were no tears only stony faces watching the procession. Once they were in the center the bodies were placed on the ground in parallel lines. The bearers stepped back and the dead were encircled by the living. The old Chief started a low chant.

Hooper watched from the outside of the circle as the lined face of the Chief looked up to the sky and he lifted his calloused hands to whatever god he was addressing. His voice, at first whispery and barely a murmur, built until a strong baritone filled every ear. Hooper marveled that the small frail man could have such a voice living inside him. There was power within it and Hooper couldn't tear himself away. It was soothing yet stirring and he didn't want it to end. But soon it did and an eerie silence filled the village.

The Chief's arms stayed extended and he closed his eyes. Hooper thought his shoulders must be burning, but the old Chief didn't falter. Finally, he slowly dropped his hands and opened his eyes. It was a signal because the women rushed forward and wailing broke out like a dam had burst. The women kneeled beside the dead men and cried. Hooper lowered his head feeling like an outsider.

Morrisey touched his arm and he gave a start. "Easy does it. We should go to Ahio's village or we'll have to make the return trip in the dark."

Hooper nodded. He drained the rest of his canteen. "I'll fill this and I'm ready."

THE WALK to Chief Ahio's village was uneventful. The four natives who were along, patrolled quickly and without fear of Japanese patrols. Hooper figured the enemy activity had dropped off because of the American offensive along the coast. Every soldier was needed to defend the line. He wondered if the Japs were curious as to the fate of the patrol Morrisey and his men dispatched a few days ago.

The patrol entered the village without having seen any sentries. Hooper thought they must either feel secure or be foolhardy. Morrisey and his men were escorted to the center of the village. The villagers weren't unfriendly, but they weren't overly pleased to see them either. Morrisey commented on it to Hooper. "Blokes seem rather cool to our arrival wouldn't you say?" Hooper was unfamiliar so shrugged. His carbine was slung, but he caressed the stock assuring it was within easy reach. Morrisey's men also seemed to pick up on the feeling, their muscles taut, their eyes flitting around the camp.

Chief Ahio was summoned and Morrisey brightened and approached him. He waved hello and in Pidgin said, "Chief Ahio, good to see you again so soon." Ahio didn't return his smile only nodded his acknowledgment. "Well, I suppose I'll get right to the point." He gestured to Corporal Hooper, "The corporal is here to collect Private Dunphy."

Ahio stiffened. He looked to the sky then back down and shook his head. In his low guttural Pidgin, he responded, "The time has not yet passed."

Morrisey frowned. "You know of our losses?" He knew Ahio had an intricate chain of intelligence gatherers just like he did. Ahio would have known about the ridge attack as soon as his own village had.

Ahio nodded, "A sad loss of life."

"Yes, the Americans lost men too and now they are leaving. They won't leave their man behind. He's one of their soldiers and is needed for their continued mission." Ahio frowned and told his men to bring Dunphy.

He came out of the jungle with a load of firewood. He looked confused being interrupted from his chores. Corporal Hooper couldn't believe what he was seeing. Dunphy had gone native. He was naked from the waist up. He hadn't shaved and he wore a native style skirt tied with a crude piece of twine. He was filthy, his white skin streaked with mud, ash and dirt. He wanted to laugh, but held his tongue.

Dunphy saw Morrisey and Hooper and smiled. He dropped the firewood and strode confidently to the group. The native men on either side of him scowled at his insolence, but since he'd been called by the Chief, didn't strike him. Dunphy sneered, "Finally getting out of this shit…"

Morrisey interrupted him, "We're negotiating your release. Keep quiet, you fool."

Dunphy clammed up quickly. This was even more surprising to Hooper who'd never seen Dunphy cowed so easily. He always had to get the last word. Maybe this had been good for him. Maybe he'd learned some manners.

Ahio spoke again, "We will keep him for two more days. Come back then."

Morrisey shook his head and the natives behind their Chief stiffened. "I'm willing to pay for his release." Ahio nodded wanting to hear more. "As you know, our village is in mourning. If you release this man to our care you and your entire village are welcome to come feast and celebrate these men's lives." Ahio looked him in the eye and Morrisey continued, "You are welcome to come eat our food and share our stores. Our villages will be as one for a day of celebration."

Dunphy and Hooper were clueless to what was being said, but they could tell Chief Ahio was warming up to the idea. The tenseness melted from the natives' body and Hooper relaxed his grip on the stock of his carbine.

Ahio paced back and forth for two minutes then stood in front of Morrisey and nodded. "I accept this offer. You may have the white man."

Morrisey smiled and nodded. "It will be an honor to have your village amongst us for this celebration."

DUNPHY WAS beside himself when he heard the news. He was fidgeting from foot to foot unable to control the smile spreading across his face. He nudged Morrisey in the arm, "Tell the fucker to bring me my clothes and weapon."

Morrisey kept his smile, but through gritted teeth said, "Mind your manners. Our languages are close enough for him to pick up you're tone. If you're not careful you may end up here another week."

Dunphy's smile faded. "No way am I staying here another minute."

Hooper chimed in, "Then shut the fuck up numb-nuts." Dunphy's eyes went to slits, but he nodded and kept his mouth shut. Hooper shook his head; he really was a changed man. If he'd talked like that a week ago, Dunphy would have tried to knock him out. "We'll get you changed out of your skirt in a minute."

Dunphy gritted his teeth and Morrisey gave Hooper a stern look. "You're like children. Try to behave." He spoke to Ahio and with the flick of his hand he sent men off to retrieve Dunphy's things.

Dunphy took his clothes and carbine to his hut. "Be back in a second." He was beaming as he ripped off the skirt and started to pull on his pants. There were hands around his waist squeezing him from behind. He jumped, but knew instantly it was Lela. She'd visited him every night. He turned to look at her, she kept her gaze down. He looked over her bare breasts with the golden-brown nipples and her tight curly hair. He lifted her chin to look into her eyes. She was still one of the homeliest women he'd ever been with, but he'd miss her skillful ministrations. "Stap gut. Mi lukim bihain." 'Stay good. I'll see you later.'

Her eyes went from sad to mad. She clenched her fists and started yelling and hitting him. He tried to quiet her, but it was no use. He had to get out of there. If the Chief knew he'd continued screwing his daughter, he'd never get out.

As she yelled and punched him, he finished pulling on his pants. The rest would have to wait; she was getting herself into a frenzy. He ran out of the hut into the evening sun with her hot on his heels, her breasts swinging wildly. She found a stick and started whacking him with it. He yelled in pain and ran to Morrisey and Hooper like a scared puppy going between its master's legs.

Chief Ahio frowned and raised his voice. She stopped beating him and stood staring at the ground breathing hard. Dunphy took the respite to pull on his boots. After walking through the jungle in bare feet for the past week they felt odd and constricting. Ahio spoke harshly to Lela. He ended with a question. Morrisey tensed and asked Dunphy, "What the bloody hell is going on? Don't tell me you've been with her again, not after the first time."

Dunphy wiped his bleeding forehead and said, "We need to get the fuck outta here. Now."

Hooper was beside himself, "Dammit, Private can't you keep your pecker in your pants for one second?"

"She came into my hut. If I didn't do it she would've told the chief I raped her. I didn't have a choice. She's frickin' crazy."

Morrisey's face went pale as he listened to Lela telling her father how Dunphy lured her into his hut and forced himself onto her. "That's what she's telling the Chief right now."

Dunphy pulled on his shirt bringing the carbine off his shoulder. The natives surrounding them tensed, "That's horseshit. If anything, she raped me."

Hooper guffawed at that, "You wear a skirt and you get raped by a woman? You're a changed man alright."

Dunphy's face went red. He wanted to kill him, but once again restrained himself. He may have all the fighting he'd want depending on how the next few minutes went.

Chief Ahio fumed, hearing his daughter's story. He shot daggers from his eyes as he stared at Dunphy. Dunphy stared back. He was done taking any more of his shit. He decided he was willing to shoot his way out of here if he had to and the first one to die would be Ahio. The natives were unslinging their ancient rifles. Dunphy figured his semi-automatic carbine would be able to take out a good number of them before he would have to change clips. He felt for the extra clips he'd had in his pockets, but they were gone. *Thieving pricks.*

Morrisey tried to say something, but Chief Ahio held up his hand for silence. He looked around at his men, tensed for combat. They looked at him as he spoke, confusion filling their faces. They lowered their weapons and stepped away. Morrisey spoke to Dunphy, "Sling your rifle, Private. He's letting us go." Dunphy made no move to do any such thing. "Do it now before he changes his mind."

Dunphy saw the other men backing down, he stood straight and slung his carbine. "Probably shoot us in the back as we leave, or hunt us down like dogs."

"They'd have a hard fight and wouldn't be able to kill all of us," he indicated his men standing at the ready. "My village would exact revenge. It wouldn't go well for them; we've got them outnumbered two to one. Trust me, he's letting us go. Don't be daft and spoil it."

More words were spoken and Morrisey turned away and walked back the way they'd come. "Don't look back. Show our trust by not looking back."

Hooper didn't look back, but it took every fiber of willpower. He expected to be shot in the back any second. When they were safely in the jungle he let out a long breath. "Holy shit, I thought they were gonna plug us."

Morrisey looked back, "Hmm, very odd. I didn't expect him to fight us, but I certainly didn't think he'd let you go after what his daughter told him." He looked hard at Dunphy. "You didn't rape her, did you?" Dunphy looked at him in disgust. Morrisey nodded, "Didn't think so. Poor girl's in love with you."

"Love? She nearly killed me back there." He rubbed the knot forming under his cut forehead.

Morrisey grinned, "A lover spurned and all that you know."
"I didn't spurn her. I only said 'see you around.' Girl's crazy."
"Well perhaps 'see you around' wasn't what she wanted to hear."
Hooper chimed in, "She's a real looker. Quite a catch."
Dunphy flipped him the bird.

## 20

On the walk back to the village, Hooper told Dunphy about the men they'd lost on the ridge. Dunphy's good mood ended and the remainder of the walk was unnaturally quiet.

By the time the group got back to the village, it was completely dark. Hooper and Dunphy were exhausted and in no shape to continue to the ridge. They decided to sleep in the village and leave first thing in the morning.

Morrisey invited them to dine with them in the center of the village. The meal was light since the following day would be one of feasting. It was still better than C-rations and by the end of the meal both men's eyes were drooping. Captain Morrisey brought out a flask and poured them each a cup of clear liquid. "We captured this off some Jap soldiers we dispatched a couple weeks back. It's awful stuff, but not bad in a pinch. I'd forgotten all about it."

Hooper smiled and took the cup as did Dunphy. "Don't mind if I do." Dunphy took a big gulp and nearly spurted it back out but managed to keep it down. "Damn, that's fire."

Hooper laughed and tipped his cup back and held it out for more. "Pussy," he said.

Dunphy looked around the group, "Hey, where's Welch?"

Morrisey gestured to a group of huts. "I've got him under house arrest until I figure out what to do with him. Probably let him go with time served."

Dunphy looked confused. "House arrest?"

"He disobeyed my orders by going to the American line, so yes, house arrest."

"That means he has to stay under guard in his hut then. Is that right? Can't leave?" Morrisey nodded. Dunphy took another bite of dried lizard meat, "You just start that? The house arrest, I mean?"

Morrisey looked annoyed, "No, he's been there all week. We've been delivering his food. He's only allowed out to defecate."

Dunphy threw an unidentifiable piece of the meat into the smoldering fire. "Then why'd I see him in Chief Ahio's village three days ago?"

Morrisey stopped chewing. "Are you sure?" he looked to one of his men and said something in Pidgin. The man darted away towards the hut.

"Course I'm sure. How many white men are there around here? And that accent's pretty hard to miss."

"Tell me what you saw and heard."

Dunphy told him he couldn't hear nor understand anything but he did see him give one of the new carbines to Chief Ahio. He told him they seemed to want their meeting secret. "I figured Ahio didn't want to share the guns."

The native man came trotting back and spoke in Morrisey's ear. Morrisey shook his head and said something else. The man trotted back the way he'd come. "Tangar checked; he's gone."

Another man trotted up and kneeled next to Morrisey. The man spoke and lowered his head. Morrisey fired off in rapid Pidgin. The man's shoulders slumped. He stood without raising his eyes and walked away.

Morrisey shook his head, "The guards have been letting him 'get his exercise' a couple of hours a day. They say he never leaves for longer than a few hours. Plenty of time to get there and back." He looked at Dunphy and Hooper, "These men are trusting, there's very little spite in them. I'm afraid this war will change that."

Hooper said, "What's going on? You think Welch is up to no good?"

Morrisey looked to the stars and rocked back and forth on his butt. Just when Hooper thought he might not have heard him he said, "Probably nothing." He stood up and stretched, "You men should hit the rack. You've got to meet up with what's left of your squad in the morning and I've got a busy day of mourning and celebrating some fine men's lives."

Dunphy held up his cup, "Think I'll stay up and drink more of this Jap hootch if you don't mind."

Morrisey nodded, "Be my guest."

Hooper clinked the hollowed out coconut cup against Dunphy's and took a long gulp.

IN THE MORNING before the sun came up, Sergeant Carver and Private O'Connor sat on the edge of the jungle looking into the village. They were surprised to come upon the village without being challenged by a native. Did they feel safe because all the Japanese soldiers were defending the line against the American advance? Carver didn't think that was Morrisey's style; he was more careful and pragmatic than that. Carver rubbed his chin, wondering if he should go in or wait for more light. He decided another ten minutes wouldn't hurt. He pointed to their back-trail and Hooper nodded. He moved up the trail a few yards to watch for any unwanted guests.

The twilight brought the scene to life in front of Carver. He could see the slain villagers lined up in the center. Each body had one female sitting with her head down, spending one last night with their husband, son, or father. He didn't see any men, including his two delinquent soldiers. He gave a low whistle and O'Connor came up beside him without making a sound. Carver turned to see where he was and almost bumped into him. He shook his head, *how'd he do that?*

He pointed to the women and shrugged. The men stood and left the safety of the bush. Their guns were slung, but they kept them at the ready until they figured out where everyone was. The women looked up, but didn't rise from their vigil. The men stood over them and looked around at the sleeping village. There were some women milling around and some coming in from the wood pile to stoke the smoldering fire. Carver waved his hand in greeting and one of the older women approached him. He tried to make her understand. "Men? Where are the men?" he pointed to himself and O'Connor, "Men." Then shrugged. She pointed to a hut, the one next to Morrisey's and pushed him toward it. Carver knew it was the old chief's hut. He couldn't remember his name.

They pulled back the door and stuck their heads into the dimly lit room. The air smelled like a combination of smoke and mint. Sergeant Carver's eyes adjusted and he saw the old chief staring at him from a chair in the far corner. Carver raised his hand and said, "Hello."

The Chief raised his hand and stood up. He didn't bother speaking, but grabbed Carver by the arm and led him back outside. He indicated he should follow as he led him to another hut, the same one he'd stayed in a couple nights before. It seemed like a lifetime ago. The chief extended his hand to the door and Carver went inside. This hut smelled decidedly worse than the chief's. He took another step in and heard his boot squelch into something wet. He looked down and scowled, his boot dripping vomit. The smell assaulted him and he grit his teeth when he saw Dunphy and Hooper lying on the bare ground, snoring. Dunphy clutched an empty coconut cup.

He kicked Hooper's foot, but he didn't wake. He kicked harder, still no movement. He called to O'Connor who poked his head in, "Get some water."

O'Connor looked around the room and picked up what was left of the Saki, "it's not water, but it's wet." He handed it to Carver who threw it across their faces. The men both sputtered and sat up. Dunphy grumbled, "Dammit, what the hell's going on?" He rubbed his face. "Ah, shit, that burns dammit." Trying to clear his vision, he said, "who the fuck did that?"

Carver put his nose to the bottle and sniffed. The alcohol was pungent. "I did, assholes. You've got five minutes to get your shit together and fall out of this hut."

Hooper sat bolt upright, wiping the alcohol from his face. The tiny cuts they'd accumulated from weeks of traversing the jungle stung like fire. "Sarge? Is that you?"

"You're damned right it's me. Now hurry up. You men are a disgrace." He threw the empty bottle and it hit Dunphy in the gut. Carver went outside and stood next to O'Connor who was bent over laughing. Even the old chief had a toothless grin spread across his withered face. Carver shook his head and smiled, "They deserved that."

Five minutes later Dunphy and Hooper stood before their sergeant trying to keep from swaying. Both men looked white as sheets and were obviously still drunk. Carver handed his canteen to Hooper who dumped it over his head, washing off the Saki. O'Connor gave his to Dunphy who did the same. Dunphy leaned forward and threw up whatever was left in his gut. The smell, the sound and the mere thought had Hooper joining him in an instant.

Once they were done Carver asked, "No more horseshit. Where the fuck's Morrisey and the rest of the men?"

Hooper looked around the compound, "I dunno Sarge." He pointed to the Chief, "Why don't you ask him?"

"'Cause I don't speak Pidgin, numbnuts."

Dunphy wiped his mouth and held his hand up, "I do, kind of." Carver looked at him skeptically, "My time with the natives; it's not a hard language." Carver nodded and Dunphy fumbled through an awkward sentence. He listened to the response. Dunphy looked confused and asked a question. The chief shook his head and gestured them to follow. "I can't make out what he means. Something about enemies and ambush and something about Welch, I think." Carver looked at him sideways, "He wants us to follow him."

They fell in step behind the chief who moved with perfect grace despite his age. When they got to the jungle edge the chief went into a crouch. The move was unmistakably combat-like and the men pulled their carbines from their shoulders, glancing at one another. Hooper licked his lips, the alcohol buzz much subdued. The chief didn't have a rifle, but he pulled a long beat up machete from his belt.

They went as silent as they could for fifty yards before the chief stopped and they crouched behind him. The chief smiled and pointed. The jungle came alive around them with men appearing as if from thin air. The squad clenched their carbines, but they were caught completely by surprise.

When they saw Captain Morrisey and his thick beard appear, they all breathed easier. He sidled up next to them and whispered, "Welcome to the show, lads."

"What show? What're we up against?" It was obvious they were waiting in ambush for some enemy force. It was no use asking a lot of questions. "Where you want us?"

Morrisey pointed with two fingers and two of his men waved them to follow. They did so and found themselves in the back of the ambush, out of the way. The natives signaled them to stay put. They went to ground lying flat on their stomachs on the lush jungle floor.

The ground was still cool from the night, but the sun was rising higher bringing heat and humidity. Soon the men were sweating. Carver could smell the alcohol seeping from Dunphy's and Hooper's pores. It was a stale, fetid smell that turned his stomach.

An hour passed. Carver was anxious to figure out what the hell they were doing. He had a mission to complete and sitting on his ass in the jungle wasn't helping him complete it, but Morrisey wouldn't have his men out here for nothing.

He felt O'Connor slap his boot lightly. He looked at him and O'Connor tilted his chin to the front. He'd seen or heard something. Carver listened and strained his eyes, but didn't detect anything. He was about to give up when he saw a slight movement. He'd only caught it because of his low angle. He focused on the spot and realized it was a human foot taking careful steps towards the ambush. He patted his carbine, knowing he could have it in firing position in an instant. The action would be in front of him though and he didn't know exactly where all the friendlies were. He would be sitting this one out unless he was needed.

He watched the foot, his eyes slits. The foot was barely discernible, but it was a bare foot, not the notched toe boots of the Japanese soldier. It looked like a native's foot. Were they that far out?

The foot moved forward, and was blocked by foliage. He lost track of it and was about to look to O'Connor, but sudden movement from all sides caught his eye. The ambush was being sprung, but there was no shooting. The natives had their ancient rifles aimed and ready to fire.

Carver stood, confusion on his face. He looked back at his men who were also standing and trying to see what was happening. Carver walked forward and stood beside Morrisey who was standing with his new carbine aimed at the ground. In front of him were thirty natives, all armed and looking from muzzle to muzzle. The natives stood in the killing zone of the L shaped ambush. Their weapons were down. There was a white man amongst them. Carver recognized Welch instantly. Carver wanted to know what the hell was going on, but kept his mouth shut.

Morrisey spoke in Pidgin and addressed a big native beside Welch. Dunphy sidled up beside Carver and tried to translate. He whispered, "He's telling them they're surrounded and they should put down their weapons." Ahio spoke and Dunphy translated again, "He's saying something about coming to eat, or feast or something."

Morrisey laughed and continued. "You always come in battle formation? And where are your women? They don't enjoy our hospitality?" he pointed at Welch, "I fear my colleague has promised you things he has no right to promise, Chief." His eyes went dark, "Now, put down your weapons and go back to your village."

Welch spoke, "You pompous ass. Chief Ahio deserves to rule both villages as it was long ago."

"I fear Mr. Welch's view of history is as false as his friendship, Ahio. He is an ambitious man who has no interest in anything except his own advancement. He's using you, coercing you to war for his own ends. He's no friend to you or your village."

Ahio looked at Welch and was about to speak, but Welch spoke first, in English. "You're a disgrace, Morrisey. You're leading your men against the very men you should be fighting for. The Japanese will win this war and the sooner you realize that, the more of your precious natives you'll save from the slaughter."

Captain Morrisey stood in stunned silence. His eyes hardened and he found his voice, "You're a traitor." He bared his teeth like a feral animal, "You. You were the one that led those yellow bastards to the village. You killed my wife and child." The realization struck him like a blow. The image of his baby boy and his mutilated wife crossed his mind. He saw red.

Quick as a jungle cat, Welch brought up his carbine and fired three quick shots. Morrisey went to his knee bringing his carbine to his shoulder with practiced calm. The bullets sliced past his ear. He fired in rapid succession, but Welch was already diving away. As Welch lunged, he fired into the surprised ambushers. Two went down spinning. Ahio's natives brought up their rifles, but Morrisey's men were ready and fired into the men at close range. Plumes of blood spouted and sprayed as men's bodies shattered.

Morrisey tried to track Welch, but he was too quick. A native was bringing his rifle to bear, but Morrisey pulled the trigger and dropped him, his mouth in a surprised 0 shape. The survivors turned and ran. Ahio hadn't moved a muscle during the slaughter. Now, in a booming voice he yelled, "Stop!"

Morrisey's men looked at him and the fleeing men stopped, heeding their leader's command. The sound of a single man crashing through the jungle faded as Welch ignored the order and continued to flee. Morrisey pointed at two of his men, then towards the sound. The two natives took off like they'd been shot out of a cannon.

Captain Morrisey stood and walked up to Ahio, who handed his brand new carbine to him. Morrisey hefted it, realizing it was one of the American weapons. Welch must have stolen it.

Ahio's men returned to his side and each man kneeled down and placed his rifle on the jungle floor. Ahio said, "We surrender to you."

Morrisey nodded and was about to speak when there was a loud wail from behind the ambush. Soon more cries filled the air and Morrisey's men started fading from their ambush positions, leaving them unguarded. Carver and his men filled in the gaps as the natives rushed to their comrades.

Morrisey, seeing the Americans had the situation in hand, turned to see what had happened. He went to the men forming a circle around someone on the ground. Lying prone was old Chief Pavu, his lifeless eyes staring into the jungle canopy above. He looked like he may be resting. The only indication of anything awry was the perfect hole in the center of his forehead with a thin trickle of blood snaking down past his nose. The men were in mourning, tears flowed from the eyes that only moments before had been hard and deadly.

Chief Pavu had been old when they were born. There had never been another chief. He seemed to never age and the men thought him impervious to the passing of time. They believed he would live forever and now the impossible had happened. He was dead.

Morrisey looked at his old friend and felt bile rise in his throat. He knelt and put his hand over his old friend's face and closed his eyes. He looked like he was merely sleeping, his lined face serene. He was at peace. He wiped a tear from the corner of his eye and went back to Ahio and his men.

They knew what had happened and were as sad as the others. Their heads were bowed, their arms hanging from their sides. They'd been excited for war only minutes before, but none of them wished any harm towards the legendary Chief Pavu. Even the stoic Ahio had his head bowed in sorrow. Morrisey clenched his jaw. *These simple men wanted war, seeing only glory. Now good men are dead and they've lost their stomach for it. Fools.*

He spoke, "This is murder and there must be punishment." He pointed into the jungle, "The man who pulled the trigger has escaped, but you, Chief Ahio are complicit in this heinous act. It cannot go unpunished."

Ahio nodded once and looked Morrisey in the eye. "I agree. I take responsibility for Chief Pavu's death." He looked around at the other men feeding the earth with their blood. "And these."

## 21

C hief Ahio and his men were led under guard back to Captain Morrisey's village. They carried their dead in makeshift stretchers they'd put together with tree branches and thick vines. Chief Pavu was carried with loving hands at the head of the somber procession. Sergeant Carver and his squad took the tail-end of the column and halfheartedly checked their rear.

When they entered the village the women and children dropped to their knees, mourning their fallen Chief. There seemed to be nothing but death here. The village hadn't seen such devastation since the time before the Colonials. The bright, warm air took on a dark feel. Sergeant Carver wanted to get out of there as quickly as possible. He had a mission to complete and the longer he took to do it the more men's lives he was putting at risk. He thought about his comrades slugging it out along the lowlands without the benefit of his eyes on the enemy.

He pulled Morrisey aside. "I've gotta get to that cursed hill ASAP. Is the best way to go back to the ridge and cross the valley?"

"As I said before, it's been a long time since I've been there, but yes, that route would make the most sense." He looked him in the eye, "My natives have some seemingly strange beliefs to our western eyes, but they usually have good reasons."

"Are you saying the hill really is cursed?"

He shook his head, "Probably not in the sense you're thinking. It might be better to think of it as being bad luck."

Carver looked annoyed "Well spirits or not, we've gotta bee-line it and report in. Wish we had more current reconnaissance on it. Seems a mighty good piece of real estate to be unoccupied. You can probably see all the way to Cape Esperance."

Morrisey nodded, "Indeed you can. As I said, the time I was there was eerie. The wind blows and makes all sorts of odd sounds. Probably just whistling through the rocks on the top, but it sounds a lot like a wailing..." he paused and looked to the sky, "Spirit, I suppose."

Sergeant Carver looked annoyed, wanting information, not superstition. Morrisey continued, "The easiest way to get there is back up along the ridge you just left, then down into the valley, yes. You'll find a footpath leading to the creek at the bottom of the valley. The trail takes up again about one hundred meters downstream. Follow it to the top. It becomes more of a game trail the higher you climb." Carver nodded his thanks. "If there are Japs up there, and there very well might be, you don't want to take the trail the last two hundred meters. It's very wide open and they'd see you coming."

Carver rolled up the map and shoved it into his inside pocket. He stepped back from Captain Morrisey and gave him a crisp salute. "It's been an honor, Sir. Thanks for all you've done." Morrisey returned the salute then put out his hand. Carver shook it, "Sorry about your men."

Morrisey nodded, "And yours, Sergeant. Someday when this bloody war's over we'll have to meet up and tip a beer and remember our valiant soldiers."

Carver nodded and released his hand. He looked to his men who were ready to tackle the next phase of their mission. "Let's get on with it," he murmured.

With each step away from the village they felt lighter, like walking from a smoke filled room into cool night air.

O'Connor took point, Carver following close behind then Dunphy and Hooper watching their back trail. Everyone except Dunphy had been along this path many times and weren't overly concerned with running into Japanese patrols. Hooper pushed Dunphy forward,

Dunphy pushed Carver, who pushed O'Connor and soon they were running flat out across the ridge. It felt good to move fast, to put the death smell of the camp behind them, to get on with a new phase, to stretch their legs.

When they got to their original outpost they hunched over hands on knees breathing hard. O'Connor was laughing. It had become a race near the end and Hooper had passed Carver and almost took O'Connor before the ridge ran out. O'Connor held his hands up in victory and did a happy dance.

When Carver caught his breath he barked, "Okay, let's cut the horseshit. Bring me the radio, Hooper. I'll check in with Division." As he called in and listened to the response, Hooper shoved O'Connor who'd been rubbing it in more. Carver shook his head, *Christ, they're like children. Hell, they are children.*

He signed off. "Alright cut it out you two. Here's the deal; they want us over there right now." He pointed to the hill in the distance. He looked at his watch. "I figure we can get to the base of the hill before dark. I don't wanna go to the top at night in case there's Japs. We can check it out in the morning. If it's empty were golden, if not, well, there are only four of us. We'll cross that bridge when we come to it."

He continued, "We need to gather our shit and get our asses moving. Division's gonna make another push two days from now and they want us spotting the Jap artillery that our boys can't seem to suppress. They think they might be up on a hill giving them the extra range they need to hit our troops without ours able to hit back. Without our help the attack may fail. You saw what happened last time." He paused looking at each man for questions. When there weren't any, he nodded, "Okay. We move in seven minutes." With that the men went to the remains of the hut and collected the batteries, ammo and C-rats stowed there.

It was past noon and the sun was at its hottest. The trail was easy to find; it started off the nose of the ridge and was well worn. O'Connor followed it easily. Soon the sparse vegetation on top gave way to thick jungle and their surroundings condensed into a few yards to either side. O'Connor kept the pace quick, but this was new territory, so he was careful. The men were spread twenty yards apart, no use having one grenade take them all out.

They made good time to the bottom of the valley. The creek was bigger than expected. The water was crystal clear. They sat in it while they filled their canteens. The water coursing around and over them cooled their bodies. The sweat and grime washed off and they felt halfway human again.

After ten minutes, Carver gave the order to move. Normally there would be bitching and complaining, but since there were only four of them, there was no one to complain to. They'd been reduced down to their smallest element, a sergeant, a corporal and two privates. They understood that their survival was in each other's hands more than it had ever been. If they lost it out here, their bodies would never be found. No one would ever know what happened to them; it would be like they'd never existed. The war would continue without them. It was a sobering thought and kept them focused.

O'Connor walked down the creek and found the trail leading towards the hill. At least he hoped it was the correct one. It was barely a trail at all, more like a game track that didn't get used much. It meandered here and there, the general direction towards the hill. O'Connor took point. His pace was slower, the jungle thicker on this side of the creek and they were traveling uphill. Soon the pleasant feel of the creek was a distant memory as the late sun beat down. Their dungarees turned a dark green as their sweat soaked through.

After an hour the sun went behind the hill and the jungle darkened. Sergeant Carver jogged up to O'Connor and halted him, "Let's get off the trail and lay in for the night." O'Connor nodded and pushed his way past thick vines and bush until he found a relatively open space. Carver nodded and informed the others they'd found their home for the evening. It had been a long day and the men were exhausted. "Dunphy, watch our back trail while the others get some chow. We'll relieve you soon." Dunphy nodded and disappeared the way they'd come. Carver watched him go and realized it was the first time he'd given the man an order without any kind of push-back. The past week of slavery had done the prima-dona some good.

Without speaking, the men tore into their C-rats. Carver did an inventory of what he had left, about three days' worth if they went to half rations. He'd give the men the news when they were on the ridge. Maybe they could find themselves a pig to butcher.

THE NIGHT PASSED WITHOUT INCIDENT. O'Connor's watch was from 2:00-4:00AM. He thought he heard human voices coming from the hill, but when he focused on the sound it disappeared. *I'm imagining things.* He'd been in the bush too long. He'd heard about guys going nuts out here. Cracking up like fragile eggs.

It was still dark when he went to where Carver was sleeping and nudged his foot. He sat up quickly with a knife shimmering in the dull pre-dawn light. O'Connor smiled and whispered, "Good morning."

Carver put his knife away, "Wake the others, eat some of the dried meat we have left and we'll get moving in ten minutes." As O'Connor turned to comply, Carver touched his shoulder, "Anything last night?" O'Connor shrugged. He was about to tell him about the voices, thought better of it and shook his head.

O'Connor was on point. The going was tough, the trail was steep and he was breathing hard within minutes. To make matters worse, it looked like it was about to rain. The sun never lit the sky. A dark cloud settled on the area and soon the first fat rain drops splattered off the jungle leaves. O'Connor looked to the sky. It looked like it was going to open up any second. He didn't have long to wait. One second he was dry, the next he was soaked. The rain came in sheets. He couldn't see more than a few feet. He felt like he was standing inside a raging waterfall. The noise was deafening. They stopped to top off their canteens. They held the open tops under large leaves and funneled the rain. It took seconds.

Sergeant Carver waved him forward. He went twenty feet and the trail angled up steeper. It was getting tough to keep his feet in the slick mud. He took a step and lost his footing on the trail, which was now more like a river. He went down and started sliding. He grabbed a branch and arrested his descent. He looked behind him searching for Sergeant Carver. He couldn't see anything. He tried to stand, but slipped again. He stayed down, gripping the vine, waiting for Carver to catch up. After five minutes he decided it was futile. He gauged the slope and released the vine. At first nothing happened, but soon gravity and physics took over and he started sliding down the path. He kept his speed under control by digging in his leather boots, but he was gaining speed. He reached for a passing vine, but missed. He was about to dig his rifle into the mud when he crashed into something solid. At first, he thought it must be a tree, but it was cussing and yelling. He came to a stop and realized it was Sergeant Carver. He yelled, "Sorry Sarge, lost control."

"Holy shit, we can't go any further until this lets up."

Carver stood and went to take a step. O'Connor tried to warn him, but it was too late. The only thing keeping him from sliding was Carver's body. When he stepped away he started sliding again. The movement dislodged Carver's foot and he crashed down on him with an 'oof.' O'Connor tried to dig his rifle butt in, but it acted more as a rudder than a brake. They careened down the path, both men reaching for branches, rocks or vines, but it was no use. They were firmly in the grip of the slippery slope.

They busted through a layer of bush and only had a second before they slammed into Dunphy, who went down like a bowling pin. He yelled in surprise, finding himself on his back and coming down behind Carver and O'Connor. Hooper never saw them coming. He had his head down, pulling his hat over his eyes in a useless attempt to keep water out of his face. He had an instant to look up before he was knocked aside and sent into the jungle like he'd been shot from a bow. They finally left the trail when it took a turn and they slid off into the jungle. O'Connor instinctively went into a ball, expecting the impact from a tree or rock any second. It didn't happen though. He stopped, uncurled and did an inventory of his body parts; all intact.

The rain hadn't let up. He looked through sheets of water, putting his hand over his eyes like shading them from the sun. He had to find the others. Carver couldn't be far. He thought he saw a dark shape off to his left, so he carefully took a step towards it, but it was a rock. He put his hand on it, relieved he hadn't hit it. He'd be dead or shattered beyond repair if he had. He heard the unmistakable cussing of

Sergeant Carver off to his right. He crawled towards the voice. It sounded like it was right next to him, but he couldn't see him. "Sarge? Where are you?"

The response was faint, but close, "Here. Down here."

O'Connor looked down, but could only see rain and bush. He took a tentative step and felt his foot break through the bush and dangle in the air. He pulled back. He was at the edge of a cliff and Carver was down there somewhere. "Carver!" he yelled.

The response was more immediate, "Down here. Hurry!"

The rain let up a little and O'Connor could see better. He moved laterally and held onto a large smooth barked tree. Now he could see the cliff. It was well hidden; he didn't remember seeing it on the way up. As far as cliffs go it wasn't much. The drop was only fifteen feet. He leaned out holding onto the tree, searching for Carver.

He almost missed him. He was covered in mud, hanging from a thick root. Water careened off the lip of the cliff and was threatening to drown him. He had his head forward trying to keep his mouth clear. O'Connor almost laughed, but didn't when he realized what the consequences of a fall would be. He'd drop fifteen feet onto a jumble of vicious looking black rocks. At the very least he'd break a leg.

He cupped his hand over his mouth and yelled, "Hold on, Sarge! I'm coming, hold on." Using the trees and vines he made his way to where he guessed he'd gone over the ledge. He cautiously leaned through the bush. He was directly above him. "Sarge, I'm here." Carver looked up and sputtered as muddy water filled his nose and mouth. He put his head back down.

O'Connor looked between his legs. The water was digging out a new rivulet which was emptying off the cliff in a spout. "Hold on. I'll try to fix the water."

He turned to the jungle, looking for something to redirect the flow. Nothing jumped out at him so he jammed his foot into the small stream. Water piled against his boot. The spigot running over Carver stopped abruptly. Carver looked up, his eyes seething. "Get me out of here," he growled.

The water was coming around his boot. He realized if he moved he'd create a huge deluge of water falling directly on Carver. The force might be enough to make him fall. He looked around in a panic. "Can you pull yourself up? I can't hold this water back much longer."

Carver attempted a pull-up. Without the water beating down he was able to pull himself halfway up, but his pack and his sodden clothes kept him from making it all the way. The water started cascading over O'Connor's boot and the flow gained volume. Carver moved laterally along the length of the root. He was able to move eight inches to the left. The water was pounding on his right shoulder and splashing into his face. He turned away and screamed an obscenity.

O'Connor yelled, "I've gotta pull my foot out so I can get to you. Get ready for more water." He pulled his foot out, but in its place a large rock appeared, dropped there by a grinning Dunphy with Hooper right behind. With the water flow stemmed, they formed a human chain and O'Connor reached down to Carver. "Give me your hand."

Carver noticed the flow of water was gone. He looked up scowling. "Get me outta here." O'Connor nodded and with his left hand holding Hooper's he reached down with his right. He grabbed his wrist and pulled. With the help of the others they had Carver on the correct side of the cliff in seconds. Carver took his pack off and laid on his back breathing hard.

"You okay?" Carver nodded, but didn't speak. He rubbed his forearms trying to get circulation back to them. His hands tingled as blood flow brought them back to life. He grit his teeth, his muscles were screaming. The rain had subsided to half of what it had been. "Where's your Thompson?" O'Connor asked.

Carver sat up looking around. He shook his head, "I lost it off the cliff, I think."

Dunphy went to the edge, laid on his stomach and peered over the side. He came back, "Yeah it's at the bottom of the cliff, the stocks shattered, can't tell if the barrels bent."

Hooper directed him to see if he could recover it. Dunphy nodded and carefully worked his way around the cliff and down the steep slope.

Carver got to his feet and looked himself over. He was surprisingly clean. The constant shower had washed away the mud. "That was some ride."

O'Connor chuckled, "It sure was. Never seen anything like it. It was like the mountain decided it didn't want us on it."

Carver thought about what Morrisey had said about the native's superstitions. He looked up the trail they'd slid down. The rain was slackening. If the trend continued it would be finished soon. "Let's try side-hilling this thing. The trail's too muddy, but we should be able to cut across the hill so we don't have to go straight up." O'Connor followed his gaze and nodded.

Dunphy returned with the Thompson. The stock was shattered and the barrel was dinged and slightly bent. "This thing's fucked."

He handed it to Carver who inspected it. He tried to eject the magazine, but it was jammed. He couldn't budge it. He threw the Thompson off the cliff and they could hear it shatter against the rocks. He pulled out his .45 caliber 1911 he had strapped to his belt, checked the action and nodded. "Let's move out, take it easy and remember, we don't know what's up there."

O'Connor took point and started side-hilling the slope. It would take longer going back and forth across the hill, but in the long run it would work out better and keep them from slipping back down the slope.

Two hours later O'Connor stopped and crouched. The vegetation ran out near the top, giving way to moss and fern covered rocks. Carver caught up and looked to the top of the hill. He couldn't see the actual top since it was over the crest. He looked down to the valley and across. The ridge they'd started from was shrouded in mist. "We're on the side of the hill. Probably a good way to approach. If there's Japs, they'll be looking the wrong way." He waved the men forward. They'd go straight up from here, carefully. When they could see the top, they'd halt and give it a good look.

The men checked their weapons. They spread out and started up fifteen yards abreast. Carver kept his sidearm holstered. He was able to move much better with both hands free. He moved from rock to rock, keeping three points of contact on the slippery rocks. Soon he was well ahead of the others. He stopped and looked behind him, catching his breath. He went another twenty yards and was able to see the top of the hill. He crouched behind a boulder and peered over the top. He dug into his pack and found Morrisey's binoculars. They were dry and intact inside the case. He scanned the top slowly then down to the ground leading up to it. Nothing but more rocks and trees. He kept scanning until the others were in line with him. He pulled out his .45 and waved them forward. They went slower now that they were exposed.

When they were yards from the top, Carver went flat and scanned the final terrain. It was as quiet as a tomb. He stayed crouched and went to the crest of the hill. He stood to his full height and waved them forward. He pointed to the other side and Dunphy and Hooper went to check it out. Carver kneeled and looked at the view. The rain was coming off the jungle in steam. He couldn't see the beach or even the ocean; he was in a fog bank that was getting thicker by the minute.

He saw Hooper's head pop up and he was signaling him to come. He stayed crouched, his pistol at the ready and went to him. When he was close, Hooper said, "There's no one here, but there sure as shit was." He moved to the other side of the hill, the part that would be facing the American lines. Carver saw the water filled holes spaced fifteen yards apart, foxholes. "There's Jap stuff all over the place, boot prints too, the ones with the funny toe notch."

Carver took his jungle hat off and rubbed his forehead. He had a decision to make. Either the Japanese that were here were long gone or they were simply on a patrol and would be returning. He asked O'Connor, "Can you tell how long ago they left?"

O'Connor shook his head, "The rain's done a number on the prints; most are washed away, just vague imprints. That rain storm would've filled those holes in a hurry. They were probably dry this morning."

"Well, at least we know they haven't been here since the rain storm, couple hours anyway. It's not like them to leave open usable foxholes though. Standard Jap procedure is to fill 'em in when they're done with 'em, just like ours."

Hooper nodded. "Probably planning on coming back. Question is, when?"

Carver continued, "We can't see anything until this fog clears out anyway, so let's find cover and see if they show. We'll dig in and have our grenades ready. We'll be outnumbered if they come back."

They dug in well away from the foxholes, in the rocky, muddy ground. After an hour the wind whipped up. The men hunkered down, feeling cold for the first time since being on the island.

The men's ears perked up when they heard what sounded like voices. O'Connor, who'd been dozing, went onto his stomach and pushed his carbine forward, his finger on the trigger. He strained to hear the voices, but they were distant and not the guttural sound he'd come to equate with Japanese soldiers. Whoever it was, there was a lot of them. The voices seemed to be vying for the spotlight, like a room full of chatty women. It was wrong somehow. The voices weren't quite right, there were no words, not even language really. He closed his eyes trying to decipher what was being said.

The wind increased and the voices got louder. He smiled and looked over to Carver who was gripping his pistol and squinting towards the sound. O'Connor waved his hand to get his attention. He mouthed the word, 'wind' and pointed to the air. Carver didn't get it and signaled him over. O'Connor crawled to him and whispered, "I think it's the wind whistling through the rocks."

Carver listened hard. He nodded, "Only one way to find out." He went into a crouch and looked to the others all hunkered as low as they could go. He signaled for them to cover him and he went forward, his pistol leading the way.

O'Connor watched him, impressed once again at how well he moved. *Not bad for an old guy.* When he got to the crest they could see him relax. His shoulders lost their tension and he stood up. He waved them up and called, "Bring the radio."

The others looked at one another, still hearing the voices, but stood and trotted to their sergeant's side. Once on the ridge the sound of the voices was obviously coming from the wind hitting the rocks. The sharp ridges and tiny holes of the volcanic rock were acting as perfect noise makers. The wind speed was perfect for sounding like high pitched human voices. Carver folded his arms across his chest and told the men about Morrisey and his native's superstitions. "I'll bet this is what they're afraid of; a little wind." He pointed, "Look at that view.

We've got a perfect view of the Jap lines from here." Indeed, it was almost too good and the men instinctively crouched. The fog had cleared. The Japs were miles away, but they were much closer than they'd been from the ridge across the valley.

They hunkered down out of the wind and Carver checked in with Division. He kept his call short, not wanting to use the precious batteries. Division informed him the push would happen the day after tomorrow at dawn and they should be ready to direct naval and air assets onto targets.

He'd signed off and spent the next hour scanning potential targets, writing down coordinates on his map with his nub of a pencil when O'Connor ran up to him and said, "Japs coming up the trail."

## 22

Thomas Welch was running through the jungle at top speed, crashing through the bush, vines and branches cutting his arms and cheeks. He hadn't heard any shooting or felt any near misses for a while. *Can I slow down? Are they still after me?*

He slowed his pace, taking more care with his steps. His breath was coming in short spurts and sweat poured from his body. He'd have to stop soon or risk dropping from heat exhaustion.

He stopped and tried to calm his breathing, listening to the jungle, listening for pursuit. He wiped his brow, only hearing normal jungle sounds. There were no gunshots, no yelling. He thought he'd come a couple kilometers from the ambush site. In the jungle, even a half kilometer was enough to disappear and he was a master at disappearing in the jungle.

He was surrounded by thick vegetation. He thought about the terrain around him, picturing his direction and speed from the ambush. He figured he was south of Ahio's village. He knew his path would be easy to follow from his headlong run. Now it was time to lose any pursuers. He'd move quietly and carefully from now on, leaving no signs of his passage. He was as skilled as any native and was sure he could make himself invisible.

He checked his new carbine. He'd fired four shots. He was pretty sure he hadn't hit Morrisey with any of them. He gritted his teeth, *how had the old fox known he was coming?* He'd most likely never know the answer. He took a drink from his canteen and thought about his next move. He couldn't go back to the village; he couldn't go to any of his old haunts. News traveled fast amongst the natives. He'd be hunted. He only had one option left and it sent shivers up his spine to think about. He'd have to get to the Japanese lines and somehow get to Colonel Araki.

He took a deep breath knowing the odds of getting through the Japanese lines without being shot weren't good. He started moving further south to bypass Ahio's village. Once around it he'd head north-west until he ran into the Japanese lines. It would help that he was fluent in Japanese, but once they saw he was a white man, would they shoot first? He'd just have to convince them.

Getting through the lines might be the least of his worries though. He cringed thinking how Araki would receive him. He'd failed at everything he'd set out to do. Colonel Araki did not take failure well. They went back a long way, but friendships only went so far in war.

As HE MADE his way through the jungle, he remembered the last time he'd been in Japan with the then *Lieutenant* Araki. It was years before the war. He'd been out of Japan for four years attending university in London. Upon graduation, he made the long trip to Japan to surprise his old friend on the day he would be accepting his commission as a 2nd Lieutenant in the Imperial Japanese Army.

The voyage had been long and arduous. Diplomatic relations between Japan and Britain had deteriorated over the years, but Welch didn't worry too much about it; politics ebbed and flowed as often as the tides. When he walked off the ship though, he was struck by how much had changed in the four short years since he'd left. The cities were bustling with feverish activity. He was astonished at some of the new buildings and more than a little intimidated with the pervasive military presence. As a European, he received withering stares from the young men in uniform. Had things deteriorated so much as to incite violence at the mere sight of a foreigner?

He'd cabled ahead to Araki's family telling them of his surprise visit. They'd written back a short cable telling him he shouldn't come. He'd been distraught. The Araki family had always been close friends; in fact, they'd been the one family he and his family had bonded with during his father's diplomatic career. It was unimaginable that he wouldn't be welcome. He'd ignored the note and decided he'd go anyway. He could stay in a local ryokan or inn. He'd see them at the ceremony and hopefully his presence wouldn't embarrass them.

The next two days he'd walked around Tokyo visiting his favorite places. He was surprised at the changes. There was an anger towards him that he couldn't understand. People that once happily sold him a newspaper or his favorite pastry, Sata andagi, with a happy word or a joke, now looked at him with suspicion and even fear. They'd look around as if searching to see if they were being watched. On the second day he was convinced he was being followed. It was never obvious, but he had the distinct feeling he was being watched.

He'd planned on staying in the city for at least two weeks, but decided he'd leave as soon as he'd seen his friend commissioned. He'd travel to the countryside and visit some of his favorite gardens. Maybe it was only Tokyo.

He'd shown up at the ceremonial garden where Araki would receive his commission. He entered quietly and sat in the back so as not to create a stir. He received withering looks from the Araki family, which made the blood drain from his face. The family that had been such a huge part of his childhood were looking at him with outright hatred; or was it fear? He was frozen in indecision. He decided he wasn't wanted and was about to leave, but it was too late. The ceremony was starting. It would be rude to leave.

He watched as each graduate received the coveted commission of a Japanese officer. When it was Gobo Araki's turn, he stood proudly before the Colonel and received his 2nd Lieutenant's patch. He saluted the Colonel with a hand that looked as though it could cut through metal. Welch was stunned at his friend's transformation. He'd always been a skinny man, but he'd filled out, his body thick and strong. He had the bandy legs of a man who rode horses.

When the ceremony was over, the crowd stood and bowed towards their newest members of the Army. Welch stood head and shoulders above the audience and Araki caught sight of his old friend. He gave a slight smile and winked. Welch felt a weight lift from his shoulders; at least his friend hadn't changed so much. He smiled back at him.

After the short reception he finally got to speak with his friend face to face. They went to a sushi bar, drank Saki and laughed. It was good to talk with his friend again. Araki told him about the changes sweeping the country. He was genuinely excited to be a member of the Army and was convinced his generation would make history and he'd be at the forefront. The talk sounded dangerous to Welch, warlike. He told him so and Gobo Araki responded. "The West has ignored us for the past decade, slowly forcing us into submission. We are a proud people and won't let our superior race be trodden on in such a manner."

Welch, feeling the alcohol, looked at him in disbelief, "Superior race? You sound like that crazy son-of-a-bitch Hitler. Since when are you a racist?"

Araki grinned, "Not racist, realist. Our Emperor is ordained by God, so of course we're superior to the mixed races."

Welch was stunned. He stood and paced, rubbing his chin. "So, you feel any gaijin, myself included, is not as pure so is inferior? Am I inferior to the street urchin selling fish at the wharf?" He was red in the face. He'd never known his friend to carry such disturbing beliefs.

Araki smiled, "I'm not going to argue something that is obvious. I'm not debating the issue." Welch shook his head not knowing how to continue. He suddenly wanted to get out of the bar and out of the country. 2nd Lieutenant Araki smiled, "I was visited by a Colonel this afternoon after the commissioning. He asked about you."

Welch raised his eyebrows, "Oh?" He looked at his friend, but he couldn't seem to focus. He shook his head trying to clear his vision. *The saki's stronger than I remember.* He grabbed the side of the table and held on as the room started to spin. He tried to speak, but couldn't seem to make a sound. His tongue felt like a bloated fish; he couldn't make it work. He released the table and held his head trying to get the world to stop spinning.

He woke hours later in a white room without furniture, except for the medical gurney he was strapped to. He looked side to side until he felt his head throb. He shut his eyes experiencing the worst headache he'd ever felt. A man was beside him and he spoke softly to him, "Relax Mr. Welch. No harm will come to you if you relax. Can you relax?"

He spent the next week and a half at the facility. At first, he was afraid, after all he'd been kidnapped, but he was released from his restraints soon after waking and he'd been treated like an honored guest ever since.

2nd Lieutenant Araki visited often and they'd sit and talk for hours about events happening in Japan and around the world. He also spoke to knowledgeable men of power with unique insight into the way they thought their country and indeed the world, should be developed. Their plans were auspicious and full of optimism and they wanted him to be a part of them. His decision to help them was sealed when they assured him he'd be well compensated, both in money and power. They rewarded his decision by putting him in a richly decorated room with a huge bed in the center. Soon he was joined by four beautiful geisha girls who kept him up all night.

He'd sailed back to England with plans to join the Foreign Service. He applied and got what was considered the bottom of the Foreign Service barrel, the Solomon Island chain protectorate. He'd spent the next four years working in the Solomons, his most recent assignment, Guadalcanal.

HE'D BEEN WALKING for three hours towards the Japanese lines. He hadn't seen any signs of pursuit. It wasn't surprising since he was very skilled at hiding his trail. Even if they were following him, it would be difficult and slow. He'd be at the lines long before they could catch up with him.

He had to be more careful now. He was close to the Japanese line.

He'd be shot on sight if he was seen. In order to survive, he had to be the one that saw them before they saw him.

He came to the edge of a small meadow and crouched in the tall grass. He listened and thought he heard voices. He melted into the jungle and listened as boots tromped through the field towards his position. There was no more talking, but he knew it had to be a Japanese patrol. Then he saw them, no more than ten yards away. They walked past his position. He thought about calling to them, but soldiers on patrol were jumpy and it would be risky. He waited until they passed out of sight and hearing, then followed their path back the way they'd come.

He had his rifle slung over his shoulder, *no reason to give someone an excuse.* He thought about what he would say. Should he call out as if he were a soldier coming in or simply walk in with his hands held high pleading his case? He hadn't made up his mind when he came to the Japanese line. He laid down and crawled forward a couple yards. He peeled back the brush and could clearly see a a foxhole occupied by four soldiers. Their rounded helmets were poking above the hole. He could make out their chatter, but no words. It was good to hear the Japanese language again.

He called out in Japanese, "Friends, I'm coming in, don't shoot. I'm your prisoner, don't shoot."

The four men put their Arisaka rifles to their shoulders and yelled, "Who goes there? Holy sun, Holy sun."

They were looking for a counter-sign that he couldn't know. He called out, "I don't know the counter-sign. I'm standing up, I'm not dangerous. I'm your prisoner." He took a deep breath. He'd either live or die in the next few seconds. He put his hands up and stood. He was fifteen feet away. The soldiers were sighting down their rifles, their fingers tightening on the triggers. "Don't shoot, I'm here to see Colonel Araki. Colonel Araki is my friend. I'm your prisoner, don't shoot."

A stocky sergeant bounced out of the hole and keeping his rifle trained on him, motioned for him to come closer. Welch did so slowly, keeping his hands up and trying to keep his smile as friendly as possible. When he was a few feet away he said, "I'm your prison..."

The sergeant was half his size, but thick and mean looking. He yelled, "Shut-up!" and butt stroked him in the gut. Welch bent over, grabbing his stomach. The next swing was across his chin and he fell to the ground, blood gushing from his mouth from several broken teeth. The other soldiers helped their sergeant pull their prize into their lines. They all punched and kicked him, taking great delight in inflicting pain. The sergeant ordered two men to stay in the hole as he and the other dragged him through the lines.

He was taken to a green, open-sided tent, pushed into a chair, his hands tied to a post and punched mercilessly until a lieutenant walked in and the enlisted men snapped to attention, stepping back from their labors. The lieutenant leaned down and inspected the bloody face. "Who told you to beat this man?" none of the soldiers responded. The lieutenant screamed, "Answer me, Sergeant!"

The stocky sergeant jumped and squirmed, "No one, Sir."

"Then why did you do so?"

The sergeant looked confused. His eyes squinting even more than they naturally did, "He's an enemy soldier, Sir, he surrendered without a fight; a coward, sir. Scum."

"I was told he spoke fluent Japanese and knows our Colonel Araki, our regimental commander."

The sergeant's face went white, "He said those things, but I think he must be a spy."

The lieutenant spun and looked down on the Sergeant's terrified face. He yelled, "Let me do the thinking, Sergeant." The sergeant cringed with each splatter of spittle upon his face. "Get out of my sight, back to your hole." The sergeant did a perfect left face and marched from the tent, followed by the private.

The lieutenant kneeled in front of the bleeding Welch and lifted his chin. Welch groaned in pain. "Who are you?"

Welch's head spun from the beating, but through blood and broken teeth he told the lieutenant everything. When his tale was told the lieutenant nodded and sent a man to summon Colonel Araki. He leaned down and whispered in Welch's ear, "If you're lying and I disturbed the Colonel for no reason, you'll be begging to die, gaijin."

Through cracked and bleeding lips he mumbled, "Tell him Thomas Welch is here. Thomas Welch. He knows me."

Ten minutes later Colonel Araki sauntered in and saw his old friend bound to the chair. Welch expected him to be angry at his treatment, expected to be released instantly, but instead the colonel crossed his arms across his chest and looked down on him. He told the lieutenant to leave and to put two guards outside the tent. The lieutenant left in a flourish of bows. "Well Thomas, it's been awhile. You were supposed to deliver the Americans to me by now. I'm assuming you being here is a sign of your failure?"

Welch pulled against his restraints. "Can you release me? I'm not leaving. I came to you." Colonel Araki only stared, awaiting an answer. For the first time, Welch was scared. He looked Araki in the eye, trying to see his old friend, but he wasn't there. He was replaced by a hard, remorseless warrior. "It's been a struggle. I couldn't convince the Americans to attack towards the hills. They were already committed to their battle plan and weren't going to change it." He looked down and shook his head. Blood dripped from the side of his mouth and pooled on his torn pants. He shook his head and whispered, "Nothing has gone according to plan. Nothing."

Araki paced, then slapped him hard across the face. The sudden violence caused Welch to cry out. Blood sprayed from his nose. "You have anything for me? Anything of use? Or have I been wasting my time all these years? Are you as useless as you appear?" Welch's shoulders heaved as tears welled. Araki yelled, "You've always been weak. You've always disappointed. I was a fool to think you could be useful to the Empire." He grabbed his chin and made him look into his eyes. "It's time to end my mistake; something I should have done a long time ago."

He went to his holster and started to unbutton his 9mm Nambu. Welch's eyes went big as saucers. He had no doubt his old friend was about to murder him. "W-wait, I have information that will help you."

Araki pulled the pistol from its holster and chambered a round. He placed the barrel against Welch's temple. "Go on."

"There's a unit, a squad of soldiers on a ridge overlooking the battlefield. They're calling in artillery and airstrikes on your positions. I, I know where they are. I can show you."

Colonel Araki smiled. He'd been taking accurate American fire over the past week. He had his men scouring the highlands, but they'd come up empty on the spotters' location. He assumed it was some high flying spotter plane's doing. He pulled the gun from his temple and called to one of the guards outside, "Bring me a map and cut this scum loose."

Welch looked at Araki and smiled. Blood soaked his shattered teeth, giving him the look of a bloodthirsty maniac. Colonel Araki scowled at him, "You look like shit, Thomas-san."

The soldier brought the map and handed it to Colonel Araki who spread it on a table. Welch was cut loose and he fell forward, rubbing his bleeding wrists. Colonel Araki looked at him while drumming his fingers. Welch staggered to his feet and joined him at the table. Araki said, "Show me."

It took Welch a moment to orient himself to the map. He put his bloody finger on the spot where they were and followed it up until stopping on a ridge. Araki nodded, "I wondered about that. It was our next searching point, but the Americans attacked and I had more pressing matters." He took out a pen from his inside pocket and circled the spot. He then brought his finger down the map to a spot in the hills far above his camp. He did some calculating in his head and nodded. "Our artillery can hit that ridge with a high arcing shot. You're sure of this, Thomas?" Welch nodded.

Colonel Araki took out a pad of paper and wrote down the coordinates. He called to the guard who was standing against the wall at attention. "Take this to the radio room. I want the forward battery on this fire mission, priority."

The private bowed, took the paper and ran outside. Ten minutes later the soft thumping of outgoing 175mm shells was heard. The barrage lasted five minutes. The ridge was hit with fifteen shells.

Colonel Araki had been outside the tent with his old friend beside him. Welch had a bandage wrapped across his jaw and his other wounds had been treated. Araki tried to see the impacts of the barrage, but the ridge was over the horizon of a closer ridge, so it was useless. He called Lieutenant Kogi over. He ran up and stood at attention. "I want confirmation on those shots. Take half of C Company to the ridge and check to make sure of its complete destruction. Then I want the ridge occupied and used as a spotter position." Lieutenant Kogi gave a crisp salute and was turning to leave. Colonel Araki asked, "Don't we have another unit in that area, Lieutenant?"

Lieutenant Kogi stopped and nodded, "Yes, Sir. A squad from D Company is on the hill to the west, due South of our position. They've recently returned to exchange radios. They had battery power, but they are stringing communication wire up to the position as we speak. I expect them to be back in position by this evening."

"Can they see the ridge from there?"

"It's across the valley, but I don't know if the jungle allows for a direct visual. When they check in I can have them scout the ridge."

"I'll send C Company anyway, but yes. Have them give me a damage report." Lieutenant Kogi bowed and went to find C Company. "One more thing, Lieutenant," he trotted back to stand in front of Colonel Araki at attention. "Mr. Welch will be accompanying you to the ridge. He knows the area and may be useful." He slapped Welch on the back, "Perhaps after our victory you can lead the company to Captain Morrisey's village."

Welch grinned, relishing the thought. He started working out just what he'd say to the arrogant son-of-a-bitch as he snuffed out his last breath.

## 23

Carver, Dunphy, Hooper and O'Connor were back on the other side of the ridge listening to the Japanese troops move back into their position. By the sound of it, there was probably a light platoon. They were far outnumbered. The evening sky was cloudy and the sun was shining through in shafts. The color infused the air with a beautiful lightness, adding a tint of pink to everything. If they weren't in such close proximity to death it would've been a glorious evening. They stayed hunkered down in their hastily dug foxholes. It was surreal listening to the enemy going about their business, completely oblivious to their presence.

The sun was just touching the horizon and the Japanese chatter had died down. The squad hadn't heard anything for a few minutes. Sergeant Carver wanted to find out what was happening. He signaled that he was going to take a look. O'Connor shook his head and pointed to himself. Carver grit his teeth, but knew it was a better choice. O'Connor was a better stalker. He nodded to O'Connor, who flashed him a thumbs up.

With his rifle cradled in the crooks of his elbows, he slithered from his hole. Soon he was out of sight. Waiting was agony for the rest of them. They expected to hear shouting, then shooting and then they'd die, but it didn't happen. twenty minutes passed before O'Connor slithered back to them. It was now completely dark. The clouds had cleared, unveiling a black sky dotted with millions of twinkling stars. Another gorgeous night on Guadalcanal.

O'Connor went straight to Carver's hole and whispered in his ear. "The Japs are all racked out in a camouflaged hut just over the ridge. We missed it before; it's well hidden. The foxholes are empty, but there's one sentry on top of the hill. He's got his back to us."

"All the others are in the hut? Are you sure? What about weapons? You see any machine guns or mortars?"

"The sentry's sitting behind a Nambu, but they must not be worried; it's not set up in a very good spot. I didn't see any mortars or any more sentries. They're sitting ducks."

Lieutenant Katayama was exhausted. His men had left this morning to replace their handheld radio with a wired unit. On their way down the sky had opened up and soaked them in an unnatural deluge of water. They had to hunker under the jungle canopy to keep from slipping down the face of the muddy hillside. It had delayed him an hour that he didn't have to spare. They double timed it the rest of the way, resupplied food, a new radio and a huge spool of communication cable. They'd used a rebellious donkey to haul the cable, but the animal proved to be more trouble than it was worth. When they got to the steep last kilometer, the donkey had stopped and wouldn't move. Finally, they unburdened the beast and hauled it up the final bit themselves. It was unwieldy to say the least. The final push had taken them two hours. They'd barely had enough time to settle in before it was dark.

Katayama laid in his hammock amongst his already snoring men and wondered if he should send a patrol to walk the perimeter. He'd put the hapless Corporal Rinko on the ridge overlooking their position with one of the machine guns. He was about to position the other one when he'd gotten the call on the new radio, asking him to report in about the ridge to the east. By the time he moved to a position where he could get a glimpse of it, the sky was darkening. He reported that it was too dark and that he'd check first thing in the morning. He'd never gotten around to placing his defenses for the night. As he slipped into sleep he felt confident in the fact that they hadn't seen any activity in their area for the past two weeks. The sound of his exhausted men's satisfied snores caressed him into a deep sleep from which he'd never awaken.

SERGEANT CARVER WENT to each man and pulled them into a circle. He let O'Connor tell them what he'd seen. They were relieved how vulnerable the usually hyper-vigilant enemy soldiers seemed to be. Carver said, "I'll sneak up on the sentry and take him out. O'Connor will lead us to the hut and we'll attack it with grenades. Everyone roll in two. Once it's done hose them down with at least a clip, then we'll finish whatever's left. Understand?"

O'Connor raised his hand, "I can take the sentry, Sarge. I know where he is. I know I can get close without being heard."

Carver looked him straight in the eye. "You ever do any wet work?"

O'Connor licked his suddenly dry lips. "I've killed lots of game with my knife. I know how to kill a man. It's easier than a wild animal." Carver nodded and O'Connor nodded back. He wondered why he'd volunteered for the grisly chore. He'd killed plenty of Japs, but this would be different. His victim would probably be sleeping and he'd have to end his life with a quick thrust of his blade into the man's brain. He'd feel the blood, the breath, the shit. He gulped, suddenly wishing he hadn't volunteered. It was too late now, he'd have to go through with it or forever be untrustworthy.

He slid forward the same way he'd scouted; he could barely hear the soft scrapes of the other men behind him. He moved without a sound. When he crested the hill, he could make out the dim outline of the sentry sitting behind the machine gun. The gun was aiming straight out into the darkness on the swivel tripod.

O'Connor stopped and realized he didn't have his knife out. He stopped crawling and moved his carbine from the crook of his arm to the dirt beside him. One of the others would pick it up for him. He reached back and pulled the knife out of the sheath at his belt without a sound. The familiar weight of the K-bar knife felt good in his hand, like an old friend. He silently prayed his old friend wouldn't let him down.

Keeping the knife in his right hand, he moved across the soft ground until he was ten yards from his target. This was the tricky part. He had to get off his belly and onto his rubber soled feet. He moved at glacial speed and after a minute he had his feet beneath him. He was in a low crouch and the slow movement had his muscles aching and sweat was pouring off his face and down the back of his neck to his ass crack. He took a few careful steps, each time searching the ground for any loose rock or twig that could give him away.

He was directly behind the man. Close enough to hear him breathing. It was now or never. He extended his arms into attack position. The knife had never felt so heavy. The man's head moved to the right slightly and he let out a long sigh. He was awake. The thought sent his heart racing. He closed his eyes for a fraction of a second, envisioning his next move, then he struck. His left hand reached in front of the man's face and clamped over his mouth while at the same time his knife plunged into the base of the neck just behind the ear. He pushed hard angling the blade up towards the brain. The sickening feel of the blade deep in the man's brain would haunt O'Connor for the rest of his young life. The Japanese soldier's body went rigid and he kicked out both legs, pushing him upwards. O'Connor kept the pressure on and rotated the blade back and forth, scrambling the brains. The soldiers' powerful backwards push almost sent O'Connor onto his back. He held on long enough for the man's last breath to escape him. He held him until he was sure he was beyond movement, then pushed him away. His right hand was covered in blood and brain matter.

Sergeant Carver was beside him, "Nice job, here's your rifle. Lead us to the hut." O'Connor took a deep breath and wiped his hand on the ground. He caught a whiff of the dead man's bowels and had to swallow the vomit rising in his throat. "Take it easy," Carver hissed.

O'Connor wiped the gore from the knife onto the Japanese soldiers' pants and sheathed it. He grabbed the carbine, took another breath and moved out in a low crouch.

They moved across the plateau. The night was dark, the stars the only light. He took them to the edge and stopped. He pointed and Carver strained to see. He leaned into Carver's ear, "It's forty yards, against the ledge."

Carver nodded and pushed him forward. He couldn't see the hut. He followed O'Connor until he stopped again. This time when he pointed he could see the well camouflaged structure silhouetted against the dark sky. He made a show of slinging his carbine and pulling two grenades off his belt. The others took the cue and did the same. With a grenade in each hand the men moved forward until they were just outside the small open doorway. They could hear the soft purr of men sleeping.

Carver held up his first grenade and pulled the pin. He didn't wait for the others; he let the spoon fly and rolled it into the open door. It was loud as it thunked the wooden floor and rolled around like a mini-bowling ball. He was pulling the pin on the second when he heard more thunks and rolling. He threw his second one in farther and turned to run. The others were beside him trying to find cover. They were ten yards away when the first grenade went off, followed in quick succession by the rest. The thatch siding of the hut muffled the sound, but it got louder as it shredded.

When the last grenade cooked off, they started firing into the dark hut as quickly as they could pull their triggers. Carver, holding his pistol, held his fire. After they'd gone through a magazine and were reloading, Carver yelled, "Cease fire, cease fire!" He crouched and the others followed suit. Their muzzle flashes had ruined their night vision. They stared into the spotty night listening for any sound of life. They heard moaning. Carver couldn't believe anyone could survive such an onslaught. They waited another five minutes until the spots dancing in their eyes settled. Carver rose, "Dunphy, get in there and check it out. We'll cover you."

Dunphy hesitated for an instant, but rose and followed orders. He stepped across the threshold and his feet slipped out from beneath him. He crashed to the wooden floor with a shout. Hooper ran forward, "You okay?"

The moaning got louder, responding to a human voice. Dunphy got to his feet and almost fell again, "Yeah, fine. The floor's slippery. I'm okay." He took another step further in. Hooper looked back at Carver who nodded for him to follow.

Inside the hut the darkness was complete. Dunphy took a step closer to the moaning. It was coming from the far corner. He kept his carbine trained on the sound. The moaning got louder, becoming a pained half scream. The floor was slippery, the copper smell of copious amounts of spilled blood filled his nostrils. Dunphy was on the edge of vomiting, but held it in by force of will. He took a step, but stumbled into something. He could barely see the outline of what was left of a man's torso. The roof had been blown away in parts and the starlight shimmered on the black blood covering the soldier's shredded uniform.

Hooper said, "Careful, he might be holding a grenade."

Dunphy looked back at him, "This guy? He's half gone."

"No, the moaner. We should shoot him just in case."

Dunphy stopped and aimed at the sound. He couldn't see the soldier, but he was only feet away from the sound. He aimed where he thought he'd be and pulled the trigger twice in quick succession. The sound within the hut seemed louder than the grenade blasts. Hooper yelled, "Goddammit, you coulda warned me. Now I can't see shit."

From outside Carver yelled, "Everything okay in there?"

Hooper stumbled out the way he'd come. When he tripped over the doorway, Carver reached out and caught him. Hooper shook him off, "I'm fine, Dunphy finished off the moaner. Fucked up my vision and hearing though." He walked past Carver and took a seat, rubbing his eyes.

Carver looked into the dark doorway, "Dunphy, you okay?"

Carver jumped back when Dunphy peered from the side of the doorway only inches from his face. "Yeah, I'm fine, Sarge." Carver stepped back as Dunphy came out and walked past all of them back to the ridge.

O'Connor watched him walk by, but didn't say a word. Dunphy

looked like he'd seen a ghost. He watched him stumble back the way they'd come and disappear onto the plateau. O'Connor looked back at Carver. "We'll leave it for tomorrow. It's too damned dark. Let's get back to our original positions and wait for the sun to rise." No one thought that was a bad idea.

IN THE PREDAWN DARKNESS, Carver woke the men and they returned to the hut. O'Connor and Dunphy dragged the dead sentry to the edge of the plateau and flung him as far out as they could. He sailed off the ledge and landed with a dull thump in the rocks. His head slapped onto a boulder and crunched. They'd have to dig a mass grave and bury the Japanese soldiers or the stink would become too much. Carver yelled to them, "Bring that Nambu down here and the ammo."

The four soldiers stood outside the still dark doorway of the hut. The smell of blood and cordite was strong. They stared into the darkness, no one wanting to enter until they could see better. Gradually, minute by minute, the sky lightened and brought color and depth to the world. The full devastation of the hut itself was evident. The walls were torn, with large pieces of thatch hanging to the ground. The roof was shredded; it wouldn't provide cover unless they repaired it.

When it was light enough, Sergeant Carver took a step to the doorway. He looked at the others, then back to the doorway and stepped through. Everyone except Dunphy followed. It was apparent what Dunphy had slipped on in the night. The floor was covered with congealed blood and unidentifiable body parts. His boot print was clearly visible on a dull white piece of what must have been intestine.

The hut was a room of gore. The bodies were strewn around, none having all their limbs. Hooper heaved over and added his vomit to the scene. O'Connor quickly followed. Carver stood there looking side to side, taking it all in. He stepped over body parts to the mostly intact man in the corner, the moaner. He noticed the shoulder boards, an officer. He kneeled down, looking into the dead eyes. The man had a large belly wound; Dunphy had saved him from a long painful death. He stood and scowled at the smoking radio still sitting on the table. He wondered how often they were supposed to check in. At least daily, he assumed. *How long before they send a squad up here to check out the radio silence?*

"All right, ladies. Let's get this shit cleaned up. We need to bury them or we'll be smelling them soon enough." He looked out the back doorway, "There's soft ground over there. O'Connor, go through their bags and see if you can find some ponchos to roll them in. I'll help you." He looked at Hooper, "See about any weapons and ammo you can salvage. We may need 'em when they come snooping." He yelled, "Dunphy, start digging a hole over beyond the hut. We'll join you soon enough." He could hear Dunphy walking around the hut. He hadn't said much since last night's attack. Every man dealt with his emotions differently.

## 24

As Colonel Araki watched C Company disappear into the jungle towards the suspected American observation post, he wondered about his old friend, Thomas Welch. Could he trust him? Probably, but how far? It was one thing to betray your countrymen, particularly when he considered Japan his home, but would he betray his race?

With his arms clasped behind him he called for his aide. "Send word to Lieutenant Katayama. Tell him to expect C Company to pass in front of his position sometime this evening." The aide bowed and quickly left. He nodded in satisfaction. *Whatever happens, the whiny rat is out of my hair for a while.*

He went back to the map table and looked over his defenses and the American line. The American Army had proven to be almost as tough as the hated Marines. They had better weapons, but poor leadership. He'd let them crash against his defenses again.

He put his finger on the map with the eight red x's. He smiled. The Americans were unable to hit his precious 105mm artillery pieces hidden in the hills. Their elevated positions allowed them to hit the American front lines without worry of counter-battery fire. He thought about the grim sacrifices his men had endured to cut the road through the relentless jungle in order to get the massive guns to the ridge. Men had died, mostly natives, but some of his own as well. The sacrifice was paying off. He had the Americans at a standstill. When they attacked again he'd be ready to push them back with his full force. He'd push them off the beaches and off his airfield. Once he owned the airfield he'd destroy the last remnants of resistance.

~

WELCH WAS GIVEN A SIDEARM, but not a rifle. At first, he took offense, but thought better of it when he saw Araki's glare. The message was clear; I don't trust you completely. Welch strapped the Nambu pistol to his belt and nodded his pleasure. He didn't relish the thought of patrolling without a weapon.

They left at dawn. They made their way through the intricate barbed wire barricades by following a guide. When they were through, they went into a single file line and followed the winding path leading up the canyon. It followed a creek which flowed clear and strong. The farther they walked the smaller and steeper the creek became.

The soldiers moved well, but he couldn't help comparing them to their American counterparts. The Americans were better in the jungle; they moved with more skill.

He'd learned through eavesdropping that the original C Company had been decimated by the American Marines. Most of the old veterans were casualties. C Company was now made up of replacements. They'd come in on what the Americans called the Tokyo express; an almost nightly reinforcement by Japanese navy cruisers. He swelled with pride thinking how the Japanese navy was having its way with the Americans. There was no way the Japanese could lose this war; the Americans were too weak. He felt certain that if they beat them here at Guadalcanal, there'd be no bouncing back. They'd sue for peace or containment and concentrate on the war in Europe. By the time they got back around to the Japanese, the world would be sick of war and the Japanese would be a formidable world power. The thought crossed his mind, *what if I'm wrong?* But he dispelled it out of hand.

As the trail steepened, the trail of men slowed. Welch was much taller than the Japanese soldiers and more used to traveling in the jungle. He was frustrated with the slow progress, but kept his thoughts to himself, a smile on his face instead.

He knew he belonged with the Japanese, but that didn't mean they knew it. To them he was a gaijin, a foreigner, no matter how well he spoke their language. He'd dealt with the same thing back in Japan. He'd ignored the looks and slights until, eventually he was looked at, not as an equal, but perhaps tolerated. It would be harder for these men; they'd been taught that all other races were inferior. To Welch this was a ridiculous twist of history, one he assumed was procreated to keep the soldiers fighting. Once the war was over and he returned to Japan, the animosity would disappear like snow in the sun.

They marched for two hours before Lieutenant Kogi called for a ten-minute rest. Instead of sitting, Welch walked past the reclining men and stood in front of Lieutenant Kogi, who was sipping from his canteen while studying a map. When he saw Welch, he nodded. Welch said, "Lieutenant Kogi, Sir," He bowed and stayed that way until the lieutenant bowed back. "Sir, I have been on this trail before. It gets steeper, then flattens out for the final mile to the ridge."

Lieutenant Kogi interrupted, "Yes, I can read a map, Mr. Welch." He shook it in his hand.

"Sir, no disrespect, but I don't think we'll make it to the top before nightfall unless we quicken our pace." He kept his eyes averted from the young lieutenant's gaze.

Lieutenant Kogi stared at him, not sure if he should be offended or thankful for this foreigner's input. The thought of not completing his mission the way Colonel Araki had laid it out made him almost physically ill. That was not a report he wanted to make. "What is your suggestion, Mr. Welch?"

He bowed again, "Sir, I could lead the patrol. No disrespect to your men, but I know this area and can get us there quicker."

Lieutenant Kogi looked at him with raised eyebrows. "You know of a faster way than the trail?"

"There are parts of the trail that take aimless, meandering turns. I can avoid these spots and take a more direct route to the ridge, Sir."

Lieutenant Kogi considered it, nodded and spoke to his sergeant, "Tell Private Asha to accompany Mr. Welch on point." The sergeant, a thick man with hands that looked like they could crush coconuts, nodded and took Welch by the arm, dragging him up the line with an iron grip.

The patrol was back on its feet and following Welch. He was moving much faster than Private Asha had been. He looked back at the panting soldier and grinned. The man had been waffling and now he was working. He'd make an enemy of the private, but a friend of the lieutenant...a worthwhile trade.

Another hour and they were past the steeps and onto the more open, flatter section. The thick jungle had given way to a forest-like setting with tall trees intermingling to block any sunlight from getting to the jungle floor. The walking was like strolling through a cushioned field of moss. Their progress increased and it was obvious they'd make the ridge with hours to spare.

When they broke out of the jungle canopy they could see the top of the ridge. Welch stopped, took a knee and waited for the sergeant and lieutenant. Lieutenant Katayama spread the men out and they slowly advanced up the hill. Welch had his sidearm out. He licked his lips, hoping they found Morrisey and his men napping, or better yet, obliterated. He let the soldiers advance past him. If they weren't napping and weren't already dead, they'd engage them at any second. *Or will they realize they're outnumbered and simply melt back into the jungle?* He hoped not.

As the forward elements got within ten yards of the top, Welch noticed the smell of cordite and smoke. There were bomb craters all around, some still smoldering. He puffed his chest, impressed with the Japanese artillery's accuracy. He crested the top, looking from side to side for any bodies. *Would they have been removed?* If there were any survivors, probably. The natives had already buried men only days before. If they lost more in the bombing, it may be enough to take them out of the war for good. He wondered if Ahio would take advantage of the power vacuum.

There was shouting from the side of the ridge. A soldier had found something. Welch went to the call. A corporal was waving the lieutenant over. Welch arrived at the same time. The soldier was pointing to a destroyed structure. It looked to be the remnants of a hut built into the ridge. The wood and thatch was shredded and parts were burned. If anyone had been inside the hut, they wouldn't have survived. Another soldier further down the slope yelled.

Welch followed Lt. Kogi. Kogi's nose crinkled as he approached the private. The air smelled fetid, like dead flesh. The private was excited. He pointed and said, "There's body parts spread all around here, Sir." The burly sergeant went down the hill fast. He inspected something, then leaned over and lifted a thick stick. It had something on the end, something shiny. Welch gulped when he realized it wasn't a stick, but a severed arm. The shiny piece was a watch. The sergeant smiled, undid the clasp and held the bloody watch to his ear. He threw the arm away like a piece of trash. He shook the watch and scowled, "Broken," he muttered. He held it up for the officer to see, "Looks American, Sir." He shoved it in his pocket; a good souvenir.

The men walked amongst the body parts looking for more treasures, but only found torn flesh, ragged boots and clothing. Lieutenant Kogi approached Welch and said, "Looks like your friends were killed to the man." Welch raised an eyebrow, and Kogi continued, "Otherwise they would have buried them or taken them away."

Welch decided not to respond, but nodded. He wondered to himself, *doesn't seem like enough men and why'd we only find white men? The natives wouldn't leave them to rot in the sun.* To Lieutenant Kogi he said, "Looks that way."

Lieutenant Kogi had his men pile the body parts in a bomb crater and cover them as best they could. It wasn't out of respect for the dead, but rather to cover up the putrid smell of their decaying bodies.

Lieutenant Kogi spread his men out along the ridge. He had them dig foxholes in case of attack and he called into headquarters. He relayed what they'd found. His chest puffed out and his chin raised as he waited to accept the praise from a job well done. But instead the words seemed to deflate him and his brow furrowed in concern. Welch was standing nearby and noticed the change in Lt. Kogi. He stayed close, hoping to hear.

When Kogi signed off, Welch said, "Were they happy to hear of the successful mission?"

Lieutenant Kogi was staring at the ground, but Welch's words brought him from his reverie. He looked past Welch and called, "Sergeant, get the squad leaders and come to me." The sergeant went to gather the men. Lieutenant Kogi spoke to Welch, "We have a new mission." He looked past Welch towards the hill in the distance across the valley. Welch spun around trying to see where he was looking. "The Colonel has lost contact with our observation post. He's worried they've been attacked. At first light we'll find out."

Welch couldn't have been more disappointed; he'd hoped to convince Kogi to attack Captain Morrisey's village. He had half a company and surprise, more than enough to completely destroy his former leader's lair. He walked away sat on a rock outcropping and took a long pull from his canteen. He gazed across the darkening valley. The hill was only half visible from the ridge. They were probably having radio trouble. They'd waste a whole day, maybe more, chasing ghosts. He threw the empty canteen to the ground.

## 25

After the dead were cleared from the hut, they got busy pooling their resources and digging in. Sergeant Carver was pleased with the number of weapons the Japanese had left them: two nambu mounted machine guns with three bricks of ammo each, twelve grenades, twenty 50mm high explosive mortar rounds and one undamaged type 89 mortar tube. It was a small caliber tube known to G.I.'s as a 'knee mortar.' It only required one man to operate and was more like a grenade launcher than a mortar. They only recovered one workable Arisaka rifle; most had been in the hut and been destroyed. Carver tested the bolt action, familiarizing himself with the rifle. He slung it over his shoulder wondering if it was sighted in properly.

He had his men dig in along the line where he thought the Japanese would come; along the communication wire. Their holes were spaced out twenty yards from each other. The first line of holes was down the hill about thirty yards, the next twenty yards and the final on the ridge itself. If they were pushed back to the ridge the only escape would be off the backside and into the jungle.

Carver had no illusions though. If the Japanese came with anything larger than a patrol his four-man unit would have little chance of stopping them, no matter how well they were dug in. And come they would. Once the hilltop outpost failed to check in, he had no doubt they'd investigate. He only hoped they'd hold off until the American attack started. Once it began, the Japanese would have their hands full and might forget about them.

While the men were busting their asses setting up defenses, Carver contacted headquarters. He'd been surprised when Lt. Smote had passed him off to Colonel Sinclair. He snapped to attention, even though he was on the radio. The colonel laid it out for him. The attack would happen soon and the only way it could succeed was silencing the 105mm pieces the Japanese had hidden somewhere in the hills. It was imperative they hold the ridge until the attack. Carver understood their position and the radio was handed back to Lt. Smote, who started taking down map coordinates of likely targets. Carver was like a kid in a candy store, relaying all the ripe targets he was seeing through Captain Morrisey's field glasses.

Lieutenant Smote assured him his fire missions were priority and he'd have naval guns and Marine air units at his disposal. Carver told him the situation with the Japanese radio check-in problem. Lieutenant Smote said he'd have fighters in the air all day flying cover for him. If he needed assistance, they were at his disposal. At night he'd be on his own, but hopefully nothing would happen and they'd be calling shots in the morning. Carver didn't put much stock in wishful thinking. In combat, nothing ever went as planned. He'd put up the best defense he could, but he wasn't going to sacrifice the rest of his squad for nothing. If it looked like they'd be overrun, he'd give the order to retreat. If it came to that, they'd be four separate men on their own, fighting for their lives in a hostile environment.

The rest of the day was spent working. The men dug their holes deep and reinforced them with whatever they could find. Each of the twelve holes were sturdy and easily entered and abandoned. Carver put the machine guns in the outermost holes. None of the men knew how to use the Nambus, but were able to figure them out in short order. Each man knew how to shoot and load the sticks of ammo, but no one knew for sure how to clear a jam.

The Nambus had deadly reputations for their high rate of fire and their reliability, so they might not need to know how to clear a jam. They'd all been introduced to the light weight knee mortars back on New Caledonia. A soldier simply braced the shaped base plate, angled the tube at forty-five degrees, indicated with a small leveler bubble window, dialed in the distance to target in meters, pulled the pin on the projectile, dropped it in and pulled the lanyard attached to the trigger. The shell would launch and explode on impact. The mortar tube was set up in Corporal Hooper's hole. The right Nambu was Pvt. Dunphy's responsibility and the left, O'Connor's. Sergeant Carver would be helping load O'Connor, but would move wherever he was needed.

By late afternoon, Carver's eyes burned from staring through the field glasses, looking for more Japanese targets. The constant drone of circling Marine fighters took on a different tone and he looked to the cloudless blue sky. There was a new sound, more engines. They were higher pitched, as if they were diving. He caught a metallic flash out of the corner of his eye. He put the glasses to his eyes, but couldn't find it again. O'Connor pointed to the sky, "Look, Jap fighters."

The Marines were rising to meet at least four Zeros diving on them. They were only dots to the men on the ground, but they knew the pilots were in a deadly battle of survival. Two to four weren't good odds. The dots closed on each other, then the darker dots, the Marines, flashed through. One of the Zeros flashed and a black plume of smoke appeared. It looked like a careless child marking a perfectly blue sheet of paper with a ragged black marker.

The dots turned together coming at each other again, but now they were lower and easier to see. The men watched as the deadly dance continued. Dogfights weren't usually this close; they happened well beyond the horizon.

The fighters slashed amongst one another and again there was a bright flash as one of the planes exploded. It was difficult to distinguish enemy from friend. The fight was taking the planes lower and lower. Now they could see the tracer fire shooting out like space age laser beams. As the fight got lower, it was obvious there was only one Marine fighter left and three Zeros.

The Marine went into a steep climb and two of the Zeros followed.

They couldn't match the wildcats' climb and both peeled off. The Marine took the opportunity to gracefully turn back to the descending Zeros; now he was on their tails. One broke off hard right and one went left. The Marine stuck with the closer one, the one that went right and soon his wings spouted flame and tracers ripped into the zero. It came apart like a toy and smashed into the jungle. A large plume of dust rose, marking its impact. The Marine continued diving and only pulled up when he was fifty feet above the jungle. He pointed his nose to Henderson field trying to make a break for it, but the Zero that hadn't climbed in the chase was waiting for him. He was at one thousand feet and he dove on the fleeing Wildcat.

The Wildcat was flying at red-line speed. The diving Zero was slowly catching up. The scene was playing out before the squads' eyes like some crazy opera. *Did the Marine pilot know he was being pursued?* It didn't seem like it. He kept his low and fast course, not altering his beeline to the east. The Zero was now at the same altitude; he'd stopped gaining the second he stopped diving. He wasn't shooting, but lining up the shot. The planes were almost out of sight. Carver pulled up the field glasses and watched them darting away. He kept the commentary going, "The Jap's not shooting. Oh wait, he is, he's firing. Shit, the Wildcat's smoking." He pointed, "He's turning back towards the beach, you see?"

Now they were coming closer to them. The doomed Wildcat was getting bigger as it flew over the American positions on the beach. A wall of tracers went up as the Wildcat passed over the friendly Army units. It looked like every man with a rifle must be firing. The Zero shuddered, then shot straight up like being pulled on a string. Both wings sheared off and it continued its upward arc, hesitated, then nosed over and sliced into the sea. The men lifted their fists in celebration.

Carver put the glasses down and suppressed his own smile, "Alright, let's get back to work."

Just before dark they heard more airplane engines. They never saw them, but the bright flashes along the beach told them they were enemy bombers giving the Army yet another pasting. Carver hated being away from the main force, but he had to admit, he didn't miss the bombing.

The men ate C-rations and watched the sun dip below the Pacific. Sergeant Carver put them on two-hour watches. If the Japanese came during the night, they'd have no chance of survival. There were so few of them, they would be outflanked in an instant. Even if they came up the expected path, they could flank them quickly with only half a platoon. Even though the men were beyond exhausted, no one felt like sleeping.

As a precaution, Sgt. Carver had the men attach their bayonets. If a night attack came they'd be hard pressed to attach them in the dark. No one particularly liked the bayonets on the M1 carbines. The weapons were small and the added weight of the bayonet threw off their aim. But if the Japanese came during the night they'd be upon them quickly and aiming wouldn't be important, stabbing and cutting would.

Carver thought about the conversation he'd had with Colonel Sinclair. He'd been careful not to say too much over the radio. He'd said the attack would come soon. *How long would it take the Japs to send a patrol up here?* If the attack didn't come in the morning he'd have to hold out another day. It wouldn't take the Japanese soldiers long to make the trek up the hill, maybe half a day. That meant if the American attack didn't happen in the morning, he could expect company by midday tomorrow. With the help of the Marine fighter cover, assuming they weren't having dogfights of their own, he could hold off one, maybe two attacks, depending on numbers and tactics. One well-coordinated flanking maneuver and they wouldn't last more than a couple of minutes. He stared into the dark night, leaned back and shut his eyes. They wouldn't come tonight. He dropped into a fitful sleep.

## 26

Corporal Hooper and the others were watching the sky lighten. It was at the edge of their perception. Morning was coming and they could all feel that their mission was concluding one way or another. The coming American assault would either fail or succeed. Their small unit would play an integral part. They all knew it and they all felt the inevitability of the path before them. There was no shirking their duty. The men on the lowlands would die by the hundreds if they didn't silence the Japanese artillery. It was up to them. The next twenty-four hours would see them succeeding or dying; there was no middle ground.

When the sun was still a half hour from rising, O'Connor whispered to no one in particular, "I've gotta take a shit, be right back."

He used his bayoneted carbine as a crutch to help him out of the hole. He stretched his tight muscles. He thought he may have gotten a couple hours of sleep. He stumbled his way west feeling for plants to use for toilet paper. There wasn't a great selection; he'd have to use a rock again. It wasn't as though there was much to wipe; he'd been mostly pissing out his ass for the past week, if he shit at all.

He went to the cliff edge, near the shredded hut and squatted. He was facing the valley and the ridge they'd occupied only the day before. As he stared at nothing, concentrating on getting the deed done, he caught movement out of the corner of his eye. He didn't look, but kept his gaze straight ahead, hoping his peripheral vision would see it again. Sure enough, there was something out there. He turned slowly to the movement. Nothing. He pulled up his filthy pants; the shit would have to wait. There was something there, he was sure of it. He crouched down, his carbine at the ready. He stared straight ahead hoping to see the movement again. The sky was lightening, shapes of rocks and trees becoming more than just dark blobs.

He tensed. There, definite movement. Definitely not natural. There were people down there. His senses went into overdrive; he could hear the small sound of boots scraping ground then the distinct sound of metal scraping on metal. If he wasn't listening for it he may not have heard it. Whoever it was, was still a long way down the hill. He scooped up his carbine and, in a crouch, ran back to the foxholes. "Sarge, someone's coming up the hill from the ridge side."

Carver gave him a startled look and popped out of his hole. He trusted O'Connor and didn't question him. "Pull the machine guns up and take one to the hut, find cover for the other. Keep 'em a good distance apart." He grabbed the knee mortar and ran it over to the other ridge. When he came to the edge he peered over, looking for the enemy. At first glance he didn't see anything so he found a medium sized rock and put the mortar behind it, aiming towards the valley. He ran back to the others and helped them move the Nambus. Hooper had an armful of mortar rounds. "Take them over there behind that rock." He pointed. Hooper nodded and stumbled his way. He deposited the load and went back for the rest.

Sergeant Carver got on the radio. "Mother, this is Falcon 6. How do you copy? Over."

There was a long pause then a scratchy response, "Falcon 6 this is Mother. read you five by five. Over."

"We have troops coming up the eastern side of our valley. Any friendlies out here with us? Over."

"Wait one, Falcon 6." 30 long seconds passed before they came back, "Negative Falcon 6. No friendlies in your area. Over."

Carver said, "You got any air cover for us? Over."

Another pause then the good news, "Scrambling a pair of Corsairs for you, should be on station in fifteen minutes."

Carver thought they could hold out at least that long. "Roger. It's gonna get busy up here real quick. Tell the pilots we'll mark our positions with smoke. Over."

"Understand. You'll mark your position with smoke. Over."

He didn't bother repeating himself, but went to the edge and looked down the slope. The sun wasn't up yet, but it was minutes away. The slope was easy to discern and he quickly acquired the khaki colored advance of a large Japanese force. He pulled his field glasses up and from behind a bush scanned them. They were coming up the hill at a slow steady pace, being cautious. *Did they know they were here? Where'd they come from?*

He swept the line then stopped on one man. He was dressed differently and was taller. He watched and said, "I'll be damned." He put the glasses down and whispered to his men. "That son-of-a-bitch Welch is down there. He's armed with a pistol. Treacherous prick." He grit his teeth. Welch had played them all like a damned fiddle. "Take off the bayonets, but keep 'em close. We'll have a coupla Corsairs up here in fifteen minutes. O'Connor, I want your first shot to be Welch. Kill that bastard."

O'Connor took off the bayonet and placed it beside him. He was lying prone and he sighted down his carbine. He found the tall Welch and adjusted his sights. Sergeant Carver spoke again, "Wait until I fire the first mortar. When it's in the air, take him. The rest of you pour it on. Make every shot count."

The line of Japanese soldiers advanced, using the sparse cover as best they could. Carver thought they looked green; they weren't moving as smoothly as seasoned troops and their uniforms looked brand new. Maybe they'd break and run. He dispelled the thought. He'd never seen a Japanese soldier run away.

He went to the knee mortar and gazed over the top at the advancing troops. He tried to gauge the distance. He pulled the pin on the shell and dropped it into the tube. He twisted the range dial to sixty meters, found forty-five degrees and pulled the lanyard. The

50mm grenade left the tube with a soft thump. He watched the grenade arc then he heard the sharp crack of O'Connor's carbine.

WELCH WAS near the middle of the reduced company. They'd come across the valley in the night hoping to make the ridge by dawn. Lieutenant Kogi put him on point first thing and he led them quickly across. He'd been on this route a few times before. He didn't know the area as well as the rest of the island because the natives were afraid of the hill and rarely visited. Nonetheless he'd led them efficiently and they'd be on the ridge with the observation unit within the hour. He wondered how long the two units would spend grab-assing before he could get back to the ridge and attack Morrisey's village. Hopefully before dark. He'd lead them back at a fast pace.

Now they were close. The unit was being as stealthy as possible. Lieutenant Kogi wanted to surprise his comrades and teach them a lesson on how to assault a hill. The inexperienced troops were doing the best they could, but in Welch's estimation they were making way too much noise. He hoped the unit on the hill would see them and realize they weren't Americans or natives. Being fired on by Japanese troops was something he didn't want to experience again.

The dawn was coming but it was still dark. Welch had his pistol holstered, not expecting trouble. The men around him were more cautious, looking at the hill as if it housed sleeping dragons. He tried to calm them, telling them there was nothing there but their own troops. The soldiers scowled at him with undisguised disgust. How dare this white-skinned heathen speak to them as if they were children. Welch decided he'd keep his mouth shut unless spoken to first.

When they were sixty meters from the top, Welch thought he heard a faint pop. It was out of place; not a natural sound. He looked up quickly and tripped on a protruding rock. He fell forward at the same instant something buzzed by his ear. The sound of the shot followed close behind. He caught his fall by thrusting his right hand onto a craggy rock. The sharp edges cut into his hand and he fell the rest of the way forward. Before he could process the buzz and the shot, there was an explosion near the front of the company, followed immediately by the popping of gunfire.

He stayed down and pulled his pistol from his holster. He looked up at the ridge, but couldn't see anything. They were being fired on by their own men. This had to be stopped before anyone was hurt. He looked to his right and saw the man he'd tried to speak to staring at him. He was about to say something when he noticed the dark blood pooling beneath the man's head.

He peaked his head above the rock he was behind and a bullet slammed into it, sending tiny rock chips into his cheek. He rolled back cussing. The men around him started rising up to take shots at the ridge. It was insanity; a deadly misunderstanding.

He heard Lieutenant Kogi yelling for his men to move forward. Welch stayed down, the last one had been too close. He felt his face and looked at his hand. It came away bloody. He felt his cheek, pulling out embedded pieces of rock. He reached into his pocket and pulled out a handkerchief and held it to his cheek. He'd sit this one out until they either killed one another or realized they were shooting at their own men.

SERGEANT CARVER PEERED around the rock to watch where his mortar landed. He couldn't tell if O'Connor's shot had killed Welch. The others started shooting using only their carbines; picking their shots carefully, making them count. The mortar landed on the leading edge of the Japanese soldiers and he saw two men fly sideways. He went back to the tube and moved it laterally a fraction. He dropped another mortar in, pulled the trigger and watched it arc away. Without waiting for its impact, he moved the tube to his left slightly and fired again. He repeated the process five more times, sweeping the mortars across and up and down the exposed Japanese troops.

He put the tube down, picked up the Arisaka and crawled to the edge of the ridge. The men were shooting carefully, knocking soldiers down then pulling back to cover. He laid the barrel on a rock and lined up the iron sights. He'd never shot an Arisaka, but knew the rifle was deadly accurate. He found a target, a soldier trying to get a better look around a rock. He fired and saw the man's head snap back and out of sight. *Whoever owned this rifle before me had it zeroed perfectly.* He opened both eyes searching for another target and saw a man's exposed leg. He pulled the trigger, but nothing happened. He cussed at himself and worked the bolt, loading another round. He fired and the leg blossomed red. *He won't be charging up the hill anytime soon.* He looked to his left and saw O'Connor shooting. The Japanese were getting over their initial surprise and were starting to put more fire out. There were too many for the small force to keep pinned down.

Between shots he yelled at O'Connor, "You get him?"

O'Connor looked behind him and noticed Sgt. Carver. He shrugged, "I had him in my sights. He went down hard, but not sure if he got hit or tripped."

It wasn't what Sgt. Carver wanted to hear. He knew he shouldn't be aiming to kill one man, but he wanted that traitorous bastard dead.

He sighted and shot another soldier who stood up to throw a grenade. It would have been an impossibly long throw. *He must aspire to be a baseball star.* Carver's shot hit him in the side and he spun, losing the grenade. It dropped feet from him and exploded, sheering his legs from beneath him like twigs splitting. Two of his comrades were caught in the blast, one wounded and screaming, the other lay still.

He saw an officer stand and wave his pistol, exhorting his men to attack. Carver brought him into his sights, but before he could pull the trigger the ground in front of him erupted with incoming bullets. He was forced to cower behind the rock and make himself as small as possible. The shots were flying by him and slamming all around him. He was too exposed. He heard the distinctive ripping sound of a Japanese machine gun opening up. At first, he thought it was one they'd captured, but the incoming rounds intensified, walking up and down his line, giving no doubt it was a Japanese owned weapon.

He yelled, "Hooper get on the Nambu and return that fire, now! You too Dunphy." He backed straight away from the rock sheltering him. The incoming fire was intense but somehow, he found cover without getting hit. He went to his knee mortar and peeked over the rock. The Japanese were up on the right flank charging up the hill. The left side of the Japanese line was laying down covering fire. They'd be overrun in minutes if they didn't get fire on those advancing troops. He was about to lob some shells their way when he saw a flash in the sky. He looked up and almost whooped when he saw the four Corsairs. He put the knee mortar down and picked up the radio. "Marine high flyers, this is Falcon 6. How copy? Over."

The calm voice came back immediately. "Five by five Falcon 6. Where you want it? Over."

"We're on the ridge facing east. The Japs are coming up the face right at us. Suggest strafing south to North. I'll pop smoke on our position. Over." He threw a smoke grenade a few feet behind him and was immediately enveloped.

"That's affirmative. We have smoke on your position. Keep your heads down. We'll start with strafing and come around again with some two hundred pounders."

Carver propped the radio against the rock and yelled, "We've got fighters coming in from the south in one minute. Keep your heads down when it comes."

He looked down the slope. The Japanese were making progress on the right side while the left flank kept up a steady hail of bullets. Dunphy's machine gun was silent, but Hooper was hammering away, despite the heavy incoming fire. Carver couldn't see Dunphy. He wondered if he was hit. He scooped up the radio, took a deep breath and ran around the rock in a low crouch. Bullets snapped and buzzed all around him. He felt a sting on his left shoulder, but ignored it. He dove headfirst into Dunphy's position. He landed on something soft.

Dunphy screamed and lashed out, punching Carver in the belly hard. Carver gritted his teeth and before Dunphy could land another punch yelled, "It's me, dumbass!"

The hole was barely big enough for both of them. Carver had to expose his legs to get himself upright. Bullets chewed up the ground around the hole, but none found their mark. When he was upright he looked at Dunphy's dirty face. "You hit?" Dunphy shook his head. "Then why aren't you on the gun, goddammit?"

"You said to get down." As if to punctuate that thought, there was a ripping from their right side. Carver risked a look over the hole and saw the beautiful sight of a gull-winged Marine corps Corsair swooping in, guns blazing. The ground below erupted as the big slugs pounded into the advancing Japanese line. Before Carver ducked back he saw Japanese soldiers being torn apart, thrown back down the hill. He leaned against the back of the hole and looked at Dunphy's searching eyes. He smiled, "They're knocking the shit out of 'em. Stay down, there's three more coming."

The first Corsair pulled up and shot into the blue sky. Another was lining up on the now hunkered Japanese soldiers. Captain Malone lined up his sights on the settling dust in front of him. He could see soldiers diving for cover. He held steady, then depressed the trigger on the yoke. The heavy thumping of his six, fifty caliber machine guns shook the Corsair. He used the rudder pedals to swing the Corsair side to side in a yawing motion, spreading out his deadly fire. He saw soldiers being ripped to pieces as his bullets found their marks. The pass only lasted six seconds, but he expended five hundred rounds of high velocity, fifty caliber bullets.

At the end of his pass he pulled up sharply and looked over his shoulder. He could see the dust and jungle foliage floating back to earth. He could see the next Corsair, Lt. Hawkins starting his run. He climbed away and leveled out behind Lt. Emmit. He'd let Emmit lead the attack to gain some much-needed experience. When the final Corsair was through with its strafing run and climbing to join up, he keyed his mike, "Nice shooting guys. This time were getting rid of our two hundred pounders. Remember there are friendlies down there, so keep it tight. If you're not absolutely sure of your shot, don't take it." He got "rogers" from the others and pulled in front of Lt. Emmit. He waved as he went by, "I'll lead the bombing run. Remember to keep your interval."

He got a terse "Roger," from Emmit. He could tell the kid thought he was being coddled too much. *Tough shit.*

Sergeant Carver slowly brought his head up and looked down the hill. Nothing was moving. The dirt and dust was settling, but the Japanese had disappeared. He knew better than to think they'd all bought it. He called to his men. "Everyone back on your guns, they ain't finished yet, I guarantee it."

Dunphy crawled from the bottom of the hole and gave a low whistle, "I don't see anyone alive down there, Sarge."

"Get on the gun and be ready. They'll be coming again." He heard the radio crackle to life. He brushed the dirt off and acknowledged the flyboys calling.

Captain Malone's voice was cool and calm, "we're coming in with two hundred pounders. Stay deep in your holes, Army."

Sergeant Carver looked at the growing dots off to the south. He yelled to his men. "Flyboys are coming in with some heavy eggs. Stay down."

WELCH REALIZED the gunfire from the ridge wasn't the heavy sound of a Japanese Arisaka rifle, but the popping of the M1 Carbines the Americans had brought. He wondered if the men on the ridge were the same one's he'd spent the last few weeks with.

After the initial surprise of being fired on, he was happy to see the Japanese troops rallying. From the incoming fire it was obvious there weren't many soldiers on the ridge. He risked poking his head up and wasn't shot at. Most of the fire was being directed towards the advancing soldiers. He watched as one of the men running forward suddenly fell to the ground. He didn't move. The Americans were few, but deadly.

He heard Lt. Kogi yell for his men to cover from the right. Every rifle on the right side seemed to fire at once. Immediately the volume of fire from the ridge subsided. When the Nambu machine gun opened up along with the rifles, the Americans were effectively suppressed. Lieutenant Kogi stood up and exhorted the men around him to advance. The entire left side stood as one and started leaping forward, trying to gain as much ground as possible while there was no incoming fire.

Welch heard the sound of another Nambu machine gun opening up, but this one was shooting down on them. The Americans were using their own weapons against them. The thought enraged him and he went to a knee and fired his pistol towards the ridge. He had no chance of hitting anything at that range, but it made him feel better. He saw better cover to his front, a depression with a medium sized black rock in front of it. It seemed almost custom made for him. He stood and ran to the hole, diving in headfirst. He rolled onto his back, rubbing his shoulder. He'd landed hard. The pain brought his rage under control and he took a deep breath. He thought, *don't get involved. Let the soldiers take care of it. You're too valuable to get killed charging a machine gun nest.*

He noticed the American machine gun had stopped firing. He hoped the shooter had been shot and was dead in his hole. He risked a glance around the rock and saw Kogi's men making great strides to the top; they'd overrun the Americans in another minute. Then the only fire was coming from the Japanese. He wondered if the Americans were trying to make a break for it.

He caught the flash of something out of the corner of his eye, right before the world erupted in violent explosions of sound and debris. He fell to his stomach and heard the ripping sound of a heavy caliber machine gun and the roar of an airplane. He covered up as best he could as the ground in front of him was literally shredded. He heard the screaming and tearing of dying men. It lasted only seconds, but it seemed a lifetime. He was just bringing his head up when another fighter slashed down and strafed. The bullets sliced and whizzed off rocks. He curled into the smallest ball he could and screamed. Two more planes strafed, then it was silent, his ears ringing in the silence.

His screams had descended to whimpers. In the silence he wondered if he were dead. *How could anyone survive?* But the pain in his shoulder returned and he realized he was alive. He came to a crouch behind the rock and peeked around the side. The scene before him was carnage. Men and parts of men were spread across the slope. The white dust was settling over the dead, giving them a ghostly quality. He looked to where Lt. Kogi had been leading his men. He couldn't see anyone alive. He looked to the left and saw men cowering. No one was moving.

He shook off the fear and realized they had to get off the slope. The planes would be back for another pass to finish them off. Was Kogi alive? It would be a miracle if he were. He took a deep breath and tried to give a command, but it came out as a squeak. His mouth was too dry to speak. He coughed and gagged and took a drink from his canteen. The briny water coated his throat and tongue and he felt his voice return. He yelled. "Fall back, fall back to the jungle line, now!"

He didn't wait for them to comply. He took off, bounding down the hill away from the ridge. He heard the grunts and breathing of the men following him. He didn't stop until he was safely under the canopy of the jungle. twenty men were breathing hard around him, some vomiting and hacking. A sergeant came up to him and said, "Sir, what are your orders?" Welch stood to his full height and turned to the sergeant, who recoiled. "You? I thought you were Lieutenant Kogi. You made us retreat against our orders. You cowardly gaijin." He swung his machine pistol in an upper cut motion, but Welch was ready. He dodged the blow and brought the butt of his own pistol down hard on the sergeant's shoulder. He grunted and dropped to one knee, but he wasn't done yet. He lunged forward trying to get the bigger man off his feet. Welch met his lunge with his knee coming up hard into the sergeants' chin. He crumpled to the jungle floor just as the position they'd retreated from exploded in a rumbling firestorm.

The men instinctively dropped to the ground and watched their old position engulfed as the four Corsairs dropped their two hundred-pound bombs.

When the ground stopped shaking they stood and looked up the hill. Another sergeant stepped up to Welch and saluted. "What are your orders, sir?"

Welch looked at the men who were now cowed by the realization that he'd saved their lives. Welch understood these men weren't afraid to die and would rather die than be dishonored. There was only one thing he could say. "We attack the ridge and kill the Americans, but we do it my way."

Sergeant Murata looked to the ridge. It was still smoking and smoldering. There was no movement from the men who'd been attacking. He had no recourse, but to assume Lt. Kogi was incinerated somewhere up the hill. Welch wasn't a Japanese officer, but he was a personal friend of the colonel's, which gave him automatic rank in Sergeant Murata's eyes. He also seemed to know his way around the jungle and this ridge. He made his decision to follow his orders, for now.

## 27

The strafing run had devastated the advancing Japanese troops. Sergeant Carver looked out over the slope, then back to the blue dots lining up for their bombing run. He thought the bombs would be enough to kill any remaining Japanese. He heard yelling coming from the slope and as he looked, he saw men starting to recover, beginning to stagger back to their feet. If they rushed they would overrun them, but the Corsairs would be there with their deadly bombs in seconds. The Japanese didn't have a chance. He heard more yelling and saw the entire left side of the Japanese line retreating down the hill at a dead run. He raised his Arisaka, but the planes were too close. He yelled for his men to get down and threw himself into the bottom of the hole on top of Dunphy.

Captain Malone was leading the bombing run. He knew the planes would be spread out behind him at ten-second intervals, plenty of time to keep out of the bomb blast of the previous plane.

He angled the Corsair down five degrees, but kept his speed steady at two hundred knots. He was slow, but he needed to be precise to keep from hitting friendlies. He timed the drop perfectly, releasing the two-hundred-pound bomb. His Corsair leaped into the sky with the sudden release of weight. He put in full military power and scratched for altitude. He felt, more than heard the air shimmer with the impact of his bomb. He turned to starboard and glanced at the fireball subsiding on the slope. *Bullseye*, he thought. He saw the next plane in line coming in on the same track. There'd be nothing left of the Japs when they were through.

Lieutenant Emmit was the last plane. He was still feeling the intense adrenalin rush from leading the strafing run. Now he was tail-end Charlie, flying through smoke and debris to get to the target. He slowed the Corsair, feeling the controls getting sluggish. He couldn't see much, but he looked to his instruments, trusting them to keep him on course. When he thought he was in the right spot he held his thumb over the pickle. He swore he felt the plane shift to the right in turbulence, but his instruments remained steady. He put in some slight aileron to correct what he felt and released his two hundred pounder.

He pulled away out of the smoke and immediately felt sick. He was flying directly along the ridge. He looked back searching for his bomb strike, praying he hadn't just bombed his own troops.

On the ground, the first three bombs struck the slope and sent carnage in all directions. The ground shook and the holes the men were cowering in collapsed all along the upper edges. The vibration shook the men down to their bones. Each man was curled into a tight ball, eyes closed hard, teeth gritted. Without realizing it, they were screaming. Their insides felt like they'd shake to jelly or their bones would break.

There was a longer pause before the fourth and final bomb was dropped. It was released late so it overshot their position, but it slammed into the ridge and exploded only thirty yards from Cpl. Hooper's hole. When the dust settled, the men slowly dug themselves out of their half-buried state. Private Dunphy felt like he'd been in the worst boxing match of his life. Every muscle ached, every joint screamed for attention. He sat on the edge of his collapsed hole and looked out at the charred, smoking slope. Nothing could have survived. Carver stood up and walked to the next hole, checking on O'Connor who was bleeding from his ears, but was otherwise okay. Then he checked Hooper.

He wasn't responding. He'd been closest to the final bomb.

Sergeant Carver pulled him out of the dirt thinking he was only staying down, but he still didn't move. He knelt beside his splayed body and slapped his face, "Wake up, Hooper." Nothing. He felt for a pulse on his neck. Nothing. He lifted his eye lids and looked into his lifeless eyes. He ripped his shirt open looking for the wound that killed him, but he was intact. Sergeant Carver started to pound on his chest trying to restart his heart. He yelled and cussed and pounded on the lifeless body.

After a minute, O'Connor put his hand on his shoulder and pulled him away. Carver looked at him with seething eyes. He went back to compressions, savagely pushing and thumping. O'Connor pulled him away and yelled, "He's dead, sarge. He's fucking gone. Stop."

Carver gave one last look at Hooper's staring eyes, stood and strode away, muttering, "Stupid eye-tie mother-fucker." He went thirty yards and sat down hard on the edge of the small cliff. He yelled, "You motherfuckers! you motherfucking sons-of-bitches!"

O'Connor and Dunphy stared, never having seen their hard-assed sergeant lose it. It gave them pause. If this hard, combat professional was cracking, they had no chance.

Carver stared down the slope for another minute, trying to get control of himself. He'd lost most of his men. The men who'd entrusted him with their lives were gone, blown to bits or shot full of holes. He'd let them all down. He'd killed his entire squad.

He heard O'Connor call, "Sarge? You okay?" No, he hadn't killed them all, not yet. He still had O'Connor and Dunphy and he still had a job to do. He shook himself and stood. He closed his eyes hard and squeezed his fists until they were bright white. He'd lost it momentarily and the thought of it drove him mad. There was something about seeing Corporal Hooper dead that had turned something inside him. He'd felt an overpowering sadness, then an overarching rage, then sadness again. He'd seen more death in this war than most men would see in four lifetimes and he'd never been bothered. Not like this. What was it about Hooper that set him off? He couldn't begin to know, but he'd have to pull it together if he wanted to get what was left of his unit through the next few hours.

He yelled, "Dunphy get me the radio, it's in our hole." He pointed at O'Connor, "Find the machine gun that was with Hooper. See if it's still operational. If not find the ammo, and anything else we can use to kill Japs."

Seconds later Dunphy ran up holding the radio in two pieces. "Radio's fucked. It must have shaken apart or something. It's useless."

Sergeant Carver held the two pieces. *How do I continue the mission without a radio?* He let it drop out of his hands and it shattered on a rock. Dunphy looked at him wondering the same thing. Carver motioned with his head towards O'Connor. "Help him recover whatever you can. Don't think the Japs are done with us yet."

Dunphy looked down the slope and saw it was still smoldering. The only evidence he could see of Japanese soldiers were smoking bits and pieces. "Don't think we need to worry 'bout them, sarge."

Carver's voice was gruff, "Saw a bunch running down towards the jungle just before the bombs dropped. They might have made it in time." Dunphy looked down the hill and ducked down. "Keep watch, but help out O'Connor. If they come they'll come from a different direction."

Ten minutes later they were huddled on the ridge going over what they had left. One Nambu machine gun with three hundred rounds, six grenades, 12 rounds for the knee mortar, three M1 carbines with fifteen clips and the Arisaka rifle. It was enough to inflict damage if the Japanese came again, but with only three of them it might be a short last stand.

O'Connor said what was on all their minds. "What are we gonna do, sarge? Without a radio we can't complete our mission. There's no reason to stay up here and die."

Carver looked at the guns and ammo, then looked each man in the eye. "If we don't take out those guns tomorrow morning a lot of G.I.'s are gonna die. Hell, we may lose the island. You wanna be left here?"

Dunphy spoke, "But what can we do? We can't call in a strike without a radio and besides, we don't know where the guns are."

Sergeant Carver looked to the west. "Division thinks the guns are on one of those ridges, overlooking the main Jap forces. If we move that way, we'll see their smoke when they fire and we can hit them with everything we've got." Dunphy and O'Connor were silent.

O'Connor scuffed the dirt with his foot. "Gotta have at least a platoon protecting those guns, sarge."

Carver continued, "We could use the knee mortar to confuse 'em, hit 'em with grenades and the Nambu, maybe disrupt 'em enough to give our guys a fighting chance. Once they're in the Jap lines they'll stop the arty." Carver wasn't sure about that last bit. The Japs tended to sacrifice their own soldiers more easily than their American counterparts. "Look, I'm not gonna order you to do this. You're right; it's got all the makings of a one-way trip, but it's our only chance to complete the mission and maybe save some G.I.'s."

Dunphy looked at O'Connor who was staring back at him. He grinned and shrugged his shoulders. "We've come this far on this fucked up patrol, might as well finish it."

O'Connor nodded, "screw it, let's do it."

## 28

Welch found himself an undamaged Arisaka rifle the previous owner no longer had a use for. He led the surviving Japanese soldiers through the jungle to the west of the ridge. The jungle canopy was thick above them, the undergrowth sparse, making for easy walking. They moved carefully hoping to keep themselves hidden from the Americans. Welch hoped they thought they were all killed in the bombing. He'd have surprise on his side and he'd roll up their defenses before they knew what hit them.

Three hours later Welch held up the men and brought his two surviving sergeants to the front. Sergeant Murata was a stocky, thick chested man with a flat nose and yellowed teeth. He'd been in almost constant combat for the past three years, a veteran of many jungle fights. He was also an educated man. Welch knew he'd been sent to England in his youth to study at one of the more prestigious military schools. He'd spent three years there before his father, a Colonel, had fallen from the graces of the military and been discharged in shame. His family suffered and the young Murata was returned home in dishonor. He never spoke English, but Welch assumed he was fluent.

The other, Sergeant Ozaki, was also a veteran, but much younger than Murata. He was short and thin, yet made up for his stature with an almost maniacal fighting spirit. His nose had dried blood from where Welch's knee had impacted him. His eyes were bloodshot and were starting to darken around the sockets. He scowled at Welch, but took a knee in front of him and listened to what he had to say.

Welch pointed up the hill. "We'll rest here for a half hour then assault the hill from here. There's good cover all the way to the ridge. It'll be slower, but we should be concealed the entire way. When we're on top, we'll spread out and sweep up the ridge. I want strict noise discipline. We won't engage unless we're seen or I give the signal. I don't think there are many of them, so we may even be able to capture them."

Sergeant Murata looked sideways at him, "We don't take prisoners, sir."

"We will if we can. I want to interrogate them before we kill them. I'd like to know what their plans are. It may help our comrades defend the upcoming attack." The sergeants nodded. *I also want to know what he knows about Morrisey.*

The half hour passed quickly. The men ate rice balls and dried meat, drank water and were ready to go. Welch had twenty men to work with, plenty to do the job. He was convinced there were only a handful of Americans on the ridge. If they could surprise them from the rear they'd have no chance. He'd have to watch his men though; they wanted blood and would slaughter them if given half a chance. He wanted them alive, at least for a while. When he'd gotten the information he wanted, they could do with them what they wished.

They left the cover of the jungle in the late morning. There were thunderheads building above the island and Welch recognized the coming of another rain storm. He hoped to reach the ridge and be done by the time the rain came. If he was late, the rain would make excellent cover for his men to advance under. Either way, the American defenders were doomed.

The men moved well, advancing slowly, using the natural cover of the car sized boulders for cover. The slope was steep, making the going slow, but they were under cover the entire way. It took an hour and a half, but they made it to the lip of the ridge without being seen. Welch went to the front and crouched beneath the ridge. He peeked over, looking for any movement, but saw nothing but shrubs and rock. They were hundreds of yards to the west of their last attack. He wasn't expecting to see the defenders.

He slung his rifle and pulled out his pistol. He waved the men forward and the sergeants split the men into separate squads and went over the cliff to the top. Welch went over, half expecting to hear the pop of the carbines, but there was nothing. He advanced with the men, crouched, using the cover. The men were covering one another, being careful not to make noise.

Welch pushed forward, wanting to be close to the front to keep them from immediately killing the Americans. He knew he was taking a risk; the Americans had obviously targeted him in the previous engagement. He doubted it was a coincidence he'd been the one shot at first. If he hadn't tripped, that bullet would have killed him. He wondered which of the soldiers had fired; probably the sharpshooter, O'Connor. He would repay him with pain if he captured the young redneck. The thought made him smile.

The clouds above were dark and ominous. *It will come any second.* If it rained soon he'd have his men push hard, catch them when they were hunkered down.

They'd covered one hundred yards with no sign. The next one hundred would bring them to where they'd attacked. He wondered if perhaps they'd abandoned the position. He hoped not. He wanted his revenge.

He was thinking about revenge when the man in front of him held up his hand and went to one knee. He looked back at Welch and pointed forward. Welch felt his heartbeat increase. He took a deep breath, getting control and made his way to the soldier's side. He pointed and Welch looked. At first, he didn't see anything, then he did. There were three men crouched behind bushes. It looked like they were packing their backpacks. Welch had the feeling they were getting ready to leave.

CARVER HAD LET the men sleep while he watched for enemy troops. It had been quiet since the air attack. He contemplated moving down the hill to see if they could recover any more Japanese ammo, but decided against it. They had plenty and exposing themselves wasn't worth the risk. They'd buried Hooper in the hole he'd died in. Carver added his dog tags to the growing wad he kept in his pack.

The weather was turning. Dark clouds were forming over the mountain and he was sure it would start raining soon. He'd woken Dunphy and O'Connor and they sat in a circle packing their backpacks. Every nook and cranny was filled with ammo and the remaining food. The Nambu machine gun was dismantled from the tripod and strapped to O'Connor's pack, the tripod on Dunphy's. Carver almost decided to leave it behind, but the firepower would be needed if they found the artillery position. He'd strapped the ten-pound knee mortar onto his own pack and taken as many mortar rounds as he could fit. He'd given one to each man as well. Their packs were heavy, they'd have to take breaks or risk exhaustion.

Initially, Carver wanted to leave at dusk, but the coming storm pushed his plans forward. It would be easier to deal with the rain once they were in the cover of the jungle canopy. It would act as a natural umbrella and moving would keep them warm and their minds occupied.

They were cinching their packs when Carver caught movement out of the corner of his eye. He instinctively reached for his rifle, but before he could bring it up, Japanese soldiers rose up fifteen yards away, aiming long rifles at his chest. He heard a voice he'd hoped to never hear again. "Drop the weapon or you die, Sergeant Carver." A leering soldier with sergeant's stripes stepped from behind Welch. Welch said, "Drop it now. These men want nothing more than to fill you with lead."

Dunphy and O'Connor were frozen by the sight of many enemy soldiers so close. They glanced Carver's way, wondering what he'd do.

Carver held the Arisaka, but knew he had no chance. He may get a shot off, but he'd be filled with holes seconds later. The thought didn't scare him; the thought of the inevitable torture did. His mind reeled. He didn't want to be captured. He told himself he'd never let that happen, but he couldn't make that decision for his men. If he made a move the others would key off him and they'd all die in a storm of lead. He couldn't decide these brave men's fate. He had to surrender. Within minutes he regretted his decision.

WELCH WAS ECSTATIC. His men had come on the unsuspecting Americans and followed his orders to capture rather than kill. He'd repay them by letting them kill the Americans slowly when the time came.

Welch knew there wouldn't be many of them, but he was surprised there were only three. His men had found the buried man; Welch remembered his name was Hooper. They'd unearthed him and in front of the three Americans cut off his genitals and shoved them in his mouth. Carver seethed, becoming unbalanced, which is exactly how Welch wanted him. Welch found the Japanese propensity for torture somewhat distasteful, but if it got him the desired results it was worth it.

Welch had them tied up and let his soldiers go to work on them with their fists. They delivered vicious blows to their bodies and faces. Sergeant Murata found a bamboo stick and used it on their shins until they were bloody messes. Twenty minutes after the beatings began the skies opened up and the rain came down in sheets. The cool water washed away the blood and gave the prisoners a brief respite from the Japanese soldiers' wrath.

Welch took the time to start his questions. "What was your mission? Why are you on this ridge? When will the Americans attack? Where will they attack?" The only answer he got was Carver's name, rank and serial number. The other two were no different. He'd have to use another tactic.

He pointed at Dunphy and his men lifted him from his crouching position by his shoulders. Dunphy winced in pain, feeling his shoulders stretched. He was separated from the others and sat down on a boulder. His hands were bound behind him and he bled from various parts of his face. His head hung to the side and he watched his tormentors through swollen, dark eyes.

Carver watched through his own slits. O'Connor slumped beside him watching as well. O'Connor had been given extra attention. Welch told him it was for trying to shoot him earlier in the day. O'Connor was tough though and took each new assault with the stoicism wrought from a lifetime of hard knocks. Dunphy whimpered with each new punch, but he was taking it better than Sergeant Carver had expected.

He doubted Dunphy would hold his tongue with more concentrated beatings, but he wasn't worried. The questions weren't important. The answers, which they didn't have for the most part, weren't important anyway. They didn't know the exact attack plan, but the Japanese knew it was coming any day and were already prepared. The answers wouldn't help them all that much. Carver wondered what Welch was playing at. Maybe he'd find out in the next few minutes.

Welch put his face close to Carver's. "Tell me about Morrisey. Is he and his band still in camp or are they nearby?" Carver scowled, but didn't respond. Welch looked to the sergeant standing in front of Dunphy with his bayonet pointing at Dunphy's chest. Welch touched his shoulder and nodded. With a yell straight from the training grounds of basic, Sgt.Murata lunged and buried his bayonet into Dunphy's shoulder. Dunphy screamed, his eyes squeezed shut in agony. A line of drool escaped from the side of his mouth mixing with the blood and rain. Murata kept the bayonet planted in his shoulder and smiled. The bayonet dripped the rain and blood mixture, making it look like a diluted red wine.

Welch continued. "I want to know about Morrisey and his men, sergeant. You'll tell me what you know or Private Dunphy pays the price."

Carver seethed and pulled against his restraints. He wanted nothing more than to get loose and snap Welch's neck like a toothpick, but it was hopeless. He was bound fast and wouldn't be able to move quickly even if he were to get loose. Carver thought about Morrisey. What did he really know? Not much, nothing that could help Welch. When the answer wasn't forthcoming he nodded to Sgt. Murata who twisted the blade. Dunphy's screams renewed, finally fading to whimpering. Carver hoped he'd pass out soon.

Through bloody lips Carver said, "What you wanna know?"

Welch smiled and held out his hand. Sergeant Murata pulled the bayonet out in a smooth motion and Dunphy fell forward, but was caught by the soldier standing behind him. He pulled him back to a sitting position. Dunphy's left sleeve was saturated in his own blood. It mixed with the rainwater and flowed to the growing pool near his boot. He was losing a lot of blood. Carver knew they'd be killed when the questioning stopped.

"Are they in camp? How many men are with him? What weapons does he have?"

Carver looked at him. These questions were inane. Welch probably knew more than he did, since he'd worked with Morrisey for years. He decided he'd go along with the farce. "He's in camp." He faltered and glanced at Sgt. Murata, whose bayonet was poised over Dunphy's heart. "He's lightly armed with old rifles and a couple of our carbines." He watched Welch's smile grow.

Welch asked, "And they're planning on attacking us from these very mountains? Attacking us from the rear?" he repeated the question in Japanese for his sergeants to hear.

Carver didn't know what he was talking about, but he seemed to want him to agree. "Yes, they're planning to attack soon. Attack your buddies from the rear while we attack from the front."

Welch smiled and didn't translate. He looked to Sgt. Murata who was staring at Sgt. Carver. Welch spoke a quick phrase in Japanese and Sgt. Murata smiled and steeled his eyes. He lunged forward and his bayonet pierced the center of Dunphy's chest. Dunphy's eyes flashed open in surprise and he looked at the bayonet buried in his chest. The sergeant leaned against the rifle, his yellow teeth bared as he stared into Dunphy's darkening eyes. He twisted the bayonet and pulled it out, a long stream of dark red blood sprayed and mixed with the rain. Dunphy's eyes rolled back and he slumped forward. This time the soldier let him collapse and he fell onto his face with a sickening crunch.

Carver screamed, "No!" and tried to come to his feet, but was slammed down by the butt of a rifle to the top of his head. The blow dropped him to the edge of consciousness.

## 29

T he rain stopped after an hour. The skies cleared and the dusk air filled with rising mist. The sun would set within the hour. Welch left O'Connor and Carver to fester where they sat. He wasn't ready to kill them yet. He might still need them.

He set the men to digging holes, which was sloppy work with the recent rain. He wanted to leave during the night and attack his old nemesis, Captain Morrisey, but he had to convince Colonel Araki of the need for the preemptive strike. He'd been pleased how Sgt. Carver had confirmed the made-up statement about Morrisey attacking their flank. He'd maneuvered him into saying it, even though he knew it was a lie. Carver had been confused, but Welch didn't think Sgt. Murata picked up on the ruse; after all, it had been in English which Murata didn't think Welch knew he understood. Sergeant Murata's own conniving had come back to bite him in the ass. Welch smiled at his own clever ploy.

He settled into the recess of a rock outcropping and told his radioman to contact headquarters. Once he had contact he handed the radio to Welch. Sergeant Murata was nearby, listening to the exchange. Welch took a deep breath and told the private on the other end about their successful attack. The private relayed the information and the next voice Welch heard was none other than Colonel Araki's. "Why are you reporting? Where is Lieutenant Kagi?"

"Lieutenant Kagi was killed on the initial assault. I took command. We lost twenty-two men to an airstrike. I led the remaining to the American flank and we captured three of them. Over."

There was a long silence. Welch thought he may have lost the connection, but soon Colonel Araki's gruff voice returned. "Well done, Thomas."

"Thank you, Sir. We've gotten some intelligence from the Americans." He glanced at Sgt. Murata, who was pretending not to listen. "Captain Morrisey and his natives are planning on attacking our rear in conjunction with the American attack. Our captives don't know the timing, only that it's soon. I would guess it to be in the morning."

Another pause, "Good work. We'll increase our rear guard."

"If I may make a suggestion, sir?"

"Go ahead, Thomas."

"Including myself, we have twenty-one well-armed men. We could move into position tonight and ambush Morrisey as he moves to your flank. I know the trails he'd take and can lie in wait for him. Over."

"Did any sergeants survive? Over." Welch gave the affirmative naming the two soldiers and Araki continued, "Give the radio to Sergeant Murata."

Welch acted offended, but handed the radio over. Murata took it and moved around the corner away from Welch. Welch could hear him speaking, but couldn't make out what he was saying. It all hinged on what Sgt. Murata believed.

Thirty seconds passed, then Sgt. Murata came around and handed the radio back to Welch who took it from him with a fabricated glare. Murata's slight nod was all Welch needed to know he'd succeeded with his farce. He keyed the radio, "This is Welch, go ahead, Colonel." He kept his voice curt, hoping to convey his displeasure over not being fully trusted.

"Thomas, you're cleared to proceed as you see fit. I've told Sgt. Murata to take your every command as if you were a ranking officer in the Imperial Army. After your successful ambush, return to the ridge and report any targets. Good hunting. Over and out."

Welch put the radio down; he couldn't help beaming. Morrisey would finally get what he so dearly deserved.

The sun was thirty minutes from setting and there was one last thing to do before moving on Morrisey's camp. "Sergeant, bring me the Americans. It's time to reward our men for a job well done." Murata gave a quick bow and went to do his bidding.

O'CONNOR AND CARVER were shivering and barely able to stand. They'd been slapped around on and off since watching Dunphy die. Carver felt each blow, but was beyond caring. He only hoped they'd kill him quickly, although he thought that unlikely. They were dragged to a small stand of trees, their hands were bound behind the tree, their feet lashed together. Carver was sure this would be where he died. The wind started up and the ghostly whistling through the rocks sounded like angels calling for him. He welcomed their call; he could finally rest.

He felt a stinging across his cheek and opened his eyes to see Welch smiling at him. "Sergeant Carver, you've been very helpful, but I'm afraid your usefulness has run its course. I'm going to give you a choice. Would you like to die first or watch your young friend die?" Carver's mouth was dry, but he conjured a bloody spit and sprayed it into Welch's face. Welch stepped back and used a kerchief. "I was going to let my men use you and O'Connor for bayonet practice. It would be a rather quick death, but if you're not careful I may let them cut on you instead. Perhaps they'll do what they did to your Corporal Hooper, but while alive."

"Fuck you, traitor."

Welch motioned his men forward. They formed a line in front of each man. Their long bayonets shimmered orange in the setting sun's final rays. "Unfortunately, I don't have time for a lingering death. Guess it's your lucky day." He raised his hand like he was starting a horse race. "Goodbye, Sergeant." He dropped his hand.

Carver closed his eyes waiting for the steel to penetrate his body, but instead he heard gunfire. The cracking of bullets passing near his head made him slouch instinctively. He opened his eyes and the soldiers in front of him were crumpling as plumes of blood sprayed his face. The gunfire increased to a crescendo of death, then abruptly stopped. It had lasted seconds, but every Japanese soldier was down.

Carver looked to O'Connor who was staring at him through swollen, black eye sockets, his mouth hung open in astonishment. There was a voice he recognized instantly. "Mighty nice of them to line up like that. Makes it easy."

Carver grinned through his torn lips and fresh blood dripped down his chin. "About time, Captain Morrisey." He felt hands on his arms then a slice and his arms were free. There was someone at his feet cutting his bonds. He fell forward and was caught by one of the shirt-less natives. He lowered him down and offered him his water flask. Carver thought he'd died and gone to heaven. The water tasted like nectar. He could feel its rejuvenating power.

After too short a drink the flask was pulled away. Morrisey was kneeling beside him, "Don't want to drink too much too fast; make you sick." He turned to look at Welch sprawled on his back only feet away, gasping with a bubbling chest wound. His eyes were open. Morrisey moved over him and noticed a Nambu pistol in his hand. It moved towards him. Morrisey calmly placed his heavy boot on his wrist and pinned his hand to the ground. He reached down and plucked the pistol from Welch's hand. He looked it over and scowled. He looked into Welch's eyes and shook his head, "Ever the disappoint-ment, old boy." He put the barrel against Welch's forehead. "I have a question for you. How you die will depend on your answer." He didn't wait for a response. "Were you responsible for leading the Japanese attack on my village before the American invasion?" Welch gave him a confused look. Morrisey moved the barrel down his body until it stopped at his crotch. "The attack that killed my wife and baby son?"

Welch shook his head back and forth hard, but his eyes showed fear. With eyes cold as steel in winter, Morrisey pulled the trigger. Welch's eyes flashed with pain. He tried to reach for his destroyed groin, but his arms were pinned.

"My wife suffered at the hands of your yellow friends for hours.

When they were done with her, they shot her in the belly leaving her to die slowly. I assure you, your pain is nothing compared to hers." His eyes went to slits, tears forming, reliving the moment. "I found her when she was minutes from death. She tried to tell me who betrayed her, but she died. I never suspected you until you betrayed me outright." He moved the gun to his belly and fired again.

Welch's eyes went to the back of his head. Morrisey leaned close and shook him until he focused on him. He pushed on his wound sending fresh waves of pain through Welch's body. He raised the pistol to his face, "Rot in hell." He shot him in the face and his head snapped back against a rock.

Sergeant Carver rubbed his wrists. He'd heard the one-sided conversation. He looked at Captain Morrisey and put his hand on his shoulder. "Too quick. More than the sadistic bastard deserved."

Morrisey rubbed his black beard and looked around in the fading light. His men were picking over the Japanese corpses filling pockets with knives, ammo and anything that caught their fancy. Morrisey threw the pistol over the ridge. "You're right, Sergeant." He shook his head, coming back to the present. "Looks like we arrived just in time." His eyes found Dunphy's body, "Not soon enough, however."

O'Connor walked to where Dunphy's body sprawled in the fading light. He kneeled over him and pulled his body so he was on his back. His dead eyes stared into nothing. O'Connor reached down and closed his friend's eyelids. The gaping wound in his chest was crusted over with dried blood. He patted his shoulder and whispered, "I'll miss you, you son-of-a-bitch." He stood up and went to where their carbines were leaning against a rock. He grabbed his and Dunphy's and handed Carver Dunphy's weapon. "We've gotta complete this mission, Sarge." He pointed, "For him, for Dunphy."

Carver checked the weapon and nodded, "Bet your ass." He walked to Morrisey and sat down. Morrisey sat beside him. Carver said, "You got to us in the nick of time. I thought that was it, I really did." He shook his head wondering how he was still alive.

He continued. "We lost our radio so our mission's changed. We're gonna find and take out the Jap artillery." Morrisey lifted a dubious eyebrow and Carver continued. "Our guys are attacking tomorrow morning and they'll be decimated unless we take out the Jap artillery. We were preparing to leave when Welch and his merry band showed up. We know the approximate location of the guns, but," He shrugged, "Were gonna be in the general area then take 'em out when we spotted their smoke."

Morrisey considered him. "Three men? That was your plan? You realize there's probably a large contingent guarding those guns?" Carver nodded. Morrisey laughed, "You're a credit to your nation, Sergeant. Certainly brave. Suicidal possibly, but brave." He looked around at his gathering men. They were fidgeting and wanting to leave the cursed mountain. "I suppose you'll want our help?"

Sergeant Carver said, "O'Connor and I'll be going whether you come or not. Obviously, our chances of success would increase dramatically with your help." Morrisey stroked his beard. "I'm not trying to convince you; you'll do what's best for your men, as it should be, but if this attack fails, it may prolong the fighting for months. Our forces will have to fall back and wait for reinforcements. More men will die."

Morrisey smiled, "What do you think we were doing in these parts, Sergeant? We weren't on our way to your aid, but on the way to the front to do what we could for your Army. Of course we'll join you. I know this area well and my men know it even better. I've a good idea where the Japs are set up." He looked O'Connor and Carver over. They were beat up and haggard, but standing on their own two feet. "You be ready to go in an hour?"

## 30

It was dark and they'd been traveling west for three hours through thick jungle. The natives were setting a fast pace, too fast for the exhausted Sergeant Carver and Private O'Connor, but they weren't going to ask for any special favors. They were already asking these men to risk their lives for them; the least they could do was try to keep up.

Every cut, minor and major, was seeping blood and puss. There wasn't a specific spot that hurt more than any other, just a constant mind-numbing throb.

Morrisey was aware of their fickle condition and made them drink water every fifteen minutes. Even so, neither of them felt the need to pee. They finally stopped and took a half hour break. Carver didn't want to sit down, afraid he wouldn't be able to get back up. O'Connor immediately fell to the ground and drained his canteen. He was given another immediately and he slurped more of the life-saving fluid. It could've been piss and he wouldn't have known the difference. It was wet and that's what his body was demanding.

Carver decided to sit beside him and slug his water. Both men were covered in a thin coat of sweat. It stung as it moved down their bodies finding each cut and scrape. "How you holding up, private?"

O'Connor nodded, "I'll make it. I'll make it." He said it like it was his new mantra he was voicing for the first time.

Carver slapped his knee and O'Connor winced, but Carver couldn't see it in the darkness. "We'll make it, no problem. Can't be far."

Morrisey approached and crouched beside him without making a sound. When he spoke, Carver flinched, "Course you'll make it and you're correct, we're in the area. We'll slow our pace from here on out." He looked at the phosphorescent dial of his watch. "We'll move for another hour or so, then wait for dawn. Don't want to stumble across the bloody Japs in the dark. That'd give away the whole show. We'll wait until they start firing, unless we come across them soon."

The half hour passed and Carver had to force himself off the ground. He felt like he'd aged fifty years since the morning. He was glad to see, O'Connor wasn't in much better shape. Sometimes being ornery beat out youth. He helped O'Connor to his feet and slapped his back. O'Connor winced again.

Their eyes were well adjusted to the dark jungle. They were able to see the natives moving like silent ghosts. They tried to mimic their stealth, but their sore muscles made them move like wooden toy soldiers and they endured withering looks with each broken branch or stumbled upon rock.

Carver tried to keep his bearings, but found it hopeless. They'd moved too far, too fast. If someone had asked him to lead the way due east, he'd have no idea. All he knew was the terrain was getting steeper, angling downhill. Occasionally they'd walk along some razor ridge, then descend again down a jungle slope. Going down was harder on his legs than going up. Each jarring step felt like needles coursing through his body. Even in the darkness he was careful to hide his pain.

They'd descended another slope and were moving along flat ground when he stumbled into the crouched form of a native. He fell and the native reached out and caught him before he hit the ground. He held his finger to his lips and Carver froze. The native eased him down and pointed forward, then cupped his ear, *listen.*

Carver strained to hear. At first nothing, only the breeze moving through the trees. Then the wind stopped and he heard the distinct sound of metal on metal and men's voices; Japanese voices. He nodded to the native and pulled himself into a crouched position. He wondered if he was expected to do something. He was the ranking American, but O'Connor was the only man under his command. Morrisey was the one risking his men; he'd let him lead. After all, he could hardly see through his swollen eye sockets. This was no time for a pissing match.

He waited and soon Morrisey was beside him. He put his lips next to his ear and said, "My men'll scout forward, see if this is what we're looking for. If so, we'll retreat and evaluate, if not, we'll go around them. Carver nodded his understanding and looked over his shoulder at the dark form he knew to be O'Connor. He could take care of himself; a good soldier.

Forty minutes passed before Morrisey was at his ear again. He didn't hear him coming again. *The man's like a cheetah.* "Confirmed target. Eight artillery pieces, well camouflaged. We'll pull back." Carver nodded and got to his feet, grimacing.

They moved thirty yards into the jungle and stopped. The natives fanned out in a defensive perimeter. Morrisey spoke to Carver and O'Connor. "There are Eight artillery pieces, probably 105mm's. My men aren't good at identifying big guns, but they said they were 'bikpela', which means big, so I'm assuming these are the ones you blokes are looking for." His white teeth flashed in the night. He looked up, the stars were obscured by the overhanging canopy, with occasional spots you could see through. "The canopy's not conducive for using your mortar here, but the ridge we passed over not long ago is clear and overlooks the Jap position. Do you think you and Private O'Connor can get up there and set up your mortar and machine gun?"

Carver squinted through the darkness trying to decipher where the ridge was, but he could barely see ten feet. "I'll take your word for that, but yes, we can make it. Is the base close enough for the machine gun to hit?" Morrisey looked annoyed and Carver said, "Sorry, course it is or you wouldn't have said it. I'm a little loopy still." Morrisey smiled at the phrase and Carver continued. "Could your men take us there? I don't think I could find my own ass in this ink."

Morrisey smiled again and shook his head. He said, "You Americans and your idioms. Yes, of course my men will take you there and they'll take the guns too, just like they've been doing all night."

Carver grinned and looked down. "Thanks Captain, thanks for everything. There's no way we could've found our way here without you."

Morrisey squeezed his shoulder, "No need for that, you may wish we hadn't in a few hours."

Walking up the steep slope to the ridge took Carver and O'Connor a long time. Each step felt like they were carrying three hundred pounds on their shoulders. The slope was slippery and they fell several times before the natives relieved them of their packs and carbines. Except for their knives they were defenseless, but neither cared. When they reached the top, sweat was pouring off and they were out of breath. They were near their physical breaking points.

The natives hustled them along and set them up in a recessed area on the ridge. While some had helped them up the hill the others had dug them foxholes and prepared their positions.

The soldiers slipped into their holes, grateful to be sitting down. All but one of the natives left. The remaining man crouched beside them and with hand signals, indicated they should set up their weapons. O'Connor nearly laughed out loud at the native's rendition of firing a machine gun; hands in a fist, shaking back and forth and sweeping side to side.

With fumbling fingers, they put the Nambu together. The knee mortar didn't require any assembly; it was ready to go. They slunk back to their holes and the native signaled they should sleep while he kept watch. Carver and O'Connor fell to the bottom of their holes and were asleep in seconds.

Colonel Sinclair and General Thornton leaned over the map spread before them on the rickety table. Neither man had slept in the past twenty-four hours and wouldn't for the foreseeable future. It was the middle of the night, but the temperature had only gone down three degrees from the height of the day. Beads of sweat dripped from their noses. Colonel Sinclair pointed at an area with tight contour lines. "This is the ridge we suspect the guns are on. It's steep and inhospitable, but reconnaissance flights show a possible area where the guns could be hidden."

General Thornton nodded. "Did they see any guns or is it just guess work?"

"The jungle's too thick to even see the ground." The General stared at him, "It's guess work. We don't have any hard evidence."

Thornton slammed his fist onto the table sending pieces across the map like a petulant child losing a board game. "Still no word from that sergeant of ours?"

Colonel Sinclair shook his head. "Nothing since the air strikes they called in yesterday. It may be their radio malfunctioned. The Marine pilots said they had good hits on the target. Whether they're KIA or out a radio, the outcome's the same on our end."

Thornton watched the Lieutenant putting the pieces back to the appropriate spots on the map. "How's our timeline? The men getting into position okay?"

Colonel Sinclair nodded. "Yes Sir, things are moving smoothly and on time. We should have everyone in place in another hour."

General Thornton looked at his watch then back at the Colonel. "I want the timeline moved up. I want our boys attacking before dawn. Let's not wait. Maybe it'll throw off the Jap's shooting if they can't see us, get our boys in amongst their troops quicker."

Colonel Sinclair didn't like last minute changes, but he understood the logic. "I'll pass it along. What time you want the attack to begin?"

General Thornton looked at his watch and made the calculation. "They'll be in place in an hour, that's 03:30. Let's move the takeoff time to 0415. That should be enough buffer for any unknowns popping up." He grinned, "Gotta give old Murphy his due."

Colonel Sinclair smiled, "Yes Sir. No doubt he'll rear his ugly head somewhere."

~

IT SEEMED like only seconds had passed, but O'Connor and Carver had slept two hours before the native awoke them. It only took his voice to wake Sgt. Carver, but O'Connor had to be poked and prodded before he opened his eyes. Neither man was happy; they felt sorer than they'd been before napping. O'Connor took a swig of water, swished it around and spit it onto the ground. "My mouth tastes like I ate a shit sandwich."

Sergeant Carver took a swig and swallowed. He only grunted. The native was crouched beside Carver's hole. Carver reached out and touched him, "Anything happening down there?" the native looked at him with a blank stare. In the darkness, Carver could see the whites of his eyes. He pointed towards the jungle then shrugged trying to get his question across. The native seemed to understand. He shook his head, but pointed to the east. It was still dark, but there was a tiny hint of the coming day. Carver looked at his watch and was surprised to see it was 0345. Morrisey wanted to begin his attack a little before light, at 0500.

Sergeant Carver got out of his hole and went to where the natives had placed the knee mortar. There was a neat stack of 12 shells beside it. It was still too dark to see his target despite the native pointing it out.

O'Connor set up the machine gun in the crook of two boulders. He sat behind the gun and worked on digging out a comfortable sitting position in the dirt. He swung the gun's barrel side to side and up and down. He would be aiming down, having to elevate his arms to get the proper angle. He adjusted his spot until he could do so with ease.

Now they waited. The night was quiet except for the constant chatter of jungle birds, insects and animals.

The time passed slowly. The night seemed to linger. The hint of light grew in the east as the morning threatened to break, but slowly. A half hour passed and the jungle noise stopped abruptly, like a light switch being turned off. The world seemed to hold its breath. Carver and O'Connor felt the tension in the air like something big and unknown was about to happen. O'Connor pivoted his gun back and forth, traversing the lightening jungle. Different shades of green started to separate themselves from the darkness. He thought he could see the clearing below where his target lay hidden, but he couldn't be sure.

Off to the east there was a muted chattering of gunfire. The sky lit up with flashes, the low rumble of explosives reached them. Carver adjusted the mortar tube and whispered between clenched teeth, "This is it. Wait for Morrisey to start things off. We're still early, looks like our guys are starting things." O'Connor nodded and raised the brim of his floppy jungle hat. He checked the ammo sticking out the side of the Nambu machine gun. He glanced to the stack of ammo at his side and took a deep breath. The native, whose name they learned was Enops, laid beside him propping his ancient Enfield rifle on a rock and jamming the stock into his bare shoulder. O'Connor looked where he was aiming and tried to see his target. He angled his barrel to follow the same trajectory.

The flashes and gunfire became more frequent to the east. There was no way of knowing who had the upper hand, only that a lot of ordnance was being expended. The guns below remained silent. A light appeared and O'Connor's heart skipped a beat. He adjusted his aim. The Japanese artillery unit wasn't as far away as he thought. He hunched although he knew they had no chance of spotting him even if they were looking. More lights appeared, extending into the jungle. The Japanese were waking up, alerted by the long awaited American attack.

Carver saw the activity, but knew things were happening quicker than Morrisey had expected. He wondered if he was in position yet. If the guns opened up before Morrisey attacked he'd have to make a choice whether to attack on his own. Every round that went out would kill American soldiers; he couldn't let that happen. He grabbed a mortar shell, pulled the safety off and dropped it into the tube. He adjusted the range dial and put the floating bubble in the center. He wrapped the lanyard trigger around his finger. If the big guns opened up he wouldn't wait.

Flashes from the sea caught his attention; they were continuous and huge. He wondered whose navy held the advantage this morning. He didn't have long to wait as the big naval shells rocketed toward the Japanese rear and exploded with bright flashes far below him, marking the headquarters area. He wished he could call those guns onto the artillery position below him. Maybe they'd see the artillery muzzle flashes and redirect their fire. He shook his head knowing the Japanese were too well camouflaged. If not, they would have been spotted and destroyed long ago.

Out of the darkness there was a much closer flash followed immediately by seven more rippling down the line of Japanese artillery. The flashes were much closer than Carver had anticipated. His night vision was ruined, but he didn't hesitate. He pulled the lanyard and was rewarded with the soft thump of a departing shell. The smell of hot cordite filled his nostrils and he reached for another shell.

O'Connor heard the mortar leave the tube and aimed down the barrel of the Nambu. He put the barrel just below closest flash and depressed the trigger. He shot a short burst, watching his tracers streak into the jungle. He adjusted and gave them a longer burst, walking his fire back. Another flash of fire from the big guns almost took his night vision, but he had one eye shut preserving some vision.

He saw Sgt. Carver's first mortar round explode near the second gun. The flash was tiny compared with the 105mm guns long tongue of flame, but the flash was enough to light up Japanese troops being flung backwards. He increased his rate of fire, knowing his own muzzle flash would be seen and he'd start taking incoming fire. He hoped Morrisey and his merry band would attack soon or his position would be inundated with fire.

THE FLASHES from the west and the rumble that accompanied it pushed Morrisey's timetable up. He'd been advancing slowly from his night bivouac position, but now his men were moving quicker. It would only be a matter of time before the artillery opened up on the hapless Americans. His original plan had been to attack the unit when they were still sleeping, catching them by surprise, but now he'd have to attack a fully alert force of unknown size. His only advantage would be the fact that they'd be busy working the artillery pieces not looking for attackers.

He was minutes from his takeoff point when the guns opened up with a deafening roar. The 105mm blast shook the men to their core, the percussion shaking their bodies, striking fear into them. He'd hoped to move his men to the side and attack from the thick jungle barrier that kept the artillery hidden. He had to reassess when he saw tracer fire arcing down from the ridge above them. Sergeant Carver and Private O'Connor weren't waiting for his attack. He saw a mortar round explode near the second gun, then more tracer fire sweeping along the guns.

Morrisey kept his men moving, not wanting to get hit by friendly fire. The fire from the ridge would take attention away from his men. They were running to get north of the Japanese position when another round of artillery went out. The men flattened instinctively, as the big shells ripped over their heads. He had them up quickly and moved them into position. He did a quick head count; they were all there.

He broke them into two units. He'd lead his twenty men to the east and Chief Ahio would lead his men against the guns in the front. He knew he could trust Ahio; he had a debt to pay. He'd sacrifice his life and the life of his men to renew his honor. Before splitting, he told Ahio to wait for his attack. Ahio nodded and melted into the jungle with his men.

Using the jungle, Morrisey moved down to the last gun. The Japanese troops charged with protecting the guns were shifting to the south towards the incoming fire from the ridge. They were returning fire up and down the line, keeping their attackers pinned down. Mortars kept raining down, but the machine gun fire had dwindled. He heard the occasional crack of a rifle from the ridge. He'd sent Enops because he was his best marksman. He was sure with every crack of the rifle a Japanese soldier was dying. More and more Japanese were moving away from the big guns, leaving them exposed.

The darkness was lifting and Morrisey could clearly see the Japanese artillery crews working like a well-oiled machine. They were in a rhythm; load, clear, fire, eject. They were putting shells out faster and faster. Their professionalism kept them focused on the job at hand and not on their dangerously exposed flank.

Morrisey wanted his men to use grenades. The natives pulled them from their loin cloths. Each man put his rifle down and got ready to throw. Morrisey waited thirty seconds. He watched the rhythm of the firing and threw his grenade at the instant right before the artillery lanyard would be pulled. His timing was perfect. The grenades went off amongst the seventh and eighth guns just as they fired, the sound masking the smaller bang of the grenades. Japanese soldiers were flung against the guns and shredded with shrapnel. Morrisey grabbed his second grenade and hurled it towards the line of soldier's backs firing on the ridge. His men followed suit. Without waiting, Morrisey unslung his M1 Carbine and charged from the jungle. He fired from the hip, killing the remaining crew on the eighth gun. His men fired, working their bolt action rifles as quick as they pulled the trigger.

Ahio and his men assaulted the front two guns hurling grenades and firing their Enfield's with devastating effect. Within a minute, four of the eight guns were out of commission. The Japanese soldiers assaulting O'Connor and Carver were oblivious to the threat. Morrisey moved his men up the line toward the middle guns which were still firing in their rhythm. The guns were the Japanese soldiers only focus; they were oblivious to the attacking natives.

A Japanese loader picked up a 105mm round and was shuffling it to be loaded when he saw a gun barrel flash behind him. He looked and saw dark shapes moving amongst the big guns. They were firing small arms. He realized they were being attacked and he shouted a warning seconds before his head snapped back with the impact of a bullet. The shell dropped from his hands and crushed his foot. He was beyond caring.

Lieutenant Tomeo heard the man's cry and looked up in time to see his head snap back. He was stunned as he was sprayed with blood and brains. His mouth hung open, trying to comprehend what had happened. He was using his Samurai sword to direct his men. It had been his father's and his fathers before him, a family heirloom.

Rage filled him as he realized what was happening. He raised the sword and screamed a battle cry, running towards the dark shapes. He was closing on a shirtless black man, a native, he realized. The man saw him coming and raised his rifle in time to deflect the sword blow. Tomeo raised it to strike him down, but was thrown back as three bullets slammed into his chest. He saw the native he'd tried to kill reach down and pick up the ancient sword. Rage filled his chest, but his body wouldn't react to his dying brain's impulse. His eyes glazed over and there was only darkness.

Ahio's man lifted the sword and smiled. He went to Ahio who was putting a fresh magazine into his Carbine and held the sword out to him. Ahio nodded and tested the sword. He swung it side to side. He slung his rifle and pointed to the backs of the Japanese soldiers still firing on the ridge. Soon they'd notice their artillery wasn't firing, so they had to attack while they still had surprise on their side. Ahio raised his new sword and ran towards the Japanese line. His men followed firing as they went, shooting the soldiers in the back.

The onslaught from behind caught the Japanese off guard. They were dying, but how? When Ahio's men were almost upon them they turned and met the threat. The natives were amongst them, using their rifles as clubs. Ahio brought his sword down and cleaved a corporal nearly in half. The finely tuned blade went all the way to the man's pelvis. He pulled the sword and swung at another man who was squirming on the ground. The blade went through his neck like butter and hit a rock. It sparked as rock chunks disintegrated. Ahio's blood lust was up. He lunged his big body into a group of soldiers who'd just shot one of his men. He swung the blade from the side like a baseball bat. It caught the first man in the side and went through him, severing his torso. Blood and gore spilled from him as he collapsed. The next man lunged his bayoneted rifle at him and before Ahio could react, sank it into his belly.

Ahio grunted, feeling the pain of steel in his gut. It enraged him and his eyes seemed to shoot fire at the soldier on the end of the rifle. The soldier held the rifle firmly lodged. Ahio lifted the Samurai Sword and lunged forward. The blade sank into the soldier's cheek, he screamed and dropped his rifle. He stumbled back holding his gushing face.

Ahio gripped the rifle hanging from his gut and yanked it straight out. A gush of dark blood followed and he staggered. He raised the sword to finish the job, but another Japanese soldier was charging from his left with his bayonet aimed at his chest. He tried to turn to the new threat, but knew he wouldn't make it in time. He braced himself, but the soldier was flung back as a bullet slammed into his chest. Ahio turned to find his men beside him, their dark torsos shimmering with sweat and blood.

Ignoring the bleeding gash in his belly, he gave a fearsome yell and led his men into the midst of the remaining soldiers.

The Japanese recovered from their initial surprise. Their bayonets shone in the morning light. A yell of "banzai" went up and they surged forward screaming.

Morrisey kept his men back at the guns. He'd already spiked two of them by putting grenades into the barrels. The thick barrels had bowed, but not bursted. He hoped it was enough to destroy them. His men were in crouched positions firing their bolt action Enfields into the line of Japanese soldiers with deadly accuracy.

Morrisey watched as the unmistakable form of Chief Ahio charged towards the Japanese line. He had a sword in his hand and his carbine slung on his back. He was yelling, exhorting his men to follow. Morrisey thought he looked like a crazed Viking. He watched as Ahio's men ran to keep up, but the big chief got to the line quicker and engaged the soldiers who were turning to meet the threat. Morrisey watched as he cut through men like wheat to a scythe. Then he saw a soldier lunge and he could tell Ahio was wounded. It was time to leave the guns and help his old friend. In Pidgin he yelled, "Sasim, sasim!" His men didn't hesitate. They rose as one and charged.

The Japanese line saw Ahio's men and were turning to engulf them. The Japanese didn't see Morrisey and his men until they were on top of them. Morrisey fired point blank into the backs of three soldiers. He stopped and picked off targets one by one. His men were too close to use their bolt actions so they used them as lethal clubs, beating the Japanese soldiers down.

Morrisey expended his magazine and kneeled to reload. A short Japanese soldier leaped up only feet away, screamed and charged, his bayonet leading. Morrisey dropped his carbine and unholstered his Webley pistol in a practiced movement. He rolled to his right, firing at the same time. The Japanese soldier's bayonet buried in the soft jungle dirt beside Morrisey. The soldier fell to the side, half his face torn away by the large caliber bullet.

Morrisey went to his knee and leveled the Webley at another charging soldier. He missed with his first shot, but as he got closer he connected. Two bullets smashed into the soldier, opening his chest. Before the man hit the ground, Morrisey was aiming at another soldier who'd just bayoneted a shirtless native. Still crouched, he fired his last two shots, but missed. In disgust, he dropped the pistol and picked up the carbine. He slammed a magazine home and shot the man in the back as he was sparring with a native. He didn't miss and the soldier fell away. The native, Taton, gave him a smile of thanks. His face changed suddenly as he looked beyond Morrisey. His eyes were big. Morrisey knew he was in trouble. He dropped to his left and rolled, bringing his weapon to his shoulder as he came to a crouch. The Japanese soldier was close and Morrisey pulled the trigger in quick succession.

The small caliber bullets ripped into the soldier, but he continued his charge like a crazed bull. The bayonet was inches from his chest when a dark flash from the right knocked the soldier away.

Captain Morrisey opened his eyes, relieved to be in one piece. The Japanese was on the ground next to him struggling to get Taton off him. Taton wasn't moving. Morrisey pulled his knife and drove it into the only part of the soldiers' body he could see, his head. The blade glanced off his forehead, but continued downward until it found the soft eye socket and sank deep into his brain. The soldier shuddered then stopped moving. Morrisey pulled Taton's shoulder to get him back on his feet, but his staring eyes were lifeless. The bayonet stuck from his side, a large pool of dark blood soaked his loin cloth. Morrisey paused, but the fight was raging all around him. He drew a bead on another soldier and fired.

SERGEANT CARVER BURNED through his remaining mortar rounds. He'd walked them back to front with devastating effect. The Japanese soldiers were dark shapes running for cover in the predawn light.

O'Connor's Nambu rounds were slicing into the Japanese lines. The tracer rounds left no doubt about their position. The Japanese were firing towards the muzzle flashes, their fire getting more accurate as they crouched and aimed.

O'Connor ducked away as rounds hit the rocks he was using for cover. Dust from the front of the rock filled his nostrils. The fire was heavy. He looked to the prone form of Enop still firing methodically. He was better protected, the only thing exposed, the barrel of his rifle. O'Connor tried to come back to the gun, but the fire was too intense. The ricochets were zinging around his head like an angry swarm of hornets. He gave up and hunkered into the bottom of his hole. He covered his head, listening to the bullets and Enop's firing. He felt useless. He thought about grabbing his rifle and crawling next to the native, but he didn't think he'd make it out of the hole without getting hit.

He heard Sgt. Carver yelling, "You okay, O'Connor?"

He hunkered lower and yelled as loud as he could, "I'm fine, but I can't move."

"Stay down, don't move. I can see Morrisey making his move he's in amongst the guns." Carver stopped firing watching the action below. The Japanese were moving towards the cover of the jungle, getting out of the exposed clearing, moving towards Carver's position. They were oblivious to Morrisey's men.

Now that O'Connor stopped firing, the Japanese didn't have a target and started spraying the entire ridge. Carver went to his belly as rounds narrowly missed him and thudded into the trees behind him. He grabbed his carbine and crawled forward. There was a large palm to his front and he crawled to the base and peered around the edge. He could see Morrisey's men overrunning the big guns. The men attacking the front guns weren't satisfied and continued forward into the backs of the Japanese. In the growing light he could see the biggest of the natives charging forward with what looked like a sword. *That big bastards gotta be Chief Ahio.*

Carver leveled his carbine and shot towards the Japanese lines. At this range he couldn't tell if he was hitting anything, but he figured he would help any way he could. The mortar was out of ammo. Even if it wasn't, with the natives mixed with the Japanese, he'd do more harm than good.

As the attack continued, the incoming fire on his position dwindled to a trickle. He yelled, "O'Connor, get on that gun. Be careful, our guys are mixed with the Japs."

O'Connor pulled his hands from around his head and noticed the incoming fire had stopped. He said a silent prayer of thanks and felt his body for any holes. Miraculously he was unscathed. He sat up and dirt cascaded off him. He poked his head up and looked down on the clearing. The sun hadn't risen yet, but it was light enough to see the entire scene. He grabbed the handle of the Nambu and checked his ammo, which was covered in dirt and dust. The gun looked operational. He traversed the barrel to the Japanese line. It was easy to discern friend from foe; the natives were shirtless and black. He lined up on a line of soldiers firing their Arisakas. He depressed the trigger, but nothing happened. He squeezed it again, nothing. He pulled on the belt of ammo sticking from the side, but it wouldn't budge. He stood and pulled back on the breech, trying to clear the jam. He couldn't move it. He pulled the weapon into the hole and immediately saw it had been hit. The left side had a gaping hole.

"The Nambu's fucked, Sarge. Took multiple hits." He threw the useless weapon over the side of the ridge and found his dirt covered carbine at the bottom of his hole. He shook the weapon, knocking the dirt off. He checked the breach and crawled forward to the notch where the machine gun had rested. He sighted down the barrel and found the line of Japanese soldiers again. He pulled the trigger methodically, correcting his aim each time. It was a long shot, but he could tell he was close when the soldiers squirmed and moved from their position. One soldier stood and his back blossomed red. He pitched forward. O'Connor looked to Enop's smoking barrel. "Nice shot," he yelled.

They continued to fire until the natives and Japanese were too intertwined. Even Enop stopped firing. As the sun rose, the battle below was easier to discern. The Japanese were doomed, their numbers down to a few men, but they fought with vigor. They charged and fought, surrender never an option. They wouldn't have been spared if they had.

After six minutes, the fighting was over. Sergeant Carver stood and looked down on the scene. Dead Japanese soldiers littered the ground. From this height they looked like toys haphazardly left on a green carpeted living room floor by a child.

They stood and without a word moved off the ridge and slid down the steep slope. As they passed through the jungle they came across native women moving towards the battlefield. O'Connor asked, "What're they doing here?"

Sergeant Carver walked with his carbine pointed at the ground. "Must be here to help with the wounded." As they came out of the jungle onto the battlefield, the smell of cordite, blood and shit filled their senses. The dead no longer looked like toys, but shredded men. Not all were Japanese. In amongst the soldiers were natives, their dark skin in stark relief against the green uniforms of the Japanese. There was a loud bang and Carver and O'Connor flinched as another 105mm gun's barrel was spiked. Smoke wafted from the shattered barrel. Morrisey's men had learned to use two grenades to destroy the barrels.

Carver looked around the battlefield, searching for Morrisey. He saw a group of natives clustered around something. He walked into the circle of silent men. In the center Captain Morrisey sat beside the hulking Chief Ahio. He was on his back, the wound in his belly seeping dark blood. Beside him was a blood soaked cloth. Morrisey tried to put it back on the wound, but Ahio looked him in the eye and shook his head. In his deep voice he said, "Let me go to my ancestors."

Morrisey nodded and sat beside him. Ahio's men went to him one at a time and placed their hands on their dying leader's head. Ahio looked each man in the eye, but said nothing. When they'd all gone through, Ahio looked at Morrisey and said, "My men have fought honorably today. Take them in the fold and forgive their treason." Morrisey nodded and squeezed his shoulder. Ahio continued, his voice quiet, "And mine."

Morrisey stood and addressed the men in a loud voice. "Chief Ahio and his men have fought gloriously and all are forgiven their treason."

Sergeant Carver and Private O'Connor couldn't understand the Pidgin, but they understood the gist.

Morrisey bent down to Chief Ahio and watched as he took his last breath. His eyes went blank, staring at the sky through the jungle he loved. Morrisey closed his eyes, stood and stepped away. The women streamed between the men and started wailing the loss of their chief. Amongst them was his daughter, the girl Private Dunphy had laid with. She looked to Sgt. Carver and searched his face. Carver thought about Dunphy's horrific death on the ridge. He gave a shake of his head, his eyes conveying sadness and Lela bowed her head and wailed in renewed grief.

## 31

It was still pitch black when Foxtrot Company of the 164th Regiment moved from the safety of their foxholes and advanced towards the bunkers of the Japanese lines. It was impossible to expect complete silence with four companies moving along such a compressed line of advance, but Captain Frank hoped they'd surprise the Japanese before they were noticed.

They'd gone forty yards without contact when the night erupted in tracer fire. In the darkness the tracers looked like glowing beach balls. All along the front, Japanese heavy machine guns opened up. They continued advancing, moving forward from cover to cover using the darkness to their advantage. The men were told not to shoot unless they had a sure target and he was proud of their fire control. Without muzzle flashes the Japanese had nothing to shoot at.

The welcome sound of friendly artillery fire arcing across the sky and smashing amongst the Japanese line pushed the men forward. Maybe this time they'd make it to the bunker line. Once past, the way would be clear to bust through to the Japanese rear and route the obstinate enemy.

The flashes of exploding ordnance ruined Captain Frank's night vision. He yelled for his men to keep moving forward. A machine gun's muzzle flash to his front was only yards away. He dropped to his belly; the three men behind him weren't as quick and were shredded and flung back. He pulled a grenade from his belt and flung it towards the muzzle flash. It exploded and the gun stopped. He ran in a crouch into the darkness, wishing he could see more than bright dots. He knew he must be close. He tripped and fell into the Japanese hole. He expected to be skewered any second. He felt bodies all around him. He thrashed and punched his Thompson submachine gun into the soft shapes, but nothing moved. His grenade had landed in the bottom of the hole and killed the three men in it. He took a deep breath.

His men flooded past him and he got to his feet trying to get himself moving. Someone grabbed his arm and his first Sergeant was beside him, "You okay, Sir?"

He got his bearings and moved beside his sergeant, "Fine. Keep the men spread out." The allied artillery was moving forward, keeping pace with the American advance. It was exploding amongst the bunkers now a mere two hundred yards away. He nodded. The sergeant said, "Don't do that shit again, Sir."

Foxtrot Company was moving amongst the forward Japanese foxholes, killing men as they passed. The first line of machine gun nests was dealt with. They'd gotten this far before, but were stopped by the Japanese artillery. Captain Frank prayed the enemy artillery would be silenced this time.

They continued to advance, but now the bunkers started hammering away at them. Men dropped as they tried to leapfrog forward. Advances were made nonetheless, men using the cover and darkness to good effect. Japanese flares filled the air, but in amongst the shredded jungle it cast crazy shadows, making targeting tough. The Japanese bunkers kept hammering away on prepositioned choke points. Even though they couldn't see the G.I.'s, they were taking their toll.

Captain Frank dove behind a fallen tree and poked his head over. He could see the winking bunkers one hundred yards away. *By God, we're gonna make it this time.* His hopes were shattered moments later when the freight train sound of incoming 105mm Japanese shells started raining down. They were coming in salvos of eight, walking along the advancing line, shredding everything in front of the bunkers not behind cover.

He put his head down as a near miss shook the ground beneath him. *Shit, not again.* He had one chance. He had to get his men into the bunkers. This was the exact scenario of the last failed attack. His men had been decimated by the damned artillery, then sent into full retreat when the Japs counterattacked. That wasn't happening this time; it couldn't. They had to break this stalemate and push the Japs off this cursed island once and for all.

His men were hunkered down, the big shells tearing apart jungle, dirt and flesh. He was about to order his men forward probably to their deaths when he noticed the volume of fire decreasing. Was he imagining it? No, the salvos of eight were now salvos of four. He yelled to his men, "Stay down, stay down." He saw the form of his radio man lit up by an exploding shell. He was hunkered behind a rock. Captain Frank yelled, "Burk, get up here with that radio."

He yelled again and this time Burk heard him and ran forward, his big fifty-pound radio pack barely slowing down his big body. He dove in beside him, the handset extended. "Vulcan 1 this is Foxtrot Alpha. We're pinned down one hundred yards from the bunker line. Can you confirm enemy artillery slackening? Over."

There was a pause, then an excited reply. "Foxtrot Alpha, Vulcan 1 affirmative, move to bunker line now. Over."

He didn't bother confirming the order. He dropped the handset and yelled at his sergeant, cowering fifteen yards behind. "Move 'em up. Move up, let's go." He stood and went around the tree in a crouch. The sky was lightening, the darkness no longer protecting them. Foxtrot Company came out of hiding and surged forward. The artillery fire dwindled as they advanced, but the machine guns in the bunker could see them and were wreaking havoc.

The company got into a rhythm, covering fire as sections advanced then covering fire for them. The bunker slits were exploding with accurate rifle and machine gun fire. The heavy weapons squad was raining 81mm mortars all around the bunkers, ruining their aim. Foxtrot Company advanced within yards. A thirty-caliber machine gun set up to the left of Captain Frank, started pouring fire into the bunker to his front. He called for a flamethrower and saw a soldier stand up with the big tanks strapped to his back. The thirty-caliber kept hammering away, keeping the occupants pinned down. The flamethrower soldier ran forward and sent a large stream of fire into the horizontal gun slit. He poured it on, sweeping back and forth until soldiers started coming through the shooting ports, engulfed in flame. They screamed and died in a withering storm of bullets.

Captain Frank waved his men forward, "Let's go, let's go." The men surged forward sensing the battle turning in their favor. They surrounded the smoking bunker, shooting Japanese soldiers as they streamed out the back door trying to escape the raging fire. It was over quickly.

Frank watched as his men jumped into the hard dirt packed trenches leading to the back door of the bunker. A private opened the door and two others flung in grenades. The first soldier closed the metal door and the muffled explosions inside killed more screaming soldiers.

Bullets started snapping over his head. He dove down and looked west to the Japanese line. They were in the open. He grabbed his radioman and pulled the handset, quickly identifying himself then calling in the grid coordinates. He ended with, "Japs in the open. fire at will."

He yelled to his men, "Take cover. Friendly arty on the way." The men hunkered and fired into the exposed Japanese soldiers.

The Japanese had been massing for a counter attack, coming out of their holes to push back the American G.I.'s just like last time. The sudden appearance of G.I.'s past the bunker line shocked them. Their only option was to attack. The officers raised their pistols and yelled for the advance. Men were falling all around as more and more American soldiers came over the top and started pouring fire into their ranks. The American artillery started exploding amongst them tearing and vaporizing the exposed troops. In less than two minutes, two companies of Japanese combat veterans were reduced to smoking cinders. The soldiers that escaped were dazed; most, wounded. They were in full retreat, the Americans right on their tails.

After weeks of punishing artillery, bombings and attacks, the

American G.I.'s were taking their vengeance. They poured fire into the backs of the fleeing enemy. They died by the hundreds.

Soon the Japanese stopped running and dropped into any cover they could find. They cowered in holes, under debris, anything they could find. They let the Americans pass over them, then they'd pop up and take as many to the grave with them as possible. The headlong advance slowed as the G.I.'s were forced to deal with each individual last stand.

COLONEL ARAKI WAS NOT a happy man. The word from every battalion was the same; full retreat. He wondered for the hundredth time what happened to his hill artillery. They should have stopped this advance before it started, but they'd fallen silent early into the attack. He wanted to send a squad of men in trucks to check it out, but his situation was suddenly dire and he couldn't spare a single man.

He grabbed his ashen faced Captain Hoshi by the lapel and pulled him close. Spittle flying, he said, "Stop this retreat. Go to the line and force them to stand and fight. Shoot any retreating soldiers. We need time to evacuate back to Cape Esperance." He pushed the startled Captain towards the front, "Do it now." His gaunt frame moved to the door, "And Captain," the Captain turned to his commander. "I don't expect to see you again." Hoshi gave a quick bow and went to perform his duty and meet his fate.

To the remaining officers, Colonel Araki's orders were succinct and to the point. Burn anything of value, kill anyone not Japanese and fall back along the coast road to the mountains of Cape Esperance for a final stand. He took one last look to the mountain, his eight 105mm guns should have been firing. He clenched his teeth. *That weakling Welch has failed me.*

## 32

With full daylight came the sounds of heavy fighting along the front line. Sergeant Carver listened to the din of battle. Even from this far away he could tell the fighting was getting closer and closer. That could mean only one thing; the Americans were advancing, pushing the Japanese forces out of their strong defensive bunkers.

The ridge top was littered with dead Japanese. The natives were busy stacking them to one side, clearing the area of their festering corpses. There was a growing stack of weapons and ammunition, an entire company's worth. Six of the eight 105mm guns had been destroyed, but the other two were fully functional. The big artillery shells were aching for a new target. Unfortunately, Sergeant Carver and Private O'Connor had no training in firing an artillery gun, especially not a Japanese piece.

They found the road leading to the ridge from the Japanese rear. The Japanese had hacked it out of the raw jungle. It must have taken months of back breaking work. Morrisey had no doubt a native labor force had been used for the task. Before the American invasion, many natives were forced to work for the Japanese. Most had not been heard of since. He wondered how many had died building this road. It was just wide enough for heavy trucks and signs of tire tracks were evident. With the recent rains the road was a muddy mess. It wouldn't be possible for truck travel, but it would be no problem for Japanese troops to move up the road out of the path of the advancing Americans.

Sergeant Carver conferred with Captain Morrisey and both agreed it would be prudent to set an ambush along the road until the battle below moved past. They moved down the road and dug in along the edge of a likely corner. Three captured Nambu machine guns were placed with interlacing fields of fire. If the Japs came, they'd be trapped on the road and mowed down.

Hours went by and the battle moved past them. Carver was about to suggest they move down and meet up with the allies, when there was movement along the road. He hunkered behind the Nambu sight and waited. Silence permeated the jungle and every man had a finger on a trigger.

The first dark shape came around the corner, full of caution. The soldier kneeled and looked at the bend in the road, seeing it as a likely ambush spot. Another soldier came up beside the first and conferred with the point man. Carver strained to see if it was friend or foe. When the second man stood he was backlit by a shaft of sunlight streaking through the jungle canopy. He could see the familiar helmet shape of an American soldier. He took his finger off the trigger and called down the road, "FRIENDLY UNIT TO YOUR FRONT GIs."

The point man dropped and brought his M1 up. The second man called out, "COME OUT ON THE ROAD WHERE WE CAN SEE YOU."

Sergeant Carver looked across the road at Private O'Connor who returned his worried look. *It would be a hell of a thing getting killed by friendlies after what we've been through.*

Carver stepped out on the road with his hands raised above his head. The point man came forward, his weapon never leaving the Sergeant's chest. Carver could see the rest of the American patrol spread out along the sides of the road, weapons covering him. Carver waited until the man was in front of him and said, "I'm Sergeamt Carver with Baker Company, 2nd platoon."

The soldier, who looked no more than seventeen grinned and called down the road. "It's clear Lieutenant, he's one of us." The soldier was surprised when the jungle around him came alive with movement as the natives and O'Connor seemed to materialize from nothing. His eyes were wide as he took in the ragtag men.

When Carver met Lieutenant Jankowski, he threw a quick salute and realized he hadn't done so in what seemed an eternity. Jankowski saluted back and said, "Sergeant Carver?" Carver nodded. "You must be the boys who took out the Jap artillery?"

Carver looked around at the natives and the approaching Captain Morrisey. "I had some help, Lieutenant. Without these men it wouldn't have happened; no way in hell."

Morrisey stepped forward and Carver introduced him. Jankowski stiffened at his rank. He wasn't sure if he was required to salute a provincial Captain, but gave him a crisp salute just in case. Morrisey laughed and saluted him back. "Good to see you. I've got wounded up there; could use some help getting them to your medics."

The Lieutenant nodded and sent his men forward. They hustled and followed the natives towards the ridgeline. Sergeant Carver said, "There's two 105mm guns up there that are operational. You have anyone that could man them? I'd think they're in perfect position to rain hell onto the retreating Japs."

The Lieutenant nodded. He called his radio man forward. While he was hustling forward with his heavy radio pack, Lt. Jankowski said, "Our arty's bogged down on the coast road. We can't bring it forward fast enough to keep up with the Jap retreat. I'll get some men up here in a hurry. Division will be ecstatic."

TWO HOURS later Sergeant Carver and Private O'Connor were sitting in front of General Thornton and Colonel Sinclair. Even being exhausted, they were still nervous in front of the big brass. As they told their story though, the officers' respect grew and they gained confidence in the telling. Carver wrapped up with, "And that's about it. Your guys got the wounded off and now we're here."

General Thornton stood and crossed his arms, "I'm putting both of you up for silver stars. Since I'm the one doing it, the process of acceptance is just a formality." He watched, expecting them to react like children on Christmas morning. Instead, they only stared.

Carver thought about the men he'd left rotting in the jungle. They'd be lucky to get decent burials. Carver and O'Connor wanted to get the hell out of there so they could get some hot chow and a rack to sleep for a week.

The sound of booming artillery coming from the ridge they'd abandoned rolled down to them. They all looked towards it. The streaking shells slammed into the retreating Japanese Army. Sergeant Carver smiled and pointed, "We appreciate the medals, Sir, but sending their own shells back at them? Now that beats a medal any day."

# AFTERWORD

The coast watchers were a valiant and invaluable asset to the allied war effort in the Pacific and particularly in the Solomon Islands. There are no documented instances of betrayal among their cadre. My portrayal of treachery is complete fiction and used as a plot point. I do not mean to denigrate their sacrifices or courage.

Keep the action going with the next book in the series:

Bloody Bougainville

26143772R00146

Made in the USA
Columbia, SC
06 September 2018